Sadjka's Way

Sadika's Way

A NOVEL OF PAKISTAN AND AMERICA

Hina Haq

Academy Chicago Publishers

Published in 2004 by
Academy Chicago Publishers
363 West Erie Street
Chicago, Illinois 60610

Printed in Canada

Library of Congress Cataloging-in-Publication Data

Haq, Hina.
  Sadika's way : a novel of Pakistan and America / Hina Haq.
    p. cm.
  ISBN 0-89733-518-X (hardcover)
  1. Mothers and daughters--Fiction. 2. Women--Pakistan--Fiction. 3.
Arranged marriage--Fiction. 4. Women immigrants--Fiction. 5. Young
women--Fiction. 6. Pakistan--Fiction. I. Title.

  PS3608.A724S23 2004
  813'.6--dc22
                                          2003022105

To Ikram—
my own personal knight in shining armor

one

HER NAME WAS supposed to be Sadik, and she was supposed to be a boy. Her parents, Akbar Khan and Bilqees Beebee, had done everything humanly possible to ensure the right sex before she was even conceived. The name Sadik had been placed along with heartfelt prayers at strategic places in the Qur'an. And before and throughout her pregnancy Bilqees Beebee had been adorned with special amulets from various holy places.

As soon as he heard the good news of his wife's pregnancy, Akbar Khan arranged for a special pilgrimage to Daataa Darbaar Lahore, the final resting place of one of the holiest men ever to live in the subcontinent, Daataa Ganj Baksh. Once there, he prayed for an entire day, eyes closed, head bent, hands outstretched; at times demanding aloud that the spirit of the great Daataa grant him his dearest wish. For extra insurance, he pledged that if a son were born he would give the poor a *daeg*, a special twenty-gallon cauldron of food.

To cap it all, every month during the last two trimesters of pregnancy, all the pious ladies of the neighborhood had come to the small Khan home to pray as a group for a son for the family.

It was all in vain.

Sadika—as she was called, since no one wanted to waste energy thinking up a more appropriate name for a girl-child— was born on a cold winter day in 1969 in Jogiapur, a remote village near Islamabad, the capital of Pakistan, to the accompaniment of her mother's hysterics and threats of suicide.

She was the third daughter born to Bilqees Beebee. The first two had not survived, but evidence was mounting that Bilqees

Beebee was incapable of bearing sons, which would make her no more worthy of respect than a barren woman. After the high hopes and expectations of her pregnancy, she found herself on the bottom rung of the womanhood ladder.

Even worse, it had been such a long, horrendous labor that Bilqees Beebee thought of doing something drastic to herself. After twenty exhausting, painful hours, as the mother's strength ebbed away, there was still no sign of the baby. Some village elders convened and decided that the only hope of a successful delivery was to frighten Bilqees Beebee's body into doing what it was apparently incapable of accomplishing on its own.

In accordance with the advice of Fakeer Baabaa, the wisest of men, the top two marksmen of the village were summoned to Bilqees Beebee's bedside with their guns. There, as they had been instructed, they fired shots into the air as close to her head as was safely possible, scaring her out of her wits.

She had scarcely had time to recover from the noise, and another contraction was coming on, when the well-meaning villagers administered yet another shock. Dressed in rags and looking as though they had freshly arisen from a muddy grave, an elderly man and woman appeared from nowhere. Fixing their fierce gaze upon her, they began speaking to her in the voices of long-dead ancestors. "Shame on you, girl, for making us come from the dead to do your task for you. You dared to disturb our peace and we are upset. Have that baby at once so we can go back to the quiet of our graves. Otherwise get ready to face the consequences."

When the terrified Bilqees Beebee did not respond, they furiously repeated their command. "Do it now, so we don't have to come back as evil spirits and inhabit your body to make you do it!"

God only knew whether her ancestral ghosts had a hand in it, but after the next few strong contractions, Bilqees Beebee was convinced that her dead ancestors were making good on their promise to take up residence in her body, and were painfully clawing their way out from the inside. Thus Sadika made her debut into the world.

Just as Bilqees Beebee was losing consciousness, she heard her mother-in-law Maanjee say contemptuously, "It's only a girl. A scrawny ugly one at that. One would have thought that after all that carrying-on, she was giving birth to at least one son, if not two."

To Bilqees Beebee, every one of the newborn's cries seemed to sound more and more like the music that would accompany her husband's second wedding. She knew very well that after this reproductive disaster, no one would object to Akbar Khan marrying a woman with a uterus more favorable to the conception of sons, if he chose to do so. Perhaps he had already told his mother of his intentions, she thought, as she lay distraught. Maanjee certainly appeared to be carefully assessing every young woman of marriageable age in the group gathered around the new mother's bed.

Bilqees Beebee did not realize that it was all a charade; that the vindictive old woman was well aware of her daughter-in-law's fears and was having the time of her life playing on them. It was not often that she had the opportunity to enjoy such power. Bilqees Beebee heard Maanjee ask about Akhtar Khatoon's two daughters: "How are dear Sughra and Kubra? I always tell my daughters and everyone that the home those two marry into is going to sparkle like polished silver." Bilqees Beebee knew that their mother was upset because these two girls were not yet married.

It was therefore not surprising that Bilqees Beebee refused even to look at the baby or nurse her, let alone think of an appropriate name for her, since that would only make the child's presence more real. She would be a permanent fixture in the household, a constant reminder that Bilqees Beebee was a miserable failure at the only major task that society had assigned to women like her: the production of a son.

"Keep that ill-fated creature away from me!" she would cry in a high-pitched voice, if she so much as caught sight of the baby. The small mob of women surrounding her, relatives and neighbors, would try to calm her down, while the younger girls lingering outside the room giggled. This was the most entertaining event in their village since the fair had come through nearly a year ago.

Akbar Khan did what he could to help create the illusion of a crisis. By nature quiet and passive, he was doing his best to play the part of a man who had been wronged. As it was, he felt burdened with the responsibility of having to marry off his two sisters, Gul Fatima and Taj Fatima. And now his burden was heavier still with the arrival of yet another female. However, he was not a very good actor and his fits of temper were unconvincing and caused more amusement than terror.

"I will murder both those females with my bare hands and throw their bodies in the woods for wild animals to feed on!" he shouted menacingly, trying to imitate the volatile hero of the Punjabi movie that had been running in the neighboring outdoor village theatre set up by the Gilleet Company. Unfortunately for him, everyone had seen that movie, some more than once. How could they not have? It was the talk of the town for more than three weeks. It became an even juicier topic of conversation when the mullahs of the local mosques met to discuss the social effect of this outrageous film, which they declared reflected a conspiracy by the West to infect the rest of the world with its sinful ways.

"Today they are promoting the clean-shaven look of the West; tomorrow they will promote their corrupt morality," the head mullah of the biggest mosque of the area had said in his sermon just last week after the Friday prayers.

"Otherwise, why would they be offering free razors with a month's free supply of razor blades? They are not your uncles from either your father's side or your mother's side. People! If you do not want your wives and daughters to end up walking half-naked in the streets and your young people to produce children out of wedlock, you had better boycott the Gilleet movie and forbid your families to view it. Any man who does not do so is not a man at all, but a jackal with his tail tucked between his legs, and an ostrich with his head buried in sand!"

People tried not to laugh whenever Akbar Khan said something that sounded like the movie hero. This was even better than the Gilleet movie, in which the hero, after shaving his chin with a gleaming Gilleet blade and mounting a white horse to track down the villain, roared ominously, "Let my woman go, or I will break both your scrawny legs like toothpicks and throw them out with the rest of your puny body for wild animals to snack on!"

Fortunately Sadika seemed to thrive without much nurturing or warmth from her parents. Her mother's hostility and her father's apathy seemed only to make her stronger. In the years that followed, she grew like a hardy weed, despite the increasing number of household chores and baby-sitting duties thrust upon her. She did not seem to be adversely affected by poverty, by childhood infections, or even by neglect.

Two

IN APRIL OF 1974, when the family of Akbar Khan moved to Islamabad, Sadika, five years old, had three siblings: Asghar Khan, a boy of four, and two girls, Zafary, three, and Sajida, two. Bilqees Beebee was now called "Khanum" by her neighbors in Gulmushk Mohalla. Akbar Khan had been allotted a small home there by the government because he had secured a job as a *chaprasee*, a kind of gofer, at a local federal office. While his family was preparing to leave Jogiapur to join him, he had moved into the new house by himself. When several of his new neighbors learned that he was a Khan, and married with four children, they had invariably asked, "So when is your Khanum coming to join you?"

By the time Bilqees Beebee arrived with her children, she had become Khanum in everyone's mind. She certainly did not object to that. The name "Khanum" was so much more sophisticated than "Bilqees Beebee." Besides, it was the last name of the country's most popular *ghazal* singer, Farida Khanum, and it implied that she was an equal partner to Akbar Khan, something that greatly pleased her. In fact, she liked it so much that after a while she asked her husband and children, too, to call her Khanum.

Sadika and her sisters Zafary and Sajida were at this time thin, wiry little girls. Although they were not weaklings, they did not brim with health like their brother Asghar. In actual fact, Asghar was nearly obese, because Khanum considered him her salvation. The girls were simply a drain, because dowries had to be accumulated for them and their reputations protected if they were to make acceptable matches. Thus, Asghar was his

6

mother's only strength, the sole balm that could keep her marriage intact and preserve her status. Naturally, she wanted more boys.

Each time she had given birth to a girl, Khanum had been plunged into deep depression. "God!" she would rage after the *Isha* prayers, sitting on her prayer mat, hands outstretched, tears streaming down her cheeks. "Why are you punishing me this way? Don't you realize what a living hell my life will become if I bear more daughters than sons? Akbar Khan will surely get a second wife. We're barely able to feed ourselves now, so tell me, how can I be expected to survive?"

Asghar's was the only name which was left as originally planned. "Sadik" had had to be turned into Sadika, "Zafar" into Zafary and "Sajid" into Sajida. Now it was Asghar, apparently destined to be the only son, who would have to compensate for all the grief Khanum would unquestionably have to suffer from her daughters. Perhaps the bride she selected for him would provide a sizable dowry to help compensate for some of her losses.

How she wished that she belonged to one of the families in the frontier region, where instead of the girl's family providing a dowry, the boy's family had to pay the girl's family a large sum of money at the time of marriage. Then she would already have been ahead of the game. The prettier, younger and more innocent the girl, the bigger the dowry that could be demanded. And Sadika, Zafary and Sajida were not bad-looking. Families with many pretty girls to marry off had actually gotten rich. But since unfortunately that was not the custom where Khanum lived, she lavished all her maternal affection on Asghar, the only one of her offspring who had any material value.

Sadika, Zafary and Sajida envied Asghar's special treatment, but they were resigned to it. In fact, it seemed to them to be the way things were meant to be. They saw often the disappointment of neighbors who had just given birth to daughters, and

the jubilation that greeted the birth of sons. They heard the
women, including their own mother, commiserating with the
aggrieved wife, telling her in detail about their own many dis-
appointments in having produced girls. "*Behen*, sister, I know
just how you feel," Khanum would say. "I've gone through this
myself. God must be testing you: to some people he sends sickness and disease; to some, money problems; and to others,
daughters to raise. But everyone has to have their share of misery in this world."

The only time the three sisters had thanked God for making
them female was when, at the age of four, Asghar was circum-
cised. It was the first big occasion their family had celebrated
after moving to Islamabad. But it was not the festivities that
Sadika, Zafary and Sajida remembered. They sat huddled together outside his room in the tiny courtyard, frightened out of
their wits by the little boy's terrible screams. It sounded to them
as though Asghar was being slowly tortured to death. They
thought their turn would come next: if the tip of a boy's penis
was superfluous, maybe some of their female parts were equally
disposable.

They felt enormous relief when they learned that only boys
had to go through this ghastly ordeal. Relief even enhanced the
taste of the delicious yellow dessert called *laddoos* that Akbar
Khan and Khanum had bought to be distributed in Gulmushk
Mohalla to celebrate the joyous occasion. Their beloved son
was well on his way to manhood. Once there, he would provide them with comfort and strength in their old age—unlike
the daughters, who would weaken them and age them prematurely.

Asghar's elevated status in the household was very evident
in the responsibilities and privileges given to the four children.
While the three girls, even little Sajida, were kept busy with
cooking, cleaning, sewing and other chores, Asghar was free to
roam the streets of Gulmushk Mohalla, to play stickball, wrestle,

and fly kites with other boys. "My boy is more masculine than three neighborhood boys put together," Khanum often commented with satisfaction when Asghar limped home with disheveled hair, torn clothes and skinned knees.

The girls started each day with a breakfast of thick wheat bread and strong tea sweetened with solid sugarcane juice, while they cast envious glances at Asghar, who was eating cream mixed with pure cane sugar given him every morning by his doting mother. They could never openly look at Asghar while he was eating, because it upset Khanum. "Don't cast evil eyes at my son, bastard females, or he will lose his appetite!" she would shout, hastily putting an old towel or sheet around the boy to shield him from invisible harm. "If he's not strong enough, who will take care of me when I am old? Your husbands?"

Even meals were planned around Asghar's activities. Khanum subscribed to the popular belief that one's daily diet should correspond to the part of the body that would be used most that day. If one were going to do mental work, he should eat calf or goat brains; if he wanted to excel as an athlete, he should be served the legs of chickens or goats. Since Khanum wanted Asghar to be better than everyone else physically as well as mentally, all brains and legs were always reserved for him, leaving his sisters to fantasize about how delicious they must be. Why couldn't they have just a taste, they wondered. After all, they helped with most of the cooking.

At dinner, while Asghar polished off roast chicken thighs and drumsticks, the three girls ate gravy flavored with chicken feet and other scraps of leftover meat. Asghar devoured calf brains in a gravy with fresh coriander leaves, and the girls were given soup made of the calf's skull bones.

The second largest portion of food went to Akbar Khan. Khanum usually ate with the girls in the kitchen, sharing leftovers with them. She was not as hungry as they were, since she did considerable sampling when she cooked. She did not of course admit that. "You should learn to be content with what you get," she frequently told the girls. "When you're married, you'll have to make sure that your family is fed before you think about yourselves."

The biggest treat for the girls was being invited to a wedding. These were always elaborate, drawn-out affairs, no matter how poor the family whose offspring was getting married. It was a matter of honor to have as lavish a wedding as possible, with plenty of food. Many people had to sell off land or borrow money to pay for these celebrations, falling into debt for years, even for the rest of their lives. The government had stopped making small business loans when it became clear that most of the time the money was being used to finance weddings.

But for Sadika, Zafary and Sajida, neighborhood weddings made life worth living. Then, apart from relief from their chores, they were able to enjoy plenty of good food and entertainment, and they also had a chance to dress up. They stuffed themselves with as much food as possible, which in fact was not all that much, since their stomachs became upset very quickly. God is so unfair, Sadika would think to herself as she visited the latrine for the third time in as many hours. Why didn't he let humans store food the way camels do? He should have realized that we would need it. If I were a camel, I wouldn't have had to worry about eating again for days instead of getting sick and not even being able to enjoy it for one day.

Because of the enormous expense involved and the symbolism of that expense, weddings often represented a turning point in a family's history. Akbar Khan's family was no exception. Moving to Islamabad had been a matter of necessity rather than choice. In early 1973, Akbar Khan, in order to provide dowries and wedding feasts for his two sisters, Gul Fatima and Taj Fatima, had been forced to sell off the small farm that had been the family's sole means of livelihood. He had been left with no option but to go to Islamabad to find work.

Three

AT FIRST, AKBAR Khan had been able to find only construction work. Like thousands of other laborers from adjacent areas, he rose at dawn and worked all day with only a half-hour break to gobble down two *rotis* with some kind of gravy that defied description, from a *khokhay wallah*, a man with a cart who visited the site around noon every day. In the evening, at a makeshift shop, he and his fellow workers consumed a dinner of thick wheat *rotis* and lentil soup or cooked vegetables washed down with strong tea sweetened with raw sugar. Finally, exhausted, he would make his way to Haji Imtiaz Ali's small ramshackle house where he was renting "*charpai* space" at two hundred rupees per month, and fall into a dreamless sleep. *Charpai* space literally meant the space taken by a *charpai*, a lightweight bed consisting of a wooden frame strung with jute fibers, an arrangement found only in the beautiful city of Islamabad.

It was almost impossible to live in Islamabad unless you were a diplomat, a government servant, or independently wealthy. Laborers from nearby villages and cities could survive there only by renting *charpai* space from people who worked at the lowest government office level and were allotted family quarters by the government. In order to supplement their meager incomes, these people often reserved one room in their very modest homes to rent out at night as *charpai* space.

Apart from Akbar Khan, there were five men renting *charpai* space from Haji Imtiaz Ali: Muhammad Zakir, Ghulam Ahmed, Abdul Ghani, Saleem Ilyas and Shakoor Aziz. Since they all came from the neighboring city of Rawalpindi, they considered themselves sophisticates, and enjoyed taunting Akbar Khan. "What are you doing here?" they asked him. "You should be in some village minding cows or harvesting crops." This made him furious, but he tried to ignore them. It was five against one, and he did not want to begin by making enemies. In any case, Akbar Khan's roommates could not know that the habits they found so amusing were the very ones that endeared Akbar Khan to Haji Imtiaz Ali and his wife Roshan Ara, and that would eventually be responsible for bettering his lot in life.

Whenever the men needed to leave their room, Akbar Khan called out, as he had always done in his village: "Men are on their way out! Women observing purda, cover yourselves now." Then Roshan Ara hastily covered her head and part of her face with a sheet or *chadar*. Since she came from a conservative religious family and was the wife of a man who had already performed the Haj, she was proud to be a devout observer of purda. If she had had her way, they would never have rented *charpai* space to men, even though they needed the money and could spare the second room since they did not yet have any children.

In Roshan Ara's eyes, Akbar Khan was the only real man and true believer of them all, because he recognized the importance of purda, when females, after reaching a certain age, are sheltered from the gaze of all adult males except those related to them. Roshan Ara was grateful to him for helping her maintain the strictness of her upbringing, and often saved some farina dessert for him from her occasional morning religious gathering of women. If he had been unmarried, she would certainly have targeted him for her younger sister Naseem Fatima: he was excellent husband material—quiet, passive, respectful, gullible, hardworking, and dull.

Bathroom and laundry facilities were not included in the *charpai* space. So every morning the workers renting space in various houses would head en masse toward the surrounding woods, where an even exchange would take place: the twigs and leaves of the trees took care of their toiletry needs, while they in turn provided that particular ecosystem with fresh nutrients that had become a crucial link in the food chain over a period of time. As people friendly with each other tended to use adjoining trees and bushes, this was often a pleasant time for bonding and conversation.

"O Shakooray!" Akbar Khan called out through the shrubbery to Shakoor, the only one of the five men he considered a friend.

"What is it, Akbaray?"

"Are you going to be able to eat a breakfast before you go to work today?"

"Not today, my friend. The *thekedaar,* the general contractor, gets upset if you're as much as five minutes late. But I have last night's leftover *roti* under my pillow. What about you?"

"I have to eat something, friend, even if the *thekedaar* kills me. Or my intestines will recite verses from the Holy Qur'an the entire morning. The *khokhay wallah* who sits at the corner of the construction site promised me fresh *roti* and tea this morning."

"Which *khokhay wallah*? The one who sings Punjabi songs all the time? If it's that one, don't drink what he gives you. All he does is dump last night's leftover tea from each used cup into one cup and heat it up. He doesn't make fresh tea or anything else till at least lunchtime."

"Oh, so that's why he kept telling me to keep it a secret," Akbar Khan replied with disgust. "'Don't tell anyone, or they'll all want this special favor.' I should have known better."

Over the weekend, Akbar Khan, along with other laborers, headed to one of the many bathhouses that had sprung up all over town to cater to the laborers who had descended on the city. There, in steaming hot water, he washed off the week's dirt, visited a barber and employed the services of a *dhobee*, who washed and ironed clothes. Thus each week he was able to remove his soiled clothes and put on the clean ones that he had left there the previous week. Then, clean and drowsy, he would buy a satisfying breakfast of thin fried bread and warm pastry from the vendor who stood outside the bathhouse, before entering the nearby cinema to watch the latest Punjabi movie.

This film experience was by far the most enjoyable part of Akbar Khan's life in the city. Never before had he felt free to whistle, hoot, and make lewd comments about the curvaceous woman he saw on the screen; never in his memory had he ever talked freely about what he would like to do with that woman. Far from it. In the village where he had lived most of his life, he had been afraid even to glance at a woman for fear that she would report him to an overprotective father, brother or husband. In fact, he had been too timid even to pinch someone's behind in a crowded place, as his friends often did to provide themselves with some measure of entertainment. He had done that once when he was a teenager, and discovered to his horror that the person in the *burqa* was a man, who had picked him up by the collar and growled into his ear, "Bastard! If I catch you doing this again, I'll break both your hands!" Akbar Khan learned later that some men wore *burqas* so they could stare at women without getting into trouble.

The Punjabi filmmakers were creative; they knew how to use camera angles and the suggestive movements of actresses so that even the raciest movies could stay within the puritanical guidelines set by the Pakistan Censor Board. There were no explicit love scenes, there was never even a kiss. But sometimes when the cinema proprietors felt safe from the vigilance of the local authorities—not that the local authorities were that vigilant, but it took a good chunk of money to keep their cooperation—they would stop the Punjabi movie, run a few minutes of genuine imported illegal X-rated film amid whoops of approval and catcalls from the audience, and then resume the regular feature. Movie houses that were known to show *totay*, as these few minutes of X-rated tape were called, were especially popular.

When Akbar Khan encountered this phenomenon for the first time—when the big screen suddenly and without warning filled with a close-up of genitalia—he did not at first know what they were. Not that he was slow. It was just that he had never had the opportunity to examine even his own genitals in such minute detail, let alone anyone else's. Certainly not a female's. Since in the village his entire family slept in two rooms, his physical relationship with his wife had been limited to hurried gropings under the sheets in the dark of night. Nothing in his background had prepared him for what was in front of him on the movie screen. Every mole, hair, even every pore of the actors' private parts stood out like a neon light in some dark alley. When he finally realized what he was watching, he sat electrified, covered with cold sweat, his heart beating wildly, convinced that somehow he was going to be arrested for witnessing what was certainly taboo. If that did not happen, he would surely roast in the most fiery regions of hell for a long, long time. After all, hadn't his village mullah condemned watching even the infinitely tamer Gilleet movies as the pastime of the devil?

However, as time passed, Akbar Khan had become a seasoned viewer who could not only watch the screen with relative composure, but could actually critique the porno stars' performances, demonstrating his sophistication and worldly wisdom. Each time he said something he considered clever, his sense of self-worth rose a notch, and he viewed with pleasure the gulf he saw widening between the simpleton he had been and the man of the world he was becoming. "That noise she was making was totally fake," he commented with conviction to Shakoor or whomever he happened to be with, using as many profane words as he could from the vocabulary he had picked up since coming to the big city. "I could tell she was all stretched out inside. I bet she could feel that man about as much as the cooking pot feels the stirring spoon."

The six *charpai* spaces that Haji Imtiaz Ali rented out were all in one tiny room, where the *charpais* were so close together that there was not room enough to get up from a particular *charpai* without invading someone else's personal space. When late at night Akbar Khan sometimes needed a drink of water, or to relieve himself against the back wall of the house, he first tried to accustom his eyes to the darkness, and then gingerly moved across the beds, stepping on the wooden frames as quietly as possible. But on occasion he inadvertently stepped on someone's hand or foot, generally Abdul Ghani's, whose *charpai* was next to his, and who loudly cursed at him, provoking a lasting torrent of foul language and curses from the other occupants. "What are you trying to do—turn me into an invalid, you bastard? Use the eyes that God has given you or I'll take them out for you!" Abdul Ghani cried, and then Muhammad Zakir shouted at Abdul Ghani, "Will you shut your mouth or do you want me to shut it for you?" and someone else yelled, "Doesn't anyone want to sleep tonight? God, this place is worse than a whorehouse!"

Akbar Khan, who felt intimidated by each and every one of them, crept silently back to bed, sorely missing his family—not so much for the love he felt for them, as for the respect due the head of the household they would give him, no matter how he treated them. So the day he managed to get a job as a *chaprasi* in a government office, was a happy and lucky one for Akbar Khan for many reasons.

If Haji Imtiaz Ali had not told him privately about the job opening in the federal office where he worked, the competition would have been tough. Not only that, Haji Imtiaz Ali had personally gone to his supervisor and recommended Akbar Khan, praising his decency and godliness to the skies, putting the odds heavily in his favor. Personal recommendation carried more weight than skill, experience, and education combined, even at this level of the government.

The new job did not pay much more than his laborer's wage, but as an employee of the government, Akbar Khan was not only entitled to family living quarters like those of Haji Imtiaz, he now had the potential to earn bribes. And that was a big deal. Even *chaprasis* had been known to become wealthy if they could do their gofering between the right offices: it was not uncommon for them to demand "wheel money" for certain files. "How can you expect this file to move," they would say, "unless it has wheels?" The expense of adding wheels to a file was of course always directly proportionate to the file's importance.

At last Akbar Khan was able to summon his wife and four children to join him in Islamabad.

four

THE LOWER MIDDLE-CLASS neighborhood into which Akbar Khan moved his family was called Gulmushk Mohalla, "the neighborhood with the fragrance of flowers." Nobody knew how that name had originated, for it was as inappropriate as it was unlikely. It had become the custom to identify neighborhoods by sectors and streets assigned to them by government, rather than by some archaic name from pre-partition India. Gulmushk Mohalla encompassed Street Numbers 12 through 15 in Sector 36. And there was nothing remotely fragrant about it. The reason being that it was surrounded on one side by a playground that was not really a playground, but had been earmarked as one by government planners some seven years earlier.

Although it was not a playground, it was put to good use by the local residents: it served as an extra latrine for them, and their children played during the day in the trenches that had been dug three years earlier to hold playground equipment. In the evenings these trenches were used by young men and women for clandestine meetings. Lavish foliage had sprung up, especially in the latrine areas, providing a convenient cover for trash dumping. In addition to all these conveniences, there was no better place to pitch a tent for special occasions—a wedding, a circumcision, or a funeral—than this playground where no rent was charged and there was no limit on the length of the celebration.

The residents had not always been so happy with the playground. In fact, there had been great hue and cry in the beginning when people kept falling into the trenches and hurting themselves, especially in the dark without street lights. Petitions had been filed and protests held outside the relevant government offices. When those actions failed, the residents had no choice but to resign themselves to the situation. No one had the energy or the time to pursue government officials who were as elusive as eels.

As time passed, people's sense of humor—an essential weapon in the arsenal of survival—had asserted itself. "The government in its enthusiasm to serve people is now providing graves that are pre-dug," they said, "just as in its enthusiasm for technology, it tries to provide clothes that are pre-stitched and food that is pre-cooked. If the grave diggers start going out of business the way some tailors and bakers have, that's okay. You can't stop progress."

Sadika was about six years old at the time the Khan family moved to House #4, Street #12 in Gulmushk Mohalla. Since she was already on her way to becoming an expert cook, babysitter and housekeeper, everyone in the family had grown to depend on her in some way. They all needed her to do something or other for them. She had little feeling for her parents, for Asghar, or for Zafary. The only person in her family whom Sadika loved without restraint and whose company she truly enjoyed was her little sister Sajida. Playful, mischievous and oblivious to family intrigues and politics, Sajida returned her sister's affection in full measure, and followed her around most of the day, a rag doll clutched to her breast with one hand while she tried to help with the other.

Whenever Sadika had free moments, the two sisters sat down with Sajida's homemade rag dolls, playing make-believe and trying to devise a wardrobe for them, much to the resentment of Zafary, who was never invited to join in since she loved to cause trouble by reporting all kinds of things to Khanum. In Sadika's skilled hands, the scraps of fabric salvaged from the local tailor shop would become tiny blouses and skirts, while the paper clips that Akbar Khan brought home from government offices provided the sisters with raw materials for clothes hangers and minuscule bracelets and necklaces.

Sometimes an envious little girl would suggest a wedding between her male doll and Sajida's female doll, with, of course, the wardrobe as the dowry. If the wedding took place, the neighborhood children would have a lot of fun with the fake ceremony, but then the rag doll would go away to her "husband's" home, and Sadika and Sajida would have to come up with another wardrobe for yet another rag doll.

As the girls grew older and Khanum assigned them more chores, there was less and less time to play with dolls. And when Sadika was registered at the local public school, the doll-playing virtually stopped, but the closeness between the sisters remained.

If it had been up to Khanum, Sadika would never have seen the inside of a classroom. But all the children in the neighborhood went to the local public school, and keeping Sadika out would have resulted in a loss of face. So even though Khanum's better judgment told her that educating girls was a waste of time, and she resented losing an excellent helper for half the day, she allowed the neighbor Hamida Aapa and her daughter Zahra to take Sadika to register in the local kindergarten.

From the very beginning, Sadika loved school. It provided relief from the monotony and drudgery of daily life and she was eager for the mental stimulation she could not find at home. As time went by and her studies improved, school became more and more of a refuge. Apart from school and her little sister Sajida, her only other pleasant relationship as she was growing up was with Zahra, the daughter of neighbor Hamida Aapa and Shabbeer Malik. Though five years older than Sadika, Zahra became her closest friend and confidant.

Their friendship had started as a matter of necessity. Both had similar responsibilities at home and both suffered from the same sense of inadequacy and helplessness. They could identify and commiserate with each other's problems and turn to each other for help whenever it was needed. When Zahra fell on the concrete road and skinned the palms of her hands so that she could not stone-grind spices without pain, it was Sadika she turned to. Similarly, Sadika relied on Zahra to sweep the court-yard when her own arms were aching from stirring the big pot of lentils and meats planned for a special occasion.

Zahra's background was not too different from Sadika's. Her family too was lower middle-class, and she too was the eldest of three children: brother Javed, one year younger, and sister Shazia, two years younger. However, unlike Sadika, Zahra had had a happy childhood: her memories were a pleasant blur of friends, work and school. Life had not started to sour for her till the ripe age of thirteen when she first became aware of the apprehension in her mother's eyes. As she grew older, her rela-tions with her mother became ever more strained.

Painfully conscious of her budding breasts, Zahra at the age of thirteen wanted only to be inconspicuous. It was as though there was an evil brewing beneath her garments, and she felt duty bound to divert attention from it. Most other girls her age proudly displayed their newly developed assets by wearing tight clothes, but Zahra took to hunching her back in an effort to camouflage her curves. When she caught Hamida Aapa glanc-ing with concern at her maturing body, she reacted by hastily throwing on another layer of clothing. She knew that the time was not far away when her family would have to worry about getting an appropriate match for her.

As her nineteenth birthday approached, Zahra could sense her family's growing nervousness. Her mother, especially, seemed excruciatingly aware of each passing week. Hamida Aapa cal-culated that when Zahra had turned sixteen she had reached the lower limit of the age range when a young girl was a prime candidate for the marriage market. Now as Zahra inched to-ward the upper limit of that range, her younger sister Shazia at seventeen had also entered the crucial time frame, and it would not be long before all hope of Zahra being settled as a respectably married young woman would be a thing of the past.

Only God knew where eligible matches lost their way. They were supposed to be there automatically when a girl reached puberty, and it was expected that she would be inundated with proposals at the magical age of seventeen or eighteen, the time when girls were noticed by the mothers and sisters of eligible young men. In fact, all the females in a boy's family, even those remotely related to him, looked at young girls with critical eyes, trying to gauge whether they had all the qualities that their beloved son, brother, cousin or nephew deserved in a wife. Unfortunately for Zahra, although she had many times been given the once-over by matrons, she had never made the final cut. Getting the approval of the matron was not her problem; it was winning the heart of the son that was difficult.

Neither Zahra nor her parents had considered going directly to the potential groom. By tradition, arrangements for the marriage of offspring were the exclusive province of the family elders. It was a system that had worked well enough in the past: prospective bridegrooms married girls recommended by the older females in the family without question, believing that they knew best about such things.

All that was changing. Thanks to Western influences, gainfully employed young men now wanted to be sweetly enticed by prospective brides before they consented to marry. This attitude had given rise to a new sort of girl, one who could better her lot in life by giving male vanity what it craved—which was really not that much: a flirtatious smile, fluttering eyelashes, a breathless whisper of sweet nonsense, were all it took for even mighty oaks to topple. Segregated society had bred a certain male innocence. Or gullibility.

Zahra, a young girl raised in old values, was not adept at playing the new mating game and had fallen by the wayside. After being recommended to a couple of boys who thought her reticence was proof not of her purity and good character but of her frigidity, she found herself out of the running. Word traveled fast in the network of small middle-class neighborhoods in Islamabad. It was now believed that Zahra was destined to remain a spinster, or to be incapable of making a good match if she did manage to marry. She was looked on as pitiable wherever she went.

It was more than her behavior that sealed her fate. She lacked the sense of style that boys had come to expect. Although not bad to look at, she was unfashionably dressed, and her thick hair, oiled and tightly braided, stood out from her head in weird parabolas. Her dowdy appearance would have been an asset in the days when matrons were looking for an innocent, pliable girl, in a time when it was assumed that one's disregard for one's looks reflected a sincere heart and a simple mind.

But with the advent of new technology and a new family order in which sons were no longer dependent on their elders, everything that once might have worked in Zahra's favor now worked against her. The result was that she was turning into a cynical, introverted young woman existing in a kind of limbo, waiting to get married. Her parents had long since given up hope of a prince charming for their daughter; they would have welcomed a janitor from the city government's custodial pool. But it seemed that even those were hard to come by.

Only Sadika's company and obvious affection for her helped to lighten Zahra's loneliness.

five

SADIKA AND ZAHRA grew even closer after Zahra graduated from the local public school: Sadika, now Zahra's only link to the school world she had once known—she was not close to her younger sister Shazia—transmitted the latest gossip about teachers and students. At the same time Zahra, at home during the day, was able to listen to the juicy conversations of the neighborhood women and to enjoy passing this gossip on to Sadika, who, younger than she, tended to be naive to the point of stupidity. Almost everything that Sadika knew about women's bodies and male-female relationships came from Zahra who, not confident of her own facts most of the time, loved the respect with which Sadika listened to her. That did wonders for her ego, besides providing her with a gullible guinea pig on whom she could safely expound half-baked theories and philosophies without fear of contradiction.

Khanum would have been horrified if she had had even an inkling of the kinds of things Zahra was telling her daughter. Khanum believed that the more ignorant young girls were about the facts of life, the better for them. Young men liked to marry innocent girls, and nothing reflected innocence more strongly than lack of knowledge. That was why, as Sadika moved toward puberty, Khanum became more and more uneasy around her. She did not want anything to destroy Sadika's air of innocence—bordering on idiocy—which she considered to be pure gold in the marriage mart.

Not that Sadika was keen about growing up. In fact, she found the prospect frightening and disgusting. If half of what

Zahra told her was true, she had a lot of bleeding to look forward to—first when she became a woman, then on her wedding night, and especially at the birth of her children when,
Zahra had assured her, blood would spout from her in torrents.

"Where will so much blood come from?" Sadika asked nervously, trying to assess the amount of blood in her seemingly
bloodless thin arms by pinching them hard.

Many of her conversations with Zahra were so sensational
that Sadika could remember them word for word and play them
over and over in her mind while she was doing her housework.
This bizarre information bounced off the walls of her brain like
popping corn and left her reeling. For example, Zahra introduced her to the topics of menstruation and loss of virginity.

"A girl's reputation is like snow-white linen. Even the slightest
smudge will show up and ruin her prospects of an advantageous
marriage forever." Thirteen-year-old Sadika listened, enthralled,
to these words of wisdom, and Zahra, enjoying the reaction she
elicited from her naive young listener, decided to spice things up.

"That's just the beginning. The hard part comes after she
keeps her reputation and gets a good match. She has to be ready
to shed a lot of blood if she wants to get somewhere in this
world, because all important occasions in her life are going to
be marked by blood. That's why nature gives her lots of practice beforehand, so she'll get used to it."

"Really?" Sadika was scared out of her wits. "Why do they
have so much extra blood in their bodies?"

"It all starts when you reach about the age you are right
now," Zahra went on, ignoring the question. "Blood starts flowing out of you every month for one week like clockwork for the
rest of your life, or until you're very, very old."

"Why? Can't something be done to stop it?"

"You don't want to stop it, stupid. It's like the flowers of a
fruit tree, not only desirable but essential. You tell me—can a
mango tree bear mangos without flowering?"

"No," Sadika replied, confused, trying to grasp the connection between the flowering of a mango tree and a bleeding woman.

"A mango tree can't bear mangos without flowering," Zahra said, "and a woman is doomed to a barren life and doesn't deserve being called a woman without a whole lot of bleeding."

Sadika, still baffled, shuddered at the prospect of bleeding. At the same time she was intrigued by the possibility of producing mangos, her favorite fruit, out of her own person. She opened her mouth to speak, but Zahra went on. "By far the most important time in her life, when she simply has to shed blood, is her wedding night, of course."

"Of course." Sadika agreed, but her mind was abuzz with questions she was afraid to ask for fear of seeming stupid. She wondered what part of a woman's body shed the blood. Her head? Her fingers? Maybe her stomach or her mouth? Or did it come out of her pores? Didn't it look strange, when she began to bleed for no apparent reason? Maybe women shed blood the way snakes shed skin or peacocks shed feathers, painlessly, and for rejuvenation. Maybe it only happened on special occasions. And how did the blood know when to come out, and when to stop coming out? And how much was enough?

She had to ask, "How much blood does she shed? As much as when you run into a prickly thorn bush or as much as when you break your head?"

"It all depends on her state of goodness," Zahra said. "The purer and more honorable a woman is, the more she'll bleed."

"Why is that?"

"I don't know. That's just the way it is. And the louder she screams, the more honorable and pure she is. Of course that goes without saying. Anybody would scream louder, the more blood they lose."

That particular conversation became engraved in Sadika's mind. When she was introduced to various laws of physics and chemistry, like the law of conservation of energy and the laws of motion, she wrote on the inside back cover of her physics textbook, "The Law of Purity of Womankind. The blood lost by a woman on her wedding night is directly proportional to her state of honor and inversely proportional to her state of dishonor. The same rule applies to the intensity and frequency of her screams."

Before Zahra gave her this piece of vital information, it had already been drummed into Sadika's head that a woman's honor was the most important thing in the world for her, her trump card in the marriage market, something to die for. But the method of acquiring this essential quality seemed fuzzy at best. She knew that she was supposed to talk, walk, and dress in a certain way to let the world know that she was an honorable female. But this was the first time she had learned about a way to demonstrate that she possessed this sterling quality, and she vowed to take full advantage of it. She said to herself, "I will somehow produce so much blood on that fateful night that people will be convinced beyond the shadow of a doubt that I am filled with honor up to my neck."

She began to devise a plan. She thought she might get some goat's blood from the local slaughterhouse and put it in bottles small enough to be smuggled into a room. That couldn't be too difficult. After all, Khanum got a whole bucketful once every year to fertilize her grapevine to make it produce the sweetest grapes. And these bottles of blood could easily be substituted for perfume and lotion bottles in a bride's makeup kit. And once she managed that, how difficult would it be to drench the wedding bed with blood so that her honor would be as obvious as the light of day? And throughout that wedding night, she was determined to emit the most bloodcurdling screams that anyone ever heard, so no one would be able to doubt her purity and goodness. In fact, she thought, I must make sure to practice those screams from time to time, so my voice won't desert me at the crucial time.

It was as a result of these conversations with Zahra that Sadika, crossing the playground alone one day, filled her lungs with air and collecting all her strength, let out a lusty scream. She had just bought a couple of spices for the morning cooking at the nearby general store, and was on her way home. The scream had not fully died in her throat when she heard four or five pairs of feet running toward her. She had not realized that people might be in areas where she couldn't see them.

The five people demanded to know what was wrong.

At a loss, she began to stammer, then blurted out the first thing that came into her mind. "Snake. A big snake. This big," she said, stretching her arms as far as they would go.

"What kind?" A ripple of excitement went through the group as they looked around for the snake and something to strike it with.

It was not often that a snake was found in this neighborhood, even though at one time it had teemed with the slithering creatures. That was until people discovered how tasty their meat could be if properly cooked. Grilled snakes, curried snakes, lime-lemon snakes, tandoori snakes, snake *tikka*, snake *biryani*, all kinds of dishes were experimented with, until the snakes were gone. Actually it was a good thing that they disappeared when they did, because the religious elders were becoming seriously displeased with the eating habits of the community, which they felt would result in some kind of punishment from heaven.

"What did it look like? Where did it go? How long was it? Was its head up or down?" Several impatient voices prompted Sadika.

"Blue, green and yellow." These were the colors of her favorite dress.

Their excitement was intensified by the thought of beating such a colorful snake to death, an experience that would provide material for tall-tale tellers for months to come, maybe for years, even for generations. They began to search the area, peering under bushes, but after a couple of hours the excitement fizzled out and the crowd finally dissipated.

Sadika made sure the next time she practiced her honorable woman scream that nobody was around.

Or she thought she made sure.

But no sooner did the blood-curdling scream leave her throat than people appeared, again apparently from nowhere, demanding to know what was wrong. A few of these had been present at her earlier practice session. This time Sadika had the presence of mind to tell them at once about the six-foot—no, six-yard—blue, green and yellow polka-dotted monster, hissing at her as it lifted and lowered its cobra-like head.

If Sadika had not been known to be calm and stable, she would have been called a liar. But creating a commotion without a reason was so foreign to her nature that no one thought for a moment that she could be making up a story about this spectacular snake. Besides, on both occasions at least one or two others, for reasons of their own, said they had glimpsed the monster before it slithered off into the underbrush. Munnoo, Zarreen's little brother, insisted that it was an insult to call such a ferocious fire-breathing creature a snake. And Lateef, the new occupant of House #8, Gali #13, swore the snake had an evil face with red eyes, and had warned him in an angry, hissing voice to back off.

When after an exhaustive search, nothing remotely resembling this snake could be found, rumors began to fly: a thousand-year-old evil jinn, an invisible, magical creature made of fire, was in love with Sadika and was following her around in the guise of a fantastic snake. Whenever he found her alone, he made himself visible to her, so extra precautions should be taken to prevent her from going anywhere by herself.

This provided a good deal of excitement. For days, people asked Sadika questions about the jinn until they finally left her alone because she seemed unwilling to cooperate. They concluded that she was trying to protect her status as the beloved of a wicked jinn. Over the next few months, the jinn was forgotten. But by then it had become a habit with Khanum to make sure someone went with Sadika whenever she went out. So she had to give up any hope of practicing her honorable woman scream.

Just as with the snake episode, everything sensational that happened in Sadika's early life was related either to school or to Zahra. Even the events that ultimately resulted in Sadika's going to America were connected with school. But only to a certain extent. In actuality, that highly unlikely event was the result of Khanum's background and psychology. It was Khanum's American connection and her almost obsessive need to solidify it that began the chain of events.

six

THE ELDEST OF two daughters and one son, Bilqees Beebee had been married off at the age of fifteen to Akbar Khan, a union eagerly agreed to by her lower middle-class parents, Zahid Muhammad and Hajra Beebee, recent immigrants from India.

Barely able to eke a respectable living from a small farm in northern India, they had been forced to migrate to Pakistan when Hindu-Muslim tensions ripped through their tiny village of Ganjia Nagar. Their finances had been a shambles and, with Bilqees Beebee approaching marriageable age and her sister Ashfaaq Beebee not far behind, they could foresee no improvement to their lot in life. Since they had always been farmers, they settled in Jogiapur on a small piece of reasonably fertile land. When Akbar Khan's mother, desperately needing a female to help out in their house and farm, proposed marriage between her son and Bilqees Beebee, Zahid Muhammad and Hajra Beebee jumped at the opportunity, not only to get one daughter off their hands but to do it inexpensively, because Akbar Khan's mother, known to everyone as Maanjee, did not demand much of a dowry.

This despite the fact that Akbar Khan, nineteen, was her only son, and her husband, Dilawar Khan, had died two years earlier of some mysterious ailment. Perhaps Maanjee's demands were reasonable because Akbar Khan had two sisters—Gul Fatima, eleven, and Taj Fatima, ten—for whom he would probably have to provide dowries. Assurances of Bilqees Beebee's impeccable reputation, cheerful disposition and dedication to hard work had sufficed, along with two not-so-fancy sets of clothes and a pair of gold earrings that Hajra Beebee had owned since her teens.

Once she was married, Bilqees Beebee's life became a maze of housework and successful and not-so-successful pregnancies. It had taken six years—two miscarriages, two stillborn daughters and one healthy daughter—for her to at last produce a son. Asghar Khan's birth gave some measure of security to a marriage that had floundered dangerously after each reproductive fiasco. Then there had been two more successful pregnancies in rapid succession, but they had not been very significant since they produced only daughters—Zafary and Sajida. It was only after the domineering Maanjee had died and the family had moved away from Akbar Khan's clan to the relative isolation of Islamabad, that Bilqees Beebee had come into her own.

Oddly enough, it was because of the grapevine in her tiny courtyard that she had eventually attained a certain influence in the neighborhood. For this reason, she sometimes felt that she loved that grapevine better than anything or anyone in the world—even Asghar. It had begun when, in order to stop birds from pecking at the bunches of grapes on the vine, she had sewn small bags for each bunch out of the fabric scraps she had found at the local tailor's shop.

One day Zahra remarked that one of the bags on the vine matched the clothes she wore for Eid, the biggest religious holiday of the year. "And those others are like the clothes Zarreen and Kausar wore on Eid," she continued, growing excited. Soon word spread that the bunches of grapes on Khanum's grapevine wore bags that matched just about everyone's best clothes. People began to drop by just to take a look at the vine, giving Khanum the opportunity to chat and gossip, along with the incentive to keep the bags on the vine in good condition. Sometimes she took special pains to dress her vine in festive bags for special occasions, when more of a crowd was expected and people were especially receptive to pronouncements on various topics.

It was partly as a result of the positive response to these pronouncements that Khanum grew more and more assertive as the years went by, eventually becoming as domineering as her deceased mother-in-law, whom she had dreaded and hated with all her heart. Khanum not only controlled her own family, but was able to exert a significant level of influence over people in all of Gulmushk Mohalla. Everyone, including her husband and children, was afraid to cross her. Bilqees Beebee was pleased by this because she had a deep-seated sense of insecurity that demanded that she manipulate everyone and everything around her, and her success at that was testimony to her ingenuity.

Nobody in Gulmushk Mohalla knew anything about Bilqees Beebee's background except that her family had migrated to Pakistan from India after partition in 1947. Thus she could create any history that came into her mind. Her family, she said, had been better than *nawab*s, rich, powerful elites in India, where they had lived in the lap of luxury. In fact, the branches of her family tree had been entwined with almost all the powerful clans of the Indo-Pakistan subcontinent at one time or another; and the history of the region would have lost at least half its luster without the contributions of many of her ancestors.

"The last Mogul emperor, Bahadur Shah Zafar, loved my father to distraction when he was a kid," she proudly declaimed to a skeptical audience. "In fact, he used to carry him around, sometimes on his shoulders and sometimes piggyback. The emperor's sons were so jealous of my father that they tried to poison him many times. Not that anyone could blame them, because the king used to talk about leaving his entire empire to my father instead of to his own flesh and blood. Well, actually of course my father *was* his flesh and blood. He was the first son of his brother's second wife."

According to Khanum, all the rich industrialists in Pakistan had been in her family's employ in pre-partition India. And the reason they had become so powerful while she herself was now poverty-stricken was that they had used stolen papers to establish a fraudulent claim on her ancestral lands. Most of her listeners doubted this story, but none had the courage to confront her and risk being cut to shreds by her razor-sharp tongue. The result was that every time she delved into her grand past, its splendor increased a notch or two.

Khanum was well aware of people's doubts, but she was not deterred in the least. She had not been given any weapons to fight for respect in the jungle of life, and if she had the ingenuity to come up with one on her own, she would not hesitate to wield it. Minimal education, a plain appearance and a mediocre family background, along with an extremely disappointing husband and three daughters, did not provide much ammunition to survive the battle zone that she considered the world to be. If the fact that her family had migrated from India in 1947 amidst chaos and anarchy, could be used to her advantage, she would be a fool not to seize the opportunity. After all, drastic situations called for drastic measures, and she considered her entire life a drastic situation.

This fabrication of her past she considered an essential strategy for survival, and she guarded it with her whole being. People who tried to question her closely about her pre-partition life received such a tongue-lashing that they dropped the subject and beat a hasty retreat. Take the time Sarwat Jahan, the wife of Haji Aziz-ur-Rahman, the richest man in the neighborhood, told a group of women who had been invited to her middle daughter Kausar's engagement party, that there were too many contradictions in Khanum's stories for them to be credible.

"How can anyone with a brain in her head believe anything Khanum says, when she says different things at different times?" Sarwat Jahan remarked, believing Khanum to be out of earshot in another room. "Were her family mansions in Maysoor or in Jaipur? And her family's world-famous banana and mango orchards—the ones that supplied fruit to heads of states and royalty—were they in Ahmadabad or in Amritsar? And about Mr. Khokhar, the big industrialist. How could he have been her family chauffeur, when he can account for many generations of his family?"

That was as far she got before Khanum descended upon her with eyes shooting bolts of lightning. One look at her enraged face was all that was necessary for Sarwat Jahan's listeners to repress any expressions of agreement, let alone their own embellishment on her comments.

"I wouldn't be so eager to throw dirt on someone else if I were you, *behen*," Khanum bellowed in a voice like a loudspeaker. "Everyone knows about the way your husband makes his money. You think people are stupid? That they don't know that no one gets rich running a fabric store? That they believe the pilgrimages to Mecca that your supposedly pious husband makes every year are really for performing the Haj? Ha! Everyone knows about the smuggling and the other shady things your precious family is involved in. Or at least *I* know! But luckily for you, I'm a very discreet woman. Many people's secrets—" here she glanced at the group assembled "—are safe in this breast—" thumping herself hard in the chest with her fist "—and they will remain here—unless of course I'm forced to give them up."

The women, who had turned to stone during this tirade, hurried to pacify her. "You get angry so fast, Khanum. You know that Sarwat Jahan didn't really mean anything she said. She's always exaggerating and making things up."

Sarwat Jahan stood tight-lipped, not daring to look at Khanum, and slowly began to inch her way toward another group of women. She had no intention of crossing swords with Khanum. Not when people more skilled than she in the art of exchanging insults had conceded victory to that woman. Khanum had made it her business to learn everything about everyone, and there were always some grains of truth in whatever she spat out in her fits of rage. Since everyone was vulnerable in some way, it was safest not to contradict anything Khanum said. Then, even though bitter words had to be swallowed and tongues bitten from time to time, at least personal glass houses were safe.

Many women even looked forward to Khanum's tirades. They enjoyed hearing some of the things she said, things that they would never have had the courage to bring up themselves. Sarwat Jahan's husband's exploits, for example, had become a source of jealousy and controversy for almost everyone. His mysterious visits to Saudi Arabia, supposedly to perform Haj, had made his family very wealthy in just two years. Rumor had it that he was involved either in drug trafficking or gold smuggling. Especially after Jahangir Ahmed, better known as Jagga, who lived in House #16, Gali #12, failed miserably in the export-import venture that he had patterned after Haji Aziz-ur-Rahman's business, the consensus was that no one could make that much money that fast in legitimate business.

The entire neighborhood had watched with interest as, at the urging of his wife, Zamurd, Jagga had conducted some dubious research that convinced him that women in Saudi Arabia were in desperate need of breast pumps. Buying a few hundred of these pumps with his life's savings, he had arranged to make a pilgrimage to Mecca. There, unable to unload the pumps that he had been assured would sell like hot *samosas,* he had looked for some item to take back that would at least pay for his airfare. Deciding that sexy lingerie would be an ideal choice for sensuality-starved Pakistani women, and that he could even sell them at his small general store, he had bought a few dozen items with the last of his money.

That backfired in a big way. Many an irate husband threatened to bash in his head if he made any more attempts to corrupt his wife by selling her indecent clothing. One man even sent knife-carrying thugs to Jagga's modest shop. "Either you make these disappear," they had thundered menacingly, holding up the offending items, "or we'll make you disappear."

It was rumored that Khanum was actually an American spy. Her younger sister, Ashfaaq Beebee, who had made a brilliant match with an educated man, a schoolteacher, now lived in the state of Pennsylvania in America with her husband Aarif Hassan, and was believed to be Khanum's American connection. No one bothered to expend energy wondering what kind of information the American government could want from a semi-literate woman who seldom left her immediate neighborhood. It was enough to believe that in exchange for whatever she was peddling, the American government sent Khanum embarrassing information about people's lives.

In a neighborhood where gossip and rumors were the very stuff of survival for ladies of the house, a juicy rumor like that not only acquired a life of its own, but became more colorful and elaborate with each retelling. Whenever something untoward happened in the neighborhood, someone would always assert that Khanum had a hand in it. Whether it was the loss of a job without any apparent reason, a sudden hike in the price of food or the mysterious disappearance of someone in the middle of the night, Khanum was at least partially credited. Some even claimed that she had had prior knowledge of the aircraft explosion that killed the former president of Pakistan, Zia-ul-Haq. Otherwise, why would she have gone shopping in that particular part of town on the very day it happened? She must have had some assignment in her work as a spy.

Khanum, who had actually spent that miserable day getting a steel pan mended, was beside herself with joy when she heard that rumor. How lucky for her that the pan had broken when it had, and that Allah Ditta, the cheapest person to make such repairs, was so much in demand that she had had to spend the entire day in Moti Bazaar awaiting her turn. She was shrewd enough to know that the wilder the story the rumor mill manufactured about her, the more daunting her image would become. So she carefully nurtured and molded each bit of gossip, keeping quiet when it served her purpose and bringing up the topic of America when that furthered her goal. Often the bits of information about America fabricated by her fertile mind and delivered by her smooth tongue in an authoritative manner, were utter nonsense.

There was, for instance, the day Hamida Aapa invited some women for an afternoon of tea and gossip. The atmosphere was relaxed because the men were not due back from work for

some time, and it was too early to worry about dinner. When
tea was about to be served, Hamida Aapa unlocked her steel
storage trunk and fished out an unopened box of imported
American cookies. Pride at being able to offer such an exclusive
treat was written on her face as she broke the seal in everyone's
presence so that no one would doubt its authenticity and fresh-
ness. After arranging some of the butter cookies on her best
serving plate, she put them on a table in her concrete verandah.
Suitably impressed, everyone but Khanum helped themselves.

When, after a while, Hamida Aapa offered them to her directly, inquiring at the same time if she was feeling all right,
Khanum began to speak in a hushed voice, looking over her
shoulder for added effect. "Do you know, America is so intent
on curbing the population growth in poor countries like Pakistan, that it secretly adds crushed birth control pills to all the
food it exports to these countries?" Pausing to shudder, she concluded dramatically, "I would rather die than touch any part of
those cookies!"

Nobody dared to mention the thought uppermost in their
minds—that she was probably past the age when she needed to
worry about the effectiveness of her reproductive system.

"I wouldn't let my children near American cookies either,"
Khanum went on in her high-pitched, irritating voice. "And I
would advise you, *behno*, sisters, to stay away from them. You
never know what the consequences could be, even at our ages.
My sister who lives in America tells me that pus instead of milk
comes out of the breasts of some of the young mothers who
have eaten these kind of cookies."

At that point, a mortified and resentful Hamida Aapa, who
had been full of pride a minute before, was left with no option
but to protest that she had had no idea about any of this when
she bought the offending cookies. Also, she quickly added, her
children, especially her daughters, had never tasted the things,
because she believed in doing most of the cooking at home. It
was good marriage training for young girls.

It was at times like these that many a neighborhood woman would have cheerfully wrung Khanum's plump neck and thrown her out in the street for stray dogs to feast on.

Over the years, her fabled connection to America had become as precious to Khanum as her fabricated past. Both were necessary props in her battle to carve out a niche for herself in the neighborhood social circle, lending her the stature and license she craved. So when Ashfaaq Beebee, her sister in America, had made a veiled suggestion on a visit some years earlier that her son Haroon and Sadika would make a good couple, Khanum had jumped at the opportunity. Not only would a match between those two lessen her burden by eligibly marrying off one daughter, but it would also strengthen her association with America.

Khanum talked about her sister and her family in America with great pride. Hearing her, it was hard to imagine Ashfaaq Beebee's husband as being anything less than president of the United States, and their son Haroon as less than a movie star and Einstein rolled into one. Khanum's joyous heart filled to bursting if she was able to bring up the subject of her future son-in-law among women who were lamenting the lack of eligible suitors for their daughters.

"Everyone living in Pennsylvania, which by the way is the best state in America, is familiar with Haroon," she would tell them. "What with him winning so many major awards, and being on half the teams in college, besides being able to speak three languages, his picture is in the newspapers all the time. Why, he has won so many trophies that my sister and her husband are considering adding a room to their house just to show them off. Of course, the biggest trophy was the one he won at the Science Fair. That's the one all world-renowned scientists win before they go on to become famous."

Khanum's words would almost always be greeted with silence. Nobody could win a match of one-upmanship with her when she was elaborating on the sterling qualities of her future

son-in-law, or for that matter, of anyone in her family. She had
honed and perfected her boasts over the years. It meant nothing
that almost no one believed anything she said. She was like a
beehive that everyone was afraid to disturb. In any case of course,
without visiting America, it was impossible to prove she was
lying.

The understanding with Ashfaaq Beebee was the only reason
Khanum tolerated Sadika's continued schooling. Without that
understanding, the girl's education would have been terminated
abruptly. Every time she thought of Zahra, Hamida Aapa's daughter next door, Khanum had to repress a shudder. That young
woman was well on her way to spinsterhood, and there was nothing her mother could do about it. If Zahra's parents had taken
her out of school early and worked harder to attract marriage
prospects, the situation might have turned out differently.

Sadika had already completed ten grades, which was more
than enough. Any grade after the tenth was considered to be
college level under the Pakistani educational system, and Sadika,
a first-year student at the government-subsidized College for
Women, was studying subjects like economics, statistics and
math, which to Khanum was sheer madness. What good would
this fancy knowledge do a young girl who was going to spend
her life serving her husband, taking care of her home and raising her children?

On top of everything else, the college was nearly a two-mile
walk from home, and in today's sinful world a girl could easily
lose her good name or good character in less distance than that.
If that happened, who would marry her? And what if Zafary
and Sajida demanded to follow in their sister's footsteps and go
to college too, even though they had flunked a couple of grades
each, and were barely able to stay in school? That would bring
a whole new series of headaches. If only it had been Asghar
instead of Sadika who was going to college, Khanum would
have felt proud instead of worried and resentful, and would
have started looking for a job for him right away. But unfortu-

nately Asghar's teachers had always treated him unfairly, with the result that the poor boy now suffered heart palpitations at the very thought of school. Luckily he had good friends in the neighborhood who spent time with him to keep him from slipping into depression. Otherwise she had no idea what would have become of a sensitive child like her Asghar.

It was not that she was not open-minded, Khanum would tell people; she was as broadminded as they came. But anyone who was not an imbecile knew that it made no sense at all to educate girls. This affected the quality of wives by filling their heads with useless information and encouraging them to rebel against their families. She could still remember how shocked she was when she found out that, among other things, teachers talked about different means of transportation between cities. How was one supposed to keep young hot-blooded people in line, when all they needed to do if they wanted to run away was consult a textbook and buy a ticket?

Sadika was about seventeen. At that ripe age Khanum had already been through two miscarriages and was swollen with her third pregnancy, while at the same time she did most of the housework, and catered to her mother-in-law's every whim. If Khanum had her way, not only would Sadika be married by now, but matches for Zafary and Sajida would be arranged as well. Granted, they were only fifteen and fourteen, but girls were like weeds—they grew up faster than anyone expected or wanted them to.

What made the situation harder to tolerate was the fact that dowries were ready for the three girls; Khanum had made sure of that. Like most of the women she knew, she had been in a state of panic ever since the birth of her daughters. Everything good or even passable that had crossed the threshold of their tiny house, Khanum had tried to save as part of a dowry for one of the girls. It didn't matter how small the item was: at the last minute there would be so many other expenses to take care of that it would be hard to come by even small things like toothpicks.

Since she sincerely believed that a seventeen-year-old girl had no business depleting the family's meager income on books when her dowry was ready and she was of marriageable age, sometimes even the food that Sadika consumed caused burning resentment in Khanum's breast. The rest of the family could probably survive for one month on what Sadika put away in a year. But there was no way to remedy the situation. Khanum would think about that after finishing with the morning cooking, while she rested on her worn *charpai* in the tiny concrete verandah shaded by her favorite grapevine. Fanning herself with an old magazine that also served to chase away flies, she regretfully conceded that if she hadn't been saving Sadika for Haroon, the burden of at least one daughter, possibly two, would have been lifted from her shoulders by now.

It wasn't that she didn't love her daughters. The very fact that she was so keen on seeing them settled before their youthful looks tarnished, or before there was a blight on their reputations, was ample proof that she was devoted to them. The city was riddled with examples of young females who had been doomed to a spinster's life because of an indiscretion or some foolish idea about the importance of education. And if some people thought that she wanted to deprive her girls of the enjoyment of their teen years, Khanum's philosophy had always been practical. She often said, "If milk sells, there's no need to turn it into cream. And if cream sells, why waste time and energy converting it into clarified butter?" In her opinion, Sadika was milk that was being turned into butter when it was perfectly feasible to unload her in the condition she was in.

The tragedy was that in accordance with custom, it was unthinkable to take steps to decide Zafary's or Sajida's future until their older sister was taken care of. Thank God the time was not far away when Sadika would be safely married to Haroon. Ashfaaq Beebee had written to say that they would be coming to visit for an entire month over the summer. And how was dear Sadika? She couldn't wait for the time when she would have the right to call her her daughter.

Khanum could not wait either.

seven

As THE SUMMER of '87 approached, Khanum's household was buzzing with activity. It would not have been so bad if what was expected was simply a visit from a sister from America. What put everyone on edge was the knowledge that Sadika's prospective mother-in-law and prospective husband were coming. And for an entire month. Even if everything went well, that was going to put a tremendous strain on the household.

What was especially worrisome was the fact that Sadika's marriage was not a done deal. Thinking about the many things that could go wrong was turning Khanum into a bundle of nerves. What if Haroon didn't like Sadika? After all, the girl was no beauty. Worse, what if he decided that he preferred some other girl he met? Or Ashfaaq Beebee might realize just what a gold mine her son was, leading her and her husband to make financial demands on the Khans that could not possibly be met.

It wasn't easy to secure an eligible son-in-law in this day and age, that was for sure. Not only were people looking to climb some kind of ladder by marrying, they didn't respect an understanding between parents the way they used to. All young men were considered fair game unless they were actually married. And sometimes even then.

To Khanum, all women with daughters of marriageable age seemed like vultures. If she had her way, she would have shot them all dead or locked them in a cage till Sadika was Haroon's wife. But unfortunately, all she could do was curse them in her heart and pray that their strategies would not work. Until Sadika's marriage with Haroon actually took place, Khanum knew that every girl who was remotely eligible would be paraded in front of him, and all kinds of discreet bait dangled in the hope that he would bite. All one had to do to become aware of that, was to visit the local tailor's shop where expensive, stylish dresses were hanging although no wedding or other big occasion was coming up. Undoubtedly everyone with an eligible daughter was getting ready to try to win the jackpot—hers, Khanum's, jackpot! There was a general feeling of expectancy based on the widely accepted belief that young men were like eggplants on a flat dish; the slightest dip was enough to totally change their position.

If Khanum was nervous, Sadika was panic-stricken, and for a different reason. She was being cast in a role for which she had no experience. Being the intended of anyone would have been hard enough. But to be regarded as the fiancée of an eligible young man of the world was almost too much to bear. How was she supposed to act? Being teased by the neighborhood girls was not a problem—all she had to do in response was act embarrassed, whether she felt embarrassed or not, and hide her face in the scarf she always wore, and that would be that. But how she should respond to *him* was a total mystery.

Traditionally, it would have been enough in any romantic situation simply to be bashfully demure. But values were changing. Young men, though not expecting a real affair, did want a romance of sorts with their intended, even in Pakistan. Sadika felt pretty sure that Haroon, a product of American society, would expect that much at least, if not more. She was not equipped to deal with even a light courtship, especially as the character of the prospective fiancé was a big question mark. Would Haroon expect a Western romance or an Eastern one? She knew he couldn't expect both, since Western and Eastern ideas of romance differed. One could find that out from immersing oneself in romance novels from both cultures, as Sadika was doing lately, during every free period in college.

She knew, for example, that in her culture, home was still the woman's domain, her main responsibility, and romance blos-

somed, at least in these novels, in domestic situations. The hero
might, for example, show up unexpectedly just as the object of
his interest finished baking professional-quality cakes and pastries, or producing an elaborately embroidered cushion cover.

In Pakistani movies, when the hero came for dinner to meet
the heroine's family, he invariably found that all the most delicious dishes—sometimes kebabs in the shape of hearts—had
been cooked by the heroine; that the prospective father-in-law's
beautiful sweater was hand-knit by her and that she crocheted
the cushions in the living room, and embroidered "Sweet
Dreams" on the pillowcases. In addition, every time the hero
made any attempt to speak to her, her shyness and innocence,
both highly regarded qualities in an Eastern female, turned her
into a stammering, bumbling idiot.

But in American culture, where Haroon was coming from,
young people seemed to be into images, into looks, so that romance bloomed when faulty zippers and skimpy clothing revealed porcelain skin stretched over delicate bones, or rippling
muscles covered well-formed parts of the anatomy. The heroine
in America might ask the hero to rub suntan lotion on her bare,
perfectly sculpted back. Or she might request that he unstick
her zipper when no one else is there to do that for her. The hero,
of course, obeys with a palpitating heart, clammy hands, and
rubbery knees, while she, brilliant, well-informed, and innocently unaware of his reaction to her, expounds on the state of
the economy, business problems in the firm where she holds a
prestigious job or on contradictions in government foreign policy.

Sadika did not know whether Haroon would be more captivated by the shy, repressed virgin of traditional Urdu romances,
or the strong, independent girl she encountered in the pages of
Harlequin novels. She finally decided that it would be best to
stick to tradition. After all, some Harlequin heroines were dam-
sels in distress, and even now in the romances of Barbara
Cartland, heroines who personified innocence and virginity always won their men. And wasn't the very fact that Haroon was

considering an arranged marriage, testimony to his being a man bound by tradition?

Often Sadika allowed herself to imagine a possible scenario. She and Haroon could have a Barbara Cartland romance with Haroon acting like a Cartland hero—masculine to the point of savagery. For most of his visit, he would mistreat and torment her because of some misunderstanding, occasionally punishing her with burning kisses and impassioned embraces, while his harsh words betrayed his perturbed state of mind. "Your innocent ways do not fool me, you worthless little gold-digger," he would say, his voice hoarse, his eyes haunted and hungry. Just as she opened her mouth to protest these unjust accusations, his lips would swoop down on hers like some graceful eagle catching its prey in mid-flight. A highly exhilarating prospect, even though the regular, intense, grinding motion of such kisses that she had observed in old English movies reminded her of Khanum's efficient movements when she was crushing spices with a stone wedge on a flat surface.

It was a good thing that the heroes and heroines in those old movies were young and strong, in the prime of life, and had strong teeth to match, she would think to herself, experimentally giving her own teeth a sharp push. Imagine how embarrassing it would be if one person's dentures fell out into the mouth of the other, right in the middle of a passionate kiss.

Perhaps being a more refined person, Haroon would inflict on her the gentler, smoother, bone-melting kind of kisses she had seen on TV in Zarreen's home, in which the mouths of the participants seemed to disappear and collapse within their joint cavity. Almost seamlessly—like the joining of two fabrics by a sewing machine, viewed right side up.

During the dramatic climax of their romance, which of course would occur when Haroon was ready to leave and she was about to perish from unrequited love, the misunderstanding separating them would suddenly and miraculously vanish, and he would throw himself at her feet and declare his undying devotion. In a voice choking with emotion, he would tell her that unless she consented to spend the rest of her life by his side, he would jump from a ten-story building or drown himself in the Atlantic Ocean. Or he would go mad with grief, tear his clothes, and disappear into the dense jungles of Africa, never to be heard from again.

At that moment, she would cover his hard masculine mouth with her soft delicate fingers and beg him to stop, his words being more than her gentle loving heart could bear. And then of course they would spend the rest of their lives in a euphoric haze.

Sometimes Sadika even fantasized about what that euphoric haze would involve: lots and lots of strapping sons with the strength of Hercules, the brains of Einstein, and the rugged handsomeness of Robert Redford, all of them totally devoted to her and guided unquestioningly by her advice. And Haroon, overcome with love and gratitude for the richness she had brought into his life, would dote on her every action and hang onto her every word.

Sadika was going through a most unsettling period, to put it mildly. The thought of Haroon's visit was causing at least as much trepidation as excitement. Her biggest fear was that, in an effort to seem all the right things to Haroon, she would end up acting like a fool. Her young siblings, on the other hand, untouched by trepidation, looked forward with unadulterated excitement to meeting their prospective brother-in-law. No thoughts of culture clashes entered their heads. Asghar was thinking about all the fun and food he would get to enjoy, since the guests would have to be shown a good time. At last he might be able to sample the lifestyle that should always have been his.

Sajida was looking forward to having a good time, while Zafary was anticipating having the time of her life. Her friends had told her all kinds of stories about the pranks that could be played and mischief that could be done to young men who came to court one's sister. She had been assured that "anything goes in these situations," and that it was only when the relationship was finalized by marriage that she needed to become respectfully cautious and polite. Zafary planned to play some of these tricks on the unsuspecting "boy," as any prospective bridegroom was called, regardless of his age. It would be funny, for example, to substitute salt for sugar in Haroon's tea and cut white soap in shapes to look like the popular dessert *burfi*. How she would laugh when he took a sip of the salty tea or a generous bite of the fake *burfi*! She had also been given to understand that it was permissible to irritate the boy by hiding his personal belongings—his shoes, his glasses and his watch. It would be great fun to see Haroon searching for his things.

The ultimate prank of course, that Zafary knew she did not have the courage to play, was to put *jamal ghota*, which caused instant diarrhea, in the boy's tea and then watch him knock frantically at the locked bathroom door. This last tactic had become a favorite after local politicians had supposedly used it to disperse an unruly crowd. It hadn't taken more than a few minutes after the consumption of the complimentary tea for the angry mob to dissipate, or so the story went.

The only disinterested person in the Khan household was the head of the family, Akbar Khan. As always, he acted more like a guest than an active participant in the internal affairs of the home, which he deemed strictly a woman's province. The only time he betrayed emotion was when dinner was late because everyone was busy whitewashing the house.

eight

THE DAY FINALLY came on which Ashfaaq Beebee, her husband Aarif Hassan, son Haroon, and daughter Ishrat, were to arrive.

Preparations had reached a peak: three new sets of clothes for each member of the Khan family, stitched diligently by Khanum and the three girls, had been completed just two days earlier. And only last week, after debating with herself, Khanum had taken Sadika shopping for a lipstick and a pair of high-heeled shoes. She did not want her sister to think that her prospective daughter-in-law was living in the dark ages, ignorant about cosmetics and high fashion. But at the same time she didn't want Ashfaaq Beebee to get the impression that Sadika flouted tradition. After all, one of the major reasons why Ashfaaq Beebee was considering making Sadika her daughter-in-law was that she wanted someone who would uphold Pakistani customs.

For the past two weeks, Khanum had been doing all she could to make sure that the family's way of living, eating, dressing, even of greeting loved ones, presented the proper mix of conservatism and modern enlightenment. After whitewashing the tiny house, cooking fancy foods and desserts and preparing the best room for the guests, the entire family spent more than three hours on the last night making garlands of fresh flowers to drape around the necks of their honored guests.

Going to the airport was an event in itself. Except for Akbar Khan, none of them had ever seen the inside of an airport. Akbar Khan had been there because his boss at the office had recruited people to greet a local political leader with cheers. Even though that had been a pleasant experience—recruits had been paid twenty rupees each, plus a free meal and transportation to and from the airport—today was different. The very thought that the entire family was not only going inside an airport, but was bringing home some people getting off an airplane, one of the twentieth century miracles, was enough to fill each and every member of the family with pride to the point of bursting.

The best part was that the neighbors all knew where the Khans were going that morning, and were probably green with envy. At least that was what Khanum liked to think. To her, life's high points occurred whenever she was able to make someone, somewhere, jealous of her in any way.

At the airport, the proudest person in the little group, fragrant with the scent of locally produced perfumes and jasmine garlands, was Sadika, who was almost dizzy with excitement and trepidation. She wore one of her new outfits, bright green with yellow embroidery at the collar and cuffs, and walked somewhat unsteadily in her brand new brown patent-leather high-heeled shoes. She had not confined her berry-red lipstick to her lips, but had spread it, mixed it with face cream, over her face, neck and hands. Zahra had told her that would give her skin a healthy but ethereal maidenly glow. Besides, the Western hero in Sadika's favorite romances always lost his heart to the girl with the Eastern values when he met her shy gaze under long black eyelashes shimmering over fiery cheeks. Zahra said that if Sadika could combine this glow with trembling moist lips and a "hesitant virginal manner," that would indeed be the last nail in the coffin of Haroon's heart.

Asghar Khan yelled "There they are!" and almost fell off his perch on top of the barricade outside the airport, when he spotted Ashfaaq Beebee's family. "Where? Where?" Khanum shouted back, and sure enough, within the space of a few minutes, Khanum's and Ashfaaq Beebee's families were standing face to face in greeting. Or rather, Khanum was greeting her sister, while the rest of the Khan family, after placing their flower

garlands around the necks of the newcomers, hung back in confusion made worse by the response they received.

Haroon, wearing blue jeans and a navy blue T-shirt, looked
withdrawn, almost sullen. Aarif Hassan, Ashfaaq Beebee's husband, a nondescript man in khaki pants and a white shirt, received his garland with cold civility, uttered a curt reply to the
salaams, and glanced with contempt at the blushing, tottering
Sadika, who was racking her brains for something appropriately cordial to say.

Haroon's younger sister, Ishrat, a feminine version of her
father in looks as well as attitude, was dressed in Western black
pants and a patterned purple short-sleeved shirt, apparently intended as a statement rejecting her heritage. Neither brother
nor sister was particularly good-looking or striking in any way,
but the unmistakable stamp of America on both made them
seem incredibly attractive.

This was more than one could say for Ashfaaq Beebee, whose
appearance everyone found amazing. She did not look like someone visiting from America, or even from a big city in Pakistan.
Rather, she looked like a woman from an isolated country village. She was covered from head to foot in a flowing robe, her
hair hidden by a drab scarf. She certainly had not dressed like
that when she lived in Pakistan with her parents more than two
decades before. She had been stylish then. In fact, it had been
her sense of fashion and style that had helped her to land her
eligible husband. Otherwise, it was generally agreed, someone
with Aarif Hassan's education and potential would never have
married her.

By the time this uncomfortable group had made their way out
of the airport and into two taxis, Khanum was experiencing the
first twinges of unease. These twinges blossomed into full-fledged
alarm during the couple of hours it took to reach home, carry their
luggage into the Hassans' room and freshen up for lunch.

Khanum had always thought that the marriage of Haroon
and Sadika was, although not a done deal, at least a highly

probable one. After all, wasn't that the entire purpose of Ash-faaq Beebee's visit—to finalize the dearest wish of both sisters? How could what seemed like a virtual *fait accompli* turn into an apparent impossibility in such a short space of time? The cold behavior of Ashfaaq Beebee's family gave the distinct impression that they could barely tolerate the company they found themselves in. So did they really want to forge a closer relationship? Was there someone else in the picture? Had Ashfaaq Beebee misled Khanum about the willingness of her husband and son to consider this marriage? A thousand questions blossomed from kernels of fear and doubt to fill her mind.

Sadly, Khanum bade goodbye to a secret dream that she had not openly acknowledged but had speculated about in the deepest recesses of her heart. What if not only Sadika found a match in Haroon, but Ashfaaq Beebee's daughter Ishrat and Khanum's son Asghar also tied the knot? It had not seemed at all improbable that Ishrat would find Asghar wildly attractive, since he was the embodiment of masculine beauty. The only disadvantage to that match was that both Ishrat and Asghar were about seventeen, and everybody knew that ideally the husband should be at least ten years older than the wife, so that there was less chance that she would end up looking like his mother after the birth of a few children. And this age difference also cut the probability of his straying when the natural juices of her body dried up in menopause, while he was still relatively young enough to demand his fun in the bedroom on a regular basis.

Khanum still remembered vividly what had happened to Noor Deen and his wife Aasma, erstwhile neighbors who were both in their forties. According to the rumor mill, Aasma had resorted to using all kinds of oils and creams to make the sexual act less painful to her and more acceptable to her husband, but to no avail. Noor Deen had been turned off by the fact that before he could even touch her, she had to take a good five minutes to apply all kinds of paraphernalia.

The harrowing day had come when he left his wildly sobbing wife and four crying children to marry a much younger
woman of dubious background. The entire neighborhood had
watched the heart-wrenching spectacle.

A few had tried to talk some sense into Noor Deen, reminding him of the days when his wife had meant the sun and the
moon to him, but his mind had been made up. Like a scene
from some vintage Urdu movie, he had pried loose the hands
clutching at his pant leg, and left without a backward glance.

So perhaps God's hand was there in preventing an attraction between Ishrat and Asghar, Khanum thought, trying to calm
down. She could only hope that the two-year age difference
between Sadika and Haroon would prove adequate. That night
she sat on her prayer mat, her eyes closed and a large gray
dupatta, a chiffon scarf, covering her head. "Please God, let
Haroon and Sadika's match take place. I will sell off one of my
four gold bangles and give the money to the poor if you will
just grant me that," she promised.

What Khanum could not know about the Hassan family
was that they always behaved in a suspicious and hostile way
toward decisions that Ashfaaq Beebee made for them, but that
they were always finally railroaded into doing whatever it was
she wanted them to do.

nine

DEPENDING ON HOW you looked at it, Ashfaaq Beebee was either a diluted or a sophisticated version of her older sister. While Khanum was loud and forever ready to launch a verbal attack, Ashfaaq Beebee had cultivated a fine veneer of softness and civility. Anyone meeting her for the first time could not help but be impressed by her sweet voice and sincere manner. Only after knowing her for a while did one discover that her tongue could be as sharp as a surgeon's scalpel, and that her sweetness camouflaged deep malice and bitterness, just as the sugar coating masked the intense bitterness of the quinine pills one took to fight malaria.

The skill with which she wielded her vicious tongue could be considered an art form. Even when cut to the bone, the victim did not realize for some time that he or she had been wounded at all. And even then, only the target grasped what had happened. Bystanders would not only be unaware of the butchery, but would remain captivated by her excessive sweetness, of which no one was more a recipient than her husband and children.

Ashfaaq Beebee often used religion to make her point or to advance her personal agenda, because chances of being challenged were few, given most people's limited theological knowledge. She dressed and talked like an extremely pious person, dragging in religious references whether they were appropriate or not, just as Khanum liked to drag in comments about America. In reality, her religion, like Khanum's, was self-advancement. Anything that could make her life easier, she somehow found a way to connect with Islam: Islam wanted women to stay at home, so she felt it her duty to do that; Islam had given the responsibility of finances to the man of the house, so she would not dream of interfering with that.

Similarly, since Islam prohibited form-fitting clothes, she did not need to exercise; Islam wanted people to eat and live simply, so she would never cook elaborate meals or exhibit any interest in decorating her home. It seemed that anything that required energy or effort was forbidden by her religion. If anyone suggested that she might be distorting Islam to suit her purposes, she reacted as though a knife had been put to her throat. When she began to gain weight and her hair lost its luster, her interest in religion quadrupled. She wore only long shapeless garments and hid her hair under a *hijab*, explaining that good women had to dress modestly.

Secretly she loved her robe and her *hijab*, believing that they gave her special advantages. She would not have traded even one of her shapeless garments for all the designer gowns in the world. No longer did she have to spend hours trying to find flattering clothes or an attractive hairstyle. It took no time at all to get ready to leave the house in the morning. All she had to do was take a shower, or if she was in a hurry, wash her hands and face and throw on her things, and she was ready. There were no bad hair days for her, or bad body days either. She acquired instant confidence, not only in her appearance but in the fact that everyone deferred to her in matters of religion, assuming that she was an expert in that field.

The icing on the cake was people's perception that she had sacrificed many of her freedoms by adopting her new mode of dress. Much to her amusement, some even regarded her as a martyr. If only they knew! If it was up to her, she would have gone one step further and worn a *burqa*, a garment that not only covered a woman from head to toe but hid her entire face behind a thin black veil. Wearing that, one never had to worry about wrinkles or unguarded facial expressions. A woman in a

burqa turned into an invisible blob for all practical purposes;
no one noticed her any more.

She loved America just as her sister loved Islamabad, because living there she too could fabricate an impressive past.
The only time she envied her sister in Pakistan was when she
considered the lack of finesse Khanum could exhibit in dealing
with her children and husband. Ashfaaq Beebee could not behave so openly. She had had to learn to manipulate her family
through intrigue and subterfuge. But by hook or by crook she
had made her marriage a stable one. Anyway, it was good to
know that even if she got divorced, as an American citizen she
would be entitled to money from Aarif Hassan to raise her children and live a comfortable life.

Aarif Hassan lamented that he had not been born and raised
in America. All men were victims, he thought, but men from
Pakistan and India were more victimized than others. Most
women were far more clever and manipulative than men, and
Pakistani and Indian women were by far the worst. Their men
were no match for them at all.

Almost invariably they started out with a façade of sweetness
and innocence that lasted only till a man was totally in their clutches.
Then, after he was completely paralyzed by a mortgage, a few
kids—after every hair on his head was tied in some kind of obligation or debt—that was when they started to show their true colors.
The man, raised in a culture where divorce was still taboo and
financial obligations were a male responsibility, was like a trapped
animal whose struggles to escape only caused him more pain.

Aarif Hassan had seen this happen dozens of times, and in
fact he himself had been victimized by it. He had been eager to
prove that he was loyal to tradition by choosing a bride from
Pakistan. But he also wanted to demonstrate his Western independence by picking a female who was not his family's choice.
Ashfaaq Beebee had seemed to be the embodiment of all his
dreams when he had first met her. Shy, timid, and reserved—
that was how she had been, calling on all his protective instincts.

Little did he know at the time that her shyness and timidity were part of her plan to ensnare him and her reserve simply reflected the fact that she had nothing to talk about.

At times he felt awed by the cunning that he thought he saw in these Indian and Pakistani women. They were more worldly wise than their men, and he believed it was because the world was a tougher place for them than it was for men. First, they had to preserve impeccable reputations to make a good match. Then came the quicksand of the marriage mart. If a girl did not have the right combination of looks, reputation and money, she was likely to be rejected by either the prospective husband, his mother, or both. If she was one of the fortunate ones who succeeded in marrying a reasonably acceptable man, the next battle front was the bearing of children, especially a male child. By the time she reached middle age, she had the cunning and scars of a general who had spent most of his life in a war zone.

He envied American men who had the option of dumping an intolerable mate and starting fresh if they wanted to, or at least to threaten that if they didn't want to. But because of the society he was raised in and his subculture in America, the Pakistani male's options died an abrupt death the day he got married. And not only that, white American men were accepted in mainstream society, while men like Aarif Hassan who had spent an entire lifetime working hard to become productive members of that same society, were still considered outsiders.

Aarif Hassan was therefore not in favor of the match that his wife had concocted between Sadika and Haroon. Why go through the hassle of arranging a wedding in Pakistan, sponsoring the new bride for a green card, helping her adjust to American culture, when Haroon would be better off married to a girl born and raised in America? If he was lucky enough to find a girl who was also blonde and blue-eyed, it would be the ideal situation. Then maybe Aarif Hassan's grandchildren would not be looked down upon as immigrants as his children were, despite having been born and raised in America. Nor would they be torn between two cultures as he himself, as well as his children, had often been.

Most of the time he kept his opinions to himself. Twenty-one years of marriage to Ashfaaq Beebee had taught him the need to tread warily. He knew that it was very difficult, if not impossible, to argue against something she wanted fervently. And even though as Haroon's father he felt duty bound to protest, he kept postponing that protest because he knew it would not accomplish much and would make his life a living hell for a few weeks at least. It had been a long time since he had gone against his wife's wishes, but his memory of it was as vivid as though it had happened yesterday.

Once, when they had been married only a couple of years, he had felt fully justified in declaring all-out war. Upset because Ashfaaq Beebee had refused to cook special foods for his diabetic father or to let his sister pay them a long visit, he had threatened divorce and engaged in a shouting match. When that failed to change her mind or lessen his resentment, the need to express himself physically had led him to pick up a flour bowl and throw it into the back yard, shouting, "Who do you think you are, you two-bit female? You were nothing when I found you, and now you're less than nothing! I'll send you back to Pakistan to rot in hell. No one will want your cursed shadow to fall anywhere near them when I finish telling them about your foul disposition!"

Instead of cowering in fright or breaking down in tears as he had fully expected, Ashfaaq Beebee had dumped the entire pot of chicken curry on the floor. The school of hard knocks she had graduated from had been tougher than his. "You try doing that," she had shouted back in a voice louder than his, "and we'll see who'll send who to rot in hell! After I'm done telling the immigration people in America about savages like you, you'll be lucky to have a job, or a place to live in!"

For a few moments he had contemplated throwing the salad or the dessert on top of the chicken curry, but then his rational nature had taken over and he had desisted. What would it accomplish, he had reasoned with himself. They were almost out of food and he could sense that it was not beyond Ashfaaq Beebee to start throwing dishes. He was not prepared to deal with that mess and expense. He knew a divorce was out of the question. He had gone against the wishes of his entire family when he married Ashfaaq Beebee, breaking his long-standing engagement to his cousin and causing his parents, who had arranged the match, to lose face. Divorcing Ashfaaq Beebee would be an admission that his choice had been wrong—he would rather die than admit that, given the commotion he had caused at the time by threatening to commit murder or suicide, or both, unless he had his way. So he had had to concede defeat. His sick father had eventually moved in with his sister, who limited her visit to his house to a few tense hours.

Ashfaaq Beebee had been far from a gracious winner. Just as the British had never let the last Mogul emperor, Bahadur Shah Zafar, forget his one act of rebellion against them in the War of Independence that they called the Mutiny, she enjoyed bringing up that isolated incident. "If it had been up to you," she would say whenever she got the chance, "I would certainly have been turned into a slave for your family. It's thanks to my learning some independence from my American sisters that I'm normal and sane today."

ten

THE VISIT OF Ashfaaq Beebee and her family lasted about a month, during which time the Khans waited on them hand and foot, deferring to their every wish as though it was a direct command from God Almighty Himself.

Every delicious treat or enjoyable jaunt within their power was provided to these guests. Every possible effort was made to satisfy their considerable desires, even if that meant dipping into hard-earned savings. When Ishrat expressed the wish to wear garlands made from fresh, sweet-smelling jasmine as she had seen worn by the heroine of a popular Urdu movie, Akbar Khan was told to go to the bazaar at once and select the freshest and the most fragrant garlands he could find. When Aarif Hassan said that he had been craving fresh sugarcane juice but hesitated to buy it from the local *thelay wallah* who probably didn't squeeze it in a sanitary manner, Khanum had procured sugarcane that very day and extracted the juice herself, with some help from Zafary and Hamida Aapa.

All Haroon had to do was utter a request and it was magically fulfilled. "I like to wear shoes that are clean and shiny," he had said. Sajida was immediately assigned the job of polishing his shoes every day and buffing them with the softest cloth she could find. And since Ashfaaq Beebee had said that her admiration for religious girls was one of the reasons she wanted her son to marry a Pakistani, Sadika had been given strict instructions to offer every one of her five daily prayers promptly and in full view of her aunt. Khanum had even lent Sadika her prized possession, a beautifully colored prayer rug, a *musalla*, that her

brother Farooq had brought from Saudi Arabia when he performed the Haj: she wanted Sadika to have as much visual impact as possible. "Make sure you dress in modest pretty clothes,"
she told Sadika when she handed her the rug. "And put the
musalla where your aunt can see you. If you can spare the time,
spend at least ten minutes in meditation after each prayer."

In addition, whenever Khanum thought that Ashfaaq Beebee might not have noticed Sadika saying her prayers, she would
be sure to point her out, and remark, "Sadika is not like most
young girls who are into having a good time. She finds contentment in prayer and meditation." Not that Ashfaaq Beebee needed
convincing. She had already decided that a non-complainer and
hard worker like Sadika was just the kind of girl she wanted for
a daughter-in-law. The match between Sadika and Haroon
would undoubtedly improve her own lifestyle as well as her
son's.

As the days passed and Ashfaaq Beebee and her family settled
into a routine, it was easy to see that they were really enjoying
their visit. They liked this better than Disney World. There they
had only been visitors to Cinderella's Castle, here they were
royalty themselves. Aarif Hassan had never felt more like the
head of a household, the embodiment of success, or the fountain of wisdom that his hosts clearly believed him to be. He
loved the way they hung on his every word as though it was a
priceless gem.

Ashfaaq Beebee was more saturated with butter than a dish of
baklava. This was not surprising, since she was the one with the
authority to dispense with that priceless treasure, her son. All the
neighborhood females who had daughters or even nieces of marriageable age were courting her with sweets and gifts. They would
show up bearing delicacies, accompanied by a young woman or
women dressed in their best outfits. Then they would sit and expound on the girls' many accomplishments and household skills,
as well as on the pleasure they felt at making the acquaintance of a
woman of the world who was also a kindred spirit.

"How do you find the time to do all the work that you must do in America while you cultivate so much wisdom and sophistication?" they would gush. "On top of that, you've managed to hold on to your values. What an inspiration you are to all of us and what an honor it is to have the opportunity to get to know you." Then seemingly as an afterthought, they would add, "We hear that you're considering Sadika for your son. She's a wonderful girl, of course. If only she had some property in her name. You never know when hard times might come your way. That's why I tell my husband that we've got to put some property in our daughter's name. Young people should have something to fall back on, I always say. Don't you agree?"

When she heard that Ashfaaq Beebee was looking for a religious daughter-in-law, Begum Faiza Hameed, who lived seven streets down in a different neighborhood, had paid a special visit to inform Ashfaaq Beebee that her daughter was a true Syed. In other words, she was a direct descendant of the Prophet Mohammed, with family trees on both her father's and mother's side going back fourteen hundred years to prove it. "I know that people like to say that it doesn't really make any difference," she said, adding in a conspiratorial tone, "But I ask you, who is more likely to go to heaven, someone who is or someone who is not a direct descendant of the Prophet Mohammed? And their spouses and children, of course."

Khanum, listening to these remarks, had to swallow the ball of resentment and rage choking her. If Ashfaaq Beebee had not been there, she would have told these so-called friends what she thought of them. How dare they visit under the guise of friendship, just to try and sow seeds of doubt in Ashfaaq Beebee's mind? This was definitely not an era of decency. Everyone was out to get something for herself. It didn't matter who was hurt in the process or deprived of their rights.

But Ashfaaq Beebee was present, and Khanum could only smile and nod at the women supposedly paying her sister a visit, while she wished she could plunge a dagger straight into their worthless hearts. Most infuriating was the fact that these same back-stabbing women had counseled her about the many things she should do to ensure Haroon's match for her daughter, advice that Khanum had taken very seriously. Now she was beginning to wonder about that advice, given these ulterior motives—and she was wondering what these women must be telling Ashfaaq Beebee when Khanum was not there.

She wished now that she had not made Akbar Khan get rid of the car that he had bought with such enthusiasm two years before. She was not sure what the make of that beat-up vehicle was, because Akbar Khan's mechanic friend had attached insignias onto its rear from all kinds of cars ranging from a Mercedes Benz to a Volkswagen Beetle. It had been torture to get it to run. First, water and oil leaked out and had to be put back in, every morning. Then it wouldn't start unless it was pushed for a hundred yards or so and the family members couldn't do it alone. So eventually most of the neighbors had taken to leaving their houses an hour earlier in the morning to avoid members of the Khan family knocking on their doors. But despite all this, it was a car. And it would have lent them some much-needed status at this time.

The visit to Pakistan was turning out to be most enjoyable for Ishrat. If someone had told her a few days earlier that she would want to spend her entire life this way, she would have said they were crazy. She had never been considered good-looking, but ever since she had come to Pakistan, she had been made to feel like a beauty queen. Unfashionably plump for America, here her healthy, flourishing look was just what the people of her aunt's neighborhood admired. At home, eating fattening food made her feel guilty. Here she could indulge herself, knowing that nobody would compare her to a beach ball.

Sweets saturated with sugar and main dishes drowning in homemade butter—anything and everything was permissible: it was a food-lover's heaven; a glutton's paradise. Ishrat was even beginning to love the clothes, the loose traditional shirt and pants worn by the local females. Why wouldn't she, when she was the recipient of whistles whenever she went out in the street in her somewhat Americanized version of this *shalwar kameez*? She could still feel the numerous pinches she had received while shopping for jewelry at Bano Bazaar. Since Khanum was furious and mortified when she found out about the pinching, Ishrat pretended to be offended too. But actually she had been pleased. She had never been pinched in America, even when she had been at her slimmest and dressed to the nines.

She didn't much care for her aunt or her aunt's family, but as their sole purpose in life seemed to be to make things enjoyable and comfortable for her, she was willing to tolerate them. Besides, they never demanded anything from her, which made them almost likable. Having Sadika as her sister-in-law was fine with her.

But the happiest visitor was undoubtedly Haroon, viewed literally as a hero. He had overheard young girls compare him to current movie heart throbs. "Look at the way he walks, as though he owns the earth, just like Nadeem in the movie *Soghaat*." In America he had never been compared even to a character in a cartoon. His mother of course had made it her mission to convince him that he was God's gift to womankind, but until now he had only half-believed her. Now he was becoming convinced. Even the primmest of young ladies looked at him with an invitation in her eyes. And if he smiled at someone, she seemed in danger of expiring.

He couldn't know that Khanum had built up a picture of him and his family over the years as perfection personified. The way he walked in his Western casual clothes, his American mannerisms and even his attempts at communicating in a mixture of broken Urdu and English, were widely admired.

"So, what do you think of Pakistan?" older people would ask him. The more he criticized America and praised the good things in Pakistan, the friendlier they became. These people seemed to have a love-hate relationship with America. They fantasized about it, and the young people, especially, wanted nothing more than to get there somehow. The parents of those same young people were attracted by the opportunities America offered, but at the same time were upset by the mere mention of this monstrous country that threatened to gobble up their young.

They knew through bitter experience that once your offspring went to that land of opportunity and voracious appetites, they were lost to you. Nothing was strong enough to pry them loose. What's more, often they turned their backs on their culture and upbringing, changing beyond recognition their priorities, their attitudes, even their appearance. So Haroon's readiness to criticize everything American raised him sky high in their estimation.

With the older women, Haroon had discovered a particular diversion. He knew they were searching for a suitor for someone they knew and loved—be it a daughter, a niece or some other relative. "I have seen how fickle the females of the West are," he would say with a sigh.

"That's why I've decided to find a wife from here. The problem is that there are so many beautiful young women to choose from, I don't know what to do." Consequently, his favorite foods would magically arrive at Khanum's house with a note saying that this traditional dish was made by So-and-So's daughter explicitly for Haroon, and that it was hoped that the distinguished guest from America would appreciate this small token of respect.

He was showered with invitations to plays, picnics and dinners at exclusive restaurants. Secretly laughing at the expectations behind all this, he would swallow all the food and attention "without even burping," as the saying went in Urdu. Younger women not quite out of adolescence were the most fun to deal with. They obviously regarded him as a bone-crunching hero in one of those bodice-ripping romances displayed in bookstores everywhere. Much to the delight of his rapidly expanding ego, a little attention from him was enough to frazzle almost any one of them. All he had to do was whisper something stupid like "Hey beautiful, where have you been all my life?" out of earshot of her mother or any other older person always hovering around, and the excitement level of the young woman would go, so to speak, through the roof. Haroon spent many a pleasant hour thinking about what would happen if he could actually get his hands on one of them.

One thing he could not understand was why his mother had selected Sadika for him. Why not her sister Zafary? He could see how a daughter-in-law like Sadika, given her house-keeping abilities, would make Ashfaaq Beebee's life easy, but what about him? Sadika didn't do a thing for him—just the opposite. It wasn't only the smell of spices, onion, garlic and ginger that seemed to cling to her that irritated him, but the fact that whenever she encountered him she would try to find a way to move away—as though he was some kind of monster or ghost or something. Not that a monster or anything supernatural would be attracted to her, he thought. With all that garlic liberally sprinkled on her, even Count Dracula would be afraid to go anywhere near her.

When he tried to have a conversation with her, she became tongue-tied, turned beet-red and started to stutter. How was he supposed to get to know her? Worse—how was he supposed to want to marry a weirdo like her, his mother's dearest wish? Zafary, on the other hand, was a different story. She was mischievous and exciting, the only female in the entire neighborhood who didn't seem to revere him. She put salt in his tea instead of sugar, substituted pieces of soap for his favorite dessert and laughed uproariously when he bit into it; she hid his shoes and clothes and followed him around while he looked for them. Finally, after much pleading on his part, she offered to get them for him in exchange for a promise to buy her one of her favorite dishes from a vendor in town.

He was exasperated, annoyed and totally bewitched. Now Zafary—he thought to himself for the hundredth time—now

Zafary could be a pleasantly acceptable wife. If only his mother had had an understanding with Khanum about him and Zafary instead of about him and Sadika.

How binding were these kinds of agreements anyway? They certainly couldn't be iron-clad or why would all the matrons of the neighborhood be trying to marry him off to one of their daughters? Maybe getting what he wanted would not be as difficult as it seemed. Right now he didn't want to rock the boat, but once they were back in America he was going to give his mother an ultimatum: he would be willing to do her the favor of marrying one of her nieces, as long as that niece was Zafary and not Sadika. Otherwise, he would have to look for an American-born wife, a prospect that he knew would chill Ashfaaq Beebee to the heart because she believed that if that happened she would lose all control over him.

Meanwhile, Sadika was looking forward to a happy future. She knew that she had probably not made a very good impression on Haroon. But marriages, once decided by parents, generally took place since traditionally young people's opinions were not given much weight. Wouldn't Haroon be pleasantly surprised when he discovered that Sadika was a much more interesting person than he had had reason to believe? Maybe he already knew, being the man of the world that he was, that she was being put in a very awkward situation and was not able to be herself.

The honeymoon would surely be a wonderful time for both of them, full of exhilarating discoveries and happy surprises.

eleven

IT STARTED OUT as a blessedly routine day.

The guests from America had left about two weeks earlier, and life was gradually returning to normal. No longer did the members of the Khan household have to look and behave their best while rushing to satisfy the whims and wishes of Ashfaaq Beebee's family. Every meal didn't have to be a feast, and fresh means of entertainment constantly devised. Also at an end was the back-breaking work of cleaning up after visitors from the neighborhood, but it was still necessary to cope with the messes left by the guests from America.

Haroon's dirty socks and underwear were still being found in unlikely places—under the bed or behind pots and pans in the kitchen—and Ishrat's personal possessions, scattered all over the house, were even now being discovered during various chores. When Asghar had found her sanitary belt in one of the comforters, he had been unable to figure out what it was. Finally deciding that it was a weapon, something like a slingshot that one of his younger sisters had concocted, he had tried hurling small stones with it at the crows sitting on the courtyard wall.

After having swept the tiny courtyard, Khanum was browning onions for the afternoon meal, while Sadika shelled peas and peeled and chopped potatoes. After consuming so many meat dishes in the past weeks, it felt good to eat vegetables. No wonder Americans were so big and meaty. Since it was Friday, a holiday, school was out, and everyone was busy with housework. Akbar Khan and Asghar had gone to the Jumaa Bazaar, a local market held every Friday, where they not only rented a spot every week to sell vegetables, but bought their groceries for the entire week. Many others in Gulmushk Mohalla did the same: that was the only day foodstuffs were available at prices lower than at the conventional shops, and one could do some business on the side to supplement one's income.

The Khan income was especially in need of supplementation because the Hassans' visit had wiped out most of their savings. Khanum thanked God that the guests had left when they did or she would soon have had to borrow from neighbors or sell off some of the things being saved for the girls' dowries.

What had begun as a routine day stayed that way only till afternoon when the long awaited letter from Ashfaaq Beebee was delivered. Not by the mailman, as expected, but by Asghar, when he found it near the entryway underneath his kite, right where the mailman had dropped it yesterday. Then all routines evaporated into thin air. It had been expected that the letter, when it came, would be a cause for jubilation. But instead it sent everyone into shock. The peace and harmony of the household was destroyed as though a bomb had gone off, forever changing life as the inhabitants of that small house knew it.

"Dear sister," Ashfaaq Beebee had written. "I do not know how to tell you this. And I am sorry to have to cause you pain, but I do not have a choice. Haroon refuses to marry Sadika. He says she just does not appeal to him. When I ask him why, he does not give me any concrete reason. 'I am a flesh and blood man. I have feelings and emotions,' he says. That is not all he says. I am almost afraid to tell you the rest, but again, I do not have a choice, so here it is.

"Haroon is agreeable to an arranged marriage of my choice as long as his feelings are also taken into account. Marriage to Sadika is distasteful to him but he has no objections to Zafary being his bride. I know that is not what you and I wanted, or even what is appropriate. But there is nothing I can do about this. As you know, boys nowadays have a mind of their own. Others here tell me that I should be thankful that he wants to marry a cousin of his at all. You might not know this, but in America it is not considered proper to marry one's cousin.

"So write back as soon as possible to let me know if a match between Haroon and Zafary can be arranged. If not, I will understand, as it is more prudent for you to marry off your older daughter first. If you want to wait, however, I am not sure even this other match will be possible. You know how the young people are today—forever changing their minds.

"Your obedient sister, Ashfaaq Beebee."

It took Sadika and Zafary longer than the others to recover from the startling contents of this letter. But after a while, as Sadika returned to her many chores with her head bowed in shame, a smile began to play on Zafary's lips.

It couldn't be denied that a terrible thing had happened to Sadika, but it certainly wasn't Zafary's fault that Haroon liked her better. Actually, it did wonders for her ego, which had been frequently battered by her teachers and her mother constantly comparing her to Sadika. "Why can't you do your homework on time like your sister did? Try taking lessons from her to make your work better." Mrs. Rahim, the social studies teacher, had said that to her just yesterday, and Khanum was after her all the time to do housework like Sadika.

This was sweet revenge. And it grew sweeter by the minute as news of the letter spread like wildfire through the neighborhood. Normally, news took a few days to make the rounds, but this was particularly juicy, and straight from the horse's mouth, too. Zafary couldn't resist taking Zarreen into her confidence, while Zarreen swore Ikra to secrecy, and so on and so forth, till everyone was asking everyone else in hushed tones if they had heard the news.

Zafary, who until now had not received any particular attention from anyone, was suddenly admired like a heroine from an Urdu movie. "I had my eye on that girl myself for my son," declared Salima Ahmad. "If I had known that her parents would agree to marry her off before her older sister, I would have proposed ages ago." Sarwat Jahan agreed that "she was the best of the batch," adding, "After she gets married, the Khan family will not have any girls of good quality to offer to the marriage market."

Khanum and Akbar Khan discussed the unwelcome letter late into the night. They could not remember having discussions like this at any time in their entire married life. This was surely one of the most difficult situations that could be faced by parents of girls of marriageable age in today's society, where there was a dearth of eligible males. Could they afford to lose Haroon, they kept asking themselves. The honorable thing to do, according to the rules of society, was to flatly reject his humiliating proposal. But what if after they refused him, they couldn't find matches for any of their daughters? That was what had happened to Jamila Bhabi after she and her husband had spurned the hand of a cousin who should have sent his proposal for the older sister instead of the younger one.

This way, at least one daughter would be off their hands. It would no doubt make it harder to marry off Sadika. But getting a decent match for her would be hard anyway, once the contents of Ashfaaq Beebee's letter became common knowledge. Aspersions would be cast on Sadika's character, her values, upbringing, personality—even her appearance.

Khanum knew enough about the malice of people to realize that Zafary's character would not be spared either. "She had an affair with Haroon and snatched that prize right out of her sister's hands," people would say. But at least Zafary would be married and in America, and nothing said in Pakistan would have the power to hurt her.

Sadika would be hurt, but there was no help for that. Although Khanum had never really cared for her, there was certainly nothing wrong with her, and she hadn't done anything to deserve this sad state of affairs. But clearly her stars were not moving in her favor. If they had been, Haroon's heart would have fallen at her feet like a ripe mango, even if he hadn't been practically engaged to her. Wasn't that what had happened to Shaheen, Khanum's brother Farooq's third daughter? She had a squint and even a slight limp. Her parents had resigned themselves to her spinsterhood, when, much to their shocked delight, the head mullah of the local mosque, a prize many a mother had tried to snare, had proposed. The very things that had made her unmarriageable in the eyes of everyone else had stirred him to want her for his bride, having decided that marrying Shaheen would prove his noble character to the world in a very concrete way.

Unlike Shaheen however, Sadika's stars were not with her; her kismet had deserted her, and there was nothing she could do to stop bad things from happening. Khanum knew that from personal experience, for she had been at the receiving end of her own kismet's fickleness many times: you just had to endure what life threw at you. Perhaps, Khanum thought, one should be thankful to God that Sadika's situation was just bad and not the worst it could be. She hadn't gotten married only to be divorced because she had proved to be barren as some women had. Now that would be a fate worse than death.

All one needed to do to have proof of that, was to look at Farhat, Hamida Aapa's divorced niece—especially at weddings, which symbolized all her failures and where she was avoided like the plague. The bride was advised not to let even the shadow of such an unfortunate female fall on her. Not only that, Farhat was strictly forbidden to participate in ceremonies like the one in which married women put blobs of henna on the bride's palm as a good omen. One couldn't help feeling sorry for Farhat, but by the same token one couldn't blame family, friends and neighbors for shunning her. After all, she had proven herself to be a carrier of bad luck, and who wanted someone else's hard luck to rub off on them?

As things stood right now, Sadika would probably never be able to make a good match. But some widower with children, or some older man in need of a second wife, or even some older man in need of some pleasant company in his twilight years, would surely accept her. In the meantime, she would just have to develop a tough hide and live her life as best as she could.

The very next day, Akbar Khan and Khanum had reached the only decision they thought possible: Zafary would become Haroon's bride, and everything else would have to be dealt with as it occurred.

"Dear sister," Khanum wrote to Ashfaaq Beebee, "I appreciate the candor of your letter. We know that it was not your purpose to cause us pain. You are as helpless in these circumstances as we are. Haroon is very dear to us. If the only way we can have him as a son-in-law is to marry him to Zafary, then so be it. As far as Sadika is concerned, we pray that God will take care of things for her. Let us keep to our original plan of having the wedding take place within six months. You are right. Young people today cannot be trusted with not changing their minds.

"Another thing that needs to be mentioned is that on your trip to Pakistan for the wedding, it would not be appropriate for your family to stay with us, as the two people getting married should not be under the same roof. You should make arrangements to stay with Farooq, as Jogiapur is not far from Islamabad. Give your family our salaams. I will get Zafary's dowry ready as soon as possible.

                    "Your obedient sister, Bilqees Beebee."

twelve

It was Zafary's wedding day.

Preparations had been at full speed for days. Special chefs, adept at cooking up huge pots of wedding fare, had already been given their supply of chickens reared in the open countryside rather than in professional poultry farms, since the latter were too tender for this kind of cooking. Also, there was enough Basmati rice, vegetables, yogurt, spinach, goat's meat, potatoes, and sugar to provide four dishes and one dessert for about two hundred people. Two big tents had been erected, one for men and one for women, on the playground that bordered one side of Gulmushk Mohalla. Inside the women's tent, a small stage had been erected where the bride and groom would be seated at the high point of the ceremony and photographs would be taken.

Guests were due to arrive any time now. Most members of the bride's family were on hand to receive them, even though they looked tired and frazzled, since they had had hardly any sleep for the past several nights. Between participating in the constant singing of traditional wedding songs that had gone on in their little house for the past week, and making arrangements for the elaborate affair that the wedding was going to be if they were to hold up their heads in the community after it was all over, every single one of them felt tense and overworked.

Sadika in purple and Sajida in blue *shalwar kameezes* liberally embroidered with gold thread, were finishing arranging rented tables, chairs, and crockery. Akbar Khan and Asghar Khan, wearing less elaborate *shalwar kameezes*, were making sure everything was in order at the cooking pots. The evening air was permeated by delicious smells of chicken cooked in special spices, mutton with spinach, potatoes and eggs in gravy, rice pudding and vegetable pilaf.

Khanum was in the house supervising the laying-out of the dowry to display it to best advantage. Zafary had been hibernating at home for the past week in yellow clothes as custom demanded. The curse of the dowry had been part of the culture for so long that most people did not even question it any more, simply resigning themselves to the idea that they would be required to produce it if they had the misfortune to have a daughter. And this was on top of making sure that the girl grew up with an impeccable reputation and appropriate domestic skills. No wonder it was not desirable to give birth to girls. Who in their right minds would want this albatross around their necks?

After some effort to reform this dowry custom, even the lawmakers had given up. Passing laws that set an upper limit on the value of things that could be given as dowry had proven even more disadvantageous, because people had resorted to giving dowries under the table, making it harder for a girl to file a claim in case of divorce.

Neighborhood women had just finished folding up twenty-one fancy *shalwar kameezes* and five saris, three embroidered and two plain, with their most decorative parts on top. The one set of gold jewelry was elaborately displayed in its red velvet case. Other items, like a black-and-white television set, a Singer sewing machine and a dinner set, lay neatly lined up in their original packaging. A sofa set and a bed had not been included as part of the dowry because Zafary was going to America and couldn't take them with her. She was being given cash for the one-way ticket instead.

It was a grand dowry by neighborhood standards. Khanum had, after all, made it a priority since the very day her first daughter had been born. The neighborhood women who had come to help out in its arrangement were suitably impressed. And they told Khanum so.

"Our Zafary is being sent off like a queen," Hamida Aapa commented, folding up a particularly festive *shalwar kameez*.

"If people had known that so many good things were lying in wait for prospective in-laws, you would have had a hard time keeping your girls single," Salima Ahmed agreed, putting a few stitches in an appropriately folded sari to hold its position.

But Khanum was not fooled. She knew very well that even if the women meant what they said, there would be a change once they were out of earshot.

And she was right.

Gossiping about wedding arrangements and criticizing them, no matter how elaborate they were, was standard behavior. In this case, it had to be particularly nasty, since Khanum had mercilessly badmouthed many weddings, finding fault with the bride, the groom, the dowry, or the way the affair was conducted in general. Not once had anyone heard her approve wholeheartedly.

So for many a woman gleefully observing Khanum's nervousness, this was payback time. But it was necessary to exercise extreme caution and discretion: it was not wise to make an enemy of Khanum, given her sharp tongue, akin to a lethal weapon. Women tried to camouflage their remarks to preserve some plausible deniability and anonymity so far as possible. Joint sessions of critiquing were safest, because if everyone said something negative, nobody would risk repeating anything to Khanum.

"How do you think Khanum was able to make such a nice dowry for Zafary? She probably gave some of her other daughters' things to her as well," Zarreen's mother Rizwana said in one of the sessions, feeling jealous of the well-organized arrangements.

"I grant you that it's nice. At least on the surface. Did you see how out-of-date the clothes are? I tried so hard not to laugh! Remember the time when the *kameezes* were supposed to be short? Imagine, trying to pass off a ten-year-old fashion as brand new." Hamida Aapa was settling some scores of her own.

"You talk of style." Sarwat Jahan was always eager to add her own cold water to lessen the fire of resentment that burned in her breast against Khanum. "I say that doesn't really matter as long as the clothes are brand new. But did you notice that the embroidery on the purple *kameez* was frayed and there was an oil stain on the shocking pink *dupatta?* It's a very bad omen to start off a new life with old clothes."

"*Behen*, I think Khanum is trying to pass off some of the clothes from her own dowry as brand new. It would have been so much better if she had given Zafary fewer clothes and gotten new ones." Bushra Bee was a matron who had given her own daughter very few clothes as dowry, and was still smarting from gossip about it.

"Did anyone take a close look at the television set and the Singer sewing machine? I felt sad for Khanum when I realized they were old. They might not even work anymore. If machines are locked up for a long time, they won't work even if they were bought brand new." Shaheena, another middle-aged woman, had her own agenda. She was still trying to argue, five years after her daughter Mumtaaz's wedding, that the food processor that had been part of the dowry had not been a used one. People had gossiped that it didn't work because it had worn out, having been used in her own household for years. Shaheena had tried unsuccessfully to explain to whomever would listen that she had locked up that appliance in a closet along with other valuables, as soon as her brother brought it from London, and that it didn't work because it had never been used. She couldn't be expected to control a fickle machine, could she?

After much effort on her part, people had seemed to buy Shaheena's story. But many believed that her brother had bought her a machine that was useless to start with and that in order to seem generous and receive his sister's family's gratitude, he had let everyone believe that it worked perfectly. After Shaheena heard these new rumors, she tried to contradict them whenever she could. But people had gotten tired of the food processor story and didn't want to be drawn into it again, so the subject was immediately changed by Rumana Butt, Shaheena's next-door neighbor.

"*Behen*, what did you think about there being no bedding, no furniture and no cookware? Granted she's going to America and won't be able to use these things. But that's true of the TV and the sewing machine, isn't it? It's the symbolism that counts. You don't want to start a new couple off with so many bad omens."

"All these bad omens and a groom from America! *Behen*, it's enough to give me heart palpitations. I don't know how poor Khanum is holding up so well. I would be sick by now." No matter what the topic, Abida Hussain somehow managed to bring her health into it. For her, the ability to feel ill at the drop of a hat was a sign of sensitivity and sophistication. Much to her dismay, people had learned to disregard her and continue the conversation as though she had not spoken, leading her to complain often about the heartlessness of modern society.

"You know, *behen*, this Haroon that Khanum is so proud of—who knows what kind of person he really is? For all Khanum knows, he could already have a wife and some children hidden away somewhere." Sarwat Jahan, impatient with all this wary treading, had finally decided to take the bull by the horns and blurt out what many were thinking.

Speculation on the accuracy of available information about Haroon had been a common theme in discussions of the up-coming wedding. People inevitably brought it up because Haroon lived in America, a country in the West where people had lost all sense of values, morality, and modesty. It had been an especially hot topic among the young women who had gath-ered in the bride's home every evening for the past few days to sing traditional wedding songs. In the breaks between singing sessions, they exchanged horror stories about arranged mar-riages between girls from Pakistan and boys from America.

"It's not wise to marry a girl off to someone in America," one young woman said.

"You can't have any idea what he's been doing there. What if he's already married? Or has a girlfriend? Or he might want to take her to a house of iniquity."

Someone else added, "My uncle's daughter-in-law's sister was married to a man they thought was highly eligible. It turned out he already had a wife and three children in America, and he only wanted to use her for a maid."

"What happened when she found out?" The whole group was agog.

"She had to stay with him, of course. Where else could she go? What else could she do? She didn't know anybody, and she didn't have any American money, even though her parents had given her five sets of gold for her dowry."

Another entered the conversation. "That's not half as bad as what happened to my second cousin's friend's sister-in-law. At least the woman you're talking about had a place to stay. This girl was left at the airport with nowhere to go and no money."

"How? Why?" a dozen voices gasped.

"Like the girl in your story, this girl had been given mostly gold jewelry as dowry because she was going to America. After they came out of customs, her husband asked her to give him the jewelry box. He said, 'It's not safe for a woman to hold it. I'll get the car and come back. Wait for me by your suitcase.'"

"Then what?" The women already anticipated the answer.

"Then he disappeared for good, of course."

Another favorite topic of conversation at the song sessions had been Sadika. Everyone loved to speculate about what had really happened to make Haroon decide to marry Zafary instead of the elder sister. As usual, the conversation began with false sympathy and went slowly downhill.

"Did you notice how pale Sadika looked today? Poor thing, she has to put up a brave front when her heart is breaking," someone began. "What could be more tragic than losing your fiancé to your own younger sister?"

"I bet she wishes that if she had to lose Haroon, at least it would have been better not to lose him to her own flesh and blood," someone else said.

"Imagine having to suddenly think of him as a brother instead of a lover and a husband," a third added.

"You can't blame Haroon. I say it was very noble of him to do what he did. Anyone else might not have wanted to have anything to do with the Khan family at all, instead of agreeing to marry the younger sister," the first sympathizer remarked.

The interest level suddenly went sky high. "Why is that? Did Sadika do something to cause what happened?"

"I hear she's not as pure as they say. That happens a lot with girls who are too interested in school instead of the kinds of things they should be interested in. Someone told me that that's why Khanum wants to marry off the younger girls while they're still young and there are no rumors flying around about them."

"That's the best policy in today's evil world, *behen*," another agreed. "Girls should be married off as soon as they get their first period, I say. Before their reputations have a chance to get tarnished."

"You're right, *behen*. The world is a bad place now. And so deceptive. Who would have thought that evil was hiding behind that Sadika's innocent face? Why, looking at her, you'd think she was the purest of the pure."

"Don't blame yourself, *behen*. We were all taken in by her. Sometimes what looks like a diamond is nothing more than glass."

Khanum's nerves were stretched to the breaking point. She had been saving and planning for this event for the better part of two decades, but there were so many details to be taken care of, and so many things that could go wrong. What if the food wasn't cooked right or the dowry didn't come up to Ashfaaq Beebee's expectations? Worse—what if Haroon changed his mind yet again and refused to marry Zafary at the last minute?

Khanum would not be able to face the community ever again and it would become almost impossible to marry off the girls after such a scandal. Well, maybe some old geezers would accept them to acquire a housemaid-cum-nursemaid, but she would lose everyone's respect and would never again be able to flaunt her connections to America.

Khanum was worried too that Sadika was still unmarried. Had it been a mistake to allow Zafary to marry before her older sister? Khanum knew the way people's minds worked and what was being cranked out in the rumor mill. Nobody had said anything to her directly, but she had caught enough women glancing at her and speaking in whispers, not to realize what was brewing.

She had overheard Hamida Aapa say to Sarwat Jahan, "Sadika's character must not be good enough. Otherwise why would Haroon choose her younger sister over her, especially if they were engaged for a long time?"

"*Behen*," Sarwat Jahan had responded, "I knew something like this would happen when I caught Sadika looking with so much interest at my son Rasheed and his friends when they were playing hockey in the playground."

Sarwat Jahan had fallen lately into the habit of mentioning past predictions that everyone knew were recent fabrications. But it was common knowledge that she had many scores to settle with Khanum, so it was not wise to challenge her predictions.

Khanum was well aware of every vicious rumor and her blood boiled, but there was nothing she could do. She couldn't help wondering if she had been too hasty in making the decision about Zafary's marriage, but in her heart she knew that she had had no choice. Who in their right mind would lose a gem like Haroon just to avoid listening to unpleasant rumors?

By seven o'clock, small colorful groups of men, women and children had started drifting, laughing and chatting, toward the tents. Weddings were the high points of the community's social life because forbidden activities like dancing, singing, laughing loudly, even mild flirting, were allowed. It was hard to find a solemn face in the crowd, especially amongst the young men and women who, dressed in their best, eyed one another as they passed the gender-reserved tents. This was an ideal time to scout for and try to make a favorable impression on prospective mates. Since this could not be done directly, young people tried to attract attention by holding animated conversations with others of their own sex.

Sometimes, with luck, opportunity would knock, and two people with a mutual attraction would find themselves in relative privacy, face to face. Then they would try to make the most of the short encounter by doing exciting things, like feverishly whispering sweet nonsense, or even touching hands. Generally, after a few clandestine meetings, attachments were formed and major decisions made, given of course that both individuals were acceptable to their families.

With the passage of time and the increase of Western influence on young minds, doing things this way was coming to be viewed more and more as a happy compromise. Dating was still forbidden and marriages were still arranged, but now the elders generally gave their offspring a few names to choose from. For older women with an eligible male to marry off, going to weddings was indispensable. Where else could one observe so many single young women unobtrusively, without visiting their homes? Weddings were where the initial screening took place and relevant information was gathered. Zafary's wedding was no exception. Matrons could be seen scanning attractive young girls with eagle eyes.

"How would that girl in pink be for my Amjad?" Salima Ahmed, on a scouting mission for her recently graduated son, asked Sarwat Jahan.

Sarwat Jahan responded with relish. "She's good-looking with a decent family, but I hear her older sister ran off with somebody at the foreign language institute where she worked.

They lived together in sin for a whole week before the parents arranged a marriage and tried to hush it all up."

"No!" Salima gasped in horror. "She's out of the question, of course. You know how it is. These kinds of germs can travel from sister to sister. Well, who's the girl in red *shalwar kameez* next to my Iram?"

"Totally unsuitable. She's the one who's in the fashion show in her college every year. And she sings. She's training to be a social butterfly—not a wife."

"Someone," Salima observed, "should introduce her to the bride's older sister. It looks like neither of them will get married for a long time." This struck both of them as hilarious. Sarwat Jahan agreed that singing and entering fashion shows made a girl as unsuitable for marriage as studying science books. Then Salima whispered to Sarwat, "What do you know about the Paracha family? They expressed interest in my Iram for their oldest son Azeem."

Sarwat Jahan had thought about Azeem for her own youngest daughter Samina. So she answered with feigned nonchalance, "I guess he's okay, but that family is always fighting with each other. That sort of thing usually tells you what kind of life he and his wife would lead. But don't let anything I say color your judgment, *behen*."

"Really?" Salima looked worried. "We had almost decided to say yes to their proposal when it came. Now I'm not so sure."

Elsewhere, Shagufta, Kausar and Farhat were discussing what kinds of questions the American consulate asked people who wanted to immigrate. These stories were almost as widespread and interesting as the ones about American bridegrooms. People, especially young women, loved to embellish the tales they had heard, to make them even more colorful.

"They utterly humiliate you," Shagufta said with enthusiasm. She was from a nearby neighborhood, and her younger sister Misbah had married an American immigrant the year before. "Nothing about marriage is sacred to these Americans.

All they want to know in these interviews is whether you have ever had"—looking around and dramatically lowering her voice to a loud whisper—"sex."

"No!" Kausar and Farhat gasped in mock horror, leaning forward in their chairs to hear better. Sarwat Jahan's middle daughter Kausar, who had been feeding her infant son, inadvertently removed the nipple from the baby's mouth. He let out a screech of protest that threatened to drown out Shagufta's voice; Kausar impatiently stuffed the nipple back, rocking him back and forth while she strained to listen.

"They call you for an interview when all they want to talk about is how and if the marriage has been consummated," Shagufta repeated.

Farhat, Hamida Aapa's married niece agreed. "She's right. My friend Nasreen married an American citizen a few years ago, and she said the same thing. Funny thing is, she didn't know American minds were so twisted, and she didn't realize they were talking to her about sex when they interviewed her."

The other two demanded to know why she hadn't realized that.

Farhat explained that the interviewer spoke very poor Urdu, and was trying not to mention the word sex.

"What did he say? What did he say?" Kausar's patience was wearing thin. She was afraid her infant would start crying again and she would not be able to hear the juicy part of the story.

"He wanted to know if she still had her curtain of womanhood. Of course my friend thought that he was referring to purda, so she said that she didn't. She said she was a very progressive lady and never really believed in having the curtain of womanhood at all. Can you imagine? She destroyed her own character without knowing it. All the interviewer wanted to know was whether she still had her hymen."

Kausar and Shagufta were giggling uncontrollably. Kausar managed to control herself enough to ask why they would do that.

"Why is sex important to immigrate to America?"

Shagufta took a guess. "Maybe they want to make sure that anybody who comes there can do it. Otherwise, wouldn't they be asking questions about a person's intelligence or education instead?"

"Wouldn't that create a lot of babies? How come they don't produce as many babies as we do?" Kausar was obviously into babies nowadays.

Shagufta replied that she was sure birth control was the answer. "Also, my sister told me that it's kind of a community effort; they keep reminding each other all the time by saying 'no kidding.' They all work together against having children."

"You know, you're right," Farhat said. "I heard two American women who work at the American consulate in Lahore say those words. I would never have guessed that they were working on some kind of a mission."

"If they had their way, people here would do the same," Kausar remarked. "That's why female doctors in town are told to give their patients these anti-babymaking-balloons." Kausar triumphantly fished out a few of these balloons from her purse, much to the surprise of her companions. Her son had drifted off to sleep, and she was free to enjoy the gossiping in peace.

"How come you carry them around?" asked Shagufta, while Farhat stared in shock. Since she had a problem in her marriage because of her inability to conceive, this sort of thing was totally foreign to her.

"They make wonderful teething rings and balloons, why else? You don't really think I would do anything so foolish as to tell my husband to use these." Kausar took one of the anti-babymaking-balloons from its package and blew air into it.

Farhat roused herself. "Our men are too manly to even consider using things that will stop them from feeling some of the good manly feelings that God Almighty designed them to feel."

"Wouldn't it be wonderful if our men weren't so manly?" Kausar asked wistfully. "Then we wouldn't have to worry so much about having babies when we don't want them."

Shagufta agreed. "You're right. I'm the one who got the balloons from the clinic. But my husband won't use them because he says they take away from his fun, so I have to come up with ways to use them so I won't get pregnant."

"How?" Intense curiosity showed on their faces.

"The same way lots of women use them in my father's village. I boil a potato, mash it, and stuff it inside the balloon. Then I slide it deep inside me."

"I've heard that women in my village do the same thing with onions and other vegetables, even without the balloon." Farhat was eager to share this interesting information. "Sometimes when they forget to take them out, the vegetables start to rot, and they don't even realize it till they start feeling sick. By then they have to go to Doctor Shahida Mastoor to have it taken out. And listen to this: Dr. Mastoor is a good friend of my mother's and she told her that nothing smells more foul than the rotting vegetables that she extracts from inside women's bodies. She has had to throw up many times. Especially since these women are not good with their hygiene to start with, and it's revolting to give them a physical exam even under normal conditions."

For Akbar Khan and Khanum, the most wonderful and comforting aspect of the wedding was its routine predictability. Not one of Khanum's nightmares materialized. No one stood up in the middle of the religious ceremony to say that the wedding could not take place because the groom had an indecent past or suspicious parentage. No one tried to stop it by claiming that Haroon had been born and raised a Christian. In Khanum's worst nightmare, a faceless ogre was always able to prove that particular fact right then and there, by ripping off Haroon's pants and exposing his uncircumcised penis to all assembled.

Ashfaaq Beebee did not take one look at the dowry and demand that unless it was improved, the wedding party would have to go back without the bride, thus humiliating the Khan family for all eternity. Nor did Haroon or Zafary run away, refuse to marry, or commit suicide at the last minute.

Everything proceeded just the way it was supposed to. There was utter chaos at dinner as everyone tried to get first crack at choice parts of the meal. And when the bride made her appearance in all her finery and makeup, people almost knocked her down in their hurry to view her to decide whether she looked pretty enough. There was hysterical laughter at the ceremonies of *aarsi masaf*, when Haroon viewed his bride for the first time in a mirror; *doodh pilaai*, when the bride and groom drank milk out of the same glass; and *joota choopai*, when Sadika and Sajida, the bride's sisters, hid Haroon's shoes and refused to give them back unless he paid an acceptable sum of money.

Even Aarif Hassan and Ishrat seemed to have a good time. Ishrat was quite pretty in her mauve-and-gold *shalwar kameez*, and Ashfaaq Beebee, looking much nicer than usual in a gray and silver *banarsi* sari with a full-sleeve blouse, kept glancing fondly at her daughter. A couple of women had already approached her that evening asking about Ishrat's future plans, and she was bursting with maternal pride in both her pretty daughter and her handsome son. She thought that Haroon looked like a prince from a faraway land come to marry his fairy princess. Not that Zafary qualified as a fairy princess, even though she made a presentable bride in her traditional red short shirt and long flared skirt.

In Ashfaaq Beebee's eyes, Zafary would not have been a match for Haroon even if she had been a world-class model. But then, neither would anyone else. Picking a docile and biddable girl like Zafary for a daughter-in-law was the way to make sure that she would be able to retain influence over her son's life after his marriage.

When she had first seen him that evening, dressed in the traditional bridegroom's long gold jacket over a thin long white shirt and loose pants, wearing the tinsel flowered headdress, Ashfaaq Beebee had wept. She debated with herself whether she should put a black mark on Haroon's forehead. Marring the perfection of someone's looks was considered by many to be the only way to protect him from evil eyes.

By about eleven o'clock that night, it was all over. Zafary was officially one of the Hassans. After a session of hysterical sobbing and embracing, they had taken her away in a rented car decorated with flowers to the hotel where they were staying.

Akbar Khan and Khanum breathed a joint sigh of relief. Their second daughter was a respectable married woman now, and a large part of their responsibility was lifted. Even if Zafary got divorced, no one would ever be able to say that her parents had not fulfilled their responsibility of marrying her off. A week from now, she would be safely in America, away from the reach of malicious gossips.

thirteen

THREE DAYS AFTER the wedding and two days before the Hassans' departure, the *valima*, the wedding reception, was held in their hotel, which had offered wonderful package deals on wedding receptions and bridal suites for clientele who could pay in dollars. The wedding night and the traditional bed with its canopy of fragrant roses and jasmine covered with a net made of the same sweet-smelling flowers, had been thrown in without charge. As had the bridal car decorated with flowers and tinsel.

The newlyweds, dressed in their *valima* finery, looked happy. Oblivious to the other guests' keen scrutiny, they kept exchanging fond glances and whispers. At dinner, they fed on bits and pieces from each other's plates, relishing the taste of delectable fingers. Apparently Haroon and Zafary were satisfied with what had happened between them, disappointing the naysayers who had predicted that the match was doomed to failure from the very start.

"Watch and see," Sarwat Jahan had said, "the bride and groom won't be able to stand each other from day one. If they say more than a dozen words to each other at their *valima*, punish me like a criminal."

This was how Haroon had envisioned himself in his fantasies: a handsome object of attention and envy. For him the high point of the evening came when Durdaana, Sadika's college classmate, asked him whether he felt he had chosen the right bride. Knowing that Sadika was within earshot, he was able to deliver the speech he had planned for just this possibility, in a voice vibrant with feeling. Of course, he made sure first that there was enough of an audience to merit the effort.

"How can you even ask me a question like that? Everyone knows about the hell I had to go through to get my Zaffo." Here he glanced lovingly at Zafary. "And only I know how much moral courage, what sheer guts, it took to defy the elders. If it had been up to them, my bride today would have been someone else. But by the grace of God, I didn't let that happen, because I knew I couldn't live with myself if I wasn't true to my heart and my soul. It required a tremendous amount of moral courage, but today I have my reward: I have my mischievous and clever Zaffo, and I have my self-esteem. And I am proud that I didn't let society punish me for not being a machine, but a living, breathing, flesh-and-blood human being with feelings."

Sadika, who had been serving cold drinks to women nearby, was frozen as a statue. What about my feelings? she wanted to scream. Don't they merit consideration? What about *my* being a flesh-and-blood human being? Throughout the evening, that silent scream reverberated inside her, as did Haroon's words, shaking her already tenuous faith in herself as a woman.

Perhaps in a country like America, where associating with a member of the opposite sex was no big deal, especially if there was no physical involvement, Haroon's behavior could be construed to be morally courageous. But in a culture like Pakistan's, where it would hurt a girl's entire future, it could not be. How could Haroon use the yardstick of one culture to measure appropriate behavior in a totally different one? Didn't he know that in Pakistan, where dating was taboo and segregation was the norm, this had been Sadika's only opportunity to test her appeal to the opposite sex? Needless to say, she felt like a total failure.

She wanted to take Haroon by the collar, shake him and demand, What kind of self-centered and self-serving morality is this, that has turned me into a victim who can't even fight back? Because the more I try to defend myself, the sorrier a figure I cut. What kind of courage is this that forces me to suffer the unpleasant consequences of your bravery, rather than you? I'm the one who will have to bear the brunt of people's speculations and jokes, while you lead a pleasant life in America with your new wife.

It was ironic. She was at least twice as clever as her sister—a quality Haroon had attributed to Zafary. The only reason he didn't know that was because Sadika thought she was his fiancée, and she had been taught that fiancées were supposed to be reserved and shy, not clever and mischievous—behavior reserved for sisters-in-law.

Anyway, it was over. Haroon would not command the tiniest bit of her heart again, ever, she thought fiercely. She would rip it out, cut it into bite-size pieces and feed it to animals before she would let that happen. And calling him an idol with feet of clay, as Zahra had suggested in an effort to comfort her, was an insult to clay. Dry hot sand was more like it. Now that he had crumbled to the ground, he would never ever be allowed a place again—either in her mind or her heart. Nor for that matter, would any other man.

By changing her circumstances, Haroon had single-handedly changed her attitude not only toward romance, but toward life itself. Her desire for romance and fulfillment as a woman had been replaced by a more basic need. She felt that her actual survival was at stake. She had to find a man, fast. Not as a woman seeking a soul mate, but as a starving person looking for sustenance. She could see that in the eyes of the world she lived in, having a man by her side was essential to validate her very existence. Without a male to call her own, she was a nonperson.

Gone were the pre-Haroon visions of the Barbara Cartland hero and the Harlequin romance scenarios. Her present need could be satisfied by any male—a leper, an invalid, or an old man—anybody would do as long as he could give her his name, hence respectability, and a means of survival in the world.

Sometimes Sadika tried to think charitably of Haroon, who, after all, was now her brother-in-law. But she couldn't do it.

How could she, when all she wanted to do was drive a stake into his worthless heart? The prospect of watching him writhing in agony and begging for mercy was infinitely appealing. As was the vision of his burning into nothingness when the heat of the sun fell like strong acid on his vampire flesh.

Unfortunately, she had to maintain a façade of civility and friendliness toward Haroon. On the day after the wedding, she could not avoid offering him pieces of succulent tandoori chicken in a pleasant manner, when nothing would have given her greater joy than to truss him up like the bird and roast him in a tandoori oven.

How dare he put her in such an awkward and vulnerable position? To become a laughingstock when she had been an object of envy; to feel like a pariah when she had always walked with her head held high. It was killing her by inches. What made the whole thing harder to bear was the knowledge that she had not even been a direct part of the sordid mess, that she had been defeated at a game in which she had not even been a player, and now probably no man would ever be willing to marry her. Especially with all the rumors flying around about her, that she tried her level best to ignore. But since she lived in Gulmushk Mohalla, that was impossible.

Just yesterday, while passing by Hamida Aapa's quarters, she had stopped dead in her tracks at hearing her name mentioned. The conversation she had overheard between Hamida Aapa and Salima Ahmed had made her blood boil and reinforced her feelings of rage and helplessness.

"What reason could a boy have to break off an engagement for an arranged marriage, and then get engaged to somebody else, unless he had learnt something bad about his intended's character?" Hamida Aapa was saying to Salima Ahmed. "I hear she tried to have an affair with him, thinking that would please him since he came from America. But sadly for her, she miscalculated. The stupid girl didn't stop to think that Haroon wouldn't want to marry a Pakistani girl who acted like an American girl, when he could easily marry a genuine American girl. Why settle for a fake when you can have the real thing? *Behen*, I always knew all that reading and learning English would do Sadika no good."

"That's not the way I heard it, *behen*," Salima interrupted. "Sarwat Jahan told me that Sadika was having an affair with a neighborhood boy, and Haroon found out. I hear that the wedding cards had already been printed when he told his family he would never marry Sadika."

"No!" Hamida Aapa gasped in horror. "*Behen*, don't accuse our decent neighborhood boys of this kind of behavior. I wasn't going to tell you this, but my Shazia saw with her own eyes what happened a few days ago. Sadika got on the back of a motorcycle, holding on tight to a man who was not from here, just like a loose woman. She tried to hide herself in a *burqa*, and even borrowed a baby from someone to make it look like a legitimate family out for some fresh air."

"Maybe it *was* a family out for some fresh air," Salima said.

"Are you doubting my word?" Hamida Aapa was annoyed. "There was no mistaking the blue dress and glass bangles that she wore last Eid."

At this point, Sadika, hearing Shazia coming, had walked on. But she knew now that there was as much speculation about her as there were people in the neighborhood. A never-ending supply of fuel had energized the rumor mill: everyone wanted to be part of the excitement by adding a scenario of her own. If they had really wanted to, they could have gotten to the bottom of these groundless rumors very easily. But then there would be no interesting juicy conversations to liven up the monotony of their lives.

The departure two days later of Ashfaaq Beebee's family, including the newly married couple, did not, as Sadika had hoped, affect the rumors one bit. They spewed out with the same intensity and irresponsibility as before, taking on new twists and turns as soon as the old versions seemed in danger of fading. If before, Sadika had been simply having an affair, now she had been pregnant and forced to have an abortion; if before she had been seen clutching the back of an unknown man on a motorcycle, now she had graduated to clandestine meetings in one of the ditches in the playground. Painfully self-conscious, Sadika felt like dying of shame and embarrassment every time she came near a group of people who abruptly fell silent when they saw her.

Adding to the turmoil were Khanum's frantic efforts to marry her off. All the matrons who had thought Sadika was spoken for, were now given to understand through various people that they should approach the Khans as soon as possible before a promising girl like Sadika was whisked away from under their noses. But of course they were not fooled. In the network of small lower-middle-class Islamabad neighborhoods, titillating news traveled fast. Everyone knew about Haroon, Sadika and Zafary. Some were willing to give Sadika the benefit of the doubt. After all, they lived in the same society she did and knew how stories were fabricated. Besides, right now a heftier-than-normal dowry could be demanded of the Khans, who would be willing to overlook even major flaws in a prospective groom.

Every time Sadika was asked by Khanum to put on the *shalwar kameez* she had worn at Zafary's wedding, or the one at the *valima*, she cringed inside. She knew what was coming. She was going to be asked to parade what she considered her woefully inadequate wares in front of a woman looking for a mate for her son or brother. And after suffering the humiliation of being gawked at, she would have to go through the final mortification of being rejected.

"She's too self-conscious," one prospective mother-in-law said. "In today's world a man needs a confident wife."

Another complained, "She's not shy and reserved enough. Her arrogance shows that she's had too much exposure to this evil world. Girls like that don't make good wives."

Some thought she was too Western and advanced; others that she was too Eastern and conservative. Some had a bone to pick with her appearance: she was too tall, too short, too dark, too thin, too ordinary, too angular, too something or other. There was concern about her as a housekeeper: how could a girl learn to be a good cook and needlewoman with school taking up so much of her time?

Begum Majid, the mother of Waseem, an especially eligible male in his last year at engineering school, had not been satisfied with meeting and talking to Sadika: she had requested that Sadika bite into a hard candy to prove that her teeth were good and strong. She told Khanum, "*Behen*, in treacherous times like these, even a goat shouldn't be bought without having its teeth checked first. What with fake hair, fake lashes, fake teeth and God knows what else out there, you never know when you might be taken in."

Even though in her heart she knew the outcome of every matchmaking encounter, Sadika put on a fancy outfit every time she was asked to. She was well aware of the unpalatable consequences of refusing. "Poor girl!" people would say. "So broken-hearted, she can't bear the thought of marrying anyone except Haroon." But with each rejection her resentment increased.

Nature had made her a human female. Chickens, sparrows, dogs, cats, cattle and other animals all had mates. Why not her? A female dog didn't have to put on airs to attract male dogs. Whenever the neighborhood bitches, stray or otherwise, were in heat, there was no dearth of male dogs wanting to mate with them. In fact, no matter how mangy or flea-bitten the female, males still had to be beaten away with a stick. The birds nesting on the peepal tree in the graveyard, and the herds of sheep and goats led for sale in the city bazaar didn't need to resort to tricks to qualify for a mate. Why did she need to?

Whenever she felt things were too much to cope with, she sought out Zahra, who was not only her friend and confidant, but someone who could identify with Sadika's situation. Zahra had been in the marriage market for quite some time now, and her case was about as bad as Sadika's. Although no rumors had ever been spread about her, she was getting to the age when prime proposals were hard to come by. And since prime proposals had not come her way even when she was younger, it was a safe assumption that they wouldn't come now. Especially as her sister Shazia, two years her junior, seemed on the verge of marriage: Salima Ahmad's graduate son Amjad had caught a glimpse of Shazia, dressed-up and laughing, at Zafary's *valima*, and had lost his heart to her.

"It's just a matter of time." Zahra offered Sadika the same hope she often repeated to herself. "Surely someone, somewhere in this God's vast earth, is meant for you. Maybe you're a Juliet who hasn't come across her Romeo yet; a Sassi whose Punnoon is looking for her; a Heer whose Ranjha is lost somewhere without her. You have just not met him yet. When you do, maybe it will be like a scene out of some movie or romance novel: eyes will meet, and just one look from hungry yearning eyes will zap hearts together, melding them for all eternity."

Sadika burst out laughing. "I hope not. I don't want to die a young tragic death like Juliet, Sassi or Heer."

Talking with Zahra gave her some comfort, but it added another heartache. Her friend was so kind and so romantic. If only some stupid male would take the time to realize that. The man who married Zahra would not only have an interesting and sincere life partner, but a hard-working one with a sterling character.

Why hadn't the Creator of the universe realized in His infinite wisdom that the system for procuring mates would get messed up for the human female, and devised a fallback alternative? For example, He could have given humans the choice of reversing sex like a species of reef fishes called wrasses she had read about in her biology textbook. For the Caribbean bluehead wrasse, the availability of eligible males was never an issue, since they were all born female. When a female was old enough and large enough, she simply changed sex and completed life as a male.

If only human beings could do that, no woman would ever have had to worry about finding an appropriate match, and the world would probably have been a better place.

fourteen

OVER THE NEXT two years, very little changed in the Khan household. Since all the good proposals were for Sajida and not for Sadika, every one was regretfully turned down. If Sajida too got married before Sadika, Sadika would surely be doomed to a life of spinsterhood. And Akbar Khan and Khanum would always be looked down on as parents who were not able to fulfill their responsibility of marrying off all their daughters.

Surprisingly, Sadika herself was no longer as upset as she had been. It was hard to feel depressed about one aspect of her life when things were going so well for her in college. Now in her fourth and final year, she was liked and respected by teachers and students alike. She had fallen in love with economics, statistics and math, the dry subjects she had chosen in order to get a good job. Given a choice, she would have liked nothing better than to live on the college campus where she could study and enjoy herself, where she was respected as someone with talent and intelligence, and not just as a spinster who could not be married off.

Mrs. Kaukab, the statistics teacher, had promised to help her find a job after graduation, right in the college, so that she could pursue graduate studies. Every time Sadika thought of that possibility, a bubble of happiness danced through her entire body. She would have given anything to be able to stand on her own two feet; to live independently away from the depressing environment of her home where she was constantly reminded that she was less than a woman.

Zafary wrote from America with regularity, reporting on the enchanting life she was leading with her husband and year-old daughter, Jalees. Haroon, she said, worshipped the ground she walked on, especially now that she was pregnant again. She and Haroon lived with Ashfaaq Beebee, Aarif Hassan and Ishrat, who were all love and kindness, taking Zafary to shopping centers and parks, helping her with housework, and teaching her about American life.

Akbar Khan and Khanum did not question the truth of their daughter's letters. They were simply relieved that Zafary had been married off to an eligible young man. Happiness wasn't the purpose of marriage anyway. But Sadika found her sister's letters extravagant and odd. Haroon was not the sort to worship anything or anyone besides himself. And unless Ashfaaq Beebee, Aarif Hassan and Ishrat had undergone a miraculous metamorphosis, they were not the sort to treat even one another with love and kindness, let alone an in-law.

Ashfaaq Beebee's infrequent letters for the most part reflected Zafary's claims, but with a twist. According to her, Zafary was ecstatic at having found someone as wonderful as Haroon, worshipped the very ground he walked on, and was deeply impressed by her in-laws.

In recent letters, surprisingly, Sadika was mentioned. In her last letter, Ashfaaq Beebee had written, "Things are great, but they would be even more wonderful if someone as capable as Sadika was here to guide Zafary and help out with the household chores. Dear Khanum. Do you think you can spare Sadika for a few months? I would be happy to send a round-trip ticket. I could even enroll her in the local community college with Ishrat. A few courses in an American college might be just what she needs to become more desirable in the eyes of a prospective husband. And Zafary would be so happy to have her own sister to help her out during her difficult pregnancy."

Akbar Khan and Khanum did not know what to make of this. It was inappropriate for Ashfaaq Beebee even to suggest that Sadika visit them, given the circumstances. Maybe, they thought, this was the Hassan family's way of making amends.

But Sadika did not believe that. These people have gotten into the habit of humiliating me, she thought to herself, and now they are doing it long distance. But it was a moot point: Khanum could not even think of sending Sadika to America. Apart from its being complicated and inappropriate, Sadika was too great a help at home. And it wasn't clear whether a temporary American experience was a plus or a minus for a girl seeking a husband.

In addition, Sadika's options in Pakistan were by no means exhausted, especially if she finished college and found a good-paying job. Many young men nowadays were looking to increase their sense of security by marrying women who could hold outside jobs. As a last resort, there was always an older gentleman wanting a young wife who could better answer his physical needs than his current wife. Sometimes this arrangement was as welcome to the older wife as to her husband, for she was as much in need of a maid-cum-punching-bag as her husband was of someone physically more appealing.

Within the next few weeks, however, a couple of things happened that changed Sadika's prospects for the worse all over again, and made Ashfaaq Beebee's American option appear very attractive. Both events were connected to Sadika's college, confirming Khanum's earlier opinion that it was not good to allow girls to be educated, and sealing Sadika's fate.

Sadika walked to and from college with two other girls from the neighborhood: Durdaana and Zarreen. She enjoyed this part of her day. Apart from the exhilaration of walking in the fresh air with nothing to do but chat with her companions, there was the unexpected entertainment provided by the peanut brittle sold by Latif Baba, the sidewalk vendor, from a rattan basket. The penny's worth of candy came wrapped in pages torn from old romance magazines that Latif Baba bought from housewives.

Sadika, Durdaana and Zarreen laughed at the extravagant declarations of love and compliments routinely uttered by the heroes of these fantasies. Secretly, however, the girls envied the lucky heroines, and dreamed of the day when a handsome young prince would rescue them from the drudgery of their everyday lives. Nevertheless, they enjoyed ridiculing the heroes' style. When, for example, one declared, "Life of my heart, I will pluck out the stars from the heavens for you, if only you will consent to be mine," Zarreen complained, "Why do these heroes always want to do worthless impractical things for their beloved?"

Sadika agreed. "What could a loved one do with a star anyway? It would probably be just something else to keep clean and dusted, just another chore. And if the loved one was a student like us, that would cut into her study time."

"I wish heroes would promise to make life luxurious and fun," Durdaana added. "I would want mine to hire gourmet cooks, janitors and skilled seamstresses with an endless supply of high quality goods, instead of going around trying to pluck out stars from heaven."

The height of enjoyment for the threesome was invariably reached with Sadika's hilarious but impressive-sounding literal English translation of the Urdu romance. English was, after all, the language of choice for socially and economically advanced people.

"Life of my desire," Sadika translated, injecting drama and extra endearments into a love letter. "These words of mine are luckier than I, my darling, as your dear eyes are tangling with them. If only I was there to personally do the tangling, soul of my soul." Or, "Our separation will surely kill me, piece of my heart. But when I am about to die, dearest one, I will request the scavengers getting ready to eat my flesh to spare my eyes, sweetheart. For even in death, beloved, I want them to be wide open and waiting for you, O Fairest of the Fair."

Love songs got similar treatment.

"Come, O my darling, into the light of the mellow moon, sweetheart," Sadika crooned in a tuneless voice. "When you and I meet, dearest fountain of delight, springtime will arrive even in the desert, my loved one. And the sky will start to sway."

Gradually, word of Sadika's ability to translate Urdu endearments into English spread throughout the college, surprising the romantics. Who would have thought a straightlaced person like Sadika would have a talent for translating Urdu romance into English? Her classmates did not know that when Sadika had thought she was going to marry Haroon, she had immersed herself in English so that she could not only communicate with her future husband, but impress him with her fluency. And she had taken special pains to memorize expressions of passion. If Haroon had bothered to talk to her, he would have been suitably impressed. But he never had, so he never was. In college, it was a different story. Sadika was a rarity among the group of students from Urdu-medium schools, and in her small neighborhood, she was unique.

In general, there was no dearth of young girls who knew English; proficiency in that language was considered a sign of intellectual and socioeconomic worth. Many young people took pride in the fact that they could communicate better in English than they could in their native Urdu. In the marketplace, in commercial centers, on street corners—there was not a place where English was not heard. Even those who were not proficient in the language of their former masters insisted on conversing in it.

"What happening in office you work?" A young clerk would inquire of his counterpart from another office, and add solemnly, "You want to go my home and speak?"

Sadika's fluency in English earned her inordinate respect because she came from a background where girls' education was denigrated. And at her mediocre public school, teaching was in Urdu, the national language. It was understood that people with money and status would send their children to expensive private schools where instruction was in English. Some public schools were English-medium, but to get into one required influence or academic excellence or both. It was ironic that the language that was considered a legacy of colonial rule should represent education and social status in the public mind.

If any of her classmates from Urdu-medium schools had to write essays or were having difficulty reading English texts, they automatically turned to Sadika. Then when word spread, through Durdaana and Zarreen, about her new talent for romance, she was contacted by girls who, despite the strictness of society, were having clandestine relationships with members of the opposite sex. In short, by females who wanted to write love letters in English to impress their boyfriends.

This situation provided Sadika with one of the happiest times that she had ever known. She had the respect and admiration of other students, as well as their confidence and trust. She also had something else which until now had been nonexistent in her life: money. Or rather, a skill which was as good as money and could be used for bartering.

It all started one day at lunchtime, when Parveen insisted on buying snacks for Sadika at the college gate where three or four vendors daily peddled their delicious wares. Lunch break was usually the time when Sadika pretended to be too busy with classwork to eat, or swallowed the few bites of the *roti* she had saved from breakfast. She had made it a point long ago to avoid the college gate because seeing the vendors made her hungry. How could it not, when it was crawling with people buying mixed fruit bits with spices from the *chat wallah*, ears of corn brushed with lemon juice and spices from the *challi wallah*, and a bun holding a round kebob from Shahji.

On alternate days, when Shahji was accompanied by his wife, Allah Baskar and her younger sister Allah Maafi, Sadika made doubly sure to avoid the college gate. The reasons were Allah Baskar's wildly popular sinus-clearing spiced kidney beans and Allah Maafi's eggs with prayers in them that brought good luck to anyone who ate them. Sadika could not afford to buy even one small bowl of beans when she had a cold, or even one special egg in case of an emergency like a difficult exam.

Although the treats sold at the college gate were mouthwatering, they were prepared and sold in extremely unhygienic conditions. "They are nothing but little packets of germs," Sadika would tell herself firmly at lunchtime. But it never helped. As with the other students, it did not matter to her that the *chat wallah* mixed the fruitchat with dirty hands; that the *challi wallah's* ears of corn were buried in the same hot sand in which he cleaned his hands after relieving himself behind the college wall; that Allah Maafi's boiled eggs were often cracked and dirty because she constantly rubbed them between her hands while blowing prayers into them.

Some claimed that the dead dogs that disappeared in the middle of the night had been taken away by Shahji to make his delicious kabobs; others had evidence that Shahji used dead donkeys that had hauled materials at a nearby construction site. This made a lot of sense, since the government agencies that dealt with this kind of clean-up were too incompetent to be relied upon. But donkey or dog notwithstanding, the stuff produced by Shahji and other vendors caused people like Sadika to dream that one day some unknown benefactor would enable them too to enjoy these goodies to their heart's content, and to be envied by other unfortunates.

But it was Parveen and others like her who became Sadika's benefactors.

One fateful day, Parveen bought a plate of beans and a couple of ears of corn for Sadika, and confided in a low voice: "*Pyari behen*, my dear sister, I need the kind of help only you can give me." After a short pause she continued dreamily, "Hashim is so cute; just like Nadeem in the movie *Baazee*. What's more, he owns a car. At least he seems to—I saw him driving it. When he suddenly hits the brakes, his head jerks forward, and his beautiful chocolate-brown hair falls over his broad intelligent forehead."

"Why are you telling me all this?" Sadika interrupted, already regretting having eaten the delectable beans, because now if she was asked to convey some sort of message to a boy living in her neighborhood, it would be hard to refuse.

"As I said, I need help that only you can give," Parveen had repeated. "You know my English isn't good. But if I write a letter to Hashim in Urdu, he'll think that I come from some backward family. *Pyari behen*, I'll be so grateful if you would translate my letter into English. Maybe we can do it tomorrow at about the same time over some kabobs for inspiration, and fruitchat for good luck."

Sadika had readily agreed. This was something she could do easily, without any consequences, and it seemed to mean a lot to Parveen. Why else would she have blown four entire rupees of her money on these snacks? And this was an opportunity for Sadika to sample more delicacies.

After only a few episodes, Sadika's reputation as a writer of magical love letters spread like wild fire amongst the lovelorn. This was partly because Parveen told everyone that the letters had produced just the desired effect, but, more important, because Hashim's parents went to Parveen's house at their son's insistence and asked for her hand in marriage. Many attributed Sadika's extraordinary talent in this area to her broken heart, caused by Haroon's marrying her younger sister.

Sadika was delighted with her new occupation. She was now more popular with her classmates than she had ever dreamed possible, although she would not entertain for a moment the notion that this happy situation had arisen because of Haroon, who had brought nothing but misery into her life. Several times during the past few months Sadika had found herself praying fiercely that somehow, somewhere, someone would cause him the same kind of humiliation and pain that he had inflicted on her; perhaps then he would realize what he had done. It was pure luck that her letter-writing had succeeded the way it had. Skill or a broken heart had nothing to do with it, she thought, all she really did was translate. And sometimes she did not do even that very well.

There was the problem with *parwana*, the Urdu word for "moth." In the literary culture of the subcontinent, there was an obsession with the legend of the candle and the moth—the candle burns out awaiting her lover, while the moth in turn loses his life trying to get close to his beloved. Farzana wanted to tell Haatim that she was waiting for him as the burning candle awaits the moth, and would wait until she expired or he took notice, whichever came first. Sadika, not wanting to admit that she didn't know the English word for *parwana*, decided to use the only insect she could think of, and produced a letter for Farzana that read, "I am like the candle that burns in wait for her mosquito. If your love is true, do not be afraid of dying in my flame, for that will give us and our story of love eternal life. Be a perpetuator of the tradition of fearlessness practiced by mosquitoes the world over, so that I, your candle, as well as your fellow mosquitoes, can be proud to claim you as our very own."

For days after the sending of the letter, Sadika, cursing her inexcusable pride, waited for the ax to fall. No one, she thought, is going to ask me to do this for them again after they hear about that ridiculous letter. But as the days went by without an attack on her reputation or a confrontation with Farzana, she heaved a sigh of relief. The boyfriends of the girls she wrote letters for were obviously in the same boat academically as their beloveds. Who knew? Maybe they thought that the candle and the mosquito had the same relationship in English literature as the candle and the moth in Urdu. Sadika's confidence in the ignorance of her contemporaries made her feel fearless and invincible. No one would dare challenge her: she could voice her opinions freely on almost anything or anyone and expect others to listen to her attentively, because no one knew when they would need her services.

She had only a passing interest in whether the letters furthered the forbidden romances. She compared herself to a poor hungry Urdu poet whose life history she had memorized for a literature test. Once on a star-filled night, he had been asked to comment on the beauty of the full moon. "What moon? What stars?" he had said, glancing at the sky. "To me they all look like pita bread."

Unfortunately, her newfound confidence made her reckless.

fifteen

KHANUM, SADIKA AND Asghar Khan went to the train station to greet Khanum's brother Farooq Mamoon, who had some business to attend to in town and was going to stay with them for a couple of days. The train was late, as usual, and Sadika and Khanum had to wait in the women's lounge while Asghar Khan went to investigate the cause of the delay. After a silence of barely a couple of minutes, Khanum started a conversation with the only other occupant of the lounge; a thin, sad-looking woman, handsomely dressed and made up, who seemed oblivious to everyone and everything around her.

What was her name? Where was she from? Why she was going there? And how many other train journeys had she taken? Was she married? With children? How many? Khanum wanted to know everything at once. The lady, who had seemed unapproachable minutes earlier, readily answered Khanum's questions, much to Sadika's surprise. What was it about her mother that made people so eager to talk? Or were all older women like her mother ready to spill their life story at the merest provocation? Not only did the sad, thin woman answer these questions, she added irrelevant details, going off on all kinds of tangents.

Her name was Rifat Ara Begum, she was originally from India, but her husband was a clerk at a government office in Lahore where he was born and where she was currently headed. They had been married more than eleven years; she had been just a child at the time. But she had made a beautiful bride nonetheless, and she had pictures to prove it. If her parents had not been in such a hurry to marry her off, she probably would have caught the eye of some very rich, influential man and be living in the lap of luxury now. And so on and so forth.

Sadika, lost in thoughts of her own, didn't pay much attention to the conversation, until Rifat Ara said in a voice sodden with tears, "I have three girls and I'm pregnant again. If it's a girl this time, my husband will never forgive me. My mother-in-law has been complaining for years that I can't bear sons; this time she is threatening to get a new wife for my Aabid. Right in front of my eyes, too. She says she will make me serve my husband's second wife like a personal maid if she produces a son. What will I do, *behen*, where will I go, if this one is also a girl?" Pointing to her nonexistent belly, she burst into tears.

Khanum, who had perked up at the mention of a pregnancy, was now at full alert. This was a subject close to her heart, because she herself had been burnt by similar actions from her mother-in-law. Besides, she had a lifetime of experience in trying to produce a son, and one of her favorite activities was bestowing pearls of wisdom on someone in dire need. Who would have thought that the train being late would provide her with such a wonderful opportunity? Leaping to life, she wrote down on the back of the woman's magazine she was carrying a lengthy incantation in Arabic that, repeated one thousand times each day at the crack of dawn and followed by a tablespoon of honey, was guaranteed to produce a son.

To further strengthen the spell, she advised that the religious man, the Peer Sahib, who resided under the oldest peepal tree in the village of Jogiapur, could make her a personalized amulet guaranteed to do the job. "*Behen,* my biggest regret in life has been that I didn't know about him earlier—I might have had four sons today instead of three daughters and one son. But see, no one told me that sometimes monsters can move into a woman's womb to stop her from conceiving a son." In a conspiratorial tone she told the eager Rifat Ara, "This Peer Sahib is expert in exorcising all kinds of monsters and at a very reasonable price too. Why, the kind of magic he can do would cost at least two hundred rupees or more in a big city. Go to him, *be-hen*, and after your womb has been cleared of all the monsters, the exalted Peer Sahib will give you a special holy water that's sure to produce a son. If I'm lying, I pray that I die the most horrifying death at the hands of cancer and small pox combined; and that my loved ones refuse to see my face in death."

Unable to contain herself any longer—human reproduction was the subject she had been studying in Biology for the past two weeks—Sadika spoke up. "Don't you know," she began excitedly, her words stumbling over themselves in her haste to inform the two women of her crucial bit of knowledge, "if you can't have a son, it's not your fault at all. Your husband is solely to blame because he didn't give you his Y chromosome. That's what makes the male baby. See, a man's body makes two types of seeds—ones that create a male baby and ones that create a female baby. And during mating. . . ."

Suddenly Sadika stopped dead. She had caught sight of Khanum's eyes, blazing with incredulous anger. Rifat Ara Begum, who had an unobstructed view of Khanum's flashing eyes, forgot all about her own troubles at this promising turn of events, visibly brightening at the prospect of witnessing a verbal blood bath between mother and daughter. Who would have thought that time spent in the waiting room of the local train station would prove to be the high point of her day? She hoped that Khanum was not one to pull punches in front of a stranger.

Rifat Ara Begum was not disappointed.

Khanum began her tirade by beating her chest with her fists and moaning, the traditional way of expressing extreme distress. "God, why am I alive to see such a day? Why didn't you call me before I could witness this tragedy? Before I could hear such sinful words come out of the mouth of this she-monster that you gave me to raise? I know she will roast in hell once she gets to you, but what am I supposed to do with her in this world?"

After repeating these questions a couple of times, rocking back and forth and beating her chest, she abruptly stopped and, pointing a forefinger at Sadika, addressed her in a high, shrill voice: "Is this the kind of garbage they teach you in school nowadays? That makes you talk like a tramp, a whore, a bastard born out of some heathen? It's a disgrace that you have this foul knowledge. But to say it to your mother's face as though she was a tramp too? I could never even lift my eyes in front of my mother, let alone lose all sense of what is right."

She turned to Rifat Ara Begum. "*Behen*, this world is turning evil. Young people have no idea of the duty they owe their parents. Last year my brother Farooq, the same one we are waiting for today, told me that his second daughter Zeenat is refusing to marry the young man he chose for her. Can you believe that? What does she expect to do? Pick out a husband herself?"

Rifat Ara Begum readily agreed, adding some fuel of her own to keep the fire burning. "You're right, *behen*. These surely are signs that doomsday is coming. In our day, children honored their parent's wishes, no matter how much they hated them. And young virgins didn't talk to old-timers as though they had the brains of grass-eating cattle."

"*Behen*, it's not my fault." Khanum was mourning again, beating her chest, rocking back and forth and moaning. "It's these city schools. I wouldn't send my girls to them, but you know how it is. All eligible boys today want a wife with an education. Now I ask you, what good is education if it makes young girls talk like prostitutes? Why should daughters be sent to school when all they need to know after marriage is how to take care of their home and family? And keep a quiet tongue in their heads, of course," she concluded, giving Sadika a murderous look.

Till the time Farooq Mamoon's chronic cough announced his arrival and Rifat Ara Begum reluctantly got up to catch her train, she and Khanum were deep in discussion, which began loudly, but after Sadika was reduced to tears, quieted down to whispers. From time to time, they glanced at her with contempt and anger. If eyes could devour, Sadika felt sure she would have become part of their small intestines by now. Then realizing that her thoughts had strayed to human digestion, a topic related to the biggest source of irritation to Khanum—education—she hastily changed her focus to the evening work still needing to be done.

But Khanum was not one to forgive and forget. No matter how many times Sadika apologized, Khanum remained inconsolable, especially since her brother Farooq was there to lend a sympathetic ear. Again and again she ranted and raved about the hellish tendencies of today's young people. If she had uttered something remotely resembling what Sadika had said at the train station when she was young, her father would have personally bashed her head open. And it was beyond her why girls today needed schooling when they made better wives without it. Sadika's behavior at the train station was proof positive. If it hadn't been for this idiotic idea of having educated wives look after kids and the household, the heavy weight of unmarried daughters on her shoulders would have all but disappeared by now.

In this illogical and difficult world, there were many pitfalls to start with. But their number increased drastically when one's daughter was too dim-witted to realize that she couldn't discuss subjects she had no business knowing anything about. How was Khanum supposed to portray Sadika as pure as snow-white linen to prospective in-laws if she went around saying all kinds of unspeakable things?

After listening off and on for two days to Khanum's rantings about the evils of education, the entire household breathed a sigh of relief when the decision was made to send Sadika away to Jogiapur to spend some time with Farooq Mamoon. Even Sadika felt some of her stress lessen as she packed. A few days, even a couple of weeks, would not set her back too much in school because the mid-term tests had just ended. No major project or test was on the horizon for another month, and her absence would surely make Khanum feel more charitable toward her.

As she left for the train station with Farooq Mamoon, Sadika's main worry was that her tattered suitcase, though bound strongly with ropes, might not be able to survive the journey.

sixteen

THE FACT THAT Khanum had even considered sending Sadika away for any length of time was proof that she was really worried about the bad influence the city was having on her daughter's morals. Sadika was her best help and making do without her was a sacrifice that was not easy to make. That is why in the recesses of her heart she was sometimes glad that Sadika had not been the first to get married. Hopefully by the time that event took place, Sajida could take over, but Khanum doubted she would ever be as efficient as Sadika.

Right now she felt she had no option. The evils of city life were getting to Sadika, and their effect had to be mitigated somehow. The only way Khanum knew to save what was left of Sadika's soul was to send her to the village to spend some days with her brother Farooq, his wife Altaaf and their five children. Maybe living in primitive conditions under the thumb of Khanum's brother and domineering sister-in-law would bring Sadika to her senses. After all, this method had worked for others. Or rather, it had to have worked. Otherwise, why would so many people resort to it as a last ditch effort when it was felt that a child's morals were being corrupted beyond redemption?

As she sat on the train, Sadika's thoughts were not as somber as her mother's. She knew that village life, even for a few days, would not be easy, specially since she was being sent away to be taught a lesson. But she was not really upset. Life in the city was no bed of roses either. It wasn't as though she was being sent away from the lap of luxury. There couldn't be more than twenty-four hours in a day at Farooq Mamoon's village. And even if every moment of that time was taken up with chores, she wouldn't be worse off—at least not in terms of the amount of work that needed to be done. She would certainly miss little Sajida and Zahra and the college, but that couldn't be helped.

As it happened, Sadika's stay at the village was much worse than she had anticipated. For one thing, she had not taken into account her new status as a fallen woman, and she hadn't realized how miserable one could be made to feel if one was regarded as a symbol of everything that was wrong with society. In the simple black-and-white value system of the village, good people punished bad people by not associating with them. If that wasn't possible, they made sure that the evil person knew exactly what they thought of him or her by their actions and body language.

Sadika was no exception. The same cousins who, when they had come to Islamabad for Zafary's wedding, had tried their best to make a good impression on her, now treated her like a leper. Her touch as well as her company were avoided. She came in contact with them only at breakfast. At all other times, and at every other meal, she was left alone with the mountain of tasks assigned to her. They would have stayed away from her at breakfast too, if it wasn't that the cooking area with its hot stove and its aroma of fresh-made pita bread and tea, was the coziest place to escape the morning chill.

And when Farooq Mamoon and his family were invited to a wedding or a circumcision, not only was no effort made to include Sadika, but no one even bothered to bring home some traditional sweets for her.

Khanum was responsible in part for this shabby treatment, because she had requested that Sadika be treated harshly to bring her to her senses. But in any case, it was convenient for Altaaf Maami and Farooq Mamoon to treat her as a slave. Especially since they could disguise it as a favor to Khanum. To say that Farooq Mamoon and Altaaf Maami were thrilled by this arrangement was putting it mildly. Secretly, they thought that this must be what city people call a "vacation," for they couldn't think of a better luxury. If only they could keep doing this favor for their dear sister forever.

Surprisingly, hard work and ill treatment were not the worst part of staying at Farooq Mamoon's house. An excruciatingly embarrassing scenario that took place each morning involving the lack of indoor plumbing, easily topped everything.

It was an understatement to say that Sadika was aghast at the latrine facilities in her aunt and uncle's home. She had moved to the city at a very young age and had not had to contend with outdoor toilets. The playground at Gulmushk Mohalla might have prepared her if she had ever had to use it as a toilet, but she never had. Besides, that was an open space distant from the residential area, while this was a tiny closed room in constant use at the side of the house.

The only time during the day Sadika could bear to use the tiny latrine was when it had just been cleaned out early in the morning by the *jamadarni*, the woman who cleaned these things for a living. That was when the stench was bearable enough for her not to throw up, and insects were not crawling over the ugly mess, making her want to close her eyes and inadvertently step in the stuff she was trying to avoid. So she made it a point to wake up at the crack of dawn. Unfortunately for her, Farooq Mamoon had the same preference that she had. So each morning, as she came out of the small stinking room, he would be waiting to go in, his resentment at not being the first person to use the facilities clearly written on his face.

She had no idea how closely he examined the contents of the latrine, or whether later each morning he was motivated by the goodness of his heart. All she knew was that at breakfast each day, right in front of everyone, he would take out his beat-up tin box of medicines, silently hand her something gray that resembled gunpowder, and announce, "Sadika has an upset stomach today, maybe diarrhea, and needs strong medicine. Luckily for her, I have some right here." Or, "I think Sadika has a touch of constipation. This spicy powder will loosen up the poison in her intestines, rinse them and wring them out, making them cleaner than if they had been washed out with Surf." That was a brand of detergent.

Mortified, Sadika prayed for the ground to open up and swallow her, or else for Farooq Mamoon to lose his voice, but neither of these things happened. Gulping down Farooq Mamoon's patent medicine, she sat through breakfast in silence, eating and drinking without really tasting anything. Then as soon as everyone left, she hid her face in her hands and gave vent to the luxury of tears. Maybe one day God would put her in a position to pay these people back for the humiliations they were heaping on her. It was said that time could alter circumstances beyond recognition. Perhaps it would work some miracle for her. In the meantime, all she could do was dread the next morning when the whole scene would be repeated.

Despite this, the two weeks at Farooq Mamoon's flew by more quickly than she had expected. She was kept so busy cooking, cleaning, sewing, looking after the younger children and doing other housework, that she had no time for anything else, including self-pity. As the day for going home drew near, she could feel her heart lighten and her spirits lift at the prospect of returning to her beloved college, and renewing her studies and her love letter writing career with all its perks, like enjoying unlimited goodies and people's confidences. Zahra must have accumulated a pile of juicy neighborhood gossip a mile high by now. And Sajida would be worn out by all the extra housework. Sadika missed even her parents and brother. Compared to her uncle's family, they treated her like a princess.

The one-hour trip to the nearest train station in a *tonga*, a horse-drawn cart, seemed as pleasant to her as it was unpleasant for Farooq Mamoon and Altaaf Maami. They were regretfully anticipating going back to life as it had been before Sadika. Their vacation was over.

seventeen

THE JOY SADIKA felt at the thought of going home would have been short- lived if she had been aware of what was brewing in her absence in House #6, Gali #15. Durdaana lived there, one of Sadika's most faithful love-letter clients. She had been having a paper romance with not one but two boys—Ishaaq and Liaquat, from a nearby all-male college. And, much to Durdaana's delight, both correspondences had progressed to the stage where marriage was being mentioned. It had been a time to rejoice for Sadika as well, since the pace of letter writing by the lovelorn increased dramatically along with Sadika's consumption of delicacies.

"Any time I see the color red, I cannot help thinking how wonderful you would look as a bride," Ishaaq wrote.

"Do not say such things, they make me feel shy," an exuberant Durdaana wrote back courtesy of Sadika, translator and confidante.

"I can't wait for the day when I will have you all to myself to do with as I please," the mischievous lover Liaquat declared.

Ecstatic, Durdaana replied, "If you write that again, I will never write to you again, or see you, for that matter!"

God knows how long the correspondence would have gone on like this if fate had not intervened. But as bad luck would have it, Ishaaq was a blabbermouth. He loved to talk about his beloved and her impressive qualities, among which was an excellent command of English. One day, Durdaana's other beau, Liaquat, fed up with Ishaaq's boasting, issued a challenge to him:

"I bet my girl's English is even better than yours, and she can beat her in any contest," he said. "Why, my Durdaana writes better than an Englishwoman!"

"Durdaana," Ishaaq repeated slowly. "What a coincidence that both of us are going to marry a girl named Durdaana who writes very good English." That would have been an very odd coincidence indeed, considering what a small percentage of girls in that small conservative community would be willing to risk the dire consequences of writing that sort of letter if it were discovered.

Growing suspicious, Ishaaq demanded to see Liaquat's letters, and Liaquat silently handed them over. The boys were jolted to see that not only was the level of English the same, but the handwriting was identical: Durdaana's exposure as the double-crossing, two-timing whore that she was, transformed their admiration into intense hatred.

It took no time at all for this juicy news to circulate, and for the entire population of the college to conclude that Durdaana deserved the most horrible fate imaginable. Justice needed to be served; vengeance was suddenly a united goal. Approaching Durdaana's family with the evidence of the letters was not punishment enough; some fabrication was essential to make sure the punishment fit the crime.

With so many young minds working simultaneously, it was easy to come up with a colorful scenario, satisfyingly sinister: Durdaana's sinful nature was slowly but surely leading young men onto the path of immorality and destruction. Ishaaq and Liaquat were only two of the men Durdaana had led astray with her false promises. Many others before them had perished from the sorrow she had visited on them. As proof, numerous sinful, damaging letters could be produced.

All hell broke loose when Ishaaq's and Liaquat's parents brought the allegations to Durdaana's mother Sakina Beebee, and her father Ghulam Rauf. The fiftyish couple, already prematurely aged by life's burdens, saw their not-so-bright future turn pitch dark before their eyes, and did the only thing they could under the circumstances.

"Please, please, for the sake of God and the Holy Prophet Muhammad, keep this information to yourselves, otherwise we will not be able to show our faces in this town ever again." Their voices quavering, tears of shame streaking their leathery cheeks, Sakina Beebee and Ghulam Rauf begged the wronged young men's families for mercy.

The two sets of parents relented. "We have no quarrel with you, but there's no place for loose females like Durdaana in a decent community. If that kind of girl is allowed to go unpunished, the entire structure of society will come apart."

"We promise that if what you have told us is true, we will personally bash in Durdaana's head and throw her out in the streets to fend for herself," Sakina Beebee and Ghulam Rauf hastily promised, seeing a light in the tunnel.

Durdaana, who with her three sisters and two brothers had been listening to this drama just outside the door, felt the blood drain from her body. She knew that she had better come up with an explanation fast or her fate would really be worse than death.

Suddenly it came to her that the incriminating letters on which the entire case against her existed had not only been translated by Sadika, but were in Sadika's best handwriting. One would have only to match them to her English notebook to incriminate Sadika and exonerate Durdaana. She knew that it was wrong to damn an innocent person and a friend, but she had no choice. It was either her or Sadika. And she rationalized that it would be much easier for Sadika, whose reputation was already flawed. Wasn't that the reason she had been sent to Farooq Mamoon's village? Durdaana's reputation, on the other hand, was pure as the driven snow and deserved protection.

When Akbar Khan and Khanum were told what their daughter had supposedly done, they were beside themselves with grief and anger. They did not defend Sadika or attempt to reserve judgment till they heard her side of the story; they reinforced the accusations by making irrational statements of their own.

"This girl has caused nothing but grief since the day she was born. Why, her birth almost killed me and destroyed my marriage. If it wasn't for my Asghar, I would have been on the street today," Khanum declared, almost enjoying the venting of old resentments. "A snake in the making, a wolf in sheep's clothing, that's what she is. We don't know what we did to deserve a she-devil like her. If we had our way, she would be sent far, far away where her accursed shadow would not fall on any of us."

"Just let the bitch come home," Akbar Khan had roared, reverting to the style of his favorite Punjabi hero, "and I'll crack her neck with my own two hands."

Satisfied that they were well on their way to achieving their purpose of appropriate punishment of the sinful, the parents of Ishaaq and Liaquat had gone home to wait for news of the final judgment.

Akbar Khan and Khanum sat down to talk about what could be done. This was the second time in their lives that a matter related to Sadika had forced them to talk to each other, and they didn't like it one bit. Why did Sadika continually make their lives so unpleasant?

It was a good thing Sadika had not yet returned from her exile to Farooq Mamoon's house, or Akbar Khan would probably have made an effort to get rid of her for good with his bare hands and Khanum's assistance. As far as they could see, there was no other way to get her out of their lives and save themselves from becoming embarrassed objects of pity and ridicule. On top of that, if word got out, Sajida's chances of making an appropriate match would be destroyed. Who in their right mind would want to marry a girl whose older sister was a proven harlot? As for Sadika, given these circumstances, even some old wreck would not accept her as a bride.

If only it was still the good old days when widowers and old wrecks were a dime a dozen. Unfortunately—or fortunately, however you chose to look at it—since the advent of modern medicine, women did not pass away as frequently and easily as they used to. Why, Khanum could not even remember the last time she had heard of a woman dying in childbirth. That was not necessarily good, even though Khanum herself had been a beneficiary of the village gynecologist's expertise during the birth of her last two daughters. While doctors and hospitals prolonged a woman's miserable existence, they also took away the previously reliable last resort and safety net of marrying off someone in Sadika's predicament to one of the ineligible widowers.

After worrying for an entire day and praying for their first-born to die of plague, smallpox, whooping cough, or a combination of all three while she was still at Farooq Mamoon's village, Akbar Khan and Khanum received a letter from Ashfaaq Beebee which they saw as God Almighty's intervention to help them out.

"Dear Sister," the letter began, "This is to give you the good news that Zafary is pregnant again. Pray that this time it is a boy. Although people tell me that this kind of thing runs in families. Since you have given birth to a lot more girls than boys, this next baby might turn out to be a girl also. But that is beside the point. What I really wanted to tell you in this letter is that Zafary's pregnancies are hard. She has been advised by the doctor to stay in bed most of the time. The problem is that it is impossible for me to do all the housework by myself as well as take care of little Jalees. After thinking for a long time, I have come up with a solution, and it has to do with Sadika. I know you must be very concerned about her as she did not get married before her sister. If she comes to America and takes a few courses at the college where Ishrat is studying, it might be easier to find a match for her when she goes back to Pakistan. You know how young men of today love to be able to say that their wives have had some schooling in America.

"For some time, while Zafary is bedridden, Sadika will have to take over many of the household responsibilities. But when

Zafary gets better, her help will not be needed as much and she can go to school as well as help out at home. In exchange for all the help, we will pay for her ticket and also for the few courses she takes at the local college.

"Let me know what you think about this as soon as possible, as I need to make other arrangements if this is not acceptable to you.

"Your sister, Ashfaaq Beebee."

Almost faint with relief, Khanum promised to offer a special prayer of thanks later that night, and husband and wife sat down to compose a letter accepting Ashfaaq Beebee's proposal before she had a chance to withdraw it. Then realizing that it would take at least seven days for the letter to reach America, and that they would have to wait at least as long for a reply, they decided that this was an emergency that warranted dipping into their meager savings. They booked a call to America that very day, and informed an overjoyed Ashfaaq Beebee that they were so concerned about their beloved daughter Zafary's well-being, they wanted to send Sadika to help out right away.

When Sadika arrived home two days later, it was to an atmosphere as grim and somber as if death had struck. Her few belongings were not to be unpacked and her airline ticket had been bought on the understanding that Ashfaaq Beebee would make full reimbursement.

Thunderstruck, Sadika asked Khanum: "What have I done to merit such a punishment? Haven't I made up for what happened at the train station by going to the village and working like a slave for Farooq Mamoon's family?"

"I wish you had never been born," Khanum spat out with so much venom that Sadika probably would have died if her mother's voice could have acquired a tangible form. "Want to know what you have done, do you? You world-class actress with the heart of a prostitute! You probably have so many immoral things to your credit that you don't even remember all of them. And you didn't think that you'd ever be caught, did you? I knew you were capable of this when I heard you spout that garbage at the train station."

"But what have I done?" Sadika tried again. As far as she knew, she had been living a modest life, even by the standards of their neighborhood. While the other girls indulged in gossip and vulgar talk, she mostly kept to her books after her tasks were finished.

Repetition of this question seemed to enrage Khanum all over again, and she began with a fresh burst of energy. "Don't try to act innocent! Not with me—the person who knows you inside out. It doesn't become you. Not after you've been having hot affairs with God knows how many young men. Oh, God! Why didn't you die before you could bring disgrace to your family! I knew you were bad news the day you were born. I refused to see you then. What I should have done was follow my instincts and strangle you."

"But what is my crime?" Sadika repeated, totally at a loss.

"What have you done? What have you not done is more like it. Ask Ishaaq and Liaquat's families whose sons you've led astray what you've done!"

"Ishaaq and Liaquat," began Sadika slowly. "I know who they are, but I've had nothing to do with them. Who ever said that I did is lying."

Khanum looked heavenward, beating her chest with her fists. "Look at this shameless creature, God," she began. "If you didn't want her to die, why didn't you take me before I could witness the day my daughter squandered away her honor and had the audacity to deny it." Glaring at Sadika, she continued, "Next you'll say you didn't write those contemptible letters, using Durdaana's name to cover up your own evil carrying-on."

At last things began to make sense. This apparently had to do with the letters she had written for Durdaana. Surely Khanum had only to ask Durdaana to explain that Sadika was innocent. . . . But what if Durdaana was trying to save her own hide by blaming Sadika? With a sinking feeling, Sadika realized that something like that must have happened for everyone to be acting this way.

"I did write those letters," she said quietly, "but they were not for me. They were for Durdaana. I only translated into English what she wanted to write."

But Khanum did not believe her. Nor did anyone else. It seemed that after the train station incident had given Sadika the reputation of a wolf in sheep's clothing, any attempt to portray her as a wronged innocent was not accepted as credible. When Sadika tried to contact Durdaana to straighten things out, her former close friend refused to talk to her.

Finally she had to resign herself to her fate, knowing that all she could do was wait for the day after tomorrow when an airplane would take her to America—far from everything and everyone who had meant anything to her: Zahra, Sajida, her friends at school, and school most of all. Every time she thought of her beloved college and the degree that had almost been hers—her passport to freedom and independence—a sharp pain sliced through her heart. This is how a dying man must feel at having the water of life snatched from his fingers just before his last breath, she thought.

The only person who had some idea of what Sadika was going through was Zahra. She tried to talk to Sadika many times, even though she had been forbidden to do so by her parents, who did not want their own daughter's reputation tarnished by association with a tainted person. God knew it was hard enough to get a match in today's world without added disabilities. Never before had Sadika felt so much love for her friend than when Zahra risked her family's anger by tying a note around a stone and throwing it into the Khan's small courtyard at a time she knew Sadika was usually alone. "I know you are innocent, and I wish I knew of a way to prove it to others," the note said. "Just believe that you can count me as your friend no matter what. Your friend and sister, Zahra."

Since it was not only Zahra, but all respectable females of the community who had been forbidden to talk to Sadika, she was not able to say goodbye to anyone. Not even anyone at her beloved school.

Left alone, and with some time on her hands, Sadika tried to decide which was the lesser of two evils: staying in Gulmushk Mohalla under the present circumstances, or going off to America where she would face a totally alien culture while living with her sister, whose husband happened to be her ex-fiancé.

Gradually, she came to believe that going to live with her aunt and her sister was clearly the better alternative. She had always harbored a secret wish to study at an American school. And if she correctly understood the contents of Ashfaaq Beebee's letter as told to her by Sajida, there was a good chance that she would be able to see the inside of an American classroom. On top of this, when she considered the fact that no one in America was aware of her supposedly checkered past, Ashfaaq Beebee's home seemed a safe haven in an exciting country.

eighteen

ASHFAAQ BEEBEE WAS overjoyed at the prospect of having Sadika live in her home, possibly forever. Wasn't that how those kinds of arrangements started? At least that was how Mrs. Qasim Waheed—a woman she envied—had found her household help. And since Mrs. Waheed was the wife of one of Aarif Hassan's colleagues, making about the same salary, it was intolerable that she should be able to live the life of luxury with a full-time maid who had come almost free.

It had been nearly five years since Mrs. Waheed had developed a back problem that required surgery. Needing someone to take charge of the household during her convalescence, she had asked Shaheen Kaukab, a widowed cousin from Pakistan, to come and stay with her for a while. Gradually, Shaheen's status as a guest had been phased out and her new status as maid-cum-sitter phased in. When she had balked at this and tried to regain lost ground by going back to Pakistan, she had found to her horror that by deciding to come to America she had burned all her bridges.

No one in Pakistan wanted her back—especially the women she knew. For them, she had become a liability the day her husband died. Not that they didn't feel sorry for her, but their hands were tied. What woman in her right mind would willingly take the risk of exposing her husband to a passably good-looking young widow who was surely seeking some man to bring her back into the mainstream of life? The result, happily for Mrs. Qasim Waheed, was that Shaheen Kaukab's visit had lengthened indefinitely, and as time passed, she had resigned herself to her new situation in life.

Wouldn't it be wonderful if Sadika became a permanent luxury in Ashfaaq Beebee's house just as Mrs. Qasim Waheed's cousin had become in hers? Though not as bad as being widowed in her youth, Sadika's situation was bad enough: she was the eldest of three sisters, and her younger sister had gotten married before her to her own fiancé. So maybe her family would not want her back in a hurry, inasmuch as her presence would make it difficult to find a match for Sajida. Ashfaaq Beebee had noticed how hardworking and skilled Sadika was in every aspect of housekeeping. That was the main reason she had found Zafary disappointing as a daughter-in-law: compared to Sadika she was unskilled labor.

How wonderful it would be to relax and have delicious homecooked meals, spic-and-span floors and clean laundry— to have a full-time live-in maid at a fraction of the usual cost. It had been clever of her to come up with such a brilliant idea, and her stars must have been in the right alignment because Khanum had immediately accepted her proposal without any objections. Now Ashfaaq Beebee would be able to have the social life she was meant for: brunches, luncheons, tea parties— she could have them all, and without lifting a finger. She had tasted the adulation of prospective mothers-of-brides on her visit to Pakistan to select Haroon's wife. Here, she did not have the attraction of an eligible son, but perhaps leisurely parties offering homemade treats fresh from Pakistan would prove irresistible.

Ashfaaq Beebee thought with pleasure of the progress she had already made when she told people about her niece's imminent visit. "You know how I love to help people out," she had said to Mrs. Qasim Waheed just yesterday. "I said to myself, who deserves a helping hand better than my own niece, my own flesh and blood? Sadika is quite backward in almost every way, you know. I thought, why not give her the opportunity to widen her horizons? Maybe she can take a few courses in some school or something and make something of herself. In Pakistan she has nothing to look forward to but marriage with some undesirable person. Here she has me and my Ishrat to guide her and better her lot in life. She might be helpful in the house too, but I'm not counting on that. Only God knows how teachable she might be."

Sadika, fortunately unaware of Ashfaaq Beebee's plans for her, was boarding Pakistan International Airline Flight 716 from Islamabad to JFK airport in New York. She was as frightened at the prospect of living in America as Ashfaaq Beebee was excited at the thought of having her there. That she had never been on an airplane before, and certainly had never before gone so far away from home, made everything worse. After tomorrow, thousands of miles of ocean would separate her from everything and everyone she had ever known. And for what? There was no eager new bridegroom waiting for her in America, as was generally the case when someone like her was sent so far away. And she wasn't being banished so that she could acquire an education or make money—the two other reasons young people left for America. Maybe she was to serve as a sacrificial lamb for some evil deo, some invisible monster, and she was too stupid even to know it.

As a child she had read fairy tales about evil deos that came from across several bodies of water. After defeating them, the handsome prince would tell them to go back to their original home and warn them never to dare show their faces again in his peaceful and righteous kingdom. Maybe America was that home, and for all she knew, deos were still waiting there, ready to avenge themselves on anyone who came from across the ocean. If only she did not feel confused and disoriented as well as panicky. If only she could decide whether she was lucky or unlucky to be going to America.

Sadika's idea about America came from romance novels, television programs and snatches of overheard conversation, and she did not see how she could find a niche for herself in such a weird society. She had overheard Bushra Bee say to Abida Hussain, about young people who had immigrated, "America is nothing but a huge den of iniquity, full of people with loose characters. All they think about is lust and illicit love. Why, I hear that all you have to do is offer a woman a box of chocolates and she's willing to do anything. *Anything*!" Bushra Bee repeated for emphasis.

"Our boys are innocent and good, *behen*," Abida Hussain responded with a sigh. "That's why they can't resist the unscrupulous whores who fling themselves on them in America."

"America is full of piles and piles of money." Sadika had heard Salima Ahmad's son Amjad imply that he himself had seen and touched the money that grew on the trees there. "All you need is a little ingenuity and hard work for it to come pouring down on you."

How America had come by these forests full of money-trees, no one knew. And if American movies and television shows were any indication, America, apart from money-trees, was a place where crime and excitement ran rampant. Criminals with guns and knives—sometimes impeccably dressed like James Bond, sometimes half-naked—filled the streets, robbing people at gunpoint, kidnapping and raping, running international drug cartels, smuggling rings, spy rings, and baby-selling rings, indulging in car chases or just going around firing at innocent people at will. How America had managed to produce high-tech products and high-rise buildings when the population was so unproductive, was anybody's guess.

Sadika would have kept to herself, lost in unsettling thoughts for the entire trip, if it had not been for Amina Mahmood and Rashida Aziz, two women from Pakistan on their way to Washington, DC. They had been watching Sadika from their seats across the aisle, speculating on why a conservative young girl was traveling alone. In the transit lounge at Heathrow Airport in London, they sat down next to her, insisting that she try some of their homemade snack made from lentils and nuts.

They were in their late forties, and were returning to Washington from a month's vacation in Pakistan. They were well-dressed, self-confident and in high spirits, although they did not speak like educated women. To Sadika, they represented kindness and affection, qualities that had been sorely lacking in her life.

"Where are you going in America, *baetee*, daughter, and what are you going to be doing there?" Amina asked, her shrewd eyes taking in Sadika's threadbare clothing and hesitant, reserved manner.

"My aunt, who is also my sister's mother-in-law, lives in Pennsylvania. My sister is expecting her second child, and I'm going to help out in the house," Sadika replied in one long breath.

"How long will you be staying? And is your sister younger or older than you?"

"I don't know how long I'll stay. As long as I'm needed, I guess." She added in a low voice, with her head bent in shame and embarrassment, "My sister is younger than I am." Sadika was fully aware of the implications of that bit of information: it had become so much a part of her identity that on the forms she had filled out for the journey, she had felt the need for a "single, with married younger sister" category. Just to write "single" did not really describe her.

"You mean you're going to help out indefinitely in your younger sister's household who is married and living with her in-laws?" Rashida wanted to make sure she had the facts straight. When Sadika nodded, she exchanged amused glances with Amina and they both burst into laughter. "Then you are one of us, little sister. Or almost," Rashida said, putting her arm affectionately around Sadika's shoulders.

"Why? Do you also help out your family?" Sadika asked, uncomfortably aware of the sudden pressure of Rashida's warm meaty arm and her intimate manner.

"Yes we do help out our families. In Pakistan, that is. In America the families that we help out are the ones who hire us," Amina said.

Seeing Sadika's total confusion, they tried patiently to explain. They each did housework for a few families in Washington. Rashida had been sponsored by one Shafeeq Ahmed, who worked for the World Bank and was allowed one servant by some kind of law. Once Rashida came to America, she worked sometimes for one, and sometimes for three families. Amina had come to America more or less like Sadika. Her rich relatives had sponsored her so that she could help with housework.

When that visa ran out, Amina had found an official at the Pakistani Embassy who got her a work visa. Now she worked for a cluster of four or five families, cooking, cleaning and doing their laundry. Each of the women earned in the neighborhood of $1000 to $1200 dollars a month, room and board included. They felt incredibly lucky and sent the bulk of that money to Pakistan where, converted into local currency, it enabled their families to live like royalty.

"My two daughters' dowries are ready and their marriages arranged to very eligible young men. Next year on my vacation to Pakistan, God willing, I'll arrange a beautiful double wedding for them," Rashida said proudly.

Amina was just as proud, probably more proud. "My older son Nazeer goes to King Edward Medical College in Lahore, the best medical school in Pakistan. After he's finished, I may be able to arrange for him to come to America by finding a good American citizen for him to marry. I've already started looking, so he doesn't have to waste valuable time after graduation. As soon as he passes the American medical exam for foreigners, I'll be able to quit my job and live like a queen."

"You should see the way we're treated by our families in Pakistan," Rashida said. "Our husbands, children, all try to get into our good graces. People throw parties for us and give us gifts. They love to listen to our stories about America and they want our advice on how to get there. We're better than visiting royalty, *baetee*. We're the geese that lay the golden eggs. By the way, *baetee*, how much are you going to get paid for your work?"

"Why would I get paid? This is family, and helping them out is what I'm supposed to do." Sadika tried to sound indignant, but she found herself stammering. Ever since she studied economics, she had thought that there was something wrong with working for someone without getting anything in return. Now for the first time it occurred to her that maybe her work should earn her money or some other advantage, even if a relative was involved. This was a revolutionary thought, because where she came from, it was accepted that women would work hard for extended families without getting so much as a thank you.

"Nothing! Nothing at all?" Amina and Rashida exclaimed in unison, exchanging glances. They looked at Sadika with sympathy, but their expression seemed to be saying, Poor foolish girl, you're so naive.

Just before they were about to disembark at JFK, the women gave Sadika their phone numbers and a final piece of advice. "Don't let your family abuse you, *baetee*. Make sure you're paid enough if you're being used as household help. If you're asked to stay as a guest and family member, then remember, others should be doing at least as much work as you," Rashida said.

Amina told her, "This world is a selfish place, *baetee*. Nobody does anything out of the goodness of their heart. You have to look out for yourself and make sure you get what's coming to you."

nineteen

SADIKA SAT ALONE in her makeshift room in Ashfaaq Beebee's basement. A partition of bookshelves had been put up, bisecting the big basement into two unequal parts, the smaller one allotted to Sadika. The damp musty smell did not bother her as much as the lack of a window, making it impossible to tell whether it was day or night. But she knew without looking at her watch that it was about ten at night, because she was physically exhausted.

Not that knowing the time would make much difference, since there was nothing to look forward to. She had gone straight from one bad situation to another. As they said in Urdu, she had fallen from the sky and gotten stuck in the date tree. When Amina and Rashida had talked to her as though she were a servant like themselves, she should have had more than an inkling of what was coming. Her apprehensions on the plane about new people, a new lifestyle and a new culture seemed laughable now. So did her worries about whether her English was good enough. Ashfaaq Beebee did not take her out even to the grocery store; it was so much more convenient to leave everything in Sadika's capable hands and go off by herself.

Sadika had been in America for three months. And, except for being driven in terse silence by her uncle in his green Subaru from JFK airport to Grantsville, Pennsylvania, she could still have been in Pakistan for all she had seen of the U.S. In fact, other than the absence of the "fallen woman" reputation and the presence of infinitely better bathroom facilities, she might as well still have been in Farooq Mamoon's village. The work was just as intense and unremitting, and the company as scarce, even though it was the home of her own sister, who looked as though she desperately needed a shoulder to cry on.

It had taken two days after her arrival for Sadika to recover from severe jet lag and an upset stomach. But from the third day on, life had settled into a dismal routine: Ishrat, Haroon and Aarif Hassan went off in the morning after breakfast, and did not come back until nearly night. Then they sat down to the nice hot meal cooked and served by Sadika, and talked about how terrible their day had been, each attempting to out-complain the others. Ishrat's college courses were too hard and all her instructors were prejudiced and unfair; Haroon's job at the local bank did not sufficiently utilize his excellent business mind, while Aarif Hassan's skills and talents were not appreciated at the high school where he taught. Even Ashfaaq Beebee, who was in and out of the house the whole day long, seemed to be having a hard time dealing with the evil side of human nature in her quest for a better social life. Only Zafary, whom Sadika remembered as being quite a chatterbox, was quiet. No one bothered to ask her what kind of day she had had, and she never volunteered the information, even when she felt sick, her feet and hands were swollen, and she had to stay in bed.

Ashfaaq Beebee's social calendar was always filled to capacity, leaving her almost no time for housework or cooking. Sadika had no idea how her aunt had managed before her arrival. Zafary sometimes lay in her room leafing through a tabloid newspaper or taking a nap, and occasionally followed Sadika around in silence. Most of the time she didn't seem half as sick as she claimed to be and was gaining weight at an alarming rate. She was eating huge meals, not, she said, because she was hungry, but because the baby needed the nutrition. While Sadika looked after little Jalees, cooked, cleaned, ironed and did everything else that needed to be done, Zafary hung around watching her and eating snacks.

What surprised Sadika was that Zafary seemed to be looking at her not with pity, but with something close to envy. At first she wondered why on earth Zafary would envy her when Zafary's situation was so much better than hers. After a while, however, Sadika saw clearly with the two eyes God had given her what her sister was reluctant to reveal.

It was hard for Sadika to believe that at one time she had considered Haroon to be the ultimate hero, that she had dreamed of sharing Barbara Cartland and Harlequin romance scenarios with him. The same lips that once had seemed sexy beyond belief, and that she had imagined pressed thrillingly against various parts of her anatomy, now seemed shaped like leeches. The mere thought of being touched by them, however fleetingly, chilled her to the bone. She imagined them sucking the energy and sense of self-worth from her sister, leaving her white and lifeless. Actually, Haroon did not need to get within touching distance of Zafary for her to wilt like last week's flowers. He telegraphed his attitude which was, Now that I, a god, have condescended to marry you, you may proceed to worship me.

Zafary's fate seemed particularly pitiable when, in front of her, Haroon told his friends how he had been persuaded to marry her. Like a soldier relating bloodcurdling war stories, he glanced at Zafary during one of these monologues as though he were describing a debilitating wound received during combat. She was his badge of courage, a cross almost too heavy to bear, but he bore it with courage and dignity.

"Do you know that in half the states in the U.S., marriage between cousins is not even permitted?" After pausing to gauge the reaction of his audience, he elaborated on his heroism. "They call it 'consanguinity', and a lot of research has been done on it. You can end up having retarded children if you marry your cousin, did you know that? The only reason I was willing to take the risk of ruining my entire life was that it made my family happy. And it was a matter of honor: see, it was very important to my mother that I marry her niece. She made that commitment to her sister in Pakistan and she would've lost face if I hadn't followed through."

If Ashfaaq Beebee was within earshot at such moments, she would throw adoring glances at her precious son.

Zafary's plight deteriorated even further when, at the end of his highly embellished tale, Haroon's American friends looked at him with a mixture of sympathy and admiration. These third-world cultures are so barbaric, they were obviously thinking. Thank God in our civilized world young people are not turned into sacrificial lambs at their parents' whim.

Although Haroon was obnoxious, Ashfaaq Beebee beat him hands down when it came to self-serving hypocrisy. Her values and beliefs changed from week to week and she tended to blurt out whatever suited her or made her look good at the time. Sadika, who cooked and served her aunt's frequent teas and afternoon get-togethers, caught snatches of conversation that sent her head spinning. Even Khanum was not as adept at changing her tune so often or so smoothly.

"I might seem settled to you," she would tell new immigrants from Pakistan or India with a sigh, knowing they were probably homesick, "but my soul yearns for Pakistan. As soon as we can, we intend to go back. We're planning for it, you know." Then she could not resist adding, "My husband has so many offers from teaching institutions that he's finding it hard to make up his mind. His reputation as one of the best has preceded him through the intellectual people we associate with. Not that we make an effort to do that—they just flock to us of their own free will. You must have heard the proverb: birds of a feather flock together. We're a classic example of that."

At other times, she expounded on the evils of Third World countries like Pakistan for the benefit of acquaintances who were already comfortably settled in America. As always, her monologue would start with the topic at hand, but quickly turn into unadulterated praise for herself or a member of her family. "The corruption is so rampant, it's unbelievable. How any decent person can survive there is beyond me. You know how straightforward and honest we are. There's no place there for people like us. My husband, who's brilliant, is convinced that nothing is done there on the basis of merit. If it was, he would probably be head of one of their finest institutions. Not that there are no examples of good and honest people at the top. You might not know this, but both my uncle and my father are top people in their professions there; my father is one of the finest legal minds, and my uncle is one of the highest ranking government officials. That's why we're treated like royalty whenever we visit."

She loved to make people jealous. And one thing she had learnt was that almost all women wished for a more amorous spouse. She used this knowledge the way Khanum used her hypothetical American connection. "I used to think that marriage is beautiful. Now that I'm married, I think it's even more beautiful. How couldn't I, when I have a wonderful husband who's handsome, cultured, accomplished, and treats me like a china doll, a delicate flower, a heroine out of some movie." She announced this to a group of women who had just been discussing how indifferent the men were in their part of the world.

"Forget gifts," Samina had said.

"I would have a coronary if my husband got me a card on our anniversary or my birthday. That's how little I expect from him in the romance department."

"All men really want from us is sex. Romance is alien to them," Salmeen observed. "The only time my husband wants physical contact with me is when he wants to practice his conjugal rights. And then he touches me the same way I touch the control panel of my microwave: he expects immediate gratification."

"Just think, one is so alone before one gets married," Ashfaaq Beebee went on. "Then you get a life partner and you don't have to spend another lonely night again as long as you live. It's so comforting. Take last night. I was cold, so I clung to my Aarif. I think being able to cuddle up to a warm body whenever you want is one of the best things about being married, don't you agree?"

To a group of disenchanted females who had just been talking about how unreasonable their husbands could be, and how
having children was one of the most unpleasant things a woman
had to do, she would utter in a dreamy voice: "Aarif and I had
our first child so soon after we were married because we just
felt so comfortable with each other. Like we had known each
other for ages. And we were eager to express our love in every
way." The group would fall silent, and watching their crest-
fallen expressions, Ashfaaq Beebee felt her chest expand with
happiness. She was very much like Khanum: convincing people
that she was superior to them made her feel more secure in a
world devoid of guarantees.

"You have such lovely jewelry," she would sweetly compliment a new bride who had just come from Pakistan, and was
obviously feeling lonely and uncertain—an easy target. "I have
beautiful jewelry too, but I keep it in the bank. Everybody here
does, you know. For one thing it's safer, and for another, it's
considered very poor taste to wear too much. There's a saying,
in Rome, do as the Romans do. You might have heard it."

If one of her children won an athletic or academic competition, she made it sound like an Olympic Gold Medal or a Nobel
Prize. But if other people's children accomplished exactly the
same thing, it was denigrated as a rinky-dink minor regional
award—the kind of thing her children won all the time without
even trying.

The peace and quiet of her neighborhood was attributed to
elegance and exclusiveness, while other areas were quiet because they were less desirable and prices were depressed. "In
far-flung areas, land is almost free and houses are worth very
little," she would comment. "Where we live, it's hard to buy
even a few square feet of land without going bankrupt."

Many women laughed at her behind her back. But nobody
confronted her. As with Khanum, they feared what she might
say about them if they made her angry.

twenty

As Zafary's weight steadily increased and her general condition declined because she stayed cooped up in the house with food as her only diversion, the sympathetic looks Haroon received from his friends increased to the point that it became torture for Zafary to be around them at all. The more desperately she tried to be accepted by them, the more contempt they seemed to feel for her. She tried using her meager allowance to buy American clothes for herself at the local K-mart, but that didn't help. Many times she caught Haroon's friends snickering or talking in low, hushed tones while glancing at her

Compared to this, life in Pakistan had been paradise. At least she hadn't been an object of ridicule. She hadn't been made to feel awkward in ill-fitting clothes, and she hadn't needed to make an effort to fit in. In fact, compared to Sadika, she had been considered stylish, good-looking, and—ever since her wedding to Haroon—incredibly lucky. She was sure Sadika must have been consumed with envy when her little sister had married Haroon. She had felt flushed with pride at having whisked away such a prize from right under Sadika's studious nose.

How she wished now that it had never happened, that Haroon had never chosen her instead of Sadika. She felt the pressure of her struggle to conceal from Haroon and his family her envy of Sadika's limited independence, while at the same time trying to save her pride by acting like a happily married woman. Every time she thought of how hard she had tried to change her circumstances, she felt like crying. Nobody would ever realize how much effort she had put into trying to develop a sense of style by studying the models in Sears and J.C. Penney catalogs; how desperately she had tried to reverse her increasing girth by exercising like a maniac. She had even joined a health club.

Jenny, the woman next door, had offered to let her join the small health club she operated out of her home free of charge in exchange for babysitting for her two children. But instead of making Zafary feel better, the contrast between herself and the trim women, smartly dressed in expensive exercise clothing, had made her feel even worse. In the wind-down period, Jenny asked everyone to close her eyes, relax, and imagine she was at the beach. "Imagine waves lapping at your feet and the gentle sea breeze blowing in your face," Jenny would say, evoking memories for Zafary of some particularly rough times during the first few months of marriage.

That was when she had thought Haroon actually felt something for her. Why else would he have married her despite all that pressure on him to marry Sadika? She had been about five months pregnant with her first child and at his mother's urging, Haroon had taken her to spend a day at the beach. Ashfaaq Beebee was concerned for the health of her unborn grandchild. Although uncomfortable with the idea, Zafary had agreed, to please Haroon and his mother.

Finding appropriate beachwear had been a feat—physically as well as psychologically. Zafary came from a culture where even bare arms were considered scandalous, and here she was, actually contemplating baring most of her body—with a child on the way too! She had felt sure that she was doing irreparable damage to her baby in order to win her husband's approval. She had heard older, wiser people say, "Committing immoral acts has negative consequences for an unborn child. If you want your child to be good, read religious books and spend time praying and meditating."

When she finally put on a bathing suit and joined Haroon for a walk at the beach, it had taken her a few minutes to muster enough courage to glance shyly up at him. She found total

unconcern instead of the pride in her courage and adaptability
that she had hoped for. As the day progressed and she saw him
blatantly ogling one female body after another, her ego had become totally deflated. The nausea she had thought had disappeared after three months of pregnancy returned with a vengeance. When he threw a suggestive look at a particularly curvaceous redhead, and received a friendly smile from her, Zafary
belched. Forced to pay her some attention, Haroon had remarked that it was a shame that the bulk she carried around
was all fat and no muscle. "You women from Third World countries are so out of shape. If you can't handle a simple walk on
the beach, how can you expect to do any real work?"

You mean like the work I used to do the whole day long,
cooking your food and doing your laundry, listening to crap
from your mother, she had wanted to shout. But she kept her
silence. An outburst like that would only make her miserable
life more miserable. Besides, living with Haroon and his family
was the only life she knew in the U.S., and going back to Pakistan was not an option. She was aware of how hard Sadika's
life had become as the elder unmarried sister and she knew that
a divorced woman's life was ten times worse than a spurned
woman's—a kind of living death.

In fact, when she had heard the term "living dead" for the
first time in a TV vampire movie, she had thought it was going
to be about just such women. Then she was caught up in the
movie and became enthralled by the lives of these beautiful supposed victims, who had turned into "the living dead." What,
she thought, is so terrible about these gorgeous women that the
entire town is trying to destroy them? It might be just a case of
people not wanting to see someone else doing better than themselves, and trying to pull them down.

I would happily trade my life for theirs any day, she said to
herself, and so would almost any woman I know: they're beautiful, forever young, and best of all, they don't have to worry
about pleasing a cold husband or an evil mother-in-law. All they

do is sleep peacefully all day, and at night they get dressed up in beautiful gowns, lure handsome young unsuspecting men into their castle, and while they're making love, sink their teeth into their attractive necks and drain their delicious lifeblood. What could be more exciting? The icing on the cake was that people were deathly afraid of them and they didn't have to worry about cooking meals or having children.

Zafary longed to go out the door in the middle of the night and encounter one of those handsome undead men, who would suck her blood and make her one of them. Then I would come back in and scare the living daylights out of Ashfaaq Beebee and Haroon with my long sharp teeth and bloodshot eyes, she thought gleefully. She visualized Ashfaaq Beebee screeching and struggling with rage, fright and pain, as her daughter-in-law effortlessly snacked away on her fat neck. As for Haroon, she would sink her deadly fangs into a different part of him altogether, rendering him forever incapable of making sexual demands on her or anyone else.

How any woman in her right mind could enjoy sex, Zafary had no idea. Right now she had a respite from her unpleasant chores, both household and bedroom, because of her pregnancy. Sadika's presence allowed her to rest the entire morning. And at night all she had to do was pretend to be tired and uncomfortable to make Haroon back off, at least most of the time. He knew how important a grandson was to his mother. So even though he wanted daily sexual release, he was unwilling to demand it at the risk of harming the baby.

But this was a temporary situation that would change as soon as the baby was born. She was already in the third trimester. The time when she would no longer have a buffer against her unpleasant bedroom tasks was approaching too fast. Then things would revert to the way they had been, at least in the sex department. Hopefully, her mother-in-law's strategy would work, and Sadika would stay on even after the birth of the baby, and at least Zafary wouldn't have to worry about housework.

In about three more months, Zafary thought with a sigh, Haroon would again feel justified in not letting her go to sleep, no matter how tired she was, till he had his sexual gratification. As always, she would feel compelled to do his bidding; as always, forcing herself to do unspeakable things to his private parts would seem the ultimate humiliation after a day full of defeat. As always, after achieving satisfaction, he would turn over and go to sleep without a word, leaving her to take care of the mess before going to bed herself, because he liked to wake up to a clean room. And, as always, the entire process would make her feel less than nothing.

How could some women complain about their husbands not performing their husbandly duties when they should be counting their blessings? Take the women she socialized with at the local mosque. "How often does your husband do right by you?" they had delicately asked her one day.

When she said, "Every night," they had let out a joint screech of envy, and demanded to know what she did to make him find her so desirable. "Do you wear a see-through negligée, put on a special perfume, perform a strip tease or what?"

Zafary told them, "I don't have any special clothes for night-time, and I guess I must smell like the garlic and ginger I eat at night for my health." They looked at her with disgust and disbelief. If you don't want to tell us your secret, that's fine, their expressions said, but don't expect us to believe that anyone could find you irresistible unless you made some effort.

If only, she had thought to herself wistfully, I was not so desirable. Prostitutes are lucky. At least they get paid for doing this unpleasant work.

She decided to quit her exercise classes. And as time went on, her looks deteriorated further because of pregnancy, lack of exercise and frustrated snacking, while Haroon became almost handsome as a result of eating healthy homecooked meals and having time to work out at a gym.

twenty-one

THERE WAS A smile of contentment on Zafary's face as she lay on the hospital bed in a reclining position with her favorite tabloid newspaper wide open on her lap. The remnants of lunch were still on a table nearby, but she didn't need to worry about cleaning up, she thought happily. The nurse, or whoever, would take care of that, as they would also take care of the next meal, and the meal after that. She didn't have to worry about anything or anyone including Ashfaaq Beebee, Haroon and Jalees.

The morning before, she had delivered a seven-pound, six-ounce healthy baby boy in the maternity ward of the General Hospital. And ever since that time, she had been in heaven. Suddenly her status, which had been nosediving in the eyes of her husband's family ever since her marriage, had taken off in the opposite direction. Where before she could do nothing right despite her best efforts, now she could do no wrong, because of the tiny scrap of humanity born to her. Her husband and in-laws actually brought her gifts and flowers, and she had heard more endearments come out of their mouths in the past twenty-four hours than in the entire three years of her marriage.

The person most transformed by little Zahid's birth was Ashfaaq Beebee. Ever since she had held him in her arms, named him after her deceased father, and put the bit of honey in his mouth to ensure a sweet nature, she had been beside herself with joy. There was a skip in her step, and her habitual frown had all but disappeared. Even her eyes, normally sharp as a hawk's, had taken on a softer look. No one would ever be able to say again that her wonderful Haroon, who was the epitome of desirable young manhood, was not man enough to produce a son. Last month when Salmeen had jokingly said, "If Zafary gives birth to another girl, maybe next time you should get someone else to impregnate her," Ashfaaq Beebee had been about ready to claw her eyes out; only the presence of other women eager for exactly that kind of spectacle had stopped her.

Now because of little Zahid, she would never have to worry about hearing those kinds of snide comments again. And since Zafary had been the one responsible for that wonderful state of affairs, she felt almost fond of her daughter-in-law. Who would have thought that Zafary, whom until now she had always thought of as "that wretched girl," had it in her to give Ashfaaq Beebee the best gift of her life.

And little Zahid belonged to Ashfaaq Beebee—of that there was no doubt—to raise and care for as she pleased. Haroon and Zafary were simply the means of getting him to her. All the mistakes that she had made in raising Haroon and Ishrat, she would avoid with Zahid. She would be stricter, more forceful, make him study harder and practice more. And when she was finished with him, he would be a world-class something or other, eternally grateful to his grandmother for having given him the right guidance. Perhaps she could find someone to get him started on his education right away. Nowadays, with the competition being cut-throat, one couldn't get enough of a head start.

Haroon was not as overjoyed at the birth of his son as his mother, but he pretended all the appropriate emotions. Babies, even his own, didn't interest him. In fact, if they didn't testify to a man's manhood, they would only have nuisance value as far as he was concerned. He wanted to look like the picture of an ecstatic father because for some strange reason that was what was expected of a real man now—not sensible skills like hunting, aggressiveness, survival abilities—but devotion to family and displays of emotion.

So he frequently held little Zahid in his arms, and lavished flowers, kisses and endearments on Zafary for the world to see.

It was the most acting he had done since he had been to camp many years ago, and surprisingly, Zafary, after the initial shock, not only recognized it for what it was, but was willing to go along with it.

"And how is my Zaffo doing today?" he crooned, stooping to drop a firm kiss on her mouth under the approving eye of the nurse, whom he addressed in a pleasant voice, "And you, I hope, are taking good care of my lovely wife. If not, understand that I'm the one you'll have to answer to."

The kindly middle-aged nurse assured him that they were doing their very best to make his beloved wife comfortable, while he arranged the bouquet of flowers he had brought in a vase and blew Zafary another kiss. As soon as the nurse left, the air whooshed out of his balloon, and his face resumed the sullen expression he usually wore when he was with Zafary. Without another word or glance, he sat down and started to read the magazine he had brought with him, till another nurse, doctor, or visitor showed up. Then the charade began all over again.

But Zafary didn't mind; she was having the time of her life. There were no unpleasant tasks, sexual or otherwise, and no one tried to dominate or belittle her. On the contrary, every effort was made to make her feel happy and comfortable, so the milk flowing from her breasts would be rich and abundant.

All she had to do all day long was lie back, accept congratulations and flowers, and smile. Even watching Haroon's transformations was fun—like seeing the hunchback of Notre Dame turn into Romeo and back again. Sometimes she joined Haroon's performance, much to his irritation, and when he said, "How is my beautiful wife today?", put her arms around his neck, and replied in an exaggerated doting voice: "Darling, now that you're here, I'm all better." After all, if he could make believe, why couldn't she? Especially now that he was not in a position to retaliate.

Amazingly, Ashfaaq Beebee's kindness and smiles were genuine. She kissed and cuddled the baby even when no one was around, and frequently asked how Zafary was feeling—sometimes going so far as to ask if she could bring something to the hospital to make her more comfortable.

Zafary's favorite time of day was visiting hours. Since it was an unwritten law in the local Pakistani community to visit someone at least once in the hospital, there were always visitors. Invariably, as soon as the men were busy elsewhere, the women started to exchange horror stories about their difficult labor.

"I was in labor for thirty-eight hours straight before my son was delivered by emergency cesarean. But by that time I had lost so much blood that I had to be literally given gallons of blood just to keep me alive," Huma, Samina's daughter, said.

"With me, it was loss of appetite. I wouldn't eat anything, and my poor husband went crazy trying to get me to eat. He would order my favorite dishes from the most exclusive restaurants in town and try feeding me himself, but nothing helped. Finally, when I fainted, they had to feed me intravenously." Rizwana from the mosque talked fast so that she could finish her story before someone cut her off.

"At least you were never in danger of losing your life," Maheen, another distant acquaintance added, as soon as she could get a word in. "My water broke during a snowstorm when phone lines and electricity were out. My poor husband had to walk one mile in knee-deep snow to get to the nearest phone. By the time he came back, the baby was almost out and there was blood everywhere. If the ambulance had arrived even five minutes later than it did, the baby and I would have died for sure."

Visiting hours generally ended with one or the other of the women still trying to enter some imaginary Hall of Fame for young women who had suffered the worst labor. And even though giving birth to Jalees had been more difficult than it had been with Zahid, Zafary felt as though she was finally a bona fide contender for that award. There had really been no point in bragging about the pain of Jalees's birth because the fruit of that labor had been less than wonderful. This time she had given birth to a son, and she could embellish her suffering to her heart's content.

How exhilarating it was to be an uncontested star, when before she had not even been in the running for understudy. Sadika, Ishrat, Aarif Hassan, even Haroon, had receded far into the background, becoming nothing more than silent spectators, while Ashfaaq Beebee seemed now to be an indulgent and affectionate supporter. For the first time in her life, Zafary understood Khanum's preferential treatment of Asghar. Little Zahid was only a few days old, but already he had done more to elevate her status among her family and friends than all her patience, prayers, tolerance and hard work put together.

How she adored her baby.

How she wished her stay at the hospital could last forever.

twenty-two

Even though the royal treatment of Zafary ceased after she came home from the hospital, there was a subtle change in her standing in the family. She had become one of them. It was now Sadika who was the only outsider—the only person not connected to the Hassan household by a solid male bloodline.

Sadika did not feel alienated only from the Hassans—she was discovering huge cultural differences between herself and the rest of America. Some were only differences in social conventions, but others were differences in attitude, perspective, pace of life and standard of beauty. In matters of social custom, for instance, it was not considered impolite to refuse food if one did not want it; just as it was not rude or gluttonish to accept a dish the first time it was offered. One was not considered a bad host for taking no for an answer, nor was a guest looked upon as discourteous for refusing something even if the hostess had cooked it herself for the occasion.

Overhearing conversations of well-wishers who had come to see the baby, Sadika became convinced that Americans felt they were slothful unless they turned into machines that got up early and did not quit till bedtime. From workplace to gym to church meetings, they always seemed to be headed somewhere in a hurry. And they were as serious about play as they were about work, meticulously planning what they would eat, where they would go, even how they would look when they were on vacation. Elizabeth, the wife of one of Aarif Hassan's colleagues, had refused to taste delicious *samosas*, ground beef wrapped in pastry, because she needed to lose weight before her Caribbean vacation, two months away. And what were they going to do on that vacation? Relax, play, and enjoy their meals. "If only I was built like you, Sadika," Elizabeth had commented wistfully, while refusing homemade batter-fried potatoes.

Sadika could hardly believe that the boyish figure that had caused her to be called "a dry rotten stick" in Gulmushk Mohalla, now made her an object of envy. The same lack of curves that had once tempted her to stuff fabric scraps into her bra, now made her fashionable when she wore clothes she had altered that had been discarded by Ashfaaq Beebee, Ishrat, and even Zafary.

She could vividly remember the first time her aunt and Ishrat had seen her in her navy blue pants suit, salvaged from Ashfaaq Beebee's shapeless navy dress and Ishrat's baggy pants, intended for the Salvation Army. All Ashfaaq Beebee could say was, "You're lucky we buy expensive clothes and think of poor people the way we do. No one else I know gives away such good stuff."

Since Sadika was no longer in school, her creativity had found a new outlet, much to the surprise of her aunt and cousins. Haroon was still reeling from the sight of the black-and-red pants suit she had worn on the occasion of Baby Zahid's first party, while Ashfaaq Beebee and Ishrat were annoyed about the positive response to the clothes from the other guests.

"Where does Sadika buy her clothes?" Samina had asked.

"Sadika must be financially well-off if she can afford clothes like that." Mrs. Qasim Waheed's shrewd eyes tried to gauge Sadika's exact status in the Hassan household.

Things reached a point where Ashfaaq Beebee, Ishrat, even Zafary, hesitated to discard their old clothes for fear that Sadika would transform them into chic designs.

In this new culture, it seemed that all Sadika's negative physical attributes had been miraculously metamorphosed into assets: her bronze complexion, so ordinary in her homeland, was the look American women sought at beaches and tanning salons; her long jet-black hair, commonplace in Gulmushk

Mohalla, was now often admired. Once when she went with Ishrat to the mall to buy baby clothes, complete strangers had commented on her loosely-tied hair. Sadika did not know what to make of it. She thought that maybe if food was scarce in America, fat people would be admired, but luckily for her this was a land of plenty, and what in Pakistan was called her "half-starved" look, was fashionable here. Why people admired her hair remained a mystery to her.

There was a downside to Sadika's transformation. Sometimes while she was tending to the children, she noticed Haroon staring at her fixedly. Considering that he treated Zafary with apathy and even contempt, this was a disturbing development. What was downright repulsive was that he had begun to find excuses to touch her. The week before, for example, when she had dropped the canister of rice in her hurry to get dinner started, he had insisted on helping her. Picking up the scattered grains, he had backed into her, apologizing when she moved hastily away. Then following her example, he had gotten down on all fours, his hands cupping hers as she scooped up the grains. When he began to brush invisible stray grains from her hands, Sadika blurted out, "Don't touch me like that. You're my sister's husband."

"Like what?" he countered wickedly. "Like this?" He laced his fingers through hers, and pulled their palms together. "Or like this?"—running his hands up and down her arms.

"I'll tell Zafary and Aunt if you don't stop right now." Panic-stricken, Sadika leaped up. Haroon shrugged and walked away. But from then on, he began to make remarks to provoke a response from her. Worse, he took every opportunity to rub against her.

His favorite time for this was late afternoon when Sadika was alone in the kitchen, washing dishes or preparing dinner. Coming home early from work, he would pretend to reach for something from a cabinet above her, blatantly rubbing the front of his body against her backside. She became so upset that she often dropped the dish she was washing or lost track of the spices she was putting in the food.

Later at dinner, Ashfaaq Beebee would reprimand Sadika for breaking the dish, or someone would comment that the food was too spicy, while Haroon, unconcerned, continued to eat, trying at the same time to find her foot with his under the table.

Even though she felt helpless and trapped, the irony of the situation was not lost on Sadika. If Haroon had acted this way when he had visited Pakistan to select a bride, all would have been perfect in her world. In fact, she would have been ecstatic. Shocked, but ecstatic. Now however, her perception of him, and of course her relationship with him, had changed, and these acts that at one time she would have found thrilling, seemed downright evil. Her heart skipped several beats when he touched her, but it was with revulsion, not excitement. She was filled with dread. What would she do? Where would she go? What would her aunt, her uncle, her sister think if they found out what was going on? Would they believe that she was innocent, or, as had happened before, would she be blamed for someone else's actions?

"Think of my sister—your wife," she pleaded with him one day after he "reached up to get my things." To her horror, she could feel his aroused body through their clothes.

"What sister? What wife?" he whispered in her ear, his cheek against her hair, his hands caressing her shoulders and dipping dangerously low into the front of her dress, while his thighs held her captive. She struggled frantically to get away.

"Don't do this," she managed to say through ashen lips. "You know it's wrong."

"Why is it wrong? We were always meant for each other. Even our parents knew it. If I hadn't been so dumb, I would've seen it too. We are each other's destiny, I feel it. Tell me you feel it too." He placed his hand over her heart. "Right here."

This time when she struggled, he released her, saying matter-of-factly, "Look at it this way. Even if it's wrong, it's a lot of fun. Besides, it's not really wrong because our religion says it's not."

"Our religion!" she repeated, aghast. "How could you think, even for one moment, that Islam would condone this?"

"Doesn't it say somewhere that as long as things are done in moderation, they're good?"

"Yes," she replied, only half listening for fear Zafary might come in at any moment. The last thing she wanted was for Zafary to think that her big sister was after her husband. Especially when nothing could be further from the truth.

"See, you agree with me. Bad is not really bad. It's actually good, as long as you don't overdo it. Isn't it?" He laughed, and then, catching her chin between his fingers, repeated: "Isn't it?" before abruptly letting go when he heard Ashfaaq Beebee's key in the lock.

Zafary was not blind to what was happening between her husband and her sister. She knew very well why Haroon's mood was much improved lately, and why he was suddenly spending so much time in the kitchen, just as she knew why he had started to keep personal items in the cabinets above the sink and stove. But she was far from feeling the emotional devastation nor-mally expected of a wife in such a situation; her romantic inter-est in Haroon had died a slow and painful death a long time ago. At this point her concerns were purely practical.

What would become of her if Haroon abandoned her? Would he and his mother let her have custody of the children in case of a divorce, given Ashfaaq Beebee's obsession with Zahid? The biggest question of all was whether Zafary had the confi-dence and the ability to survive and provide for her children in America without a husband's protection. Although it would be wonderful never to have to worry about satisfying Haroon's sexual needs again, and never to go through another day feel-ing the sting of his contempt, Zafary was aware of the sad truth that she had no marketable skills, no means of survival. She did not even know English very well. As far as she could see, her only option if Haroon abandoned her would be to support her-

self by providing the male population with the same service in
bed that she provided to Haroon.

But she had reason to believe even that option was not open
to her—not because of pride or morality; she had passed that
point long ago—but because she was hopelessly inadequate at
it. In fact, if Haroon was to be believed, her sexual ability was
not even as good as her English: "It's only because I'm so much
a man that I can make do with you," he said. "An ordinary
man would have to be blind and drunk to be satisfied with
what you have to offer—you're ugly and undesirable, and I wish
I didn't have the misfortune to call you my wife."

At first she had chosen not to believe him because she knew
he always enjoyed belittling her. Then one day she had found
the porno magazines hidden underneath his mattress, and after
leafing through them, had conceded defeat. She was not even
remotely familiar with the kind of sex she saw in them. To her,
the young women in pantyhose, garter belts, high heels and
little else, handling all kinds of paraphernalia that she supposed
were essential for an exciting sexual encounter, looked like they
were acting in a horror movie. If this was standard in the sex
lives of Americans, it was a miracle that Haroon had not abandoned her long ago in favor of a more experienced and knowl-
edgeable partner.

How she wished she had married one of the simple men
who lived in Gulmushk Mohalla. Then at least she would not
have had to worry about this aspect of married life, since he
would have been as ignorant of this sophisticated stuff as she
was. Or maybe not. Maybe this was the way men were and she
had just not known it. Hadn't there been some scandal involving the local bookstore and sex magazines around the time of
her wedding? The police had confiscated all the porno material
in question in a sting operation, and they had been so concerned
about the morals of the general population that they had refused to release it for inspection.

Actually, her situation was not so bad, considering that she was an immigrant—the owner of a green card—and that she had the power to grant the person who married her the same permanent immigrant status as hers. Last year, everyone in the mosque had been talking about Jabeen, Rizwana's twice removed cousin who had been a cleaning woman. Jabeen had married a Pakistani medical doctor wanting to practice in America, and was now living like a queen in some six-bedroom mansion in New Jersey.

Maybe if she tried hard enough, she could marry someone much more satisfactory than Haroon; someone who demanded sex only once in a blue moon. Perhaps a medical doctor too busy making money to indulge in foolish meaningless pastimes. She would not only be provided with money to spend, but be left free to find a niche for herself in the exciting world of her favorite tabloids. A world filled with sex tapes, sex scandals, alien abductions, alien babies and people playing musical beds with each other's spouses. Where women didn't have to starve themselves to lose weight; they could do it painlessly, even plea-surably, by going on a diet of chocolate, steak and pasta.

Why couldn't Haroon have been some kind of celebrity? He certainly had been portrayed as one in Pakistan by his mother and hers! Then she could have given her side of the story to the tabloids and torn his reputation to shreds. Oh, what juicy de-tails she would have provided about his private life and private parts. She would have magnified and elaborated upon every disgusting demand he had ever made of her in the bedroom. And she would have enjoyed making her mother-in-law regret every mean, belittling thing she had ever said and done to her.

It wouldn't have mattered that Haroon wasn't a celebrity—in fact it would have been even better—if he had been brutally murdered by some eccentric millionaire. Not only would she have been rid of Haroon for good, but she could have sued for millions for having all the joy ruthlessly removed from her life.

And she would have played the part so well. Just as she had seen the actress Babra Sharif do in some of her favorite Urdu movies. Looking beautiful, slim and regal in black, smiling sadly, she would have become a role model, both in America and in Pakistan.

Perhaps her reproductive ability was her key to financial independence. She might be able to earn a living being a surrogate mother like some women she had read about. Maybe all she needed to do to survive on her own was to agree to have someone's baby every year. Or even more, if she took fertility drugs. Her womb could end up making her independently wealthy by cranking out babies at the rate of thirty thousand dollars per baby per year.

And Sadika was more than welcome to Haroon. He probably should have married her in the first place, because she seemed much more suited to life in America than Zafary ever was. Maybe God was punishing her for coming between Haroon and Sadika. With a pang of regret, Zafary recalled how excited Sadika had been at the prospect of being engaged to Haroon and how hard she had tried to hide her feelings. Perhaps Sadika was still dying inside of unrequited love, in which case Zafary would be glad to step aside. In fact, she would not feel even the tiniest bit of envy of her older sister, only the deepest sympathy for her.

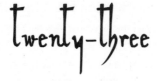

twenty-three

"WHEN YOU CALLED me to America, it was with the understanding that you would help me get an education in exchange for household help. I have held up my end of the bargain. Now you should either hold up yours, or send me back to Pakistan." That was quite a mouthful coming from Sadika, who was generally quiet as a mouse in the presence of Ashfaaq Beebee.

To say that Ashfaaq Beebee was thunderstruck was an understatement. She had convinced herself that she would never hear any demands from Sadika, legitimate or otherwise. It was just not in that stupid girl's fearful nature to speak up. Ashfaaq Beebee had congratulated herself many times in the past few months on her brilliance in bringing Sadika to America. For just as she had planned, she had succeeded in hiring a maid-cum-cook-cum-baby-sitter for a fraction of the usual cost. What's more, she had felt perfectly justified in doing it.

After all, Sadika was not good for anything else. Marriage was out, because no eligible man in his right mind would marry a girl whose fiancé had dumped her for her younger sister. Even before that stigma, she had not been a desirable prospective bride. Otherwise, wouldn't Haroon have complied with his mother's wishes? As for higher education: how academically inclined could a girl be who had been educated in a Pakistani Urdu-medium public school?

No doubt about it. Staying at home and helping with housework and child rearing was plainly what God Almighty had designed Sadika for. Not marriage, not belligerence and certainly not the giving of ultimatums. Only the immoral climate of this screwed-up country could have brought about such a drastic change in Sadika, Ashfaaq Beebee was sure of that. Her earlier policy of not allowing Sadika outside exposure had been right. If only she had been able to maintain that wise policy during the hectic time of Zafary's stay in the hospital. But what was done was done. The clock couldn't be turned back. Perhaps if she just pretended to forget about this aberration, Sadika would do the same. And things would go back to the way they had been for the past year: pleasant and relaxed.

But Sadika did not forget. In fact, once the words were out, it became easier for her to say them over and over. She was fighting for her sanity, her very survival, and that gave her the courage to confront Ashfaaq Beebee with her demand every time she encountered her. And each time, Ashfaaq Beebee was shocked, as well as convinced that Sadika would eventually drop it. She couldn't bring herself to believe that her assessment of Sadika's character had been so wrong, that someone who had always followed instructions without question could be capable of giving out challenges at every turn.

Ashfaaq Beebee would not have been incredulous if she had been aware of the intense frustration and soul-searching behind Sadika's demands. And she would have been furious if she had known that, but for the promiscuous character of her beloved son, Sadika would have kept quiet, just as she had predicted. For Ashfaaq Beebee was correct: Sadika had been raised not to question authority figures; she was accustomed to doing what she was told without question.

Finally, unable to ignore her any longer, Ashfaaq Beebee decided to give in. Sadika was too great a help to risk losing her. Life had become too comfortable. For the first time, Ashfaaq Beebee could wake up at any hour she pleased, and do whatever she wanted once she was awake. She had even started inviting ladies from the mosque to brunches and lunches, till she realized that it was in her personal interest to limit Sadika's exposure to other women.

Sadika's thin fried bread was a hit, as were her spiced chickpeas, *halva* farina dessert, and ground beef *samosas*. Everyone had commented on how tasty these were, and how lucky Ashfaaq Beebee was to have such a cook living right in her home. The popularity of Sadika's cooking had increased, as had the number of people vying for invitations to Ashfaaq Beebee's parties— a wonderful circumstance, if Ashfaaq Beebee had not caught several of the women observing Sadika the way a dog eyes a steak bone.

So, regretfully, she had given up the morning social gatherings at her house, and chosen instead to give the occasional big dinner party, when Sadika was kept too busy to socialize, because she knew very well that people would try their best to snap that gullible girl up if she became available. And at real wages too, rather than the small allowance that Ashfaaq Beebee was giving her.

Even if that didn't happen, meeting people would make Sadika aware of other options, and that was a potential disaster. A big disadvantage of living in America was that there were jobs available everywhere for anyone who wanted to work. Granted, they didn't pay much by American standards, but by Pakistani standards, the money was extraordinary, and it allowed people to stand on their own two feet. No wonder American parents were losing control of their offspring right and left. How could you hope to exert any significant degree of control, when access to freedom was there all the time?

The words coming out of Sadika's mouth with alarming frequency were proof positive of that.

"Register her in the most difficult course you can think of at your college," Ashfaaq Beebee finally told a sullen Ishrat. "Let her realize how inadequate she is for an American classroom. Better still, enroll her in the most difficult course you're taking, so you can keep tabs on how miserably she's doing. I want this going-to-school nonsense to end as soon as possible."

"If that's what you want," Ishrat said with a shrug. But as she thought about it, her expression brightened considerably. This next semester could be very enjoyable; it would be a lot of fun to watch Sadika fall flat on her face; it was time that moron realized exactly how much distance there was between her and her civilized cousins.

Satisfied, Ashfaaq Beebee turned away, muttering to herself. Whoever heard of an illiterate, primitive person going to school in America? Next she'll say she wants to be a movie star. What does she think I am, a magician, a miracle-worker? No doubt about it, that girl's head is filled with cow-dung instead of brains. Well, she'll come to her senses soon enough. Only I wish there was some way for her to do it without my spending money on her. Or taking the risk of making my Ishrat look bad in college by associating with someone like her.

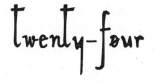

twenty-four

ON THE FIRST day of Fall semester, 1991, when Ashfaaq Beebee saw Sadika and Ishrat setting off to start school, her heart, already heavy at the prospect of spending the morning doing housework, sank like lead. She had to admit that Sadika looked good in Ishrat's altered clothes. Ishrat hadn't looked that good in them when they were brand new. To make matters worse, Sadika didn't carry herself like a Neanderthal female encountering civilization for the first time. Far from it. Much to Ashfaaq Beebee's discomfiture, it was Ishrat who suffered by comparison, not the other way round.

That Sadika had been so obviously lost and disoriented on registration day two weeks ago, had done Ashfaaq Beebee's heart a world of good, apart from reassuring Ishrat about the amusement awaiting her in the approaching semester. The American system of education was a total mystery to Sadika, who had needed Ishrat's help in filling out the simplest forms. At least three times she had asked Ishrat what courses she should take. Even after she had signed up for economics and calculus, she was still confused, asking, "What are prerequisites?" At the Government College in Islamabad, there was a limited set curriculum. With no choice of courses, there was no need for prerequisites.

Later, at the dinner table, Ishrat described Sadika's less than perfect registration experience with relish, and everyone except Sadika and Zafary burst out laughing. Zafary knew her sister's academic abilities too well to believe that what happened on registration day was any indication of the future.

"How can she expect to pass when she has no idea what courses she wants to take, or if she has the prerequisites for them?" Haroon said at last, wiping the tears from his eyes.

"Maybe," Ishrat said, "she thinks cooking and sewing are what you need to do well in American colleges. How she's going to cope with tough courses like economics and calculus, I don't know."

"Economics and calculus?" Haroon broke into laughter again. "While you were at it, you should have enrolled her in . . ." he leafed through the catalog on the table. "Let's see . . . Social Forces and the Law, or Small Business Consulting and Entrepreneurship. Here's the perfect one: Fundamentals of Biomedical Engineering and Science. I'm sure her near-perfect round *pooris*, and her equilateral triangular *samosas* are a good background for any engineering course—or how about architecture?"

Ishrat agreed, joining the general hilarity. "She could learn to design buildings that look like her *pikoras.*"

"Don't make fun of Sadika," Aarif Hassan interjected. "Who knows? If she works hard, she might pass both courses. But I'm surprised Ishrat didn't help her pick easier courses for her first semester."

Ever since Sadika had won her right to enroll in the local college, Aarif Hassan had developed a new sympathy for her. He was a conscientious teacher himself, respecting education as a worthwhile goal, especially commendable in tough circumstances like Sadika's. Going against Ashfaaq Beebee's wishes was no mean feat.

"Don't tell me you're going to blame your daughter if Sadika fails!" Ashfaaq Beebee was visibly upset. She didn't want to hear words of encouragement for Sadika. The faster she dropped out of college, the better for Ashfaaq Beebee. "How is my Ishrat to blame if Sadika is too stupid to realize she doesn't belong in an American college? When I wrote to Khanum about her taking courses here, I meant cooking and sewing, not economics and calculus. I felt sorry for her, and I thought maybe some man would marry her if she got some American schooling."

"Maybe someone will still marry her for taking courses in America. She doesn't have to tell them she failed," Ishrat said.

Throughout this discussion, Sadika was quiet, and much to everyone's surprise, apparently unperturbed. That she didn't seem upset that she had obviously bitten off more than she could chew and was already a laughingstock, could only be more evidence of her stupidity.

Actually, Sadika might have panicked if Ishrat had not left her alone for a little while that day to run an errand. Sadika had gone into the nearby college bookstore and found the textbooks assigned for her courses. Glancing through them quickly, she could hardly believe what she saw. For someone who had already had almost four years of college, majoring in economics, statistics, and math, this was basic stuff. The economics was child's play, while the calculus was only a little more difficult. She thought she could easily have handled more advanced work. But Ishrat had kept telling her how difficult everything was, on the assumption that she couldn't have learned anything in Pakistan.

But maybe it was just as well. She probably needed to get used to the American community college without undue stress. She did in fact enjoy the classroom environment with its challenges and stimulation, and she liked her teachers. Eric Johnson, the economics teacher, said that he was always available to help. Dr. Davis, the calculus teacher, announced that she would hold weekly help sessions in the library. As far as Sadika was concerned, one could ask for nothing more on the campus.

As the weeks passed, Ashfaaq Beebee's foreboding blossomed into full-fledged dread. Sadika didn't appear the least bit frazzled. If anything, she seemed more focused than her two cousins had ever been. That girl read her calculus textbook with rapt interest as if it were a steamy novel. She swiftly finished her housework and spent the evening studying. It was as though some fairy had waved a magic wand and turned her into an academic Cinderella. Either that, or Pakistan's Urdu-medium public school system was the world's best-kept secret. What Sadika had once found irresistible—altering clothes, going to the movies or the mall—seemed to have taken a back seat to—of all things—calculus problems and economic theories.

Ashfaaq Beebee's fears were more than justified, for Sadika was having the time of her life at the community college. Her hard work and enthusiasm were appreciated, and her conscientious, respectful attitude, combined with her obvious insecurity and vulnerability, had won her the affection of her teachers. By the time the first major exams for the semester were over, Sadika had established herself as the top student in both her classes. Much to the horror of her aunt and cousin, instead of feeling like a duck out of water as they had hoped, she seemed at home even in what they had thought would be the hardest classes. While Ishrat was struggling to maintain a B- average, A's were becoming commonplace for Sadika.

Perhaps Ishrat would not have been so resentful if she hadn't observed Sadika's success firsthand. And if she had not told Diane, her best friend, who was also taking calculus, that she expected to have to hold her backward cousin's hand throughout the semester. On the first day of class, Ishrat had told Diane, "She probably doesn't even know basic math. I hear that all good teachers end up leaving Pakistan because they're not respected. That's what happened to my father. Girls over there aren't serious about getting an education anyway, because they can't have careers. I hope Sadika doesn't expect me to spend a lot of time helping her—I've got my own work to do."

When the results of the mid-term exams came in, Sadika had scored highest in her class, while Ishrat had barely passed. "Doesn't look as though Sadika needs you to hold her hand," Diane commented to Ishrat, who seethed with rage and frustration. The last straw came when right in front of Diane, Dr. Davis told Ishrat, "You should take advantage of the wonderful resource you have right at home. With Sadika there, you don't have to worry about hiring a tutor. Ask her if she has time to give you some help." Ishrat could feel her face burning.

At home she let herself go. All her pent-up anger and resentment burst forth in the form of accusations as outrageous and colorful as they were groundless. She couldn't think of vile enough things to say about Sadika. Especially scandalous was the story she concocted that Sadika was having an affair with Mr. Johnson. She let her imagination run riot.

"The way your niece sucks up to teachers is disgusting," she told Ashfaaq Beebee in a voice dripping with spite. "No wonder she's doing so well in school. I'd be getting straight A's too if I was having an affair with the economics teacher. I heard Roger Benson say he overheard Sadika tell Mr. Johnson, 'I love the way my naked breasts feel when I rub them against your bald head.' It must have taken a lot of practice for Sadika to get so familiar with a teacher so fast. No wonder Haroon was turned off by her in Pakistan—that must be the kind of thing she tried on him. If I were a man I wouldn't marry her either. God knows how many men, how many different nationalities, can call her their hand-me-down."

Unfortunately for Ishrat, Ashfaaq Beebee knew her better than she realized. Ishrat had grown up in America, and they didn't share the same language or culture, but mother and daughter were very much alike. Ashfaaq Beebee knew that her plans had gone awry as soon as the words came out of her daughter's mouth. If Ishrat felt the need to make up these wild lies, obviously Sadika was doing much better than expected. And if Ashfaaq Beebee did not want things to get farther out of hand, she had better devise a brand new strategy—fast.

"You want me to talk to the head of school or whomever one complains to about such things?" Ashfaaq Beebee asked her daughter casually, but with a sinking heart, trying to gauge the extent to which her plans had backfired.

"No, no, of course not." Ishrat's hasty response confirmed Ashfaaq Beebee's worst fears.

"Let the stupid bitch fall flat on her face all by herself. If you go to the trouble of complaining to people it will only make

Sadika feel more important. And that's the last thing you want someone like her to feel."

Although Ashfaaq Beebee had correctly recognized that her daughter's feelings stemmed from hurt vanity and pride, she had not gauged their intensity, nor the depth of Ishrat's insecurity—something that had plagued Ashfaaq Beebee herself all her life. It was ironic that the same religious fundamentalism that gave Ashfaaq Beebee a sense of identity and provided her with an anchor in choppy waters, had taken these things from her daughter. This was a result of the division in the local Muslim community, which comprised two distinct groups: the fundamentalist group and one opposed to it. In the loosely knit community, the two were dubbed the Fundee Party and the Fun Party.

Most older people, including Ashfaaq Beebee, belonged to the former while the younger set had joined the latter. In Ishrat's and Haroon's case, their hearts belonged to the Fun Party, but they had been dragooned into the Fundee Party by their mother. And in classic sour grapes fashion, both, along with other young people in a similar situation, had grown up denigrating what had been withheld from them. People in the Fun Party, they said, were simply non-believers who would surely roast in hell with other sinners, especially since they enjoyed music and dance parties.

In point of fact, the Fun Party were moderates, trying to find a happy medium between the culture they had come from and the one they found themselves in. They feared that their children would have a hard time fitting into the American mainstream if they were too different from others. The music parties did not involve orgies, as the Fundees suggested. No alcohol was served—that was forbidden by Islam—and the songs and dances were traditional.

It was testimony to the success of the Fun Party that younger Fundees always tried to crash their celebrations, religious and otherwise, much to the dismay of their elders, especially Ashfaaq

Beebee. Not only had Ishrat and Haroon always been among the party crashers, they were invariably the ones caught doing it. And despite lectures, threats and dire warnings from Ashfaaq Beebee and Aarif Hassan, including gruesome details of life after death, they had continued to crash Fun activities, not only at parties, but at their school.

Both Ishrat and Haroon, frustrated, had frequently asked their parents, "What are we doing here, if you think the American way of life is so sinful?" Aarif Hassan had always responded: "You should thank your lucky stars for the opportunity to get the kind of education children in Pakistan can only dream about." Ashfaaq Beebee had added, "When you're all grown up, you'll see how far superior to your relatives in Pakistan you are and you'll thank us."

The prospect of one day meeting her illiterate cousins from Pakistan and condescending to them, was one of the things that sustained Ishrat through the difficult years. Whenever she had been mercilessly teased by her peers because of her stodgy dress or other social ineptitude, she imagined herself handing out the same treatment to her backwoods relatives. So when Sadika, of all people, did better in school than she, it was much more than a slap in the face for Ishrat: it was a disaster.

And it was insulting! Sadika was regarded by the Hassan family as a maidservant; a female who would not be able to function at all on her own in civilized society, let alone excel in one of its institutions of higher learning. The day Sadika became a success in America, not only would there no longer be a valid reason for Ishrat and Haroon to have spent miserable childhoods trapped between the values of two different worlds, but the self-images of both would suffer a staggering blow. They could no longer consider themselves virtual martyrs who had endured sinful American life in exchange for an education.

Ashfaaq Beebee was aware of all this and it added fuel to the fire of resentment already burning within her. That day when Sadika came home from classes, Ashfaaq Beebee handed her a long list of tasks, apart from the daily housework, that had definitely to be completed within the next week. "And don't tell me you don't have time," she concluded, knowing that Sadika did not have time, because she was studying for final exams.

Surprised, Sadika glanced at the list of important chores, noting that every one of them could be postponed for at least a week, if not longer. The dining room chandelier had been dirty for so long that it would not be a catastrophe if it stayed that way for a few more days; and there really was no reason for the glass cabinets in the living room to be cleaned or the silver to be polished, since no party was planned for the foreseeable future. Similarly, the blinds in the family room could easily be left un-washed for weeks, if not months.

It was obvious that these "important" jobs had been trumped up. What was not obvious was why. Sadika knew that Ashfaaq Beebee was well aware that final exams were coming up. Wasn't that the reason she had forbidden Ishrat to go shopping, Ishrat's favorite pastime, over the next few days? Wasn't Sadika en-titled to some consideration? It looked as though Ashfaaq Bee-bee was attempting to sabotage her.

Sadika had tried hard not to resent the special treatment given to Ishrat before even a minor test. Maybe that would have been justified if her cousin had been a good student. But not only was Ishrat uninterested in her classes, it seemed that study-ing was something she did as a favor to her parents. Although she had been given no responsibilities so that she could devote her entire time to school, she acted like a victim every time she had to open a textbook to study for an exam.

Based on conversations Sadika had overheard between Ishrat and her friends, Ishrat would not even have been taking these courses if it wasn't for her almost total dependence on her par-ents. Chemistry, biology, calculus, and physics were, in her opin-ion, the most ridiculous subjects in the world. And scientists were crazy people who made up theories about atoms that were there but couldn't be seen; stars that weren't there but could be seen; animals that must have been around because of what had been dug up; and monkeys that Adam and Eve must have been intimate with if they were everybody's ancestors.

And what was the big deal about ladders leaning against walls, people riding vehicles on inclines with friction, gravity and wind dragging them down? It seemed every textbook dealing with numbers was filled with problems that were a variation on the same theme. All physicists and mathematicians must be residents of the same rundown neighborhood.

The problem was that Ashfaaq Beebee and Aarif Hassan were obsessed with the idea of Ishrat becoming a doctor. No member of the household was allowed to disturb her concentration by as much as a sneeze, if her parents thought she was studying. Ashfaaq Beebee and Aarif Hassan had no way of knowing that she often read light novels inside the covers of her textbook. Ishrat hoped that when they realized there was no way she could get into medical school, they would also realize that it really wasn't her fault. She had tried, but as with Haroon, it just wasn't meant to be. In the meantime, no one could blame her for enjoying the little perks of her situation. She loved the way Ashfaaq Beebee made farina dessert just for her before every exam, blowing special prayers into it as she added heavy cream and nuts.

And whenever she felt her daughter needed extra brain power, Ashfaaq Beebee put her on a special diet. Almonds crushed in milk at the crack of dawn to stimulate the mind, yogurt with fruit in mid-morning to keep it crystal clear, and vegetable concoctions during the day to help it stay cool and serene while it assimilated knowledge. And, of course, plenty of roasted calf brains at dinnertime to replenish the supply of depleted brain cells. Just before bedtime, Ashfaaq Beebee, her head wrapped in her prayer scarf, would enter her daughter's room with a bowl of raw egg beaten in warm olive oil. Draping an old towel around Ishrat's shoulders, she would massage the brain-strengthening mixture into her head till she felt sure it had seeped in, all the while muttering prayers and blowing them at her head.

Sadika, an envious observer, felt sure that if Ishrat studied half as hard as she pretended, she would have become a genius by now. If only her aunt and uncle would realize that Sadika deserved some attention too. Perhaps her final grades would do the trick. Or perhaps not. Maybe it was time to revise her opinion of her aunt as a well-wisher, something she had resisted doing so far. Where Sadika came from, it was understood that one's exterior was not truly representative of what was inside, especially when it came to matters of affection. Certain people, particularly those closely related to you, wished you well whether they showed their emotions or not. That was why you loved and respected them, even if they acted cold and remote.

But Sadika had noticed how, gradually, her household duties had been increased ever since she had started doing well in college. Instead of one main dish, the evening meal now had to have two; the furniture needed to be dusted twice a week instead of once, because Ashfaaq Beebee had suddenly discovered she was allergic to dust; and unless the carpets were vacuumed and the floors mopped every other day, the house smelled strange. What's more, Ashfaaq Beebee had abruptly decided that the dishes and silverware weren't dishwasher safe after all.

As if the increase in work was not enough, Haroon was coming after Sadika with renewed vigor, finding new ways to harass her. Lately, he had taken to hiding her notebooks and textbooks, forcing her to ask him for them. It had started two weeks earlier, when, seeing Sadika searching frantically through her book bag, he innocently asked, "Are you by any chance looking for your economics notes? Because if you are, I think they somehow got mixed up with my papers. Come with me to the garage and I'll give them to you." Reluctantly, she followed.

At the garage, much to her disgust, he "accidentally" bumped against her, and kept touching her. The last straw was when, getting out of the car, he hit his head against her breast. She was furious and frightened.

"What do you think you're doing?" she asked through clenched teeth.

"Which part didn't you understand?" he said, unfazed. When she warily backed away from him, he casually admonished her, "Be nice to me. Or I might be forced to tell my mother about the passes you keep making at me."

"But you," she stammered, "you're the one—"

To which he replied slyly, "Who do you think she'll believe? You or me?"

She left without answering, but to herself she said, Without question, you! Her own parents had not given her the benefit of the doubt, so what could she expect from an increasingly hostile aunt?

By the time Sadika finished the housework and coping with Haroon, there was little time or energy left for studying, even on nights before exams. Her enthusiasm and dedication did not flag, so she kept up her grades, but the circles under her eyes were deepening, and she often dozed off in the bus.

Something had to give, that was for sure. Either she had to find a better environment, or she would have to consider leaving school—an alternative too depressing to contemplate. As in an Urdu proverb, she was at a stage in life where she could neither swallow what she had bitten off nor spit it out.

twenty-five

ONE MONDAY, WHEN Sadika was on her way to the college for a review session, bleary-eyed with lack of sleep, she could think about nothing but her situation. Her mind seemed to have lost its resilience. That is when the words "roommate wanted" posted on a bulletin board caught her eye. She stopped short and looked at the various notices. She had never realized how many people were looking for roommates. And within walking distance of the campus too.

What she wouldn't give to be one of the people looking for a room, she thought wistfully. If she had an income of her own, she would surely answer some of the promising ads. But there was no way Ashfaaq Beebee was going to let her move to one of these places. That would be paradise—better than paradise: freedom to come and go in a place of one's own sounded more appealing at the moment than lakes of milk and honey in heaven.

If only money was not a factor in all this. And if only she had not turned into a whipping boy, full-time maidservant, babysitter and cook all rolled into one. Ashfaaq Beebee would be out of her mind to go back voluntarily to the inconvenience and hard work of her pre-Sadika days.

Sadika was still lost in her melancholy reflections when another notice on the board caught her eye. This one had to do with employment. A full-time person was needed for the Xerox room. The salary was not much, but it entitled the person to subsidized housing near campus and waived partial tuition. Now that's something I could handle, she thought excitedly, jotting down the phone number.

The person currently in charge of Xeroxing was a girl named Charlene. She was in Sadika's economics class and the two of them often sat together to compare notes and chat. Once, flattered by Sadika's interest in her Xeroxing work, Charlene had suggested jokingly that maybe Sadika should apply for her job next semester when Charlene graduated. At the time, Sadika had not paid much attention to that, but she wondered now if her friend could actually help her get that job. It could be the answer to all her problems and the realization of all her dreams. She would be free from Haroon, Ishrat, Ashfaaq Beebee, Aarif Hassan, and yes, even Zafary and her two adorable kids. For the first time in her life she would be answerable to no one but herself—a thought almost too exciting to bear.

Charlene did in fact talk to her boss, and was able to assure Sadika that the job was hers if she wanted it. That night at dinner, Sadika mentioned the possibility that she might be moving out. As she expected, all hell broke loose. "It's hard for me to study here, Aunt," Sadika said, trying to ignore her racing heart, cold, clammy hands and perspiring forehead. "Besides, Zafary is well now, and she's able to take care of herself and the children. So the reason for my staying here doesn't exist any more. You told your friends many times that I might make something of myself by getting an education. I'd like to try."

It was as if the words coming out of Sadika's mouth cast a spell on all of them: Zafary, just entering the room after putting the children to bed, stood frozen, as though turned to stone; Aarif Hassan's fork, heavy with pieces of succulent chicken and vegetables, hung suspended in mid-air on its way to his open mouth; Haroon's jaws, working on a big piece of chicken, stopped moving; Ishrat nearly choked on a glass of water; Ashfaaq Beebee's fingers, about to dip a piece of *naan* in gravy, looked glued to the bread.

After a few moments, Ashfaaq Beebee was the first to break the silence: "So you're willing to abandon your family for the sake of a little convenience?" she demanded through clenched teeth. "Is this the thanks you give me for bringing you to

America, paying your fare, housing you, clothing you and feeding you? You should be ashamed even to think such ungrateful thoughts. Tell me, why didn't you jump into a river and drown yourself in shame as any decent girl would have done as soon as you had these disgraceful thoughts?"

The Sadika of only a year ago would have listened in silence to these criticisms, perhaps weeping. But many months of frustration had given her courage. Also, once she began, she found it impossible to stop. "I think I have repaid you for everything you've done for me by working for you almost for nothing. I realize that I'm family and so I shouldn't expect to get paid to help you, but I haven't been treated like family by any of you. If I were, the work would be more equally divided and I wouldn't be the only one doing everything. Some students I know get a lot more money for doing much less work."

Ashfaaq Beebee, shrewdly realizing that it would not be possible to keep Sadika forever, began to think about how long she could hang onto her. She was particularly concerned about a dinner party for some twenty people planned for next month. Sadika didn't even know about it, but invitations had already been mailed out. She would be lost without her niece's help.

"*Baetee*, daughter," she began in a new soft voice, trying to buy time so she could think more clearly and avoid this catastrophe, while everyone else looked on in fascination, not moving a muscle for fear it might call attention to them in what promised to be a bloody battle. "It seems to me that something must have happened today to upset you. I'll disregard what you just said because I'm sure it was not you talking at all, but your nerves."

Noting Sadika's grimly determined expression, Ashfaaq Beebee was at a loss for words for the first time since she had known her niece. But her mind was working at top speed and within a few seconds she decided that the best strategy would be to get what she could out of the situation and cut her losses. If Ashfaaq Beebee had been in politics or business, she would no doubt have had a brilliant career. "On the other hand, if your mind is made up, I won't try to stand in the way of what makes you happy. I'd like to ask you not to desert me suddenly, because I've taken on certain obligations, expecting your help. I feel that as your aunt who loves you, though I might not always show it, I deserve that much."

Sadika, steeled for her aunt's ear-splitting rage, was disarmed. She had to admit that she should have given more notice, but she hadn't foreseen that things would fall into place so fast. And even though she wanted to move out as soon as living arrangements were complete, she said she was willing to help out for a reasonable time. But she had to tell them that they must get used to the idea of life without her.

The fact was that getting used to life without Sadika was easier said than done. Everyone at the table felt sick at the prospect of going back to the way things had been before Sadika. The arguments and tension that had all but ceased would surely return with a vengeance, especially after such a long hiatus. It was hard to remember what everyone's assigned chores had been, let alone when and how they were to be done.

Haroon was wondering whether he had been the impetus for this drastic change. Maybe he had been too aggressive. Repressed, frigid types like Sadika needed time to appreciate these things, marriage to Zafary should have taught him that. If he had used more patience and finesse, Sadika would have fallen at his feet like a ripe mango, instead of bolting like a startled mare. Hopefully, he would still get the chance to finish what he had started. It would be a crying shame if someone like Sadika, who at one time was his for the taking, suddenly sprinted out of his reach forever, leaving him to wonder for the rest of his life how it would have been with her.

Ishrat felt sick with envy and dread: envy for the freedom that Sadika would have, and dread for the loss of her own freedom and comfort. She had always wanted to live on her own, but her mother had never permitted it, insisting that exposure

to the sinful ways of the outside world would corrupt her irre-
vocably. Since Sadika arrived, Ishrat had come to enjoy being at
home. It was like living at a good hotel, only better: room service, no responsibilities, excellent meals and no rent. Who could
ask for more? Now this life of luxury would come to a screeching halt.

Zafary was frightened, too. But it was not housework she
was dreading, but her husband's unpleasant temper. Without
Sadika as a distraction, her reprieve would be over in more ways
than one: Haroon's playful attitude in the evenings would surely
end, as would his preoccupation with the kitchen. He would
return to his former surly moods and regular-as-clockwork
sexual demands. Worse, his aborted attempt at whatever he had
been trying to brew with Sadika would add to his frustrations
and rotten disposition, and Zafary would have to bear the brunt
of it.

The only people who were genuinely disappointed because
they would miss Sadika herself, were Aarif Hassan and his two
grandchildren. Aarif Hassan had come to regard Sadika as a
kindred spirit, because, like him, she worked tirelessly for his
ungrateful family. And the children loved her because she cared
for their needs, gave them affection, played with them and read
them stories. Also, with Sadika there, the others seemed more
relaxed and approachable.

That no one had expected such independence, courage and
resourcefulness from Sadika was evident in the expressions of
the people at the table. Who would have thought that a mousy
timid female would dare to take on a steamroller like Ashfaaq
Beebee, and what's more, beat her hands down! It gave them
food for thought. Perhaps, with the proper approach, Ishrat would
be allowed to move into a dormitory and Haroon into an apartment of his own. Aarif Hassan had always convinced himself
that in the interest of harmony, he could not go against Ashfaaq
Beebee's wishes. But come to think of it, what could Ashfaaq
Beebee do if he put his foot down—cut off his allowance?

The biggest change in the Hassan household, caused unin-
tentionally by Sadika's decision to move out, was a loosening
of Ashfaaq Beebee's iron hold on her family. And for as long as
she lived, Ashfaaq Beebee would never forgive Sadika for that.

twenty-six

SADIKA LOVED THE small apartment in the run-down building close to the campus. Not because it was particularly attractive, but because it enabled her to experience life to the fullest for the first time. Now she was responsible for no one but herself, accountable to no one but herself. And if she did something for someone, it was not taken for granted, but appreciated as a favor. Unencumbered by the demands of a family, she could meditate, reflect, soak up and saturate her mind with impressions of this wonderful new country. How did the people here live, eat, entertain? What was important to them? What were their values? Her mind wanted to absorb everything like a thirsty sponge.

Sadika liked her roommate Susan. Each had her own room, but they shared the bathroom, the minuscule kitchen and living room. Rent, utilities and housework were split, including grocery shopping and cooking of simple meals. Sadika augmented her small salary by waitressing a couple of evenings a week.

In the first few days after she moved in, Sadika had tried to model herself on her roommate's behavior, including her eating habits. But after eating pizza, hamburgers and hot dogs four days in a row, she found herself yearning for lentil soup, spicy cooked vegetables and thin round bread. Inevitably, she began to buy groceries from a local Asian store and cook for herself, offering to share with Susan.

Within a very short time, she had developed a reputation as a gourmet cook and her roommate was considered lucky beyond words. Sadika did not mind cooking for Susan at all. In addition to praising the food to the skies, Susan insisted on paying for most of the groceries, and ate fewer hot dogs—a food which Sadika found especially revolting. She understood that people had different tastes and preferences, but, she asked herself, do they really have to eat that part of the dog? A starving beggar on the streets of Islamabad would not voluntarily consume any part of a dog—and certainly not that body part. What kind of dogs would generate such huge genitalia anyway?

Perhaps, she thought, the key word was "hot." The dogs must be the counterparts of bitches in heat, and were castrated in their prime, at the height of sexual arousal. Perhaps it was a difficult art, requiring the ruthlessness of a headhunter and the precision of a gemologist. And judging by the numbers of hot dogs that Americans consumed, somewhere in North America there must be an enormous population of huge castrated dogs.

Or maybe not. America was, after all, a wasteful country. Maybe the poor dogs were thrown away after their genitals were cut off, as minks probably were after being skinned, and rabbits after being depawed. Otherwise wouldn't she have heard of dog stew, rabbit soup or mink burgers?

This wastefulness was an American flaw that Sadika found very hard to accept; especially the waste of food. Accustomed to Khanum's, and then Ashfaaq Beebee's, thrifty habits, she was shocked when she saw perfectly good food thrown away. How could people bear to discard cakes, cookies, pizza, just because they were no longer hungry? They knew they'd get hungry again, didn't they? Susan's explanation that she did not want to gain weight was not convincing. Wasn't the next slice of cake or pizza just as fattening as the one that was thrown out? Why not simply save leftovers instead of buying new food and trashing the rest of that as well?

Often Sadika found herself strongly tempted to take food out of the garbage and save it. She had learned from Khanum how to turn rotten fruit into delectable desserts and make wonderful soups and gravies from the most unlikely animal parts,

like washed-out intestines, stomach linings and feet. Khanum
would have had a field day with the contents of American garbage cans.

Sadika was relieved to find that some of her fears about
being on her own were proving groundless. She had been nervous about communicating effectively, since her English was
stilted and possibly not fluent enough. Doing well in a classroom situation didn't mean that she would be able to function
well in everyday life. In a last-ditch effort to convince Sadika to
stay, Zafary had gone to her older sister on the day she was
leaving and put into words Sadika's own fears: "What makes
you think people will even understand what you are saying? Or
that you won't be lost without someone to talk to in Urdu?"

Much to her relief, Sadika had discovered that language
was, for the most part, no problem, since she could understand
and speak English well enough. Her accent was a little strong,
but that was no big deal. It was only when she thought in Urdu
and translated these thoughts into English, that she said things
that sounded ridiculous. Once she had told Susan how much
she still missed Pakistan: "When I think of my old neighborhood and my friends at school, I feel as though a dagger has
plunged into my liver."

"You feel that a dagger has plunged into your liver?"

"Yes," Sadika said. Then noticing Susan's confusion, she
tried again: "The memories of my native country produce holes
in my kidney." This time it was Sadika who looked confused as
her companion burst out laughing.

"I'm sorry," Susan said, wiping her eyes. "I think you mean
that the thought of what you left behind breaks your heart."

"That too," Sadika readily agreed, but she did not understand what was so funny. Why should her memories affect only
her heart, when her other organs were just as vulnerable?

twenty-seven

WHEN SHE LIVED in her aunt's house, Sadika had had an inkling that America was different from the way most people in Pakistan perceived it, or even as she herself had expected it to be, but she hadn't realized how different it was. She had thought that people committed X-rated and semi-X-rated acts right on the streets, but in actuality that didn't happen. Sometimes people kissed or hugged in plain view, but compared to what had been in her mind, that was nothing. Besides, everyone was so busy here that they probably didn't have time to do half the stuff she had imagined them doing, even if they had the inclination.

One thing was certain, though: even if it was not what she had expected, America was very different from what she was used to. In fact, she was still reeling from the impact of going from a society where there was strict segregation of the sexes, to one where there was no segregation at all. Whenever she saw a male student in her class, which was all the time, she felt as though some animal that was supposed to be in a cage was being allowed to run free. It was scary and exciting—like being on a huge safari where humans had free access to dangerous beasts, and vice versa.

What was even odder was that these beasts did not realize they were beasts—that they were a different species from the humans they were allowed to mingle with. All males seemed to think it was absolutely normal to associate freely with females. Like the cat Heathcliff and the dogs Snoopy and Marmaduke in the comic strips she sometimes read, young men treated young women as equals. Not like in Pakistan, where everyone knew their preordained place in the order of things; where some seats or sometimes entire rows of seats were set aside for women whenever members of both sexes needed to congregate at the same place.

When Sadika had first enrolled in the community college, she was at a loss to understand what was going on. Institutions of higher learning were places where she had hoped immoral acts, like free commingling of the sexes, did not take place, at least not in broad daylight. What made matters worse was that it didn't seem important to the males sitting next to her in class that she was right beside them, within easy touching distance.

She wondered, What kind of men are these that they remain unaffected at the proximity of a woman? Maybe they had been castrated at birth, like the eunuchs in old Chinese palaces, so women would be safe around them. Otherwise it would have surely dawned on these nonchalant members of the opposite sex that young attractive females were within close physical range—and their hormones would have gone berserk.

She finally decided that their hormones must be hibernating. Hadn't she read somewhere that in cold climates hormones wake up much later in life? But that didn't explain the attitude of the female students, an even greater mystery. How could young women laugh and talk so casually with these men? Didn't they realize that these males had the means of divesting them forever of their honor, which was dearer than life? In which case, what would become of them? Who would want to marry them? No man liked to marry a woman who was equivalent to soiled linen, that much Sadika knew, because it had been dinned into her head since childhood—first by her mother, than by Zahra. And from what she could tell, some of the female linen at the college was downright filthy.

Could it be that people in America didn't care about that? That it might even be desirable for linen to be somewhat soiled? What else could explain the deliberate meetings between males and females, many times set up—supposedly to study—by the females themselves? Who in their right mind would believe that young men and women of marriageable age could be getting together to—of all things—prepare for an upcoming test? To study, one needed to concentrate and focus: exactly the two things that the company of even moderately attractive members of the opposite sex would prevent.

It was as if everything that Zahra had told her in Pakistan was null and void. As if the Law of Purity of Womankind was not even operable. Sadika had heard people at college talk about their sexual encounters with the same casual detachment with which the merits of planting corn as opposed to potatoes, were discussed in her native country. As far as she could see, no one was concerned about being able to prove her state of absolute honor to anybody. She would never forget the evening Susan had invited her boyfriend Bob to their apartment. "Why don't you go study at the library?" Susan had said to Sadika with a wink. "It should be much quieter there, and you'll be able to get a lot more done."

Sadika had readily agreed, but once in the library, her conscience had not let her read her textbook in peace. You should save your friend from folly, it had admonished. Go back early, even if Susan gets upset, since right now, in the throes of red-hot emotion, she's not capable of rational thought. You need to make sure she isn't led into a temptation that could ruin her chances of a good life forever.

Giving them just enough time to finish the simple meal that Susan had bought earlier for the occasion, Sadika had slipped back into the apartment, using her key. Much to her surprise, the unopened boxes of Chinese food were still on the table, while the strangest sounds emanated from behind her friend's closed bedroom door.

Trembling, she armed herself with a paring knife, and stood outside the bedroom door. Maybe Bob was forcibly wresting her honor from Susan—or maybe not. It was hard to decide. There was no sound from the bedroom except what seemed to be muffled laughter, so Susan could hardly have been suffering those painful moments that turned a girl into a woman. If Susan was paying the price of womanhood, she certainly seemed to be doing it willingly. Maybe even enjoying it.

She stood listening at the door, ready to burst in and somehow save her friend. But her doubts about what was going on prevented her. Finally she put the knife back in the drawer and returned to the library, and when she came home much later, she was thankful that she had restrained herself. She saw a glowing Susan not looking at all like a forcibly defiled woman. "We decided to skip dinner and get right to dessert," Susan confided with a grin.

Sadika had had no idea what Susan was talking about, and was too embarrassed to ask. But that night her mind flooded with questions and thoughts that kept her awake for a long time. She liked Susan, but she found her behavior upsetting. How could she go into the bedroom with that boy, alone with him with the door closed? Possibly nothing was going on in there—maybe they were just having an innocent conversation. Wasn't Susan worried about losing her honor?

There might be something after all to Zahra's theory about a woman's honor being housed in her body, and every woman being honorable to a different degree. Maybe there was a gadget somewhere for measuring a woman's honor. What if on a scale from one to ten, Sadika ranked a three on womanhood, and a one point eight on honor, or something like that? What if that was why Haroon had not married her: had he had a way of quantifying her honor and womanhood and found her wanting? No, she dismissed that last thought immediately, because knowing Haroon, he would have found ways to torment her with that knowledge; he would never have kept quiet about it.

As she tried in vain to get to sleep, she thought about Kausar Sultana, a pretty girl who had been in the final year of college in Pakistan when Sadika had been in the first year—the girl who had lost both her legs to the Almighty God of Honor. One day while she was walking home from school, Kausar had been forcibly abducted by some men who knocked her unconscious and sold her to a shop in the red light district of Lahore. When Kausar recovered consciousness and realized that she was in the beauty market, as such places were called in Pakistan, she frantically looked for a means of escape. She had somehow climbed to a small window high in the wall, and with utter disregard for her safety, jumped from the second floor and landed on the concrete road with both legs broken. The beauty market people, not wanting to have anything more to do with her, dumped her outside the emergency room of the closest hospital.

Kausar barely survived and remained an invalid. But after her story was known, she became a heroine-cum-saint in the eyes of the community. Major newspapers published her story and many magazines carried interviews with her. For a long time, she was held up as the ideal that all women of honor must emulate. Mothers, including Khanum, constantly told their daughters, "A virtuous girl should be like Kausar: ready and willing to die in honor rather than live in dishonor."

Secretly Sadika had thought even then that, faced with a similar choice, she would have preferred the use of her legs to the preservation of her honor, whatever that meant. Many times it seemed to her to be just another name for a woman's hymen. She had heard of the life of dependency and despair that Kausar was leading, and was convinced that given the same choice again, even Kausar's decision would have been different. But she had kept her opinion to herself. Not to wholeheartedly agree with Khanum would have left the impression that her own honor was not dearer than life to Sadika, an implication that would have evoked one of Khanum's fits of hysterical rage.

But that night Sadika was reminded forcefully of the futility of Kausar's sacrifice. The concepts of honor were apparently so arbitrary that an act thought honorable in one culture might well be considered the height of idiocy in another, and vice versa. Maybe it was foolish to sacrifice even the tip of one's little finger over something as meaningless and artificial as honor, let alone two fully functioning legs.

twenty-eight

NOT SURPRISINGLY, AFTER she moved into the apartment, Sadika began to think quite a lot about sex. It was, after all, a subject that was taboo where she was raised and now she suddenly found herself in a culture where people not only thought about it, but tried their best to stimulate others to think about it. The ease and freedom with which sex magazines and movies could be acquired was mind-boggling: copies of *Penthouse, Playboy* and *Hustler* were sold right in the college bookstore and X-rated movies could be rented in broad daylight at $1.99, five minutes from the campus.

If Yasmeen, the only other Pakistani student in the community college besides Sadika and Ishrat, was to be believed, porno movies and magazines were becoming increasingly available in Pakistan as well. Maybe they had not yet pervaded the Islamabad neighborhood of Gulmushk Mohalla, but in many areas of the city, porno material was freely available to people of all ages if one knew where to look for it. Yasmeen's own mother had caught her ten-year-old brother with a *Penthouse* and the boy had confessed that his best friend's older brother was running a secret rental business right next door. All that was required for the rental of a movie or magazine from the hugely popular business was a ten rupee bill. More than half the neighborhood boys were among his clientele and they regularly spent their lunch money on their viewing pleasure. In many traditional homes, boys apparently could choose from worldwide pornographic material, while girls couldn't witness even a simple kiss on TV because of the strict policies of the censor board.

Sadika had been such a girl. Watching television in Zarreen's house, it had been quite common to see a man and a woman move toward each other, only to walk abruptly away as soon as they got within touching distance. But even though the sight of couples embracing or kissing was simply snipped out of the film by the censor board, imaginations often worked doubly hard to substitute the steamiest scenes for the ones that had been removed. Sadika hadn't realized the disparity till she watched reruns of "Bewitched" and "I Love Lucy" in America: the censored parts that she thought had been nothing short of full-fledged orgies, were in fact extremely tame, even dull.

Even the sinful contents of sex magazines, exposure to which was supposed to guarantee a place in the most fiery regions of hell, were anti-climactic. Not that they were not every bit as shocking as Sadika had expected, but the sky did not fall and volcanoes did not erupt when she read them, courtesy of Susan. What's more, she did not develop any serious rashes or pimples, as she had been assured she would if she read filth. Maybe it was because people didn't really do half the things they said they did. Sadika couldn't imagine how they could discreetly carry them off. For example, everyone seemed to brag about the dimensions of her lover's private parts. It was a mystery how those people knew this to the nearest quarter of an inch. Maybe they took measurements, stopping by mutual consent in the middle of an encounter to take readings.

Mrs. Ghani, Sadika's high school physics teacher, always insisted on at least three readings. Did that hold true here too? How many types of measurements did one need to take anyway? Was knowing the length enough, or did girth count as well? Did one measure girth by means of the gadget called vernier callipers, which according to Mrs. Ghani was the most reliable way to figure out the girth of a cylindrical object?

One thing was certain: whether true or false, fabricated or simply exaggerated, in America sexual language was explicit and direct. Sadika wondered whether it was easier to convey sexual content in English than in Urdu. *Love or Delusion*, the only Urdu "sexually explicit" novel she had ever read, had been a hot item in her eighth grade class. Tasneem had given it to her in a brown paper bag, whispering, "Durdaana wants to read this so bad, but I said that I promised it to you first, so she'd have to wait."

Sadika could hardly wait for that day to end. When at last everyone was asleep, she took the flashlight from the kitchen shelf, put the novel under one end of her pillow in case she would have to hide it in a hurry, and opening it with hands shaking with excitement, began reading in the dim light. After forty-five minutes, her excitement had turned to disgust. She thought that this might be Tasneem's idea of a joke—how was Sadika supposed to get a big thrill out of the love scenes if she couldn't find them? She couldn't even decide if this was a romance or a jungle story, the kind Asghar sometimes brought home about the hunter Jim Corbett, who loved to hunt maneating lions and tigers in the jungles of Pakistan and India. It had certainly started out as a romance, but then without warning and at the parts that should have been the most thrilling, just when the hero and the heroine seemed to be getting somewhere, "the arrogant lion descended into the lush valley," leaving Sadika totally mystified. Where had the lion, arrogant or otherwise, and the valley, lush or barren, come from, in a story that was supposedly set in the dusty flat city of Lahore? And where were the hero and the heroine during all this?

It was very confusing. Maybe one was supposed to know somehow that the main characters had escaped into a jungle where they had been chased by a lion into a lush valley. That would certainly explain the abundance of "love-dew" on the breathless hero and heroine. In another chapter, a king cobra, appearing out of the blue, "buried its fangs into its unwilling victim." And then "the mongoose engulfed the sneaky, dangerous snake, draining all vitality out of it."

Both Tasneem and Durdaana tried hard to convince Sadika that she had really read a dirty book. If they considered that book dirty, Sadika, sitting in her room in the apartment she shared with Susan, could not imagine the response of those two to the mountains of smut they could easily find in America.

twenty-nine

SADIKA HAD HAD no contact with any member of Ashfaaq Beebee's family for a month. Ever since she had stopped going to her aunt's house to help out, all communication had ceased: Ishrat pretended not to see her in the college corridors, and even Zafary had little to say to her when Sadika sometimes phoned in the morning to ask how she and the children were doing. Ashfaaq Beebee had phoned a few times to ask Sadika to give her some help on a regular basis, but the atmosphere in her aunt's house had become so strained that Sadika couldn't bear to go there, despite threats and then pleas from her aunt to do her duty and not behave like an ungrateful wretch.

Now life had become so pleasant and comfortable that Sadika often felt like pinching herself to make sure she wasn't dreaming. Her job at the Xerox room was going smoothly and she enjoyed waitressing, which gave her enough money to add a course. As her tensions lessened, she blossomed in the general atmosphere of admiration, friendship and encouragement. She looked almost beautiful, and her self-confidence, sorely tested during her stay at her aunt's, began to revive. She was still plagued by doubts about her value as a woman, but now she was beginning to think that a man could be a possible soul mate, rather than an appendage necessary for survival in the world.

Maybe it's is not too late for me, she told herself. Maybe one day, as Zahra predicted, my eyes will meet someone's across a crowded room and that person, not able to fight the strong force of mutual attraction of two soul mates in the same space, will move inevitably toward me. Who knows? Maybe I'm not a human being at all; maybe I'm a female cobra in the guise of a human female who has forgotten the spell to change herself back.

According to legend, a cobra acquired magical powers when it reached the age of one hundred. For example, it could turn itself into a human being and back again, and it could convert everyday objects into gold. Since the cobra mated for all eternity, if it lost its mate it spent forever searching for it. Perhaps somewhere in the world an ancient cobra was moving heaven and earth to reach her. Maybe that cobra was currently a prince or a millionaire and would soon whisk her away on an ornately clad elephant or private jet, to his magnificent kingdom or villa.

As Zahra had foreseen, so it was—well, almost. Sadika's eyes did meet Michael's across a crowded room—or rather a crowded classroom. As for being an ancient cobra in the guise of a human—who knew? One thing was for sure: if he was a snake he was certainly a good-looking one: nearly six feet tall and blond, with piercing blue eyes. Dr. Moore, who taught Marketing, had asked students to form groups of three or four for presentations in the final weeks of the course. Sadika and Michael had been in the same group and had become good friends.

Not only did they share a work ethic: they seemed to find the same things interesting despite the differences in their backgrounds, and they often had trouble sticking to their assignment without going off on a tangent and discussing everything under the sun. In many ways, both were rejects of the cultures in which they had been raised. It was ironic that the characteristics of each that were not considered particularly desirable in one culture would have drawn compliments in the other. For instance, Michael's pale skin, blue eyes, slight paunch and receding blond hairline seemed bland as boiled squash in America. But in Pakistan his complexion would have been much admired, not only because it was unusual there but because centuries of British rule had given it superior status. In Pakistan, his thinning hair would have been looked upon as a sign of experience and wisdom, just as his slight paunch proclaimed him to be a mature man of means.

On the other hand, Sadika's skin, commonplace in Pakistan, had the bronze glow that Americans sought to duplicate on beaches and in tanning parlors; her long black hair was admired in America; as was her boyish figure that had often drawn ridicule in Pakistan—or at least in Gulmushk Mohalla, where they thought she looked half-starved and overworked. Even her classmates at the Women's College in Islamabad had made fun of her. "God's workers were tired when they made her," Durdaana said, laughing,. "That's why they didn't bother to give her different measurements for different parts of her body." Her friends joked about her flat chest, long waist and narrow hips.

When Introduction to Marketing was over, Sadika did not see Michael for a few weeks. Without the excuse of preparing for a presentation, each felt too shy to seek the other out. Then one day she came across him at an International Students Association meeting where he was one of the few Americans. At these meetings, held every month to help foreign students acclimate themselves, notes were compared on the various restaurants in the area, on campus accommodations, on the values and lifestyles of different countries and cultures, and anything else of interest. As usual, many students complained about living in America—Sadika could not understand these complaints, but she listened carefully, as did Michael, fascinated by the variations in physical appearance, mannerisms and accents. Sadika wished she had the self-confidence to say in public that for her, America meant escape from an unbearably stifling atmosphere.

But she kept quiet, trying to look noncommittal to mask the embarrassing thrill she felt at finding herself in such an exquisitely beautiful group. Actually, in her opinion "beautiful" was not a strong enough word to describe the appearance of some of these men and women. With hair in varying shades of gold, eyes sparkling like fine sapphires and emeralds, and satiny skins the color of milk, sometimes with a touch of honey, they seemed the personification of everything precious on earth. No wonder some people in Pakistan thought that Western women were the female angels that God Almighty had promised in the Qur'an as a reward to the righteous and the pious. Where she came from, even one of these physical characteristics would have earned admiration. Perhaps countries like America were thriving because their people had so many angelic creatures to inspire them.

Sadika found it hard to imagine that someone like Michael, who was himself blond, blue-eyed and fair-skinned, would consider someone ordinary like herself to be even marginally attractive.

thirty

WHEN THEY WERE both in a Business Law class, Michael and Sadika began to take a serious interest in each other. It was not Sadika's academic ability or intelligence that impressed Michael, but her obvious lack of worldliness. And it was not Michael's looks, background, or intellect that drew Sadika, but his behavior in an embarrassing situation that resulted from the Business Law instructor's repeatedly telling off-color jokes in class. Most students seemed to find them amusing. Sadika, caught unaware each time, didn't realize Mr. Roth was joking till it was too late and she had, much to her consternation, made a fool of herself.

The first time Mr. Roth told one of these stories, Sadika was sure it was a trick legal question. Asked whether the steaming mug in his hand contained hot chocolate or coffee, he had answered, "Neither. It has tea. But steaming cups don't always have tea or coffee—or hot chocolate for that matter." Taking a generous sip, he went on, "Why was Dracula looking for a used tampon in a trash can?"

Eager to please and not knowing what a tampon was, Sadika raised her hand. "He was trying to investigate whether it was defective so he could sue the company." The tea spurted out of Roth's mouth like a geyser as he and most of the class burst into laughter. "I don't know whether I should even tell you the answer. This young lady's reply is more amusing than anything I could come up with. But I'll tell you anyway. Because he wanted to make tea for himself."

Sadika, mortified, turned beet red, much to everyone's amusement. If only she was not sitting front row center right where everyone could see her.

The next time Mr. Roth made a joke, she was taken in again.

"What do you think this is?" he asked, making a flying motion with his hand, his middle finger extended. When nobody ventured a reply, he said with a grin, "Superman flying over a nudist colony." Sadika, confused, raised her hand and asked, "Is that from the chapter that we're covering now or have you started the next chapter?" Everyone in the class exploded with amusement once again, even Michael, but his eyes met hers with an expression of sympathy.

"See if you can find it in the chapter on contracts," Roth said finally, wiping away a tear.

Bending her head in embarrassment, she met Michael's eyes again. She understood now what was meant when people wrote about drowning in someone's eyes. She would have given anything to drown in Michael's. He was moving his lips, addressing her silently. "Don't worry about it," he was saying. "I'll explain it to you later."

Sadika was never comfortable in that class again, because those two incidents had set a pattern. Even though she no longer asked questions, she became the center of attention and entertainment whenever Roth was in a mood for humor. The class found it so amusing to watch her blush and bow her head that it became a ritual: first would come the joke, then her embarrassed reaction, followed by laughter as the entire class focused on her. She began to sit in the back row to avoid notice, but when that didn't work, she tried to control her facial expression as Michael suggested. "They're not going to stop looking at you till you stop providing them with entertainment," he said.

In due course, she became proficient at it. No matter how raunchy the joke, her face did not reflect one grain of her reaction, and she almost lost her entertainment value. Almost, but not quite. Sometimes when caught unaware she could not help betraying her discomfort, so people continued to cast hopeful glances at her.

Business Law was the first class in which Sadika made an effort not to ask questions. It was difficult, because one of the things she liked best about the educational system in America was that an inquisitive mind was considered a blessing and not a liability. But she felt that all Roth's students were laughing at her because they thought she was stupid. All except Michael. She began to sit next to him for moral support and for the boost to her ego from his show of interest in her. At least, she said to herself, he doesn't consider me a weirdo like the others in the class do.

In fact, Michael enjoyed talking to her. He wanted to know more about the society that had produced this sweet and naive person. What he learned fueled his interest even more. How could that repressive, punitive culture have produced such a bright, conscientious girl? It defied logic. Or maybe adversity helped to develop character and bring out sterling qualities. Before he met Sadika, Michael had thought his life difficult at times, but compared to hers, at its worst it had been virtually a bed of roses.

While he and his peers had been learning the dating game, had she really had to stay away from members of the opposite sex because they could only bring dishonor and heartache, soil her reputation and make her an unworthy competitor in the marriage market? Did the society she had been raised in really discourage an understanding of male-female relationships and curb any curiosity one might feel about them, in order to ensure that a woman would remain one hundred percent innocent and virginal? "A woman's reputation is like pure white linen," Sadika told him, quoting her childhood mentor Zahra. Than seeing Michael's confusion, she elaborated. "At least in that society it is. Even a very faint smudge stands out like a neon light. There's no room for mistakes—one mistake is all it takes to ruin a girl's chances forever."

It was ironic that the reputation that Sadika had been so concerned about was damaged forever through no fault of her own. Because the Haroon fiasco had forced her out of the marriage market for which she had been carefully groomed, she was punished by being given household responsibilities and limited exposure to the outside world. Michael had the impression that even now Sadika was upset that the stains on the clean linen of her reputation were merely figments of people's imaginations. In retrospect, she thought that a few real but discreet smudges here and there on that white linen would probably have helped rather than hurt her situation. For one thing, she might have been better equipped to cope with Haroon. For another, she might have learned how to make herself more attractive to prospective husbands.

By the end of the Spring semester, Michael and Sadika were involved in a courtship of sorts, even though one that often needed a jump-start because it was studded with cultural impediments. Courtship, they were finding out, was not instinctive. It was based on learned behavior; a function of one's culture, values one acquired along the way. Even though these two cared very much for each other, each time one of them tried to create a romantic setting, the result was a near-fiasco.

There was the time Michael decided to surprise Sadika with a candlelight dinner in his one-bedroom apartment. She asked anxiously, "What's the matter? Is something wrong?" when she entered the room to find it lighted only by two candles on the small table holding take-out containers of wonton soup and tai-chin chicken. In Pakistan, a burning candle was a sure sign that the government was conserving electricity for its more productive users by turning it off in households. Even though she was no longer in Pakistan, Sadika still associated the sight of burning candles with an electricity outage.

The food, which Michael found spicy enough to cause fire alarms, was bland by Sadika's standards and not thoroughly cooked either. The vegetables actually crunched between her teeth. When he confided that she was the first woman for whom he had gone all out like this, she couldn't help thinking to herself that the whole dinner was rather stupid. After all, it wasn't as though they were living in some remote area without access to electricity. Why would anyone choose to subject himself to the hassle of lighting candles when all he had to do was flip a switch?

In Farooq Mamoon's village, people who did not have electricity tried their damnedest to hide that fact from others, especially from the lucky ones who had it. Special events were held during the day in natural light. Sometimes, if the occasion was important enough, like showing a prospective bride to prospective in-laws, people were known to go to the trouble of borrowing electrical appliances to put at strategic places in the house to give the impression that they had access to electricity.

Besides, Sadika thought, unless the host had something to hide, wouldn't he want his guest to be able to see what was on her plate? Good food was supposed to be a feast for all the senses, one of which was the sense of sight. No food, even if cooked to perfection, would taste its best unless one could see it, smell it, and touch it with one's fingers. American customs had forced her to give up eating with her fingers, but it would be a real shame if romantic conventions prevented her from seeing her food as well.

On another occasion, when Michael suggested they go away for a weekend, Sadika was insulted. He thought that would be fun, a relaxing jaunt, but for her the connotations were downright evil. What kind of woman does he think I am? she silently raged. Apparently the type who has no regard for her reputation. Or maybe he thinks my reputation is a shambles to start with and can't be protected anyway.

They didn't speak for a whole week as a result of that disastrous suggestion. After they reached an uneasy truce at the end of a miserable seven days, Michael suggested a day at the beach. "It'll give us a chance to get to know each other all over again," he said. Unwilling to relive the bleakness of the past week, she

didn't tell him that the one place on earth bound to be excruciatingly uncomfortable for her was the beach, because she was
accustomed to modest covering and it would be traumatic for
her to wear a swimsuit. Where she was raised, a respectable
female hardly revealed her forearms or ankles, let alone her
arms, legs and back.

Besides, she didn't like the sun. In Pakistan, the sun blazed
almost every day. People tried their best to avoid it; no one
would deliberately sun himself. Sadika felt in a romantic mood
not when the sun was shining in a clear blue sky, but when
there were black clouds heavy with rain and a cool breeze was
blowing. That had something to do with the predominantly
agricultural economy of Pakistan, where well-being was associated with the rains that brought life-giving moisture to the crops.
The monsoon season was the season for lovers.

Luckily, the day before they were to go to the beach, Sadika
developed a heavy cold and was able to get out of it.

Finally, in a last-ditch effort to find an activity they could
both enjoy, Michael suggested a camping trip. In separate tents,
of course. He thought that Sadika, coming after all from a Third
World country, would surely feel at home communing with nature. For all he knew, that was what constituted prime entertainment in Pakistan. After gathering information about possible camp sites, Michael told Sadika enthusiastically about his
plans for the upcoming long holiday weekend, confident that
this time he had chosen wisely.

But Sadika's silence when he unveiled his plans told him
that something was wrong. She was in fact thinking about more
than the negative aspects of camping, like getting bitten by bugs
and using bushes as a toilet—she didn't know facilities were
provided for that—and what she was remembering was the time
she had spent in Farooq Mamoon's house as a fallen woman,
when personal privacy had seemed almost a matter of life and
death. The camping suggestion seemed, like the candlelight din-

ner, to demonstrate that when a society advanced to the point that amenities like electricity, running water and indoor plumbing were taken for granted, their absence could be considered exciting. But Sadika had not reached that point yet. She enjoyed the comforts of life and had no desire to be involved with primitive conditions.

How could she tell someone like Michael that every time she took a shower she hurried, for fear that the water might quit in the middle of a shampoo or when she was rinsing soap from her body? That she never waited till dark to begin studying for an important exam for fear that the electricity would go off? Ironing, washing dishes and cooking were all done promptly, not because she was compulsive, but because she didn't want to risk a power failure.

She knew her fears were irrational, but humans were not always rational creatures. Sometimes she wondered if people born and raised in America had fears like that. Or if they were even capable of understanding them. Since coming to the U.S., she had heard of fear of flying, fear of crowds, fear of going up in an elevator, fear of commitment and many other fears which were called phobias, but she had never heard of a running-out-of-water phobia or an electricity-shut-off phobia.

Maybe if these were unexplored phobias, she could become a psychiatrist and research them. Who knew? Possibly one day, like a new species of plant, there would be a phobia with her name on it, her ticket to fame and fortune. There had to be other immigrants like her out there with similar phobias. For all she knew, there was an underground epidemic going on right now in America that health care officials were unaware of; a virtual pandemic affecting people's mental health and consequently their behavior and well-being, as surely as other recognized psychological conditions did. Sadika knew of at least one victim: herself.

She would have loved to linger in a deliciously invigorating shower, but she couldn't overcome the image of standing in a bathtub all soaped up under a suddenly dry shower head. "Some-one get me some water from somewhere, please!" That frantic plea kept ringing in her ears as she hurried to finish and get out of the tub. And if she decided to put off studying till late in the evening, she would suddenly think that the lights might go out and the next day the instructor would ask her embarrassing questions about the material she was supposed to have read.

"Where should we go today? What would you like to do?" Michael had asked her for suggestions many times. "What do lovers do in Pakistan?" he had once asked, exasperated by her unresponsiveness.

"I don't know. In movies they dance, sing songs and chase each other around," she said finally.

"That could be very interesting," he countered after a moment's reflection, his intense blue gaze alight with specula-tion. He had become quite a talker since he spent so much time with Sadika. Maybe it had something to do with her being even more inhibited than he, or maybe it was because she seemed contented just being with him. All he knew was that for the first time in his life he felt ten feet tall—a suave, charming, intensely masculine man of the world.

"You want to chase me around or you want me to do the honors?" he asked her.

Once again, Sadika didn't respond. For one thing, she didn't have the courage or the experience to explore where an answer to that lighthearted question might take her. And for another, she hesitated to tell him that there were no declared lovers where she came from, since dating was forbidden. Those who dared to conduct love affairs against society's dictates spent all their time trying to find ways to meet without being caught. That was heady stuff in itself. It was hard to explain all this to some-one who had never been subjected to the constant insistence that great evil could come from association with members of the opposite sex. She thought often of telling Michael that she was happy just to be with him and didn't need any other enter-tainment. The fact that he obviously found her desirable was excitement enough, giving her wonderful new feelings of self-esteem, confirming her value as a woman in her own eyes as well as in the eyes of the world.

She couldn't count the number of times her fingers itched to smooth the frown lines between his eyebrows or push back the unruly strands of goldspun hair from his forehead. She enjoyed dreaming about the day when she might have the right to kiss him on his sculptured lips. But since she was too shy to tell him how she felt, she tried to come up with an answer to the question he kept asking her. She racked her brain trying to think of what young lovers in Pakistan did when they were able to be together.

She knew from her experience as confidante to lovelorn fe-males that they didn't indulge in physical intimacy, at least not in the American sense. They might hold hands, embrace, even exchange a few chaste kisses, but for the most part that was it. Few couples went "all the way" before they got married, and often even after they were married it took them a while to work things out because of their inexperience. That was why wed-ding nights were so momentous and intimidating.

She tried to think of the way lovers behaved in what were considered great love stories in Gulmushk Mohalla. From what she could remember, all those lovers did was talk. Maybe after the enormous effort required to simply meet alone, they had no energy left for anything else. It could also be that, as they liked to claim, their love was so pure and spiritual that the very thought of polluting it with physical acts, no matter how loving, was abhorrent. Or maybe their conversations when they were to-gether were so stimulating and interesting that they didn't need anything else. Although how this could be was puzzling.

She thought about some of the legendary love stories of the subcontinent: Sohni and Mahinwal, and Heer and Ranjha. She remembered reading about how both couples met, but never about how they spent time together. Did they discuss politics, play catch or what? She was at a loss to say. What could Sohni, a potter, have to say to Mahinwal, a prince and an experienced man of the world, that would enthrall him? Unless of course, he was interested in making pottery. Similarly, Ranjha, a rich man masquerading as a shepherd to win his beloved's heart, could not have found much to say to Heer, a country girl.

Sadika thought about Heer and Ranjha in the hit Punjabi movie *Heer Ranjha*. She still remembered the film vividly because it was the only one she had been allowed to watch in a movie theater. But all she could come up with were the words of two songs they sang to each other as they were falling in love: "Whenever you whisper my name softly, I feel as though I could perish on the spot," and "When I hear the sweet sound of your flute, I perish."

Maybe it was just as well that these tales of true love had had tragic endings. Heer was forcibly married off to some villainous character, leaving Ranjha to die of a broken heart. And the inverted clay pot with the help of which Sohni crossed the river to meet her lover was sabotaged by her jealous sister-in-law. It fell apart, and she drowned with Mahinwal's name on her lips. Mahinwal, too, drowned when, hearing his beloved's cry, he jumped into the river to try and save her.

These doomed lovers had lived a long time ago. But where Sadika was raised, love affairs were as exciting today as they had been then, because they were forbidden. Reshman, one of the girls in her college class in Pakistan, had started an affair with a neighborhood boy and had taken great pride in entertaining her friends with tales of the resourcefulness, escapes and near-death experiences involving secret meetings with her boyfriend.

Sadika's favorite was a story Reshman told about sometimes dropping a laundered shirt from her window on the second floor, so she could slip outside and pick it up and return later unnoticed. If anyone questioned her, she would point to the shirt. Reshman had gone on and on about her courage in taking risks and the excitement of not only being able to meet secretly with a male, but of sometimes actually performing the forbidden and therefore excruciatingly thrilling act of touching—and even of kissing.

The teenage girls listening to Reshman tried to imagine feeling the pressure of ripe male lips and envied Reshman—if only they could have had just one adventure like those that Reshman seemed to be having constantly, they thought they would cherish the memory forever. They were not like Reshman: they couldn't handle being dropped from a world of adventure into a sea of sensuality and back again. They believed that James Bond himself couldn't have handled that trauma—at least not if he had been raised in Pakistan, where the simplest contact between the sexes seemed more exciting and illicit than a completed sexual act in the West.

There was the time that Mr. Aasim Mahmood, the Social Studies teacher in the only co-ed middle school in the area, had decided to start a photography club. When the time came to develop films and use enlargers, he had taken a group of young boys and girls into the darkroom with him. People had been scandalized when they found out about it. How could a teacher do something as immoral as putting boys and girls together in a room and turning off the lights? What was he planning to do next? Provide beds for their convenience? Surely this was one more sign that the world was ending and the Day of Judgment was near.

Many parents had withdrawn their children from the school rather than expose them to such a sinful atmosphere. The alarmed principal, Mr. Qadir Baksh, had hastily declared that he had had no knowledge of the depravity taking place in his school. The unfortunate Mr. Mahmood had been made to apologize publicly, and was fired despite his fifteen-year seniority. Needless to say, no other school would dare touch him with a ten-foot pole.

Sadika, having been raised in that environment, could hardly believe that a young man would ask his beloved what she would like to do to make their time together interesting.

thirty-one

IN THE END, Michael decided that things were never going to warm up between him and Sadika unless he was willing—and able—to change their relationship.

What brought things to a head were letters that Khanum was writing to Sadika with alarming frequency. Apparently, ever since Sadika had found employment and was anticipating getting a degree from an American college, prospective mothers-in-law had started to approach Khanum. Many of the same families that had once considered Sadika beneath consideration were now more than eager to discuss a possible match between her and their sons. A delighted Khanum was not sure how long this good fortune would last.

Normally, the most promising prospective brides were culled in their teens. The second cut was made when women were twenty to about twenty-two years old. Females left over after that were looked upon as inferior and had to settle for anyone willing to accept them—a wastrel, a ne'er-do-well, a widower with children, an old man, or anyone looking for a housemaid-cum-nursemaid. Sadika was now twenty-four, an age at which decent marriage proposals stopped altogether. She was lucky that the reverse had happened in her case, but one never knew when her luck would run out. Khanum urged Sadika to come back so a marriage decision could be made right away.

Sadika ignored her mother's letters. For the first time in her life she was tasting not only freedom and independence, but even love—heady stuff. And she was not about to give that up, certainly not to the same people who had once rejected her after forcing her to parade in front of them in her finery. But Michael, who knew about the letters, didn't know that she felt that way. She hadn't told him, and he was afraid that she could slip away if he didn't ask her the question that had been on his mind for days. So whether she was ready or not, before anything happened to whisk away the opportunity from him forever, he was going to give it his best shot.

Their big moment was played out in a highly predictable setting. So predictable that if Sadika were not so insecure, she would have known what was coming as soon as she stepped into the private corner of the Italian restaurant, where a vase of red roses rested between lighted candles on the festively set table. Michael, handsome and sophisticated in a dark suit, rose to hand her a perfect long-stemmed rose.

Throughout the meal, she had no idea what she was eating. Surely there was no reason to feel so nervous at a simple dinner, she thought, trying to drag herself back to the real world. Her heart kept thumping and her mouth was dry.

When Michael took the little box out of his pocket and reached across the table to take her hand, she thought about what that could mean. She knew that this was the traditional way for men to propose in the West, but surely, that couldn't be happening. When someone like Haroon, who had been practically engaged to her, had refused to marry her despite the tremendous pressure from his family, how could someone so much more attractive than Haroon choose to do so of his own free will?

But Michael held out the open box with the diamond ring and asked her to marry him. She saw that he was pale and his hand was shaking. He was her dear friend and confidant, providing comfort and boosting her flagging self-esteem whenever a boost was needed. She was not sure about the thing called love, but her heart was brimming with gratitude toward him. His stature in her eyes was tremendous and she hated to see him so nervous in front of her like this. Wordlessly, she extended her left hand to him and watched him slip his ring on her finger.

thirty-two

AFTER THAT EVENING, a certain wariness crept into the relationship. While till then they had simply enjoyed each other's company, now each seemed to be trying all the time to decipher the other's inner feelings and expectations. Sadika's restrained reaction to their engagement was especially disturbing to Michael. He asked her frequently whether she was happy, and wasn't satisfied with the slight smile and nod she gave him in response. He looked at her thoughtfully, trying to decide whether she really meant she was happy. She certainly didn't sound enthusiastic. Was it a cultural thing or was she really not happy with their engagement?

He himself was ecstatic. He wanted to fold her in his arms and do all the wonderful things that he had fantasized about for weeks and months. If she were an American, all barriers would have been breached by now. His brother Steven had been living with Caroline for years before they decided to tie the knot. His kid sister Amy and her fiancé Richard were all over each other all the time; it wasn't hard to imagine what they did as soon as they were alone. But here he was, engaged to be married and not even a decent kiss to show for it.

And it wasn't from lack of trying on his part, either. Each time he put his arm around her in even a casual way, her entire personality changed. Gone would be the charming, sometimes funny and sometimes solemn woman he had fallen in love with, replaced by a tense person rigidly waiting for something unpleasant to happen. He didn't know what to make of it. If it had been anyone else, he would have thought there might have been sexual abuse in the past. But with Sadika it could be anything: her obvious insecurities and inhibitions, her lack of experience, her cultural background.

It was funny. Steve and Amy had warned him against her when they had met her in the fall. Who knew, they said, what her background really was, and what she was really after. Maybe a green card? Money? What kind of relatives did she have and would she try to bring them over? You had to give it a lot of thought before you got involved with someone from a Third World country.

Sadika could see that her lack of physical and verbal affection was hurting Michael, making him doubtful and insecure, and with all her heart, she wanted to change, for she cared a great deal for him. But she didn't know how: in Pakistan no one worried about personal happiness, maybe because most people were too poor to think beyond survival or because society did not see personal happiness as a goal. All she knew was that when she was growing up, she heard a lot about duty and obligation but nothing about happiness. Love and happiness were childish things that didn't matter and that certainly couldn't last. "The love-monster has taken over this person's senses," the elders would say of someone who was happily infatuated. "The responsibility of a spouse and a few children is just what he needs to set his mind straight."

Most of the time this seemed to be true. The love-struck person forgot about that emotion after becoming saddled with a family, perhaps because the struggle to make ends meet was too overpowering in a society where opportunities were few. Or maybe the emotion of love was transient to begin with and the elders in their wisdom knew that. Hadn't Sadika herself believed she was in love with Haroon when she expected to be married to him? Now the thought of having anything to do with him caused her to shudder.

Could you trust your own emotions? Today she was sure that happiness was being with Michael, but hadn't she felt at one time that being married to any appropriate person would constitute happiness? In fact, if the situation portrayed in Khanum's letters had existed a couple of years ago, Sadika would probably have been in seventh heaven. Who would have thought then that she would ever become a hot commodity in the marriage market? No wonder Khanum wanted her back as soon as possible—before people changed their minds. She had sent photographs and information about various prospective grooms in each letter. Bemused, Sadika had looked closely at the photographs before dropping them in the wastebasket. Why were these people suddenly so eager to marry her? Wasn't she the same person whose sinful ways had supposedly led astray several young men of sterling character?

Sadika would have gone on simply avoiding a direct answer to Khanum's urgent appeals if the choice had not been taken away from her. The letter was written in Asghar's sprawling hand: "Our mother is dying, and as her daughter it is your duty to come to her at this time. You know she will never forgive you if you do not. Her instructions are that if you do not make it in time you should not be allowed to see her dead face."

When Sadika handed Khanum's letter to Michael that evening, she had already decided to take the earliest flight to Pakistan.

Michael did not say much, but he was visibly upset. It was hard for him to believe that a piece of paper covered with what looked like squiggly worms could abruptly change everything like that. He wondered whether Khanum's sudden terminal illness was not just a ploy to get Sadika back. Once in her family's clutches, would Sadika have the strength to pull away? She had never once told him outright that she loved him. What if her sense of obligation to her family was stronger than her feelings for him? What would become of their future together? He couldn't bear to think that he might have to give up the idea of building a life with Sadika. He certainly couldn't say outright that her mother might not really be on her deathbed. There was always the possibility that Khanum was really sick and if she died, Sadika would probably never forgive him for talking her out of going.

Despite her decision to leave for Pakistan as soon as possible, Sadika had to delay for one week. With only two semesters left before graduation, she had set up job interviews with companies that paid low salaries in return for sponsoring employees for the coveted green card. Unfortunately, these interviews could not be rescheduled. Michael protested that she didn't need to do this because when she married him in the near future, she would get permanent immigrant status. But she didn't want anyone, especially Michael's family, to be able to say that she had married him from ulterior motives. She wrote to Khanum about the reason for the delay, not realizing that by mentioning job interviews and green cards, she had further elevated her status in the marriage market and unleashed a new storm of marriage proposals.

As the day of Sadika's departure neared, Michael's frustration with her attitude toward their engagement grew. He no longer expected to see her afloat in a euphoric daze, but at least she should have exhibited some kind of glow or something. Maybe it was beyond her to fling herself in his arms and cover his face with passionate kisses, but surely she could manage a peck on the cheek once in a while. Even holding hands more often would have been nice. From the way she seemed reluctant even to look at him, one would think that he was walking around stark naked or had suddenly sprouted horns or whatever the equivalent of that was in Pakistan.

Michael could not know that Sadika was behaving the way an engaged woman was supposed to behave in the culture in which she had been raised. Awkward shyness was expected from a woman of impeccable character who had never had a serious relationship with a man. In fact, in Pakistan an engaged couple could not set eyes on each other till their wedding day. The conventional wisdom was that this not only fostered romance, but decreased the chances of things going wrong. It was so much easier to dream about someone you didn't know well and to believe he had all kinds of desirable qualities if you were forbidden to see him, let alone have a conversation with him. More often than not, a traditional couple would feel that they were head over heels in love by the time they got married.

One might even call it conditioning: men and women were conditioned to fall in love with their parents' choice just as people in the West were conditioned to feel romantic at the sight of lighted candles. For example, Shehla, a girl two years older than Sadika, had gotten engaged to Haseeb, a man she had never set eyes on before. She had started out by liking the sound of his name better than any other. Gradually during the ten months of their engagement, after a few clandestine meetings, stolen caresses and smuggled love-letters, things had progressed to the point where they had been wild to catch a glimpse of each other or even to hear the sound of each other's voice.

Many times when Sadika heard her American friends talk about how cold and calculated arranged marriages were, she couldn't help being amused. If only they knew! Those "cold and calculated" arrangements could be fully as red-hot as anything anyone over here could ever imagine. In fact, Aarif Hassan believed that if marriage was the objective, American society was going about it the wrong way by allowing people to date, and even to live together.

How could anyone be expected to want to marry a person whose flaws he or she knew intimately? It was a miracle anyone took the plunge at all. Aarif Hassan didn't tell Sadika this, of course, but it was a fact that if he had known Ashfaaq Beebee even fractionally as well before marriage as he did now, he would have run for his life. But he had eagerly walked into that trap—and like a mouse craving cheese, had thrown his life away for a measly crumb. By the time he realized his blunder, it was too late: he had turned into a husband and father, and divorce, especially at that stage, was taboo.

Sadika's demeanor belied her intense excitement about her engagement; Michael had come to mean the world to her. Marriage had always been her goal and now it was what she desired above all else in life.

Before she came to the United States and met Michael, she had wanted a male by her side because that was the only way she could become socially acceptable and respected. More than gaining a prospective soul mate or a meal ticket, it was a requirement for the chance to go through life with pride and dignity. No matter how professionally advanced, financially secure or personally fulfilled a woman might be, she was not really respected if she was unmarried.

Benazir Bhutto had been prime minister of Pakistan, but in many people's eyes she was an object of pity till she married. By the same token, Sadika's youngest sister Sajida, an impoverished orderly's wife, was considered set for life because she was married, even though she was miserable. According to Khanum, Sajida's husband was cruel and insensitive, treated her with contempt and suspicion, and even beat her occasionally.

Before she left Pakistan and Michael came to mean so much to Sadika, it had not been marriage but the label of a "settled" woman that she had hungered for, along with the respectability and privileges that went with that label. She had longed for the right to put a blob of henna on a bride's palm as part of the wedding ritual: only seven married women with living husbands were allowed that privilege, to assure the new bride a long, prosperous and happy marriage.

Sadika had wanted her mother to be able to say that her daughter was settled, with a child on the way, instead of Khanum's being forced to try to come up with a plausible reason why she, unlike her younger sisters, was not yet married. Sadika had wanted to be able to discuss the hardships of married life in low conspiratorial tones with other married women who would consider her a comrade-in-arms in the battle to produce sons in order to achieve some degree of marital tranquillity.

She had wanted to be able to carry on about her wedding night being so difficult because of her innocence. "It was so hard for a woman like me, who has led such a sheltered life," she had imagined herself saying. "I had never even held hands, let alone kissed a man before. And of course viewing the male body unclothed had been out of the question. So everything was just so shocking for me. It was a miracle I didn't have a coronary. I bled for days afterward, you know. Not that I wasn't fertile, mind you." To make sure that it was understood that her innocence in no way detracted from her being a highly functional female, she would add, "Poor me! I got pregnant on the very first night!"

In Pakistan, and before she met Michael, a major reason for wanting children had been so that she could contribute a horror story of her own to women's gruesome childbirth stories. "I lost about five and a half pints of blood," she imagined herself saying. "The doctor and the nurses were soaked, but still the baby wouldn't come. He was just too big, too well nourished, while I of course was so slender and petite. In desperation, the world-famous gynecologist who was doing my case free of charge because of the numerous complications involved, ran down the hospital corridor yelling hoarsely for help with tears streaming down his face. Finally, with the aid of two other world-renowned doctors—a heart surgeon and a brain surgeon who happened to be passing by—he was finally able to pull out my ten-and-a-half-pound, healthy, screaming son, while the nurses cheered and my grateful husband looked on."

Before Michael, she knew that she had to have a husband to save herself from being viewed as a freak and an anomaly, in her own mind as well as in the eyes of the world.

Now she could hardly remember half the reasons for marriage that had once seemed so crucial to her, and those that she could remember had lost their significance. The stories that she had been planning one day to tell an audience of her peers were becoming hazier by the minute. All she could think now was that her marriage to Michael, which would take place at some future date, promised warmth, security and love in a world that had been harsh, frightening and devoid of tenderness.

She was afraid to dwell on that wonderful future because she knew in her heart of hearts that it was too good to be true, that it could never happen. She tried to discourage Michael from making specific plans because she was sure that if he thought enough about it, he would realize how impossible their situation was and he would make the dream disappear even while she was still trying to hang onto it.

Thirty-Three

HOW DIFFERENT SHE was from the young woman who had stood at that very spot some three years ago, inwardly shaking in her boots, expecting some kind of calamity. Today she stood calmly by the conveyor belt amidst the bustle of the Islamabad airport, waiting for her elegant luggage—a gift from Michael—to arrive.

She wondered who would come to meet her at the airport and how they would behave toward her. Then, realizing with a pang of guilt that she was thinking more about herself than her sick mother, she decided that if Khanum was so ill that no one would be able to come to the airport to get her, she could go home by herself. Even as she thought that, Sadika realized that her parents' home was not her home anymore—that the idea of home was now associated with Michael, whom she longed for among these strange men who were mentally undressing her even though she was wearing the traditional Pakistani *shalwar kameez*. Michael alone could make her feel cherished and protected.

She came out of the concourse to find what seemed to be a sea of familiar faces. Sajida, Asghar, Khanum—Khanum!—Akbar Khan, several neighbors, and a few women she distinctly remembered rejecting her as a prospective bride, were waving excitedly at her, holding garlands of roses and jasmine. The self-assurance she had been so proud of a moment earlier threatened to desert her. She blinked several times to clear her vision. Could the rules of the society she had left behind just three short years ago have changed so drastically?

"My daughter! My loved one! The peace of my mind! The joy of my heart! You've come back to me at last!" screamed

Khanum, tears coursing down her plump cheeks; her arms extended toward Sadika as though to pluck her into the crowd from a distance of twenty feet. Some of the other women, while silent, displayed great emotion. Even Parveen Majid, who had once demanded that Sadika bite into hard candy to prove that her teeth were healthy, was dabbing her eyes with the corner of her scarf.

In spite of herself, Sadika was deeply moved. This was the first time anybody had ever shed tears for her, crocodile or otherwise, and brought her garlands of flowers. In a daze, she went from one pair of outstretched arms to another with barely enough time to catch her breath between embraces, or to register the identity of the embracer. She had no idea who took her luggage or called the cab to take them to Gulmushk Mohalla. She was in a state of shock—as much from seeing Khanum hale and hearty as from this emotional reception.

At House #4, Gali #12, Gulmushk Mohalla, nothing had changed. The four chairs in the small living room next to the entrance were still slip-covered in the light-green fabric Sadika had sewn and embroidered. The curtains, also sewn by Sadika, were in about the same condition as when she had left; no one had bothered to mend them after Asghar's friends had torn them playing hide and seek more than three years before. The only thing different was the large wicker basket filled with pastries sitting on the small table. When she was told that the room that had been given to Ashfaaq Beebee and her family nearly five years ago was allotted to her—she herself had whitewashed the walls—it was obvious that Sadika's status had changed: she had become a coveted commodity. She guessed that she must have acquired tremendous money-making potential in people's minds.

When everyone sat down to eat in the living room, where the coffee table doubled as the buffet table, Sadika was able to observe her little sister Sajida and her husband Razzak, for the first time. She found it hard to believe that Sajida was married—especially to this person who resembled a gorilla. What was even more amazing was the fact that in Sajida's eyes, Razzak was everything a man should be: "strong, virile and forceful," were the words she had used to describe him in the letter she had written Sadika. Her only lament was that she had not been able to provide him with a healthy son by now: "Someone as masculine as my husband should be surrounded by strapping sons."

Sajida had changed in appearance as well as demeanor. Wearing a festive yellow *shalwar kameez* embroidered with red silk thread at neck and sleeves, presumably from her dowry or a gift from the groom's family, she had gained a good thirty pounds after two miscarriages and one stillbirth. She looked much older than her twenty-one years, and a far cry from the mischievous tomboy she had been only three years before.

Is my favorite sibling really hiding somewhere inside this quiet, overdressed young woman? Sadika asked herself for the dozenth time. Had marriage and childbearing destroyed her forever? Where was the youngster who used to burst out laughing at the most inappropriate moments, who stole onions, *roti* and pickles from Khanum's cooking area and hid underneath her cotton comforter to eat them, who didn't care whether she was dressed in rags or velvet? She had been married only two years. Why had she changed like this?

Sadika glanced at Razzak and, as before, her gaze was caught by his enormous mustache: thick and bushy, it extended a couple of inches from either side of his face. He kept stroking it and looking at his reflection every time he lifted his polished stainless steel water glass.

Sajida had said that the mustache was Razzak's pride and joy, and she confided that he spent a lot of money on it. In addition to the twenty-rupee mustache allowance that the Pakistani army gave soldiers with imposing mustaches, he spent another fifteen. After every meal he massaged his mustache with a special oil custom-made for him by the local folk healer, wiped off the excess, combed in some homemade starch, and, taking out the small ornate mirror that he kept in his pocket for that purpose,

carefully shaped the mustache. To protect its beauty, he avoided
rain, wind, sweaty physical exertion and kissing. Sajida said she
could count on her fingers the number of times her husband had
kissed her over the past two years. His fear of ruining his mustache apparently does not extend to eating, Sadika observed silently, as she watched Razzak wolfing his food.

He seemed very self-confident, at least in his wife's family's
home where he had high status, not only because he was the
son-in-law, but because he was considered saintly since he refused to take a second, more fertile, wife. One of his favorite
pastimes was telling his in-laws about his mother's and sisters'
efforts to talk him into a second marriage. He liked to talk in
general, and since Sadika was not only a newcomer but a female who had apparently been subjected to sinful Western influences, he felt compelled to show her the error of her ways
and make her aware of him as an authority figure.

After his hunger had been assuaged and he had had a few
moments to lean back and pick his teeth, he addressed her with
dramatic intensity: "The day of judgment is near. All you have
to do is look at the women of the West if you want proof positive—their skimpy clothes, their evil behavior—they're nothing
less than the agents of Satan himself." As Sadika did not respond, he went on, "I think anyone who chooses to live in a
sin-infested place like America is furthering the devil's work. I
was very happy to learn that you've come to your senses and
you're here to marry one of your own kind. A woman needs a
husband to guide her and protect her from her own weaknesses
and her fickle nature."

Sadika suddenly began to give him her undivided attention.

"What do you mean by that?" she asked, trying to keep her
voice free of the hostility she felt toward this newly discovered
brother-in-law.

Glancing around the room, she noticed that Khanum looked
uncomfortable, as did her brother and father. There was more
going on here than she had been aware of. The pastry on the

side table, Parveen Majid's prolonged hug at the airport, Sadika's reception there as an honored guest . . . everything pointed to preparation of something. A wedding maybe? Hers?

She turned accusing eyes on Khanum, who was concentrating on her food with a new intensity "Were you ever sick at all?" she demanded in a direct and very un-Sadika-like manner. "Or was that just a scheme to get me here? And now that you do have me here, what is it that you think you're going to persuade me to do?"

"Whatever parents do, they do for the good of their children, I know you realize that," Khanum told her. Sadika's defiant attitude was certainly proof that girls should be married off early, before their tongues learned to wag. "It's not as though we're planning something that you didn't want in the first place. I remember how you rushed to put on your best clothes to make a good impression on Waseem's mother. Now that she's finally chosen you for her son, it's time to rejoice and stop acting as though something shady is happening."

Khanum paused, debating with herself whether to continue. Then she said, "We've tentatively decided that the engagement will take place next week. Nothing fancy—just some neighbors and close friends. Of course there's no hurry for the wedding. It can even take place next year, to give you time to wind up your affairs in America."

The past flashed by Sadika: her rejection by Haroon and by her parents—by her entire culture in fact—and the shabby treatment she received from her relatives in America. In a voice laced with sarcasm, she said: "Are you saying that you have arranged for me to get engaged to Waseem without even consulting me? If you have, then let me tell you that you have no such authority. Any rights you had were lost the day you sent me off to America as a maid and baby-sitter for your sister."

It was against Khanum's nature to remain passive in the face of defiance, especially in front of witnesses. "I wouldn't be so quick to hurl accusations if I were you, you ungrateful girl!

You are what you are today because I had the foresight to send you to America, where I knew with my sister's help you could become something. If you were a proper daughter you would have drowned yourself in shame before telling these lies to me."

Sadika stood up. "You have a very convenient memory," she responded vehemently. "I don't remember concern for my well-being ever being part of the picture. You were scared to death of what people would say if they thought your older daughter was not only still unmarried, but having affairs with half the boys in the neighborhood. Sending me to America was a way to get rid of me—nothing else! And if I'm something today it's due to my own efforts. If your sister had her way, I'd still be a baby-sitter and a maid in her house."

She drew a deep breath and went on more calmly. "I don't know why I'm saying all this, because at this stage it's beside the point. It's a good thing I didn't unpack. You're obviously not sick—and you certainly don't need me. So I'm going to call a taxi, get my luggage and get out of here."

Experience had taught Khanum that she possessed two very effective weapons: threats and tears. One or the other almost always worked. Since her threats had failed, she tried the other weapon in her arsenal and burst into tears. "I'm an old woman whose time on this earth is nearly done," she sobbed. "All I want to do before I die is fulfill my responsibilities, to see all my daughters married and my grandchildren playing in my lap. You tell me, Sadika, why is that so terrible? Mark my words—if, when I die, you're still unmarried because of your foolishness, I'll instruct everyone not to show you my dead face." She couldn't resist concluding with a threat.

Then, alarmed because Sadika continued to stand facing her, she tried a different tactic. "Sit down, my daughter," she began in a gentler tone. "We all wish you well here. No one's going to force you to do something that will make you unhappy. But if you go away now, everyone who's been looking forward to seeing you is going to be disappointed. We all want to know what you've been doing in America." Khanum waved her hand toward all the members of the household. "Sajida, her husband and her mother-in-law are staying with us just so Sajida can be with you, and Zahra has been stopping by every other day to find out when you would be here."

She's right, Sadika thought reluctantly, it doesn't make sense to go back when I just spent all my savings to get here. No one can make me get married without my consent—and I really want to spend time with Sajida and Zahra. It's not as though I can't leave whenever I want to.

thirty-four

SADIKA DISCOVERED VERY quickly that being a successful returnee from America meant that people reacted strongly to her: they were either fascinated or wanted nothing to do with her.

Among the young women who were her contemporaries, some regarded her as courageous and fortunate, and others as someone who had betrayed her culture and its values and would surely be punished one day by meeting a horrible fate. And if that didn't happen, God would personally attend to her on the Day of Judgment—which, by the way, would undoubtedly arrive pretty soon, because people like Sadika were flushing the world down the toilet. Interestingly, both points of view were represented right next door in the persons of Zahra, Sadika's childhood friend, and Durdaana, her old nemesis.

Zahra, whose situation had not changed during Sadika's absence, was as delighted and proud of her friend as though she herself had some part in Sadika's good fortune. On the other hand, Durdaana, who was now married to Zahra's younger brother Javed, was angry that Sadika had come back and was being treated as if she were a heroine. In any social situation when Durdaana could not completely ignore Sadika, she confined herself to curt nods and avoided eye contact.

Changed beyond recognition because she had put on so much weight after having one child and a miscarriage, Durdaana was always appropriately covered from head to toe and proud of her respectable married status. "Married women like myself," she often said, "are the cornerstones of society." It was hard to remember that she was the same woman who had once endangered her reputation by having paper "affairs" with two neighborhood boys at the same time.

Zahra had not changed much physically, but she was well on her way to becoming a frustrated and bitter woman. From what Sadika could tell, the process had started about two and a half years earlier after her father's death and Javed's wedding. That was when she had become a servant in her own home, courtesy of her brother, her new sister-in-law, and her mother Ameena, a semi-invalid.

There was nothing specifically wrong with Ameena, but she complained constantly of aches and pains. Her audience generally consisted of other older neighborhood women who also suffered various bodily ailments as colorful as they were unique. They all often got together to sympathize with one another during the day while everyone else was working. Every morning after breakfast Sadika went next door to spend time with Zahra and, while helping her friend in the kitchen, listened in fascination as the old ladies indulged in a game of pain upmanship—a match in which, despite the tremendous effort expended, there were no winners.

If Zahra's mother started out by saying, "*Behno*, lately I've been having these pains that spiral upward starting in my heel. And a pain that starts out like a pounding hammer in the center of my brain and then spreads into a throbbing network through my entire head before it drips in drops through my neck into the rest of my body," she was immediately countered by Saffia's grandmother, who cleared her phlegm-filled throat with noises that sounded like two roosters fighting, before launching into a description of pains that defied medical science. "*Behno*. All I know is that mine start between the bones of the shoulders and arms. After they begin, the shooting pains sometimes rush and sometimes move slowly to the tips of my fingers—I can't pick anything up or put my hands in water."

That was as far as Saffia's grandmother was permitted to go before being topped by Zarreen's first aunt: "I am a victim, *behno*. I am a victim," she moaned, beating her bony chest with clenched fists. "I get these mysterious pains that begin like shooting stars in parts of my liver and spleen and then burst out, tearing away bits and pieces and making my insides bleed like a fountain."

Frequently Zahra's mother, dissatisfied with the response she evoked, tried again. "That sounds like this strange ache that I have sometimes—the one that starts deep in my insides like some evil sphere that keeps growing bigger and bigger and stronger and stronger and starts moving toward my neck or my head and then it bursts and shreds of it spread all over through my weakened bloodstream."

Zarreen's first aunt, annoyed at having the limelight stolen from her, returned to the fray. "I know exactly what you're talking about, *behen*. Tell me—does it cause a tingle near your heart? Because mine does. It's a very treacherous tingle too—unpredictable and cunning—it changes its face like an unfaithful woman—first just a little ache, gently constricting my chest, then it turns nasty and attacks my insides like the claws of some horrible monster."

Sadika listened spellbound from the relative anonymity of her perch near the stove, taking care not to let them know she was paying attention because they would clutch onto any new listener until they were ready to let go, which was generally a very long time. A similar fate was met by anyone who made the mistake of inquiring about the health of anyone in the group. Sadika knew this from personal experience.

Feeling sorry for the trio of sick old ladies when she first heard about their morning meetings, Sadika had brewed tea with ginger and cardamom and, despite Zahra's warning looks, served it to the delighted women along with some pastries. "So how are you feeling today, father's sister-in-law?" she had asked Zahra's mother, handing her a cup of the aromatic tea.

"I don't know how to answer you, *baeti*," Zahra's mother moaned. "There are so many things wrong with me that it's not possible to go into all of them at one time. But I'll try. See how drawn I look, and yet my face is flushed? It's because old age has eaten up most of my blood. What little I have is not distributed right—"

She was interrupted by Zarreen's first aunt. "I know what's wrong with you. I told you before, but you're so stubborn you won't listen. You have the same thing I had five years ago. Your liver has started to fall apart. All you need is soup made from goat's feet to glue your insides back together. If you took my advice when I gave it to you, you'd be fine by now."

Annoyed, Zahra's mother tried to ignore Zarreen's first aunt and talked to Sadika. "*Baeti*, come and feel my hands and tell me if even a rhino's hide is so rough and leathery."

At this point, Saffia's grandmother, silent until now, spoke up. "*Baeti*, feel mine. If hers is like a rhino's, mine is like the rhino's grandfather's. And this even though I eat right—not like Ameena . . ." Here Saffia's grandmother waved her finger at Zahra's mother, who sat sullen, seething with anger and frustration. After all, it was her health Sadika had inquired about. How dare the others interrupt?

Sadika hastily tried to pacify all three women by saying she would make sure to remember them all in her prayers, and she hoped they would feel better the next time she saw them. Then, pretending to hear her name called, she escaped into the kitchen where Zahra said, "I told you." Sadika sank with relief into the low chair next to the stove and the two exploded into stifled laughter.

Zahra's mother's mysterious ailments had started at about the time her husband died and her son married Durdaana. No longer the wife of the head of the household, she could fall back only on chronic sickness to avoid joining her daughter Zahra in the role of domestic servant. She was powerless to alter Zahra's fate, but she herself refused to spend her days toiling over a hot fire and wrestling with all kinds of dirt. Her strategy was successful: now no one dared ask her even to walk a short distance, let alone to do any real work. Her family had learned to be grateful that she was not one of those who required frequent visits to the local hospital.

Unfortunately for Zahra, she did not have the excuse of old age or frailty. Her chances of getting married, slim before, were now nonexistent because of her advanced age—nearly thirty—and because her younger sister, terrified of sharing Zahra's dismal fate, had worked tirelessly to make a match for herself. Since most people felt that a loose character was genetic, Zahra had become even more undesirable as a prospective wife after her sister's love marriage. And, people reasoned, if Zahra had been worth marrying, wouldn't someone have married her by now?

Since no one made any effort to attract an appropriate match for her, it was highly unlikely an eligible male would fall from the sky one day. And even if for some inexplicable reason someone did ask for Zahra's hand, nothing could come of it because her dowry was already gone. Durdaana had begun to use the linen and comforters when relatives visited from Multan, and Zahra's set of gold jewelry had been sold off to pay doctors' bills for Ijlaal, Javed and Durdaana's son.

Zahra's subdued looks had faded further, but she was still a fount of information—especially on the subject of Durdaana. Apparently she had never had the chance to air her true opinion about her sister-in-law and she was more than ready to express it to Sadika.

"Don't let Durdaana's altered looks deceive you," she told Sadika. "She's as much into having affairs today as she was the day you left. How do you think she became my sister-in-law? My mother certainly didn't choose her, and neither did I. After you went to America, she kept coming down here to sympathize with Khanum about the worthless female you turned out to be. Imagine the nerve! First she made you take the blame for what she did, and then she used that to get a husband for herself.

"Five days. Five measly days. That's all it took for her to snare Javed. And she did it in a way that makes him think to this day that the whole thing was his idea. You should have seen the letters she wrote him when they were engaged. Sickening! 'I am like the lake whose depths have never been plumbed by anyone. And I am like an open book that no one has ever read.' Ha! As though I didn't know! If she'd been a lake, all her fish would have died of pollution. And if she'd been a book, the pages would have fallen apart from use. But my dim-witted brother believed each and every one of her lies. You should have seen how he had tears in his eyes when he read those letters. He used to quote them to us as proof of her spirituality. That's how I know. I tell Javed that he's lucky she's become so ugly, or she'd be auctioning off our family honor in the streets of Islamabad today. Nothing is beyond her kind. Nothing!"

As she had done in the past, Sadika agreed with whatever Zahra said, trying to give her what comfort she could. The fate of her childhood friend was tragic, Sadika thought, and she was justifiably bitter about her meaningless and desperate life. It was a good thing that she didn't realize the true extent of her misfortune, or she might not have been able to bear it even as well as she did. Sadika couldn't help thinking about Michael, about her own good fortune, and what Zahra was missing.

The memory of the goodbye scene with Michael at her apartment before they left for the airport, sent thrills through her body. That was the first time in their relationship that Sadika had not only returned each loving gesture in full measure, but initiated some of her own. And when her flight had been announced at the airport, it had suddenly struck her that she would not have Michael to share things with anymore. Oblivious to the crowd, she had blindly reached for him, closing her eyes tightly as they embraced. It was probably going to be several weeks before she would see him again, this wonderful man who had a hard time keeping his hands off her, but whose code of decency forbade him to make advances without her permission.

Why hadn't she realized how acutely she would miss him, how much she had relied on feeling cherished and protected by him? It seemed that any time she couldn't make sense of some-

thing, she expected—almost needed—him to tell her not to
worry. "I'll explain it to you later." And to think that one day
she might have him for a life partner. Surely no woman in the
world was as lucky as she. And Zahra would never know any
of these feelings.

Sadika could still remember Zahra coming to her with freshly
washed hair, giving her a bottle of oil and asking her to saturate
her hair with it because her own hands were too tired. Even
then Zahra had considered her hair a monster—impossible to
confine in a braid unless it was well oiled, since no matter how
tightly it was braided, it would escape in a matter of minutes.
Now no one would admire Zahra's hair, even though it was the
kind of hair any female would cheerfully kill for: glossy, thick,
and reaching almost to her knees. Unoiled, it was like raw shiny
silk with a life of its own. Sadika's hair, which had earned her
many a compliment in America, was nothing compared to it.
But no man would ever change Zahra's mind about her appearance.

What a shame.

What a waste.

thirty-five

ZAHRA WAS NOT the only contender for Sadika's attention. Sajida needed a shoulder to cry on and a sympathetic ear just as much as Zahra did, if not more.

Sajida was married, but she couldn't find peace and happiness because she had not been able to complete a successful pregnancy, let alone produce a male child, in almost two years of marriage. Why, she often asked herself, is Razzak so desperate for a child? It wasn't as though he was a king in need of an heir. As far as she could see, his name wasn't even worth propagating. The town—in fact the entire world—was riddled with Khans. There were several in their neighborhood alone. But she kept her opinion to herself.

"I haven't succeeded in winning my husband's heart, *Aapa,* elder sister," Sajida had confided in a small, sad voice. "I try so hard, but nothing seems to work."

Maybe because he doesn't have a heart, Sadika thought. Maybe all he has is a huge big stomach and a mustache-making machine. But she encouraged her little sister to talk, to vent her frustration. That was probably all she could do to help Sajida.

Ever since she married him, Sajida had, apparently, been preoccupied with finding sure-fire ways to make her gorilla of a husband fall in love with her. At first she had tried reaching him through his stomach, as many a seasoned wife had advised her. After culling unusual delicious recipes from various sources, she had planned wonderful dinners for an entire month. Razzak was dumbfounded—he had never even heard of the strange foods his wife cooked, let alone tasted them. Nevertheless, each evening he wolfed everything down without comment while a hopeful

Sajida looked on. In a moment, she thought, he will look up with the spark of love in his eyes. But nothing happened.

Then on the fifth day of Sajida's gourmet month, when Razzak came home to a dinner of chicken livers, kidneys and hearts mixed with egg and coriander leaves, he had erupted into a volcano of suspicion. "What kind of nonsense is this," he bellowed. "Are you trying to kill me by feeding me these bizarre things? I put up with your madness for a few days, but no more! You can keep your cheese *koftas*, your carrot puddings and ground beef and onions wrapped up in bitter melons! From tomorrow, I'm going somewhere else for some real food. I know what you want. You think you can poison me by hiding the poison in this crazy food so you can get all my money!"

"But you don't have any money," Sajida said, trying to calm him down. But this remark only made him angrier and he walked out of their small house carrying on about the treachery of women. Needless to say, Sajida never again cooked new and interesting dishes for her husband. However, she didn't give up hope, and within two months was trying another way to capture his heart, a way highly recommended by Samina, Sarwat Jahan's youngest daughter, whose best friend had tried it with one hundred percent success. And after that, Hamida's daughter Sidra and Zammurd's sister-in-law had both gotten wonderful results with it.

"Before my friend tried this, her husband used to find her so repulsive that he left the room as soon as she came in," Samina had told Sajida. "The poor girl's face would fall like an overripe fruit. But now he's her slave and all she has to do is express a wish and it's taken care of. She says she's in the mood for a few *samosas* and he jumps up and rushes across the street to the vendor. Once she said she had a headache that could only be cured if he bought her an emerald ring. And guess what her husband did! He went out to the market that very instant to buy an emerald ring for his wife. And she isn't even passably good-looking. Far from it, *behen*. Her face is crooked and covered with zits. Not only that, she squints so no one can tell where she's looking. You have to be very careful when she's around."

Eagerly, Sajida begged Samina to tell her what to do.

"It's very simple. You have to make your husband drink some fluid that comes out of your body. Mother's milk works the best, but Zammurd's sister-in-law says urine is what produced results for her."

"That's not simple," Sajida said, deflated. "That's impossible." It was common knowledge that her husband was a glutton who was willing to eat or drink almost anything to fill his bottomless pit of a stomach. But this was ridiculous.

"He doesn't have to know about it, silly. You slip it in his food or add a few drops to his dessert."

That seemed doable. So for dinner that evening, Sajida carefully prepared Razzak's favorite dish—goat meat with onions—adding saffron flavorings and extra spices to camouflage the urine. Then she waited expectantly while Razzak consumed almost the entire pot without comment before demanding his after-dinner tea. When he showed no sign of affection even after he had his tea, she decided that the change of heart was not supposed to be obvious. Inside, he must be burning with love for me, she told herself.

"You know, I have a craving for some of the *samosas* that Baabaa sells down the street," she said, testing him.

"Do I look like a servant to you?" he thundered, putting a damper on her hopes. She should have known better than to think urine would work on someone like Razzak, who had no taste buds at all—just a huge stomach. Next time, she decided, she would try something more potent.

While she was mixing choice tea leaves with some of her menstrual blood as she had been instructed, her heart pounded with the anticipated euphoria of her husband's finding her irresistible. Please God, let this work. I will read the Qur'an an extra hour every night for the rest of my life. Just please, please, let me be successful this time. She had prayed with all her might.

After the leaves had dried in the sun, she once again took extra care in making Razzak's dinner, especially his after-dinner tea. He didn't notice any change in the taste, but he didn't turn into her love slave either.

The third and final foolproof method Sajida tried was a fiasco. And that was what was causing her extraordinary stress right now. "How was I supposed to know something like this would happen, *Aapa*?" she sobbed hysterically on Sadika's shoulder, her words harder to understand with every passing moment.

"Like what?" Sadika had spent the last hour listening to her little sister going on about all kinds of superstitious nonsense and her patience was wearing thin. When after another five minutes, she finally grasped the point of Sajida's story, it was so fantastic that she didn't know whether to laugh or cry.

A few days earlier, Sajida had paid a visit to Professor Khatib Sheikh in the neighboring town of Rawalpindi. It had taken her six months to gather enough money to pay the famous magician, astrologer and healer for his services. In actuality, Professor Khatib Sheikh was not a professor at all—he wasn't even a high school graduate. But his devout followers believed that he had found a direct connection to God Himself. His amulets could turn a heart of stone into hot runny wax; his enchanted stones could cure the worst terminal disease; he could grant sons to the most infertile of women, and the power of his special chants could enable students to get good grades without opening a book, to find a good paying job in any chosen Middle East country without even trying, and to put the coldest beloved at one's feet with minimal effort. Exactly what Sajida needed.

It had taken a lot of effort to get to the professor. She had had to pretend that a childhood friend was on her deathbed before Razzak would let her take the bus to Rawalpindi. But after a day filled with noisy buses, dusty, bumpy streets and small congested neighborhoods, she had accomplished her goal and returned home with the magical chant that the professor had concocted especially for her.

The magic words of the chant sounded like a string of non-sense sounds, but she committed them to memory as required, checking to make sure she had done it right, for the effective-ness of the magic depended on the accuracy of the chant. Also, since this was a one-shot deal—the professor had made it clear that if she needed to use it a second time, she would have to get a fresh version from him, at a discounted rate of course—Sajida had to make sure she got it right. Following the professor's in-structions, she had taken special care in cooking *kheer*, rice pud-ding, Razzak's favorite dessert, before chanting *atte shugame choom chana dere na tadare daani tarre tadare daani shaham shaharee shabree thass thadar thada* twenty times, and blowing thrice into the bubbling pudding pot.

After dinner she put the bowl of magic pudding in front of her husband. Then, to allow him to eat his dessert without dis-traction, she went off to wash dishes. That was when disaster struck. Her supposedly sick mother-in-law, who had been in bed in the neighboring room, had gotten a whiff of the *kheer*, her favorite dessert as well as his. She had gotten up and taken the bowl away from her son, saying, "I want to see if your wife can make good *kheer*," and gobbled down most of it.

When Sajida came back into the room and saw the almost-empty dessert bowl in her mother-in-law's hands, she realized at once what had happened and feared she was about to have a heart attack. How could you do this to me, you evil old woman? she wanted to scream. If it had been in her power, she would have shoved her hand down that old woman's throat into her stomach and pulled out the *kheer* she had plotted for and cooked so painstakingly for her husband. Her mother-in-law had de-stroyed her carefully laid—and expensive—plans.

It had taken a good couple of hours for Sajida's anger to cool. Then rage was replaced by sudden panic. The eater of the *kheer* was supposed to find her irresistible. She didn't know whether it was irrespective of sex—the professor hadn't said anything about that and of course she hadn't asked him—and how could she have foreseen such a calamity? Now she was terrified that her mother-in-law would find her irresistible. It would certainly have been helpful if her mother-in-law were to come to love her as a daughter, given the old woman's influence over her son and over household matters. But what was tormenting Sajida was the possibility that her mother-in-law would find her physically desirable in the way a man desires a woman.

Fueling her fear was the fact that her mother-in-law, who had never liked staying at Sajida's parents' house, had been doing so for the past week of her own free will, despite the uncomfortable cramped quarters. And completely contrary to her nature, she had never once complained or said a harsh word to Sajida. Just the opposite: she seemed to be trying to get into her daughter-in-law's good graces.

Something was very much amiss.

Sajida had heard about such women: they were called lesbians. And the thought that she might not only have inadvertently created one, but had made herself the object of this evil desire, was driving her crazy.

Of all the people in the world, it was her mother-in-law whom Sajida dreaded and despised the most. It would be too much to bear if instead of her husband, it was her mother-in-law who could not keep her hands off her. This, she thought, must be how lesbians started. What else but magic gone astray could make a woman have lustful feelings toward other women? It certainly wasn't natural.

Sajida spent her days minutely watching her mother-in-law for signs of lechery. Every time the toothless old lady smiled, which was a lot lately, Sajida would slide more deeply into depression. Where was the sour old grouch? What had happened to the constant taunting about Sajida's childlessness? What would be the next step—a lover's words? A lover's touch?

Sajida was at her wit's end and Sadika was her last resort. Maybe her older sister had learned something in the far-off magical land of America that could help her.

Thirty-six

SINCE THE SCENE in the living room on the day of Sadika's arrival, there had been no further mention of an engagement or a wedding. But Parveen Majid, the mother of Waseem, the neighborhood's most eligible bachelor, had been a frequent visitor at their house.

It was turning into a real annoyance for Sadika: Mrs. Majid showed up at all times of day, wreathed in smiles the size of the Grand Canyon as soon as she laid eyes on Sadika. Then would come the extravagant compliments: Sadika was more beautiful than a movie star, the woman who was a better housekeeper than Sadika did not exist, the family that had the good fortune to call Sadika their daughter would never want anything else.

The times when Mrs. Majid held up Sadika's face to the sun as though examining a rare jewel, were especially disconcerting. "What a lovely girl you are," she said. "And what a sense of style you have. We're so lucky to have you to set a good example for our daughters. Who would have thought that a shy bud could blossom into such a glorious flower?"

It was hard to believe that this was the same woman at whose insistence Sadika had bitten into rock-hard sohan halva, who had declared that she wouldn't buy a goat without making sure its teeth were strong, let alone choose a bride for a favorite son. I bet she wouldn't care today if I wore dentures on false gums in a fake jaw, Sadika thought.

Parveen Majid was not the only female trying to engage Sadika in conversation and paying her extravagant compliments. Many women, even Sajida's mother-in-law, were doing it.

All this reminded Sadika of that visit of Ashfaaq Beebee and her family. Like Haroon then, Sadika was being assiduously courted because she had come to represent opportunity, money-making potential and the magical green card. And just as Ashfaaq Beebee had then, Khanum was thoroughly enjoying the status that the eligibility of her offspring bestowed on her. Most evenings she swaggered from one gathering to another, dragging Sadika with her whenever she could. She talked end-lessly to hopeful mothers about the tremendous influence she had over her daughter, and how she might be induced to use that influence on behalf of someone's son. This was as good as having an eligible son to marry off.

Some of the people who were after Khanum for her daughter's hand were doctors who wanted to practice in America, and engineers who wanted to study there—people who at one time would not have considered having anything to do with Sadika or her family. Khanum was elated and amazed. Who would have thought that the child whom she considered the cause of most of her grief would become responsible for her achieving a position in society that until now she had only dreamt of? The same women with super-eligible sons who once had shunned her were now most eagerly seeking her out. She had suddenly become like a sister not only to Parveen Majid, but to a host of other women who had recently discovered what a wonderful person Khanum was and how much they enjoyed her company.

After two weeks, Sadika had had enough. There was obvi-ously nothing wrong with Khanum. The "she is dying" letter had been exactly what Michael had suspected it was: a ruse to bring Sadika back so she could be married off. Clearly, Khanum and Akbar Khan had mistaken her for the Sadika of three years ago who could be manipulated into doing whatever they wanted.

She no longer had a life in the neighborhood. As more of an honored guest than a family member, she was not allowed to work in the house any longer. All her school friends were mar-

ried and most had moved away with their husbands. Some still
in the area had their own lives to grapple with and, after once
or twice attempting uncomfortable conversation with Sadika,
had simply stopped making the effort.

The truth was that nobody could identify with her anymore,
not her family and not her friends. Their lives were very different, as were their perspectives and hopes for the future. They
didn't know what to say to her or even how to regard her: she
was not the excellent housekeeper or the bright student they
had always turned to for help. Nor was she a fallen woman.
The role of a highly eligible spinster was too new for anyone to
accept comfortably. Added to the unuttered apology they owed
her from three years before, an unbridgeable gulf existed between them.

The person who most resented the situation was Asghar
Khan. Wasn't Sadika the same female who had almost succeeded
in chopping off the proverbial family nose single-handedly?
Wasn't she the same daughter who Khanum used to wish had
died at birth? The same sister who had been a curse on the
entire family? How dare she strut about like some eligible bachelor! And worse, how dare everyone treat her like one while he,
the real eligible bachelor of the family, seemed to have been
forgotten. The time would soon come, he told himself, when
people would realize their mistake and shove Sadika back where
she belonged—into the gutter. Meanwhile, it was just really
exasperating that he was forced to watch people make fools of
themselves.

Mrs. Qureshi, for instance, had been furious when Asghar
had made known his desire to marry her daughter. She told
several people, "Does Asghar really think that I would even
consider a poor slob like him for a rich and educated girl like
my Shagufta? Why, he's not even a high school graduate, and
my daughter is in her second year of college. It would be different if he was independently wealthy, but who wants to get stuck
with a good-for-nothing-bum like him?"

And now that same Mrs. Qureshi was interested in Sadika for her son Shafique, an electrical engineer.

Sadika had a way of corrupting people's minds, that was for sure. Asghar couldn't wait for her to go back to America, out of their lives and minds—forever.

If Asghar had known how desperately Sadika wanted to leave, he would have been a happy young man. But no one knew that Sadika stayed only because Sajida had begged her to, that Sajida had convinced herself that the only thing holding her mother-in-law's lechery at bay was Sadika's presence. "Only God knows what horrible fate will befall me if you leave, *Aapa*," Sajida said. "This much I know—if that old woman lays a hand on me that way, I will surely die of disgust." But Sadika was beginning to realize that the longer she delayed her departure, the harder it would be to leave: Sajida was becoming too dependent on her, and her parents were developing unrealistic expectations. That was apparent from the way they talked about the future and acted toward Parveen Majid. Sadika had overheard Khanum ask Mrs. Majid whether they should consider renting a hall for the auspicious occasion.

Apart from everything else, Sadika couldn't believe how much she missed Michael. She worried that a physical barrier had been breached the day she left for Pakistan, and that things were not going to be the same as they had been before—that if their relationship became physical, they might discover that the feelings evoked that day had been a fluke, a one-time thing. She feared that their affinity was too good to be real, too good to be true. At the same time she was afraid that she might never be able to fully experience those feelings, that something unforeseen might happen, that somehow she might be trapped into staying, and lose Michael and the life that he offered. Whiling away time in Pakistan might tempt fate to wreck her future.

Suddenly Sadika could not wait to go back. Before she left, she had put Michael off when he pushed for a definite wedding date. Now she knew that she wanted to marry him as soon as possible. There was no reason to wait; there was no one in the world she would rather spend her life with. She had no desire to be the means of bringing someone to America to further his education or help him get a good job. She couldn't imagine being part of any family or household without Michael.

When Sadika told the family about her decision that very day at lunchtime, it caused bigger shock waves than she had anticipated. Khanum, who had decided that the time was now ripe to bring up again the subject of Sadika's upcoming engagement to Parveen Majid's son, immediately had one of the heart attacks she reserved for dire emergencies. Sajida burst into tears and ran sobbing from the table, followed by her mother-in-law. Akbar Khan and Asghar Khan looked on with rapt interest—the former wanting Sadika to stay to raise his status in the community, while the latter hoped just as fervently, and for the same reason, that she leave.

"How can you do this to me?" Khanum began, recovering with remarkable speed. Beating her chest with her fist, she became more and more worked up, raising her voice louder and thumping her chest harder with each question: "Me—who carried you in my womb for nine exhausting months? Me—who almost died giving birth to you? Me—who made your dowry? Me—who taught you cooking and sewing and cleaning so you could be a good wife and mother? Me—who guarded your reputation, and even had you sent to America so you could have a better life? Haven't you already caused your family enough grief? Now that you're in a position to remedy some of that, you're leaving? Like a jackal, you're tucking your tail between your legs and running away?" She screamed at Sadika, who, instead of cowering in fright as expected, was looking more grimly determined than ever. In fact, much to Khanum's consternation, the same sort of tirade that, no matter how unfair, would once have evoked an apology, now seemed to be acting as a catalyst.

Without a word, Sadika got up from her chair and left to go down the street to Zarreen's house where there was a phone. There she called the airport to reserve the earliest flight back to America. Then, thanking the intensely curious family for the use of their phone, she returned to her own stunned family, still seated around the small living room table.

"I am leaving for America tomorrow night," she announced calmly and sat down again.

As she was packing her suitcases later that afternoon, Sadika had only one regret: that she was leaving Zahra and Sajida behind.

Earlier, there had been tears in Zahra's eyes when Sadika had gone next door to say goodbye to her old friend. "Now I wish you had never come, even though you're my one true friend in the entire world," Zahra had said in a quavering voice, while her spice-scented embrace tightened. "Now it will be so much harder to accept my life the way it is without you."

The image of a sobbing Sajida running from the room also haunted Sadika; it broke her heart to realize that she was the cause of her beloved sister's tears. But again, there was nothing she could do. She couldn't spend her entire life trying to be a human shield for Sajida.

"*Aapa.*" Sajida's voice, vibrant with happiness, jolted Sadika from her guilty brooding. She turned to find her sister's face glowing with excitement.

"She cursed me, *Aapa,* and she hit me!"

"What?"

"She called me the tendons of an owl, the consumer of a bastard's food, and the daughter of a pig—just like she used to!"

"Who?"

"My mother-in-law, who else? And she said I had no brains or looks or money—just like she used to. She said she couldn't imagine why she let me marry her son—just the way she always talked! And then she said something she never said to me before: that she's glad I haven't given her a grandson, because any son of mine would look like a chimpanzee.

"The best part is that she yanked me by my hair, and tried to put my face in the water boiling on the stove. She never did that before. And look at my cheek! She hit me so hard I thought she knocked my teeth out. She hates me more than she did before, I'm sure of it. Isn't it wonderful?"

Sadika thought that if someone had told her two short minutes ago that she would feel happy that Sajida had been mistreated by anyone, she wouldn't have believed it. But here she was—not only happy to hear about Sajida's mother-in-law's cruelty, but incredibly relieved. A great burden had been lifted off her shoulders. Her presence would no longer be important to Sajida, whose life had now returned to normal, however abnormal that normal might seem to anyone else.

"Everything sounds well and good," she told Sajida, "but it doesn't explain why your mother-in-law was so nice to you. And what changed her mind now?"

"It was all because of you, *Aapa.*"

"Me? I never even met her before I came back. Why would she treat you any different because of me?"

"She had her eye on you for her younger son," Sajida said with a sigh. "And she was expecting to have me sweet-talk you into it. Now that she knows there's no chance of that happening, she's her old self again."

After a moment's reflection, Sajida said, "You know, if you had decided to go back sooner, my mother-in-law would have started acting her usual self much earlier. So even though you thought you were doing me a favor by staying here longer than you wanted, you were really not doing me a favor at all."

thirty-seven

A MONTH AFTER Sadika returned from Pakistan, she started a part-time job with what the foreign students called the "green card company," because it hired foreigners at low wages in exchange for sponsoring them for a green card. Sadika and Michael decided to marry as soon as possible because their relationship was too stressful. No matter how hard she tried, Sadika could not help feeling she had compromised her "white linen" status every time Michael touched her, and Michael of course wanted their relationship to be consummated. They tentatively decided on a spring wedding, about six months ahead, when both would have graduated and with luck would have found gainful employment.

To say that they had their work cut out for them was an understatement. Both sets of families and friends had to be notified. And then there was the wedding itself. Six months was a short time to plan even an ordinary wedding and, given the cultural and religious differences of the bride and groom, this wedding would not be an ordinary one. Both Michael and Sadika decided that introducing Sadika to Michael's family was the logical first step. Since it was not possible—or even desirable—at this stage for Michael to meet with Sadika's family, they would have to be told by mail.

Sadika was nervous about making a good impression on Michael's parents, but Michael said repeatedly that accepting her was their problem: "We can't be expected to live our lives to suit them."

She wasn't sure whether Michael's attitude reflected his background or his personality. All she knew was that even though rationally she agreed with everything he said, emotionally she couldn't accept it because in her country family ties and involvements were simultaneously revered and despised. What relatives thought, especially a husband's relatives, was of earth-shattering importance.

She had heard somewhere that the language of a culture was a reflection of its values, that whatever was important to a people could be determined by studying its language. The reason why Eskimos, for example, had numerous words for "snow" was that snow was critical to their survival. Now she understood why generic English words like "uncle" and "grandparent" did not exist in her native Urdu. In English there was apparently no need to employ more specific words for family relationships. In the Pakistani culture these relationships represented unbreakable chains, while in the West they were often strings that could be cut with some degree of impunity.

Gradually, Sadika had gotten used to these generally descriptive names for relatives, but when she had first heard them she had found them irritating. What did someone mean when he talked about his uncle? Was he referring to his *chacha*, his father's younger brother, his *taayaa*, his father's older brother, or his *maamoon*, his mother's brother? When he said "sister-in-law," did he mean *jithaani*, a husband's older brother's wife; *devraani*, the husband's younger brother's wife; *nand*, the husband's sister; *bhabi*, the brother's wife, or *saali*, the wife's sister? When someone went to visit her grandfather, did she go to her mother's father, *naanaa*, or her father's father, *daadaa*?

While she had nightmares about Michael's *khala*, his mother's sister, or his father's older brother, *taayaa*, disowning him, Michael was incredulous at the very idea that his aunts or uncles, or anyone outside his immediate family, might take it upon him- or herself to raise an objection to their marriage.

"Why would Uncle Dan and Aunt Abby be upset?" he asked, looking at her as though she had lost her mind. "I don't really mean anything to them. The only reason they might feel an-

noyed would be because they'd have to take the trouble to go
out and buy a suitable wedding present."

What Sadika found even more amazing was that Michael
didn't seem more concerned about his family's response: if worse
came to worse, he said, he would lead his own life and they
would lead theirs, which they did anyway, apart from major
holidays and some family occasions. "We're the ideal American
family in that sense," Michael had told Sadika. "Everyone is
independent; no one relies on any other family member for personal fulfillment."

Sadika was thanking her lucky stars that they were not in
Pakistan where not only her family but the entire neighborhood
would have been having fits and coming up with ways to punish them for daring to want to marry each other. "How can she
be so selfish?" she could imagine people asking. "Doesn't she
know that her actions will reflect on all the women in her family? Anyone would think twice before proposing marriage to a
girl in a family with a female like Sadika who has so few morals
that she not only became involved with a man from a different
faith and a different culture altogether, but ended up marrying
him. How can Sadika want children who are bastards in the
eyes of her faith and her people?"

As the days passed, Sadika's apprehensions lessened. Michael
kept telling her that only the two of them mattered, that what
people might say shouldn't bother her. "People's reaction might
surprise you," he said. "Some might react strongly at first, but
chances are they'll settle down once they realize they can't do
anything about it."

Maybe he's right, Sadika thought. Khanum will be violently
opposed to the match, but she might be happy after she's had
time to think about it. After all, her daughter will be getting
married without her having to spend a single rupee; she won't
even have to worry about a dowry. And what she saved up
could easily be sold or bartered and she could keep the money
or whatever she gets. Michael might even turn out to be her

ideal son-in-law: because he was American and was far away, Khanum would be free to fabricate things about him to her heart's content. Her American connection, so dear to her heart, would be strengthened and more important than ever.

A week later, Sadika and Michael spent the day with his parents at their house in an upper-income suburb in eastern New Jersey. Michael had told them over the phone that he was planning to come down for a visit and bringing along someone very special. "We'd love to meet this special friend of yours," his mother had said, adding in a light, teasing tone, "Exactly how special is this special friend?"

"You'll see," Michael responded. "Pretty special."

She was happy to hear that. Michael's younger brother had taken the plunge and his sister was in the process of taking it, while Michael had apparently not even gotten his feet wet. His mother worried that if he stayed a bachelor much longer, there might not be any suitable girl left for him to marry. Most of her friends' daughters were marrying at an alarming rate and the available pool was shrinking.

The Glenns were taken aback when Michael came in with Sadika. Who exactly, they wondered nervously, was this exotic creature, and what was her relationship with Michael? Maybe, they hoped, she was some foreign student whom he had taken under his wing. Michael was soft-hearted; his mother remembered how he had gone out of his way to protect Danny Bugleo from the class bully in the sixth grade. Andrew and Ellen Glenn, accustomed to dealing with awkward social situations, greeted Sadika warmly, and everyone passed a pleasant afternoon talking about college life and the state of the world in general. Ellen decided that Sadika was really a sweet, harmless little thing— polite, shy, timid as a mouse, and probably just someone whom Michael had decided needed a friend in her new surroundings.

Feeling well disposed toward her guest, Ellen took her through the house, starting in the family room where she pointed out some country antiques that she had inherited from her mother; she liked them, although she knew they didn't fit into the relatively austere modern interior that she had chosen as a good background for her abstract painting collection. These must be her prized possessions, Sadika thought, amazed. Most things like this were still in use in Pakistan and if someone offered to replace them with something up-to-date, the owners would have been overjoyed.

There was a lantern like those in constant use in Gulmushk Mohalla when the electricity went out; and a wooden commode, serving here as a planter, was the same kind still being used by a privileged few in the village of Jogiapur. In fact, when Farooq Mamoon's mother-in-law had become bedridden, he had sent for a similar contraption from the city and only the invalid was allowed to use it. Anyone unable to resist the temptation received a severe scolding from the old lady herself. "This society is doomed," she would mourn in her plaintive voice. "Nobody has any regard for the elderly. You mark my words—these bastards are going to roast in hell." She predicted this with conviction, not caring that the people who would suffer this horrible fate were her own flesh and blood.

Ellen led Sadika through rooms hung with abstract paintings, explaining that she loved these pieces and enjoyed supporting young artists who were not afraid to experiment with fresh concepts. To Sadika, these paintings made even less sense than the antiques, which at least had at one time performed some useful function, and which she could understand had nostalgic value. The paintings looked to her like odds and ends glued together, wild daubs without any point.

"Modern art is the most irrational thing in the world." Sadika could still hear her Pakistani art teacher's declaration. Miss Rahman wasn't really an art teacher; she was an extracurricular teacher, which meant that all nonacademic activities were her province. "Be especially suspicious of modern paintings," Miss Rahman had said. "What looks like a pineapple could very well be a voluptuous woman, and what seems to be a field of sugarcane could turn out to be a bunch of people worshipping idols."

"What do you think of this?" Ellen asked. Sadika looked intently at a mass of wires, cardboard and metal that resembled an imploding robot. "It's very interesting," she said finally.

"And guess what this is?" Ellen pointed to a painting of what looked to Sadika like the contents of a garbage can.

"A lot of things really," began Sadika lamely.

"You're absolutely right," Ellen said, rather surprised. "It does represent a lot of things—complicated industrial society."

The house had recently been remodeled and Ellen was particularly proud of her closets. "Anything I haven't worn for the past six months I give to charity," she said, opening the door to the large walk-in closet in the master bedroom.

"It's beautiful," Sadika exclaimed, thinking that this closet was bigger than her bedroom.

"Our Amy's a pack rat," Ellen continued. "She hordes everything. I'm sure she never wears half the clothes in her closet. I've tried to get her to clean it out, but it's no use."

Sadika had been raised to believe that the ability to save everything was one of the greatest virtues a woman could have. That was certainly one of her mother's biggest virtues, since it helped a small income go a long way. Ellen was happy to get rid of things; Khanum was happy whenever she managed to produce a long-forgotten item from the bottom of some battered suitcase or box, just when it was needed.

"Remember this?" Khanum would triumphantly hold something up. "How many of you know what it is?" If everyone was at a loss, she would be delighted. After all, it was this ability to save that had earned her the label *sughar*, good housewife, and enabled her to come up with decent dowries for all three of her girls on Akbar Khan's meager salary.

"We give up. What is it?"

"This is the cellophane bag the living-room furniture came in," she would say. Or "This is the fabric Maanjee gave me when Asghar was born." Or "This is the shirt I wore before I got pregnant with Sadika. It will go very well with Zafary's blue *shalwar* now."

Nothing was ever thrown away in Khanum's household: old containers, magazines, empty jute sacks, scraps of fabric and whatever else crossed the threshold of that tiny house was carefully saved on the chance that it might be useful some day. And it generally was.

Khanum would be aghast at the idea of getting rid of something just because it hadn't been used in the past six months. Sadika's old coat had been handed down to Zafary and then to Sajida. When it became too worn to serve as a coat any longer, Khanum had taken out her old Singer sewing machine and turned it into a vest and socks for Asghar. Almost all their clothes were hand-me-downs. A new article of clothing was a rarity, a cause for jubilation. Khanum's old clothes were worn by Sadika, Zafary and Sajida in turn. By the time they reached Sajida, the cloth was generally threadbare and easily torn. "These girls are more like ponies than human females," Khanum would grumble. "Only God knows why they're always galloping about and doing wild things."

If Asghar needed more than Akbar Khan's old clothes, his new ones were made big so that he would not outgrow them quickly. Consequently, Asghar's shorts reached nearly to his ankles, while his pant legs, folded several times, looked as though hoops were sewn into their ends. Each year as Asghar grew taller, the folds were let out a little, but the let-out sections, less faded than the rest of the pants, looked like extensions with somewhat smaller hoops sewn at the ends.

When at last they sat down to dinner, Sadika breathed a sigh of relief, only to discover that she had relaxed too soon. Her place was set with several knives, forks and spoons, as well as four different plates and three glasses. Am I expected to use all these things? she thought to herself. Or are they here just for show? In Gulmushk Mohalla, it was common practice for women to wear all the jewelry they owned and even borrow some if they wanted to impress people on special occasions. But the Glenns could have had no desire or need to impress her.

Maybe the extra plates and glasses are in case I break any, thought Sadika. After all, they weren't like Khanum's sturdy metal dishes and glasses. Those wouldn't break if a bullock-cart ran over them. Maybe with this flimsy stuff you needed plenty of extras so as not to embarrass the guests if they broke something. And of course when you have so much china, you have to have enough silverware to go with it.

Fortunately, Sadika decided to watch the others and do as they did. During the entire meal she did not have a single awkward moment that anyone could notice. She was so preoccupied with the table settings that she didn't join in the conversation and she was too nervous to eat much. She was almost as hungry at the end of the meal as she had been at the beginning, but that was a small price to pay for coping with all those dishes.

We're so different in every way. How will this ever work? Sadika wondered later in the evening, as she sat in the family room quietly sipping a cup of hot chocolate with Michael and the Glenns in front of a roaring fire. Marriages were hard enough to work out when two people had similar backgrounds. With so many differences, this marriage would be impossible. Wouldn't it?

At that moment she looked up and her eyes met Michael's. All her doubts vanished like soap bubbles under a shower. As always, his expression was gentle and full of understanding and humor. Our marriage will be more than all right, she thought with sudden conviction. It will be perfect. How can it be anything else when Michael is such a decent, sincere and wonderful human being? He always seems to make me feel good about myself and at peace with the world. She smiled at him and his blue eyes carried a message of intimacy as exciting as it was disturbing.

Ellen, on whom this little exchange was not lost, suddenly felt sick. This couldn't be happening, she thought. How could Michael consider a serious relationship with someone like this, a nobody from God knows where who had been doing God knows what with God knows whom? She hadn't believed Amy's story that Michael was interested in a Muslim girl from, of all places, Pakistan. Surely Michael wouldn't disappoint his mother in this, as he had in almost everything else.

She went on being pleasant to Sadika, knowing that warning young people against something, especially relationships, only made them more determined. Like a dam on a river, an obstruction increases the water's force.

Michael and Sadika were satisfied that the meeting with Michael's parents had been a success. And Sadika had mailed two letters earlier that week—a short one to Akbar Khan and Khanum, informing them of her decision to marry an American with a different faith and cultural background, and asking for their understanding and blessing, if possible. And a longer one to Zahra telling her about the wonderful man she had met, how she was looking forward to spending the rest of her life with him and how she hoped to introduce him to Zahra one day.

Although they were not religious, the Glenns always celebrated the Christmas holidays, a time when the family would be together. Since the children had grown up, conflicting schedules often prevented real family gatherings. But this year Michael's brother Steve and his wife Caroline, Michael's sister Amy and her fiancé Richard, were all going to be at the Glenn house on Christmas Day. And Michael, who wanted them all to get to know Sadika in the warm, cheerful holiday atmosphere without any tension, had decided to postpone telling his family about their plans till after the first of the year.

"Christmas brings out the best in all of us. What better time to forge new bonds and foster new relationships?" he said to Sadika. Then, catching himself, he added sheepishly, "I know you don't celebrate Christmas. We always have, even though it doesn't have much religious significance for us. How about you? Do you mind celebrating Christmas?"

She smiled and shrugged—her standard response to questions about the holiday season.

thirty-eight

THE FIVE BATCHES of holiday cookies Sadika had baked were neatly packed in the trunk of Michael's car with the wrapped gifts and luggage.

Michael was excited at the prospect of the first real family holiday celebration in four years. He was confident that everyone would fall under Sadika's spell; he was sure they wouldn't be able to resist her. It wasn't often that one encountered someone at once so beautiful, so innocent, so mature and so inexperienced. One shy look from those chocolate warm-honey eyes should be all it would take. And Sadika would like his family too, when she had the chance to get to know them.

"They're brilliant," Michael told her proudly for the umpteenth time. "And good-looking too!" As often before, she smiled while her heart ached for him, because she could tell that he didn't regard himself in the same light. They were alike in so many ways, she and Michael. Both came from families that considered them to be less than good enough. Hers, because of her sex and her inability to make a good match, and his, because he was not an outstanding student or good at sports. She gathered from things Michael said that he had been considered below par for most of his life. His mother and father had been bitterly disappointed with his grades, especially since all their friends' kids seemed headed for Ivy League schools.

When he was in the fifth grade, his parents had him tested, and it was found that he had a learning disability. They gave him special tutoring and occupational therapy and he was able to work around his disability, trying his level best not to disappoint his family academically or otherwise. But his younger

brother and sister did not have his problems, and a pattern had
been set. Michael never received the respect and high expectations usually accorded the firstborn. Sadika suspected that their
engagement would deliver the coup de grace to his standing in
the family. Despite the fact that Ellen often told her children,
"All we want is for you to be happy," what she really meant—
possibly without realizing it—was that they could be happy only
if they lived lives and found spouses acceptable by her standards.

Ellen had often imagined saying to her friends, "Michael
has met this really nice girl at school. She's from an interesting
family, you might have heard of them. . . . The kids are in love
and they want to get married as soon as possible, so I've started
to help them plan their wedding. Nothing elaborate—just her
family and ours and a few close friends, so we can all get to
know each other. They're wonderful people, you know; they
haven't let their money go to their heads."

Now Michael was going to destroy this fantasy forever.

If Sadika had not spent her life keeping her opinions to herself, the holiday weekend would have been a disaster, even on
the surface. But her restraint, coupled with the good manners
and gracious attitude that the Glenns displayed no matter what,
made everything go smoothly and look like the smashing success that it was not.

The decorations and lights were beautiful; the Christmas
tree with its crystal ornaments exquisite; the turkey with all its
trimmings delicious; the thoughtfully chosen gifts impressive in
their red and green wrappings. But all through the festive meals
and the exchange of gifts ran an undercurrent of hostility.
Michael's family believed that he had settled for Sadika because
he was too insecure to try to attract someone more appropriate—that was apparent when Steven and Amy joked about his
always being a "laggard in love." Something, they said laughing, had been wrong with every one of his girlfriends; he had

always had a penchant for attracting deprived females. These remarks, supposedly intended as good-natured family banter, raised Sadika's blood pressure. She had been considered a lesser human being in one culture and was outraged to encounter this denigration in another. She couldn't bear the thought that Michael could be looked down on because of his association with her; she had worked too hard and come too far for that to happen. But she didn't know how to put a stop to it.

Her attempts to make conversation was met with silence or a polite snub. She thought that the family seemed almost offended when she tried to talk about the holiday celebrations she had diligently studied to work up conversation for this occasion. When Caroline commented that it was interesting that Christmas and Hanukkah were celebrated at about the same time, Sadika remarked that she had read that Hanukkah was almost prevented by the rabbis from becoming a religious festival because it commemorated the Maccabeean War where human blood was shed. "God said, 'Thou shalt not kill,' in the Ten Commandments. So there are no references to war in the celebration."

After a pause, somebody changed the subject.

When Steve talked about how he loved to see Christmas trees light up everywhere, Sadika said, "They put up a very special one in our college this year. It's really tall and the ornaments are beautiful. Even students have gotten into the spirit of things and some of them put up small trees in their dorms."

"That sounds very nice," Steve said dismissively, and changed the subject.

Trying again later, she mentioned to Ellen that she found the tradition of the Christmas tree interesting, that she had read that the tradition had actually started in Germany or somewhere in Northern Europe as a pagan festival. Ellen expressed happy surprise that Sadika knew so much about the holidays, and changed the subject. Sadika gave up, wondering whether they resented her enthusiasm for what they may have thought were holidays that belonged to them. Maybe they thought she was trying to pass herself off as something she wasn't.

That was not the only thing that made her uncomfortable: Amy and Richard couldn't seem to keep their hands off each other. While to everyone else this was apparently accepted as the predictable behavior of an engaged couple, to Sadika it was a source of amazement that a daughter would think nothing of indulging in physical intimacy right in front of her parents. Khanum would have suffered a heart attack, Akbar Khan, despite his interest in steamy movies, would have reached for a shotgun, and a couple acting that way on the streets of Pakistan would have been arrested.

She wondered whether people realized that letting consenting adults do whatever they pleased short of sexual intercourse, in plain view of everyone, was unacceptable in some cultures. It certainly was unacceptable where she came from. A brother with any sense of family honor would have chopped off his sister's feet for what Amy was doing to Richard with hers underneath the dinner table. They would never turn a blind eye as Michael and Steven did.

thirty-nine

As they rode home, by unspoken mutual consent neither Michael or Sadika mentioned their apprehensions. Instead, they talked about how great the food was and how well everything had gone off. Sadika was going to have a tough act to follow.

"When are Amy and Richard getting married?" she asked.

"They haven't decided." He added with a laugh, "Looking at the way things are with those two, I hope it's soon."

"I hope so too," Sadika said, and lapsed into silence. She was too uncomfortable about her future sister-in-law's behavior to discuss it with anyone, especially with Michael. For the rest of the drive home, Sadika pretended to sleep, but her mind was abuzz with conflicting thoughts about the behavior of engaged couples. She felt almost ashamed that she was more worried about physical intimacy than about profound issues like marrying a man with a different faith, being part of a biracial couple and bringing mixed-race children into the world.

She thought back to the previous Tuesday when she had gone to visit Ashfaaq Beebee to tell her about the upcoming wedding. For a few moments, her aunt had been in shock. Then she asked about Michael, his background, family, and future prospects. After learning that he was a handsome, eligible young man with bright prospects from a good moneyed family, she had paused again before she rallied and said, "Right now, love has blinded you. Later on, when it's time to raise children, you'll realize how inappropriate this match is. Your kids will be without a race, religion, or even a country! And they'll curse you for bringing them into this world. You mark my words."

Ignoring this outburst, Sadika changed the subject by inquiring about Zafary, who was not at home and who had irritated her aunt by taking a part-time job and issuing all kinds of threats and ultimatums. "I'll take the children and leave," Zafary had said just recently. "And I'll sue your entire family unless they start showing me some respect."

Ashfaaq Beebee was beginning to wish she had never come to live in America where young minds were inexorably and inevitably poisoned beyond redemption.

Her aunt was not the only one who commented on the insurmountable differences between the two faiths and cultures. Letters from traumatized relatives and friends were trickling in from Pakistan, and, with the exception of Zahra's, they all contained veiled and not-so-veiled references to the dire consequences faced by people who married outside their own kind. There were hair-raising stories of how these couples, shunned by society, reached the point where they could not stand the sight of each other. There were tales of children who had totally disowned their parents, or—worse—had done bodily harm to family members because of confusion about their identity and heritage.

It was strange. What so concerned others didn't bother Sadika at all. She wanted to hold Michael's baby in her arms. Apart from the fact that their children were bound to be healthier, stronger and more beautiful than others, they would be truly cosmopolitan because their background would include two major world religions. They might understand better than anyone the true essence of a Higher Being, since they could pray to God Almighty in different ways. Hadn't she heard somewhere that the more ways of communication you find with someone, the better and richer the relationship? Why wouldn't that apply to God?

And being from two cultures might not be the obstacle that people made it out to be. Multiculturalism was getting to be quite the rage in America, while in Pakistan, since the invasion of Western civilization via television and satellite, mixed-race individuals were coming to be considered a "beautiful amalgam of East and West."

So Sadika's worries had nothing to do with culture or children. They had to do with her feelings of inadequacy and confusion about physical intimacy. She was having a hard time overcoming the attitudes, expectations and behavior of her native country, where physical relations without marriage were unthinkable. And since gender separation was a way of life, by the time they grew up young people had fantasized so much about the opposite sex and were so enthralled at the idea of being permitted to engage in a physical relationship, that marriage seemed the culmination of all their dreams. Sadika knew that, contrary to the American image of arranged marriages, the romantic excitement surrounding these marriages in Pakistan was ten times more potent than anything Western brides and grooms might experience.

"Was the bride a true innocent?" and "Was the groom man enough to do the deed?" were questions of earthshaking importance to be answered on the wedding night, the night when the bride and groom were so fatigued and stressed-out from the ceremonies that it was a miracle they were not carried to bed on a stretcher; the night on which the probability of their indulging in orgiastic behavior was about as great as that of someone participating in the Boston Marathon immediately following open-heart surgery.

But in America, young people had no qualms about engaging in sexual activity before marriage. Couples who had not yet consummated their relationship—or had they?—looked at each other like starving dogs eyeing a sirloin steak. Amy and Richard, for instance. And they were not the first Sadika had seen behaving like that. At college she had found disturbing the way couples seemed oblivious to everyone and everything but themselves. They shouldn't be left alone, she often said to herself. What if they get completely carried away and do irreparable damage to each other?

When she had first mentioned her fear to Michael, he laughed and said, "Surely you can remember the way it was the first time you had the hots for someone?"

"No, I don't, because I never have," she replied.

As soon as the implication of her words sank in, he became serious and asked point-blank what he had always suspected: "You're a virgin, aren't you?" Whispering the word.

"Yes," she whispered back.

After that, he treated her with extra consideration, walking on eggshells around her as though casual responses would somehow damage her virginity. Maybe he has confused virginity with an inflamed appendix, Sadika thought in exasperation, ready to burst and spread its poison in the body at the slightest provocation. That night she lay awake for a long time, perplexed. What was it about virginity that made people from different cultures react to it so differently? In Pakistan, it was a commodity precious enough to die for. Its absence turned a woman into a liability, and no self-respecting man could possibly marry her. In America, people acted as if it was no big deal, but Michael's reaction seemed to suggest that it might be.

Maybe, she thought, Pakistanis knew something that Americans didn't. Maybe when a woman's hymen broke, it uncorked the genie from the bottle. Everyone knew that a genie couldn't be put back into the bottle. Even in America everyone knew the story of Aladdin.

Or maybe it had nothing to do with a genie. Maybe it was something like "imprinting" that she had read about in Psychology 101. Just as ducklings took anything they first laid eyes on to be their mother—a duck, a person, or a ticking clock— perhaps a woman's insides were somehow imprinted by the first male to penetrate her, making her his for all eternity in some mysterious way.

The genie theory, however, was more consistent than imprinting. Zahra had once told Sadika about it when she was still a child. "A woman's honor is enclosed in the tiny space in her vagina," Zahra had said. "If it's breached by the wrong man, it flies out of her and can never be recaptured. But if the right man enters that sanctuary, the honor not only stays put, it gets bigger."

"Why did God stuff all the honor in one little space?" Sadika had asked.

"He's God. He can do what He wants. Who are we to question Him?"

"Where's the man's honor housed?" Sadika had asked hesitantly; she did not want Zahra, her only fountain of wisdom, to be upset with her, and she had noticed that Zahra tended to become irritated if she was asked questions for which she had no ready answers. But in this case Zahra replied without hesitation.

"Why do men need honor? They're not the ones who have to keep their reputations pure as driven snow, they don't have to hope and wait for someone to offer them marriage. All these difficult things are reserved for women." As an afterthought she added, "Maybe men are lucky because they don't have a cavity in their bodies big enough to hold honor."

"They have belly-buttons," Sadika said.

"Not big enough," was the emphatic reply. "God must have decided that instead of giving them such a tiny bit of honor, He wouldn't bother to give them any."

Sadika had resentfully accepted that answer. It made perfect sense: she had heard scores of times of a woman losing her honor at the hands of a man, but never the other way round. But she couldn't help wondering why God hadn't come up with a fairer and more sensible way to hand out something as valuable as honor. He could have thought about chemistry classes. Something like a litmus paper test would have worked fine: why couldn't a simple change of color signal honor or dishonor? Like when a stick of litmus paper was put into a test tube, the honorable person would turn blue and the dishonorable one green or vice versa.

Even creating a separate honor-filled organ inside each human being would have made more sense. The honorarium would be filled with the appropriate level of honor just as the brain was filled with thoughts, the heart with feelings, and the stomach with food. Then, whether it was a man or a woman who became dishonorable, the honorarium could burst open like a rotten appendix, and release its poison into the body.

But for some reason, God in His wisdom hadn't done either of these things. Instead, to make matters worse, He had really been partial to men and very mean to women by installing a messed-up system of rewards and punishment. Otherwise, what kind of reward for taking good care of one's honor was physical pain? If a business used incentives like that for their workers, they would surely go under fast. If staying pure for one's mate was such a wonderful thing, shouldn't the result have been pleasure and not pain? Shouldn't the "honorable woman scream" that Zahra told her about have been a shriek of extreme pleasure instead of pain?

Or since disease was the price of promiscuity, why hadn't God put some kind of seal on a man's organ—like the protective covering on a medicine bottle—that had to be broken open before that body part could be used for sex the first time. Broken accompanied by burning pain, of course. That way, not only would the sexes have been able to identify with each other better, but women in general would have felt a lot less like victims.

She wondered now about women like Zahra, who were going to go through life with no sex at all. What became of their honor? Did it improve in quality with time like some vintage wine? Or did it decay with age, like eggs in an ovary?

forty

As DAYS PASSED, and the heat in Michael's eyes grew in intensity, Sadika's fears and insecurities increased. She had nightmares, not only about her body accidentally giving up her honor instead of keeping it, but about the mechanics of sex. What if her insides were not velvety but coarse as burlap? What if only gently reared people had velvet-lined insides, and working-class people like herself, with rough skin, had a similar texture inside? And what if her responses were wrong—no hard nipples, no shallow gasping, no wet private parts? What would Michael do? What would he think? Could she successfully fake those things?

Michael was certainly aware of Sadika's fear of intimacy. Every time he held her too close, or caressed her too intimately, she became tense. So he always held back from showing her more than friendly affection. But he longed for the day when he would feel free to explore with her a whole treasure trove of forbidden emotions and pleasures. And it would be as much for his benefit as for hers.

Before Sadika, Michael had never understood what the hoopla was about: his few sexual encounters had not come close to satisfying his hyped-up expectations. He had wondered whether he was actually capable of experiencing the deep thrills that he kept hearing about. People talked about fireworks and the Fourth of July, but he had experienced, at best, a couple of lousy firecrackers. Maybe it was because he hadn't really cared much for his partners, or because he had always felt that he was competing with some unknown person and was going to be found wanting. Many of his friends were on their second or third serious relationship, and he was beginning to feel like a freak.

With Sadika, he knew it would be different. For one thing, she would be happy with his sexual prowess as long as the experience wasn't too unpleasant, since she was clearly expecting something really dreadful. For another, his confidence level was high because he knew he wasn't going be compared to another lover. If his performance was mediocre, Sadika wouldn't know it. There was a lot to be said for virginity.

But basically the two of them were just plain good together. Whether they were sitting and reading or taking a walk or just talking, they enjoyed each other's company. How could more of the same be any less?

He determined that he would make it a sensual feast, a twelve-course banquet. By the time they finished, he promised himself, her sensual circuits would be on overload, and she would never again look at him with fear in her eyes.

forty-one

SADIKA WAS SURE that despite all her apprehensions, fear of physical intimacy was something that time would remedy. What time might not be able to remedy, at least without some help, was the Glenn family's attitude toward Michael. She deeply resented that. How dared they not value him as they should? And how dared they regard him as going downhill further because he was engaged to her? Somehow she had to make people value Michael as the superb catch that he was and understand that their relationship was enviable.

She knew it could be done. Khanum had done it all her life—instinctively recognizing that fabrications could be as effective as facts if they were reasonably consistent and resisted exposure. Even though there had always been doubters over the years, most people had bought at least part of Khanum's story about her impressive background and her important American connection.

In Sadika's eyes, Michael was a knight in shining armor. It was nobody's fault that God hadn't granted him academic brilliance, taut muscles and a full head of hair. He was a beautiful rose disguised as a cauliflower. But thanks to marketing skills learnt from her mother—a born marketer—the world was going to recognize his true worth. Sometime in the future, after they had become a family, Sadika intended to devise a marketing plan to refurbish Michael's image in the eyes of the Glenns, just as she had created the right image for a new soft drink for a project in Marketing 101.

She thought that if she carefully studied her target market—in this case, Michael's family—she could devise a strategy that would convince them that he was the personification of drive, virility and financial success. By the time she was done, Michael would not need an Ivy League degree, a trim, hard body or a head of hair like the Amazon forest to win acceptance. And of course she and Michael would lead a life filled with romance, gift-giving and protracted, mind-numbingly passionate love-making.

She didn't care much for what passed as romance in American culture. If Michael had bought her a sexy negligée or underwear, she would have considered it in extremely poor taste. But she could give the impression that he had bought her those things and that he took her to expensive restaurants where he kept telling her between courses that he loved her—never mind that secretly she considered eating in restaurants a reflection on her cooking, and constant love talk less satisfying than companionable silence. She would tell everyone that Michael sent her masses of flowers, while privately she looked on flowers as useless gifts that made a lot of extra work and wondered why people didn't bring their lovers something that made more sense, like a leg of lamb.

Who could challenge her? Unless someone had been following them around with an invisible video camera—no one!

Michael was her hero. And she planned to refurbish his image so that everyone would think so too, instead of saying he was a geek or a nerd. When she had first heard Amy call him a geek, Sadika had thought she meant a Greek—like a Greek god. But when others had delighted in speedily correcting her, her heart had ached for Michael.

Once they were married, no one would have the nerve to call him as a geek again—not if she could help it. Because they were going to live like royalty. If Khanum could make dowries for three girls and maintain their tiny household on what Akbar Khan brought home, Sadika did not see why she should have a problem creating a splendid life for herself and Michael on what they could earn together. And if a near-illiterate like Khanum could make people believe that she was an American spy with access to governmental secrets, how hard could it be to make people believe that Michael had a brilliant career going?

In addition to revising Michael's image, Sadika had to decide how she was going to celebrate the traditional American holidays after her marriage. She didn't really enjoy them—as Michael and so many others had appropriately pointed out, they weren't her holidays. Or were they?

She had felt in the past that she could enjoy Christmas because she didn't have to do anything while others were killing themselves shopping and hanging decorations. But now that feeling was gone. It had been highly presumptuous on the part of Michael's family, and even of Michael, to think that she didn't celebrate that holiday, even though she didn't.

Whenever she thought of the wonderful sense of self-worth and self-esteem that she had developed since she had come to America, she felt fiercely possessive of everything American. This great country, with its tradition of personal freedom and autonomy, had given her so much that she wanted to embrace everything about it. Or at least to have the choice of embracing everything about it—including Christmas, Thanksgiving and the Fourth of July.

Where did it say that she had to belong to a certain religion or have a certain ethnic background to join in holiday festivities? Celebrations and traditions of a country were an integral part of the culture of that country. And as of now, all American celebrations were hers since America was hers. It was true that at this point American traditions were not part of her cultural heritage, but they would certainly be part of her children's heritage, and now was the time to start joining her new country's culture so that the next generation would have a head start. No one, she felt, should question her or condescend to her if she served a big Thanksgiving dinner, and she shouldn't feel a need to apologize or explain.

America was a melting pot in which she was one of the ingredients. As such, it was her obligation as an American to contribute her unique essence. From now on, she would try and celebrate all American holidays and all Pakistani ones as well. In fact, since America was made up of people from all over the world, she would pick and choose the celebrations that she liked from each part of the world. From Pakistan, she would choose the two Eids, major religious occasions with traditional foods, rituals and festive clothes, and Basant, the festival that heralded the coming of spring.

She had always loved Basant, but as a female she had never been able to participate in it fully. Now she could celebrate it to her heart's content. Just as she had seen men and boys do in Pakistan, she would fly the colorful kites with the string made stiff with starch and water and covered with powdered glass. In her new country, she would be the one jumping up and down with excitement—instead of Asghar or some other male—when her kite string with its sharp edge cut down the most kites in a contest. She would be the one climbing the roof of the tallest house so her kite could reach the best air current, while others enviously watched her graceful kite seem to come alive, fluttering, dancing and swaying in the wind, jerking now and then when she pulled the string.

From the Christian tradition, she would have a Christmas tree and roast turkey with cranberry sauce and plum pudding, and from Jewish culture a Hanukkah menorah signifying light and truth. And since life in America would not be complete without celebrating Thanksgiving, Halloween and New Year's Eve, she would celebrate them with gusto.

If she felt up to it, she would even make it a family tradition to celebrate festivals that she found fascinating, like the Hindu fire festival of Holi with its red-colored water-squirting, and the harvest moon celebration of Kwanzaa. And of course, any children belonging to her and Michael would love, if given the chance, to celebrate Mardi Gras with its carnivals, masquerades and parades.

And if someone had trouble understanding why she lit menorahs and set up Christmas trees at the same time, well, tough, as Susan would say. This was her country and those would be her celebrations of choice.

forty-two

IF THEIR COLOR, race, nationality, faith, education, socioeconomic level and physiques had not been so different, Akbar Khan and Dr. Andrew Glenn could have passed for twins. They were virtually alike in attitudes, perspectives, values, even in temperament. Neither wanted to have much to do with his wife and children, or for that matter with anyone else. Their attitude announced to all and sundry: "Leave me alone. You can do whatever you please as long as you don't demand anything from me."

Each liked to project the image of a family man, while he secretly longed to lead the life of a playboy. Each considered himself a martyr, forced to accept subsistence-level sex with his wife while finding enjoyment only in a fantasy world where women were fast, loose and willing to do anything and everything. For Akbar Khan, it was the latest Punjabi movie star he had taken a fancy to. For Dr. Glenn, it was a scantily clad blonde like Marilyn Monroe.

"I'm concerned about Michael's grades in college," Dr. Glenn told colleagues. "It's a tough job market out there. I wish I could make life a little easier on our kids today." In fact, all he wanted to do was tell his friends what he thought they expected him to say. In the same way, Akbar Khan often remarked to his friends: "It's very difficult to be the father of a girl in today's world because young men are ruthless. A father has to be forever concerned about exploitation. Sometimes I can't sleep at night thinking about what my children might have to face." He never lost a moment's sleep worrying about the fate of his daughters, or even of his only son.

Since Dr. Glenn and Akbar Khan were startlingly similar in their attitudes, priorities, and values, even though they lived continents, even worlds, apart, it was not surprising that both had similar reactions to their offsprings' decision to make an inappropriate marriage. Both men were concerned that this marriage would damage their standing in their community.

Dr Glenn summoned Michael to his office, while Sadika received a threatening letter from Akbar Khan; the first time in his life he had ever written to anybody.

"Have you taken leave of your senses?" his father thundered at Michael. "You were never too bright to start with, but recently you seemed to be showing some promise. I should have known better. Unfortunately, you're part of our family and when you do stupid things, they reflect upon us." He paused for a moment, as much for effect as for collecting his thoughts. "I want you to give up this foolishness immediately. For all you know, this girl could be connected with terrorists, or anyway they have customs you haven't even thought about. Mark my words, if you ever get into a disagreement with her or one of her relatives, they're capable of killing off your entire family. Is that what you want? Nothing is beyond them. Nothing! You should know that. Don't you read the papers? Don't you watch TV?"

Michael was more puzzled than upset. He hadn't expected such strong reactions from his family. His mother had had a tearful session with him earlier in the week, and Amy and Steven had made it obvious that they thought he was doing himself and them a great disservice by pursuing his relationship with Sadika. As far as he knew, he had never been important enough for anyone to get that frazzled about any decision he might make about his life. It was not as though his parents didn't have other children who had met, and even exceeded, their expectations. His brother and sister seemed to be right on track for what their parents had in mind for them. And Steve and Amy had never cared that much about anybody he dated. So why did they object so strongly now? The answer was obvious.

"You're mistaken about Sadika, Dad," Michael said at last with a calmness he didn't feel. "You don't know her or you wouldn't hurt me by saying things like that about my future wife. Anyway, it's not as though I need your permission to marry. Whether you accept my choice or not doesn't matter. It would be more pleasant if you gave us your blessing—but that's up to you."

Dr. Glenn was clearly upset; he couldn't remember Michael ever defying him openly. He was surprised, but his reaction was not entirely negative. When had that slow, insecure child metamorphosed into this young man who stood his ground with quiet determination? If Sadika had had anything to do with it, he might have to take his son's advice and revise his opinion of her.

Akbar Khan's letter to Sadika was much stronger than anything Michael heard from his father. All the dramatic anger and contempt he had seen in his many years of watching Punjabi movies came to Akbar Khan's assistance. In his mind he was the wronged hero whose innocent daughter had been led astray by the son of the local landlord—who, true to the movie tradition, had been sucking dry the lifeblood of local peasantry for years, while his ignoble son, a worse specimen of humanity even than his father, practiced serious debauchery on the local female population.

"You are the black dot of shame on the forehead of society," Akbar Khan wrote to his daughter. "An insect that thrives in the sewers and gutters of life. Haroon was smarter than I ever gave him credit for—he must have sensed these immoral tendencies in you when he refused to marry you. I would have strangled you with my own hands at birth if I had the slightest inclination of the shame and degradation you would heap on the family. God has given you this chance to atone for the grief you have caused us. But instead of choosing the respectable way of marrying an eligible man of your own faith as you have the choice of doing, you are opting to live a sinful life with an infidel. This vile union will not only damn you to eternal hell-fire, but will create children who are bastards in the eyes of God. The only way for you to avoid perpetual shame and the wrath of God is to recognize your duty and come back home."

Calmly, Sadika folded the letter and put it in a drawer with one from Khanum that said, among other things, "Shafiq's mother came last week with her son's proposal for you. Before that Parveen Majid, Waseem's mother, as well as Bashir's family, did the same. As you know, Shafiq is one of the most eligible young men in the community and you are very lucky to have the option of marrying him—especially at your age, when as a rule choice proposals have long since stopped coming. Take it and you will not only lift the cloud of shame that not being able to marry you off has put on your family, but you will make us all proud of you. Leave it, and we will have to wash our hands of you and you will cease to exist for us."

In a postscript, Khanum added: "If you do not want to reconsider your decision for us, do so for all the young women of the community. No family will ever trust a daughter to get an education outside their supervision again if you marry someone from a different faith and race. And your conscience will never leave you in peace for as long as you live."

The only person genuinely pleased for her was Zahra. In a long letter, she expressed her joy and pride in the way Sadika had defied her family and gone against the wishes and expectations of the community. It was as though in her mind it was she and not Sadika who was the rebel: it was Zahra who had gathered the courage to break the mold and exert her independence; it was Zahra who had found the strength and the means to stand alone in the face of ostracism.

"In the end, you will prevail," she wrote, "because the people who are trying to stop you are not right, and they do not care about you; they do not want you to be happy because they are miserable. Your courage makes them feel like cowards for not going after what they themselves wanted at some point in life and your happiness makes them feel alone in their misery. So do not worry about what anyone says, as they will eventually come around. Just follow your heart—for you as well as for me."

Even though Sadika didn't hear from either of her sisters, she knew she had their silent support. Just the fact that they didn't join in the condemnation told her that they were with her.

The first few weeks after they announced their decision to marry were difficult ones for Michael and Sadika. But after the first angry outbursts, things seemed to quiet down. As time passed, conciliatory gestures were offered by some who just a few weeks earlier had threatened extreme measures if this disgraceful wedding was allowed to take place.

Khanum was the first to relent, once she realized that no American connection could be stronger than that to one's own offspring. Khanum's domineering personality eventually brought everyone else around. "I don't see what my daughter is doing that's so wrong," she said. "How is spreading the true word of God sinful? She's talking to Michael. Once he converts, they'll be able to work together to spread Islam. Don't you know that's the way Islam is spreading all over the United States?"

Nobody knew anything of the kind, but they were not stupid enough to reveal that to Khanum and risk having her cut them to shreds with her razor-sharp, diamond-edged tongue.

The Glenns, not having heard that Michael was on the verge of accepting Islam, decided to resign themselves to the marriage and began to do their own damage control and image-building. "She's the sweetest girl imaginable, and she'll make Michael a wonderful wife," Ellen told her friends. "Especially since she's so crazy about the American way of life. She'll certainly be very active in the community after the kids come." Then with a conspiratorial wink, she added in a dramatic whisper: "They're very fertile, you know, women from that part of the world."

Ellen had decided that Sadika should be included in Amy's wedding party the following winter. Both Steven and Amy had been told that they had to make the best of a bad situation. "Try to make her feel comfortable," Ellen said. "I know it's hard because we're different as night and day, but there's no help for it. We have to think of Michael. He's hell bent on marrying her. Though God knows Julie Knight would have been perfect for him." She sighed. "I had so hoped they'd get together. Maybe if I'd tried harder, things would be different today."

A couple of months later, it seemed as though the impossible had been accomplished. The wedding was not only going to take place, but it looked as though things would go smoothly.

Akbar Khan and Khanum had written to say that they were willing to accept the marriage as long as the ceremony was performed in a traditional way under the guidance of Ashfaaq Beebee. And Ellen decided to take Sadika under her capable wing; the girl had seemed promising when she first came to visit with Michael. Perhaps the situation was salvageable. Maybe, with proper guidance and polish, Sadika could be made to pass muster and even rise creditably to the occasion.

The reality of how far the situation had progressed was brought home to Sadika when her aunt arrived at her door, holding in one hand Khanum's letter begging her to do the best she could for Sadika in this trying situation, and in the other a deluxe edition of *Beheshti Zewar*, *Jewels of Paradise*, bound in red velvet. Ashfaaq Beebee gave both to Sadika along with the assurance of her cooperation.

Jewels of Paradise was given by conservative Pakistani families to their daughters some time before their wedding day, to enlighten them about what was going to happen on their wedding night. It was a relic from a fairly recent time when it was assumed that the bride would lack all sexual knowledge if, as she should be, she was pure and impeccably brought up. *Beheshti Zewar* still performed this function for many a young Pakistani bride.

When Susan asked Sadika about that neat-looking book, Sadika could not resist translating some of it for her: "A woman's

body houses three things in the area directly underneath her na-
vel . . ." Susan rolled her eyes and they both burst out laughing.

forty-three

WHEN THE WEDDING was only two months away, it was becoming painfully obvious that things were getting nowhere. Far from getting together, Ashfaaq Beebee and Ellen Glenn seemed to be spending all their energies trying to avoid each other, with the result that most arrangements had not yet been made. The only thing decided so far was that the event would take place on the top floor of a big local hotel—Michael's suggestion because he had once attended a wedding there. Everything else was still up in the air. Michael and Sadika were told that they should concentrate on their studies and leave everything to their elders, so it looked as though everything would stay up in the air.

Ellen wanted to hire a caterer that she and many of her friends had used. But Ashfaaq Beebee disliked the idea. Whoever heard, she asked, of serving bland Western food at something as colorful as a traditional Pakistani wedding?

"What traditional Pakistani wedding?" Ellen said stiffly. "The groom is my son, who by the way, is paying for most of the wedding."

"My niece is the bride and she's paying for it too. I know she won't feel right about the wedding unless there is *biryani* made with good quality goat meat and Basmati rice, and *murgh korma*—chicken cooked with just the right combination of spices."

Ashfaaq Beebee knew nothing of the kind, but she had been given authority by Khanum to do whatever was appropriate and necessary under the circumstances. When she saw Ellen flinch at the mention of goat meat, she decided to elaborate further, since she was enjoying herself immensely.

"We know a very good shop where the owner himself goes to a local farm and personally slaughters choice goats and sheep. Then he cuts up the entire animal right in front of your eyes and packages it. He does a good job with the feet and brains too. Not everyone has the skill to do that, you know. Have you ever eaten goat's feet or brains?"

Ellen maintained a stony silence as Ashfaaq Beebee continued, undaunted.

"They're delicious! I'll cook some for you with my own hands sometime. Only don't let my son know—he'll gobble up the whole thing before anyone else has had a chance to try it."

Ellen became more and more tense about the whole affair. What a weird wedding it was going to be. Civilized people didn't eat goat brains and feet, she thought with a shudder. Ashfaaq Beebee was surely the most unreasonable person she had ever had the misfortune to meet. That woman didn't want to compromise on anything. It almost seemed that she was being difficult and unpleasant on purpose. From the arrival of the guests to the departure of the couple in a car decorated with a net of roses and other flowers, Ashfaaq Beebee insisted on doing everything the traditional Pakistani way. Just the thought of talking to her was enough to bring on a major migraine.

Unfortunately, Ellen's suspicion that Sadika's aunt did not really have any interest in cooperating or making the wedding a dignified, lovely occasion, was correct. Ashfaaq Beebee was hoping that people would find the occasion ridiculous, because she wanted to humiliate Sadika and all the Glenn's guests as well. She felt fully justified in pursuing that end.

Wasn't Sadika the ungrateful wretch who had taken advantage of her aunt's generosity to make a place for herself in the world? She had managed to get a good education, an excellent job and now she was marrying an eligible bachelor from a prominent family. In the process, she had flouted the predictions of Ashfaaq Beebee and made her look silly. While Ishrat was still struggling at the community college with no hope of a good match in the foreseeable future, Sadika was living it up with her boy-friend and planning an elaborate wedding when—if there was any justice in the world at all—she should be roasting in hell.

Worse yet was the fact that Sadika had filled Zafary's head with all kinds of nonsense, so that she was becoming more as-sertive with each passing day. It had started after Sadika had stood up to Ashfaaq Beebee and demanded that she be sent to college as promised. Things had not been quite the same since: Ishrat's sullen moods and uncontrolled outbursts, which had been relatively rare, had become more frequent; Haroon kept threatening that he would move out of the house unless things were done his way, and even Aarif Hassan was deferring to her less and less.

The worst of the lot, however, was her good-for-nothing daughter-in-law Zafary, who was becoming lazier and less man-ageable by the minute. Just a few days ago when she had been asked to shovel some snow, Zafary had threatened to go to the authorities and charge Haroon with wife abuse and Ashfaaq Beebee with daughter-in-law abuse, if there was such a thing. The miserable girl seemed to have forgotten that if it had not been for Ashfaaq Beebee, she would probably have been rot-ting in some remote village in Pakistan as the wife of a dirt-poor farmer, and so would her precious older sister Sadika.

Unfortunately, nobody would take that into consideration if Zafary did go to a newspaper or some government agency. Given the way the authorities and the media relished negative stories about Muslims, Ashfaaq Beebee was afraid that Zafary would become some kind of heroine if she did get through to one of these agencies. She could just see the headline: "Woman Exposes Abusive Muslim Practices in Pennsylvania . . ."

Wasn't that what had happened to poor Mrs. Ilyaas Pirzada? She had been crucified by the media for arranging her daughter Nuzhat's wedding against her will to a highly eligible bachelor. Instead of commenting on how ungrateful Nuzhat was, and how unappreciative of her parents' efforts and their concern for her well-being, the newspapers had written about the un-civilized practices still existing in many Muslim communities today.

There was no doubt about it: Sadika had shamelessly used Ashfaaq Beebee. But she was sadly mistaken if she was stupid enough to think that Ashfaaq Beebee was going to go out of her way to make things easy for her. In fact, Sadika would soon be getting her just desserts: chances were that after this wedding fiasco, the Glenns would not want to have anything further to do with her.

Each time Ashfaaq Beebee came home after a meeting with Ellen, she found her entire family, with the exception of Zafary, eagerly waiting to hear all about how she had once again foiled that snobbish matron's efforts to come up with a "proper" wed-ding and how Sadika was surely going to look like an idiot on her absurd Pakistani-American wedding day. This was the first time in her life that Ashfaaq Beebee had gotten so much posi-tive attention from her family, and she loved every moment of it. The more she exaggerated the difficulties and humiliations in store for Sadika, the heartier was the laughter and the more she was applauded. The result was that she made every mole-hill look like Mount Everest, and every disagreement sound like a world war—increasing their anticipation and soothing their damaged egos in the process.

When Haroon had first heard that Sadika was marrying one of her classmates, he had reacted as though this was the worst thing that could happen to a decent Muslim woman. Sadika must have resorted to this on the rebound from him, since he wouldn't wish a fate like hers on his worst enemy. In fact, if he had known that that was how the poor girl would end up, he might have married her himself. At least then his conscience would not be bothering him right now. Later, when he learned that there was no reason to feel sorry for Sadika, he exhibited cool contempt, while inside he seethed with frustrated rage. How dared Sadika go on to lead a new life instead of slowly dying of a broken heart as women of her background were supposed to do? And if she had to give a contemporary twist to her life story, why couldn't she have done it by having a flaming affair with her brother-in-law?

Apart from everything else, Sadika had set a bad example for Zafary, and for that Haroon could never forgive her.

Gone was the timid, quiet creature whose only goal in life was to do her husband's and mother-in-law's bidding, whether in the area of sex or housework, and in her place was a person who thought nothing of refusing Haroon his conjugal rights, demanding extra money for unforeseen expenses or taking a nap when there was work to be done. What's more, whenever she was displeased, she made thinly veiled references to American laws and institutions which were very protective of women and children in abusive situations. Not too long ago, she would not have dared even to think of such nonsense.

How he would have loved to get his hands on Sadika, skin her alive slowly, then dip her in a tub of burning acid.

Ishrat too had been immersed in black thoughts ever since she heard of Sadika's engagement. In her opinion, it was events like these that were responsible for sending America into decline. What else could be expected of a country that allowed maidservant types like Sadika to assume the role of members of elite society? She comforted herself with the thought that Sadika's fiancé would undoubtedly come to his senses one day, but by then it would be too late. When that day arrived, it was possible that he might come to cry on Ishrat's shoulder. And, wise and nurturing as she was, Ishrat would advise and console him in his hour of need.

Aarif Hassan privately believed that Sadika was doing the right thing, and wished his own son and daughter were as clever and sophisticated. She had found a surefire way for a young person to assimilate into American society, and her children would probably be considered a lot more American than his own grandchildren.

Zafary was genuinely happy for Sadika and hoped that the wedding would go off without a hitch. She knew what Sadika had gone through and felt that she deserved happiness if anyone did. Especially since she had brought some measure of satisfaction into Zafary's own life and shown her that it was possible to stand up for oneself, and that if worse came to worse, one could build a life from scratch. Zafary would have thought anyone was crazy who had predicted even a few months ago that Haroon would become less verbally and sexually abusive and that Ashfaaq Beebee would seem almost intimidated by her. But that had happened, and she had Sadika to thank for it.

The time between an engagement and a wedding is supposed to be filled with happy plans for a wonderful future. But for Michael and Sadika, the time was like a whirlpool in which they were helplessly swirling, headed directly for the drain. One planning fiasco after another, accompanied by bickering between his mother and her aunt, were contributing to the disaster that their wedding was surely going to be. Ellen certainly foresaw disaster. Michael, thank God, refused to arrive on a horse rented from a nearby stable, as Ashfaaq Beebee had requested, but he gave in to her insistence that he wear a *sehra*, a festive gold tinsel headcovering with streamers and flowers.

After a lot of argument, compromises were reached. In order to avoid a religious donnybrook, it was agreed that it would be a civil ceremony performed by a judge who was a friend of the Glenns, that Sadika would dress in Pakistani red and American white, and that Michael would wear the *sehra* with his formal tails. Since Ashfaaq Beebee had insisted on Michael wearing the *sehra*, Ellen had dug in on Sadika wearing the traditional white veil. When Ashfaaq Beebee argued that a bridal veil would not go with the colorful traditional Pakistani bridal jewelry, Ellen lost her temper, something she rarely did. "Come hell or high water," she said grimly, "Sadika is going to wear a white veil if I have to personally glue it onto her hair with Krazy Glue. If she doesn't do that, I for one am not going to the wedding."

Adding injury to insult was the amount of money that would be required to put together this comedy of errors. Sadika's unusual dress would have to be custom designed, and food, being catered by two different companies, would cost an arm and a leg. Tandoori chicken, *biryani, korma* and *raita* would be ordered from a Pakistani caterer, while Ellen's caterer would supply hors d'oeuvres and other American dishes. The food service would have to be handled diplomatically, since the caterers had already expressed sullen resentment of each other. Then there would be the expense of providing music for the guests.

As if there was not enough conflict already, Ishrat had spoken up during one of the painful planning sessions, eager to do her bit to escalate the friction. "I don't think a Pakistani wedding would feel right without some good-natured insulting nonsense songs to liven it up," she said. "We'll need to translate them into English of course, so everyone can understand them. I've already started working on a few, and I can sing them for you when they're done—even before the wedding if you like."

"Good-natured insulting nonsense songs. I don't quite get your meaning," Ellen said coldly and politely. "Could you give me an example of one of these songs?"

Ishrat was not intimidated by Ellen's tone. "I still have to work on them, you understand. But I'll tell you what I have so far, and I think your friends will really enjoy it. It goes something like this: 'Darling, the bells will ring out/ and then we we'll go a dancing/ Your brother, my brother-in-law/ he has a stomach like a drum/ we'll play drums on it/ and then we will go a dancing/ Your sister, my sister-in-law/ she is like the trash on the street/ we will throw her out/ and then we will go a dancing.' As I said, this still needs work."

Ellen found the strength to say curtly, "Neither I nor any of my friends have the slightest interest in these so-called songs, I

can assure you. Why don't you just get them out of the way
before the groom's family arrives at the hall? After they've been
pronounced man and wife," she continued with a shudder at
the prospect, "we will of course have the traditional toast to
the bride and the groom, and then after dinner for the dancing,
we have to decide whether we'll have someone play tapes or
live music—-"

"Hold on a minute." Ishrat held up her hand as though she
couldn't bear to hear another word. "The songs have to be sung
in the presence of everyone—that's the whole point. And no
one is going to drink alcohol at my cousin's wedding. It's
haram—that means it's totally unacceptable in our religion.
We're not going to burn in eternal hellfire because of your customs. And what are you trying to do to my poor mother by
making her watch the type of vulgar dancing that people do
nowadays? Give her a heart attack?" Ishrat had really gotten
into the spirit of things.

"Maybe I don't have to watch the dancing," Ashfaaq Beebee interjected hastily as Ellen's face flushed dangerously red
with anger. She didn't want Sadika's wedding to go well, but
neither did she want the responsibility of causing someone to
have a stroke or a heart attack. "Let's talk about more pleasant
things, like the bride and groom drinking milk from the same
glass, the bride's sisters and friends hiding the groom's shoes . . .
Young people always enjoy those traditions, and I say the appropriate time for them would be after the dancing."

"What on earth are you are talking about?" Ellen demanded.
Why couldn't Michael have eloped instead of putting his family
through this trauma? Then at least his mother wouldn't have
been forced to plan her own humiliation and nobody would have
needed to know much about Sadika or her maniacal family.

Ashfaaq Beebee explained that traditionally the bride and
groom drink milk from the same glass before or after the groom
has licked a blob of dessert from the bride's palm. Only seven
licks were allowed, she added helpfully.

"The sisters and friends hide the groom's shoes, and don't give them back till the groom gives them money," Ashfaaq Beebee continued. "It's a lot of fun to watch the groom haggle to get the shoes back. Tell Michael not to give the asking price. He has to bring it down to at least half what they ask." Ashfaaq Beebee was in a good mood. Sadika's wedding was going to be a complete disaster, she could feel it in her bones. So she could afford a little generosity.

Unfortunately this generous gesture was lost on Ellen, who had run out of patience. Michael couldn't know what kind of fool these people were going to make of him, or he would never have agreed to this wedding. Suddenly she felt sure of that. With a surge of hope, she decided that it might not be too late to exert her maternal influence and extricate him from this mess. He had to be brought to his senses, because these people were making everyone's life a living hell.

Thanks to several frantic messages Ellen left on his answering machine, a worried Michael paid her a visit the very next day.

"Oh, thank God you're here," she cried, throwing her arms around him. He followed her into the family room where they sat next to each other on a loveseat, his hand held in both of hers. Something must have happened to his father, he thought, feeling sick. Or there was some other tragedy.

To his surprise, instead of collapsing into tears, she was looking at him almost angrily. "I can't take this anymore," she said.

"Can't take what?" he asked, surprised. He had never seen his mother in such distress.

She said she had tried to hold off because both he and Sadika had been spared involvement in these horrible wedding arrangements so that they could concentrate on their studies, but she could spare him no longer. She launched into an emotional and disjointed tirade: all she wanted out of life was to see her children well settled and happy; she had devoted her life to them; but she had to say that this wedding looming over them was going to be the equivalent of doomsday. If he knew the kind of things Sadika's relatives were planning, he would realize that he was making the biggest mistake of his life.

While Michael stared at her in disbelief, she described her meetings with Ashfaaq Beebee. But his reactions were all wrong. What should have seemed outrageous to him apparently struck him as funny. When she told him about the good-natured insulting songs, he burst into laughter. He said he would get a kick out of seeing the guests' reactions to them. And the rest of it sounded like fun. Maybe people should lighten up at weddings, he said, maybe his wedding would start a trend in that direction.

Appalled, Ellen dropped the subject and retreated into stony silence. She responded to Michael's attempts at jocularity with monosyllables, and he finally left, feeling most uncomfortable. She went up to her bedroom and burst into tears. She was sure that Michael was the victim of some kind of sexual obsession that was going to ruin his life.

She had always thought that one day she would plan the perfect elegant wedding for at least one of her children. Steve and Amy had both decided on simple informal gatherings, but Michael's, she had thought, would begin with elegant engraved invitations; there would be bowls of full-blown roses on every table with white linen cloths, crystal and china, and handwritten place cards. Guests would admire the baskets of flowers throughout the hall. The food and wine would be carefully chosen; the wedding cake would be an architectural marvel, and the ceremony conducted by the prominent minister would be heartwarming and unforgettable.

Later, Michael and his beautiful bride, in her lovely gown of antique lace, would circle the dance floor to their favorite song, gazing into each other's eyes while everyone stood admiring them.

The whole thing would be videotaped.

Before the wedding, there would have been the pleasurable excitement of the bridal registry and getting everything organized, and in the days afterward, while the couple were on their honeymoon, Ellen would keep track of the gifts and make sure that the proper monogrammed cards were ordered so the bride could write her thank-you notes.

Now none of that was going to happen.

forty-six

WHEN MICHAEL LEFT his mother, he felt uncomfortable, realizing that he had been less than sympathetic, and that he should have tried to express his understanding of her predicament. Because he really did understand her; he knew that for her the respect and admiration of her circle was a central concern, the core of her world. And Ashfaaq Beebee was certainly outside that world; in fact, Ashfaaq Beebee existed in her own world. He could see what he should have seen earlier: that it had been a terrible mistake to expect these two to collaborate on anything as traumatic as wedding plans.

Now his mother had begun to dread dealing in any way with anyone associated with Sadika, and probably that feeling extended to Sadika herself. For all he knew, the Pakistani contingent felt the same way about him and his family.

Amy and Steven were more responsive to their mother's tale of woe than Michael had been. They were even more pessimistic than Ellen about the marriage itself. "Six months tops, that's what I give it," Amy said, after hearing about Sadika's relatives' demands.

"Six months?" Steven repeated, incredulously. "I'd be surprised if it lasts six weeks."

Ellen agreed that the prospects for the marriage were not good; she was concerned about a pre-nuptial agreement. "Michael is so touchy that I don't know how to bring it up. The last thing we would want is for this Sadika to get hold of his trust fund. Though God only knows what those people would do with that kind of money. Have a goat meat banquet, I suppose. Or maybe get their teeth capped with gold."

It's a no-win situation, Michael thought, as he and Sadika contemplated the two major events in their lives that should have been cause for celebration. The wedding was still almost two months away. But graduation was just around the corner, and Ashfaaq Beebee had already told Sadika to make sure that their family got better seats for it than the Glenns. Ellen had flatly told her son that she absolutely refused to sit anywhere near the Hassans.

"They'll all come around after we're married. You'll see," Sadika said, with a confidence she was far from feeling. Even though by being passive she and Michael had allowed their wedding to be turned into a three-ring circus, no one was appeased. If anything, the situation had grown worse.

"They'll never come around, you know that," Michael replied, with genuine conviction.

Sadika had to agree. "I'm afraid," she said with some hesitation, "that my aunt is not acting out of conviction. I think she has never forgiven me for leaving her house, and this is her way of paying me back."

"My God," Michael said. "I have to admit that I thought some of the stuff she wanted was crazy, but I told myself that people have customs—"

"You don't know her," Sadika said. After a long silence, she remarked wistfully, "Wouldn't it be wonderful if we could skip graduation and just go away and get married without that big wedding?"

Michael was suddenly energized. "You're absolutely right. It would be wonderful if we could skip graduation and the wedding. And you know what? That's exactly what we'll do! We were crazy not to decide to do that in the first place." The more he thought about it, the more he liked the idea. "In fact," he said, "why just go away for the graduation and the wedding? Why not start a brand new life far away from here, where we don't have to deal with relatives at all? What do you say?"

For a second, Sadika's heart seemed to stop. Could they really get married right away? That would be wonderful. But that also meant that she would have to contend with the issue of sexual fireworks much earlier than anticipated. She would surely die of mortification if the passion that was supposed to blaze out of control simply fizzled. In Pakistan all anybody worried about on wedding nights were a few bloodstains on a sheet.

"Can we really do that? Where would we go? How would we live? How would we get married?" Sadika, like Michael, had not considered this option before, or even thought it might be possible. Just as she hadn't realized that Michael had more than an inkling of Ashfaaq Beebee's motives behind her involvement in the wedding plans.

He was right of course: if they disappeared, they could start their life together in peace. Just the two of them, away from family intrusions, demands and expectations. Not only that, but the worry and exasperation—to say nothing of the expense—of the wedding would be circumvented. Maybe the placement office at the college would help them find jobs even before they moved.

The best part of eloping would be depriving Ashfaaq Beebee of her revenge, frustrating Ishrat and Haroon, and getting far away from the pessimistic expectations of the Glenns.

Michael, who had been reading Sadika's thoughts in her face, knew her answer even before she said in a voice that shared his excitement: "Let's do it!"

forty-seven

Ashfaaq Beebee was in a good mood. Wearing one of her more elegantly embroidered robes, she had even plucked her eyebrows and bleached her moustache, a thing she did only for special occasions.

You look pretty good, she said to her reflection, after viewing herself from different angles in the full-length mirror. Aarif Hassan was a lucky man. And she deserved a medal for doing the thankless job of running a home and putting up with unscrupulous people like Sadika who went out of their way to take advantage of her.

She smiled as she thought of Sadika. Things were finally looking up on that front. Not only were Sadika's future in-laws thoroughly depressed and disgusted, but Sadika's roommate Susan had asked her to come to their apartment as soon as possible. That sounded bad. Maybe Michael had left her for someone else, or his parents had put a stop to the wedding and Sadika had gone into deep depression or committed suicide. Ashfaaq Beebee was headed there right now to find out.

At last everyone connected with Sadika was beginning to realize how important Ashfaaq Beebee was, she thought with pleasure as she got into her Volkswagen. She was after all the person in charge of the bride's interests. Or rather the female's interests, she hastily amended. Just the thought of that wretched creature being a prospective bride was enough to cause her to feel ill. But anyway, Sadika was going to get what she deserved soon enough. Disaster was going to strike in the form of a botched-up wedding, if the wedding was still on at all, and Sadika

would be made to pay in some small measure for all the suffering she had caused her well-intentioned aunt.

If it hadn't been for her, Ashfaaq Beebee, Sadika would probably be married by now to some old man with one foot in the
grave, she would be slaving away in dusty hot weather in front
of an antique stove, her hair and skin a mess, wearing rags that
were a far cry from the stylish clothing that made Ishrat look
dowdy. Or maybe she would have been able to make herself
look good—shameless tramps had a knack for that; they were
born with antenna for picking up potential tools of the trade.

If only Ashfaaq Beebee had known what she knew now,
things would have been so different. During a recent visit to
Pakistan, Salmeen, one of the teachers at the mosque, had stayed
at Gulmushk Mohalla and uncovered the entire sordid story of
Sadika's affairs with the neighborhood boys. Ashfaaq Beebee
had relished telling her family, including an uncomfortable
Zafary, about how Sadika had left Pakistan in disgrace.

I should have been suspicious when Khanum agreed so fast
to send Sadika to America, she thought. If only I had investi-
gated, I would have treated Sadika the way she deserved to be
treated, instead of making her welcome in my home like some
honored guest. I would never have provided her with those
golden opportunities, and that girl would still be in her rightful
place today—in my kitchen.

But it was too late to cry over spilt milk. What was done
was done. Things were in God's hands, and at some future date
He would surely reward Ashfaaq Beebee for the goodness of
her heart. Maybe her palatial home in heaven would be up-
graded from gold and silver to rubies and diamonds. And she
would be carried there by angels.

Sadika had been trash then and she was trash now. Haroon
must have sensed that when he refused to marry the girl—the
wisdom of that boy never ceased to amaze his mother. Maybe
some wrongs could still be righted. She would start by doing

the world the favor of revealing Sadika's true character, so that no one would ever again be taken in by that façade of innocence. She would do it subtly; first surrounding Sadika with humiliating circumstances, and then telling the truth about her to everyone. Things were already moving in the right direction: Sadika's prospective in-laws could not stand being under the same roof as anyone associated with her, let alone in the same room, and it was obviously pure torture for Mrs. Glenn to be forced to discuss wedding arrangements with Ashfaaq Beebee.

These Americans were so gullible! Mrs. Glenn believed Ashfaaq Beebee was really obnoxious, never considering that there might be good reasons for her behavior. One could safely assume that the woman had never lived in an extended family environment, had never been exposed to family politics and intrigue. If it had been her Ishrat instead of Sadika who was engaged to Michael, Ashfaaq Beebee would have been so sweet and accommodating that Ellen and all the Glenns would have fallen completely under her spell.

At the apartment, Susan let her in and waved a piece of paper in her face, saying, "See this? They've fled!"

"Who's Fred? Who are 'they'? Who has Fred? What does this have to do with me?" Ashfaaq Beebee was confused.

"Not 'Fred'—*fled*," Susan said. "As in disappeared, eloped. Michael and Sadika have eloped. And now the big wedding is off."

Sadika had finally done what Susan had always hoped she would do some day—escaped from the clutches of her relatives, and Susan was eager to watch Ashfaaq Beebee squirm.

Ashfaaq Beebee, however, did not squirm in public. She was of course deeply disappointed that her well-laid plans to avenge herself on Sadika had been frustrated. But she saw instantly that Susan wanted to witness that disappointment, and she would rather have been bitten by a poisonous snake than oblige her. The best defense therefore was a good offense—the way to thwart her enemies was to make things so uncomfortable for them that they had to start worrying about their own hides.

"That's a lie! You're lying so people won't know about the despicable things you have done to destroy my niece," Ashfaaq Beebee said loudly.

"What in the world are you talking about?" asked an astounded Susan.

"Next you'll tell me that you didn't plan with Michael to have her abducted so that her honor could be shredded to pieces. My poor innocent niece!" Ashfaaq Beebee noted with satisfaction that Susan was no longer smiling; in fact she was enraged.

"Are you crazy? You're responsible for this, you vicious old woman! You and that mean, ugly daughter of yours, and your good-for- nothing son!"

"I won't talk to you anymore till I have witnesses, a lawyer, and the police, so they can all hear the slanderous things you're saying." Ashfaaq Beebee had not religiously watched "People's Court" on TV and spent the better part of her life in America for nothing. She knew that in this litigious society the best way to intimidate someone was to threaten a lawsuit. "Then I'll see how you can talk your way out of it. But listen to me—no matter what you say or do, you'll never convince me that my poor niece went with Michael of her own free will. We, the women of the East, would rather die than part with our honor. Unlike Western women like you."

She went on in this vein till a fuming Susan dared her to call the police, and rushed into her bedroom, banging the door shut behind her.

Ashfaaq Beebee promptly dialed 911 and in a voice loud enough to be heard by Susan, reported an abduction, a kidnapping, a probable rape and murder. After having been assured that an officer was on his way, she immediately dialed the Glenn number.

Morning was Ellen's favorite time of day. From the moment her alarm clock went off at six o'clock to her emergence from her room at eight, freshly showered, invigorated by her routine exercises and wearing light makeup, she was in control of every aspect of her morning—doing everything just the way she liked it.

She sat at the breakfast table, drinking coffee and scanning the newspaper, paying special attention to the sales. Weekend mornings were especially pleasant because the maid was off, and her husband always played tennis at the club; she could relax and enjoy the serenity of her neat peaceful kitchen.

Then the phone rang.

She picked up the receiver and heard Ashfaaq Beebee's detestable voice telling her that she should now consider her son a criminal because that was how he would be perceived by the police once they heard what Ashfaaq Beebee had to tell them. What's more, she, Ashfaaq Beebee, had seen the germs of criminal behavior in Michael from the very start, so this was no surprise to her at all. No wonder her beloved sister in Pakistan had been so concerned for her poor daughter's welfare. Ashfaaq Beebee's only regret was that, because she had tried too hard to spare Sadika's feelings, she had not been forceful enough in letting her know her true opinion of Michael. Otherwise they might not be facing this tragic situation today.

With trembling hands, Ellen hung up and dialed the club. When Andrew was finally located, she told him they were facing an emergency of epic proportions. "Unless we get to Sadika's place right away, there's no telling what that horrible woman will end up doing—what outrageous lies she'll make up, who she'll talk to. Something like this could get out of hand—it might even get into the newspapers!"

It was only when Andrew asked, "What about Michael?" that it occurred to Ellen that Ashfaaq Beebee's hysterical attack must be based on something that Michael had done, and the logical conclusion was that the wedding was off—that would certainly be the silver lining in this ominous cloud.

The scene that greeted the Glenns at the apartment defied belief.

Ashfaaq Beebee, Susan and an exasperated uniformed policeman stood in the living room. Susan kept trying to say something, but she was drowned out by Ashfaaq Beebee, who was rocking back and forth, beating her chest with her fists. "My beautiful niece, what have they done to you?" she was wailing in a loud shrill voice, not unlike Khanum's. "My dear sister in Pakistan—however will I face you now? After all the trust you put in me, how am I ever going to tell you about our poor Sadika's tragic, tragic, horrible, horrible fate? I know you put her in my charge; but it wasn't my fault, dear one! It wasn't my fault! How could I have known that the stars were conspiring against her? If I had had that knowledge, I would have locked her up and guarded the door of her prison with my life. But I didn't know, sister, I didn't know. Dear sister, forgive me, forgive me. . . ."

She stopped suddenly in mid-tirade when she spotted Michael's parents entering the room.

"Terrorists!" she spat at them. "Terrorists! I knew your entire family was up to no good. You thought you could hide behind your fancy clothes and cars. But my eyes saw right through to your cruel hearts. And I warned my loved one. But she wouldn't listen. She was blinded by infatuation for that good-for-nothing boy. Now look what happened! He's kidnapped her and stolen her virtue. These men are all alike. I could see in his eyes that that was what he was after all along!"

Andrew Glenn raised his voice, cutting off Ashfaaq Beebee, and also Susan, who was trying to talk to him. "Officer," he said, "you can certainly see from this woman's behavior that her niece had everything to gain from an association with our family, and anyway the girl is well beyond the age of consent—"

"If anyone talked anyone into anything, it was probably not Michael," Ellen broke in, shaking with anger.

Ashfaaq Beebee turned to the policeman and lowered her voice. "You know, officer, I'm psychic. When my mother died, I dreamt about it for days before it happened. I saw my husband's car accident in a dream too. I warned him, but the fool didn't believe me. I had another dream last night and I know exactly what happened to my poor niece. Michael took her in his car and raped her over and over—"

"This is ridiculous," Ellen said. "If anything happened to anybody, officer, I think we should try to find out what these terrible people have done to Michael—"

"For God's sake," Susan said. "Will anyone listen? Look, I've got this note! Michael and Sadika have left town, they've fled, they're going to have a quiet wedding, and they don't even want any of you people to know where they are."

It was four long months before the Khans and the Glenns heard from the newlyweds. Since before that, no one knew anything about them, everyone was able to come up with the scenario that he or she preferred.

"Michael has become a devout Muslim," was the story that Khanum, Akbar Khan and their children told everyone they knew. "You know how these converts are—more dedicated to their religion than the ones born to it." Khanum had a field day with the subject of her brand new son-in-law, even when she was not sure she had one.

"Why, he has become a fanatic about saying all his prayers, and at the right time, too. How many people wake up at five every morning to say their *Fajr* prayers, and do not go to bed till their *Isha* prayers are done? My son-in-law does—and he says the long version, too. Besides that, he fasts the whole month of Ramadan, gives to the poor, and he's handsome as a Hollywood star. His hair is like spun gold, his eyes blue as sapphires, and his skin white as milk from a lake in Paradise. We couldn't have found a better match for our Sadika if we had personally scoured the world, and the moon and the sun had given us the light to do it in."

Khanum and Akbar Khan loved to tell everyone in Gulmushk Mohalla how their eldest child kept begging them to pay a visit, now that she and her husband had just bought a new house that was really a mansion. "And she keeps insisting that we consider settling in America—she would love to sponsor us," they would add as an afterthought.

Sajida liked to increase her importance in her in-laws' eyes by telling them how Sadika wished that her favorite sibling was living nearby to give her tremendous moral support in a strange country. Maybe sometime Razzak could find a way to earn a living in the gold mine that was America. And when that day came, Sajida would ask her older sister to sponsor her for a green card.

Asghar Khan had given in to the temptation of increasing his status in the community by bragging about his well-settled beloved sister and his influential brother-in-law, who was deeply impressed by him. "Michael wants me to teach him all about Eastern cultures," he told everyone.

"Maybe I should pay my sister a visit," Zafary would tell Ashfaaq Beebee when, in the middle of planning one of her parties, she assigned Zafary more than her share of work. "I haven't seen her for a long time, and I need a break." Khanum had told her sister and her daughter the same stories she told everyone about getting letters from Sadika.

In the first weeks, Ellen, although infinitely relieved that the burden of the ghastly wedding had been lifted from her shoulders, had felt uncomfortable pretending to know all about where her son and daughter-in-law were, and what they were doing. But she couldn't possibly tell her friends that the pair had apparently vanished without a word except for the note they left with Susan. She had to make up a story—they were too much in love to wait for the wedding—and then she realized that now she could assign Michael the brilliant career and material success that she had always wanted to brag about, and she felt much better.

"I hear from them fairly often, but the truth is that those two like to keep to themselves," she told people. "I don't blame them, of course—newlyweds are like that, and these two are especially wrapped up in each other. They're really happy: Michael practically runs the company he works for, and Sadika has a great job at a bank."

In fact, Michael and Sadika had settled in southern California. She had found a job as a lab technician for a biological research company, and Michael was working for the State Department of Education as a grant supervisor for learning disability programs. After a couple of nights during which Michael exhibited great patience and sympathy, Sadika learned to the great relief of both of them that the physical side of marriage was neither painful nor frightening, but was in fact more than pleasant.

Three months later, Michael suggested that it might be time to contact the families. "If you don't want to get in touch with yours," he said, "I can understand it. But I really feel that I ought to talk to my mother. She had a pretty upsetting time over that wedding."

Sadika had in fact been thinking a great deal about Sajida and Zafary, and even wondering how Khanum was getting along. She rather missed hearing from them, and she really wanted to write to Zahra, but she had hesitated to broach the subject with Michael. "I'm glad you said that," she told him. "I think it's time to get in touch."

So Michael phoned New Jersey, and Sadika wrote to her family, to Zahra, and to Zafary. It was a smooth transition: Khanum had told everyone the couple was in New York and the Glenns had said they were settled in Texas, but it was a simple thing to announce that they had moved to California.

And there were snapshots of them looking as happy and prosperous as everyone had already been told they were.

Shortly after that, Sadika discovered that she was pregnant.

All the stories now had real credibility and the family net-
works were restored at a safe distance—at least temporarily.
"I'm so happy for them," Ashfaaq Beebee said. 'I can't wait to
see them. After the baby's born, Ishrat and I are going to take a
trip to California."